WIT

Having worked in the law, journalism and numismatics,
K. J. Parker now writes and makes things out of wood and
metal (including prototypes for most of the hardware
described in this book). Parker is married to a solicitor
and lives in southern England.

Find out more about K. J. Parker and other Orbit authors
by registering for the free monthly newsletter at
www.orbitbooks.net

K·J·PARKER

THE BELLY OF THE BOW

VOLUME TWO OF
THE FENCER TRILOGY

www.orbitbooks.net

ORBIT

First published in Great Britain by Orbit 1999
This edition published by Orbit 2000

9 11 12 10 8

A CIP catalogue record for this book
is available from the British Library.

ISBN 978-1-85723-960-7

Typeset by Solidus (Bristol) Ltd
Printed and bound in Great Britain by
Clays Ltd, St Ives plc

Papers used by Orbit are from well-managed forests
and other responsible sources.

MIX
Paper from
responsible sources
FSC® C104740
www.fsc.org

Orbit
An imprint of
Little, Brown Book Group
100 Victoria Embankment
London EC4Y 0DY

An Hachette UK Company
www.hachette.co.uk

www.orbitbooks.net

For my mother
(Who *hated* the bit about the rabbit)

And Tim Holman
(In compensation for all the pork pies he'll never eat)

Author's Note

All the bows described in this book are based on prototypes I've made myself; except for one (you'll know
which one when you get to it) which was inspired by a
description of something fairly similar in Jim Hamm's
book *Bows & Arrows of the Native Americans*. To the best
of my knowledge, the project is technically possible; if
anybody ever succeeds in building one, I'd really rather
not hear about it.

KJP

CHAPTER ONE

The sergeant was pulling at his sleeve. 'Get out of here, Father,' he said urgently, only just audible over the shouting and the nearby clatter of weapons. 'They're coming. You'll be killed if you don't get out now.'

Doctor Gannadius stared at him and grabbed his wrist. It felt solid enough. 'This is wrong,' he mumbled. 'I can't be here.'

'Get *out!*' the sergeant screamed; then he pulled his wrist free and set off at a clumsy skidding run down the corridor, crashing into a book-case as he went and scattering book-rolls on the floor. In the other direction, far away but getting nearer, Gannadius could hear more shouting - orders, by the sound of it, yelled by an officer at the end of his tether, but he couldn't make out the words or tell whether it was the enemy or his own side.

'This is wrong,' Gannadius repeated softly. 'I was never here. I left before this happened.'

A few yards away from him, a shutter flew open and a man's head appeared through the window, backlit in orange. It was a nightmare face, foreign and dangerous, and Gannadius instinctively shrank away. Logically, he should be running. Very far back in second place was the notion of grabbing one of the discarded weapons that lay on the floor and trying to kill this intrusive stranger before he got through the window. Gannadius couldn't do either. In the back of his mind, he was making a note on the effect of blind terror on the unwarlike, sedentary

1

individual: paralysis, involuntary bladder activity, an apparent extension of the moment, as if time was frozen or no longer applied.

'But this is *wrong*,' he insisted loudly, except that his voice didn't work. 'I escaped from the City before it fell. I was never here.'

'Tell it to the judge,' grunted the enemy soldier as he wriggled his left shoulder through the window frame. 'I expect you've got a note from your mother, too.'

An enemy soldier shouldn't be talking with a strong City accent, using City phrases. But on the other hand, Doctor Gannadius, Perimadeian refugee currently domiciled in Shastel, shouldn't be here talking with him. Someone was breaking the rules, he thought, how horribly unfair; but once he'd been killed, who would ever know?

The sordid and uncomfortable feeling of piss running down his leg, and the smell of burning bone filtering through the window – how much more real can it be? I'm here. Damn.

'Please,' he said. The enemy soldier grunted again, swung one leg through the window and put his foot to the ground. 'Go on,' he said, 'run. Well?'

'I'm sorry,' Gannadius replied. 'I can't. I don't seem able to move.'

The enemy soldier shrugged and reached behind his back for an arrow. *I'm not really bothered*, his eyes said, *one way or the other. You can run if you like, or I can kill you now. You're dead anyway.* Gannadius closed his eyes: it would be too horrible to watch the arrow actually coming towards him, and with time running slow like this he was sure he'd be able to see it in the air, observe for himself the operation of the phenomenon known as the Archer's Paradox, whereby the arrow actually bends round the bow at the moment of loose. A true scientist would want to see that. *Not me*, he said aloud, but the words didn't work any more. *I don't understand. Unless this is some horrible mess-up in the operation of the Principle, which means that instead of going forward, I've*

*been hauled back, maybe to where I should have been all
along. Is that the way it works? We think we can spot the
flaws in the Principle, prise open cracks in the points in the
future where momentous things happen and slide in our
acts of intervention. But what if it works both ways, and the
flaw's closing up on me? In which case it's all Alexius' fault,
and mine for getting involved. Perhaps—*

Something prompted him to open his eyes; and he
saw the enemy soldier staring at him, his face suddenly
contorted with a fear that mirrored Gannadius' own.
There was an arrow in the man's chest that hadn't been
there before.

'Loredan,' he said, then turned round. A man stood in
the archway, a short black bow in his hand, his face
frustratingly in shadow. Loredan, yes; but which one?
Not that it mattered if he was safe now, but there were
two Loredan brothers, and one was good and one was
bad, and the elder of them was taller and bald-headed
(but he still didn't know which one he was looking at).

Whichever Loredan it was took a step forward, then
called out, presumably some warning. It came too late,
because Gannadius could see the arrow coming, spinning
elegantly around the axis of the shaft—

So I died here, after all. How ironic.

Someone touched his arm, and he jerked round. It was
a girl, one of his students, not the most promising of
them but terribly enthusiastic. She was smiling, amused
to see an old man fallen asleep in his chair, so peaceful.

'Doctor Gannadius,' she said. 'I'm here for my tutorial.
It was today, wasn't it?'

His mind was still fuzzy with sleep, because he replied
with something like, 'I thought so too, but it turned into
then, and now it's now again.'

'Doctor Gannadius?' She was staring at him, eyes
puzzled and worried; very sweet she looked, too.

'I'm sorry,' he sighed, stretching his legs and finding
them afflicted with pins and needles (maybe they explained the arrow). 'It's this hatefully comfortable chair.

The moment I sit in it I'm fast asleep, and there doesn't seem to be anything I can do about it.' He had a splitting headache, too.

'If you like, I can come back later.' Oh, how disappointed she looked, and how brave she was trying to be – was he ever that enthusiastic about anything, ever in his life?

'That's fine,' he said. 'No, stay. I'm awake now. Please, sit down.'

She was one of those awkward perchers, the sort who balance on the very edge of a chair as if they're afraid they'll break it or that the person who's really entitled to it might show up at any minute. Her name – absolutely no chance, he admitted to himself, of remembering her name this soon after waking up. Machaera.

Fancy remembering that.

'Remind me,' he said. 'What were you doing for me this week?'

She straightened her back even more until she looked like a human plumb-bob. 'Projection exercises,' she said. 'Like you showed us.'

(*Hah! Savage irony, if you like. You want to stay well clear of projection exercises, my girl. They're not safe. In fact, they could be the death of you.*)

'I see,' he said, steepling his fingers and trying to look as if he had a clue about anything. The truth was that these famous secret Perimadeian projection exercises, which were basically what had got him this superb job, were little more than his garbled attempts to duplicate the techniques by which Alexius and he had (accidentally) managed to achieve a number of projections (with disastrous effects) shortly before the City fell. About the only thing that could be said in favour of these exercises he was now teaching was that they didn't work. At least, he devoutly hoped they didn't, or they were all due to be in ever such a lot of trouble.

'Shall I . . . ?' she mumbled. She was embarrassed, like a patient taking off her clothes in front of a doctor.

Gannadius nodded. 'When you're ready,' he said.

'All right.' She huddled up in her chair, as if she was out in the rain without a coat, her eyes squeezed painfully tight. He could almost feel the gigantic effort of will she was making – counter-productive, of course. Which was all to the good.

Nevertheless: 'Relax,' he said, 'try and—' How to describe it? Not a clue. 'Try and make everything seem as normal as you can. If you think about it, all you want to be doing is standing still in a room or a street somewhere, which is about as mundane as you can get. The only difference would be, you'd be out then and not back now. Chances are you won't feel any different at all. It's not magic, remember; it's a perfectly natural phenomenon, like dreaming.'

She relaxed – relaxed *savagely* – and Gannadius had to make an effort not to laugh. 'Ah,' she said. 'Oh, I *see*. Yes, I think it's working.'

It can't be, surely. 'Are you sure?' he said, forcing himself to stay calm. 'Just look around you and tell me what you see.'

'I'm not sure,' she muttered. 'It's somewhere I've never been. The nearest place to it I can think of is the library. And there's—' She lifted her head, her closed eyes directly in line with his (although he'd moved since she closed them; how did she know where he was?). 'Doctor Gannadius, you're—' Suddenly she screamed, a horrible, shrill, painful noise that seemed to vibrate along the very same nerves in his head that the headache was affecting. He jumped up and grabbed her hands, which she was paddling wildly in the air like a drowning cat; she pulled her hands free and pushed him in the face so hard that he fell over on his backside, and swore.

'Doctor *Gannadius!*' She was gazing at him with a mixture of horror and terminal shame, and her eyes were as big as catapult-shot. 'What did I *do?*'

He picked himself up and made a humorous play of dusting himself down. 'It's all right,' he said. 'Nothing broken that I've used in a long time. Tell me what you saw.'

'But Doctor—'

He sat down and looked at her. 'Tell me,' he said quietly, 'what you saw.'

She found a handkerchief in her sleeve and started twisting it. 'Doctor Gannadius,' she said, and the horror was already tinted with just the faintest flush of pride, 'I think I saw the fall of the City. You know, Perimadeia. And—' She swallowed and took a deep breath, as if she was about to dive off a high rock. 'I think I saw you get killed.'

Gannadius nodded. 'I see,' he said. 'Tell me, how's your head?'

She felt the back of her skull. 'You think I might have banged it and I'm seeing things? I'm sure I—'

'How's your head?'

'Fine. Well,' she added, looking down at her hands, 'I do have a bit of a headache, but apart from that—'

'How did I die?' Gannadius asked. He was perfectly still and his voice was perfectly even; only the palms of his crumpled-up hands were sweating. 'It's all right,' he said, 'I won't be offended.'

'You were shot,' she replied in a tiny voice. 'An arrow hit you in the face, it went right through—' She stopped and made a succession of alarming noises, which sent Gannadius scurrying for a big copper bowl that usually held fruit. He made it back with the bowl just in time.

'That's all right,' he said. 'It was the stress, it can take people that way sometimes. I should have warned you.'

She looked up, the lower part of her face muffled by the handkerchief. 'So you do believe me?' she said. 'Oh, I'm so *glad* - oh, that sounds such a stupid thing to say, what I meant was—'

'I know what you meant. If it's any comfort,' he lied, 'I was sick the first time too. And I didn't even see anything horrible.'

'Doctor Gannadius—' She stood up, sat down, stood

up again. 'I – please, do let me wash out the bowl for you.
I am so terribly *sorry—*'

Not half as sorry as I am, Gannadius reflected, once
he'd finally shooed her away to her cell. I think disasters
must follow me round like a sausage-maker's dog. A
natural, someone who can break through into the Principle *at will* ... A really sensible man would follow her back
to her cell and cut her throat at once. But.

'Damn,' he muttered, flopping onto the bed and curling his legs round. As he closed his eyes, he thought of
his former colleague Alexius – apparently still alive, by
some miracle, and cooped up on the Island, miles away
from this war and presumably safe. For a while he toyed
with the idea of trying to reach him by projection – *Are
you out of your tiny mind? You don't stop a fire in a
timber-yard by setting light to your neighbour's oil store.*
Remarkably soon under the circumstances he fell asleep;
and though he had vivid dreams, he couldn't remember
anything about them when he woke up.

Towards the evening of the second day they found a
single straight ash tree growing in the ruins of a derelict
cottage.

'It's not perfect,' he said, 'but it'll have to do.'

Bardas Loredan let the reins slip through his hands
and sat for a while looking at the ruins, the stones
standing out through the light sprinkling of snow like
elbows poking through a frayed sleeve. Burnt down, by
the look of it, maybe fifty or sixty years before; even
after all that time, the marks of fire were plain enough.
This high up in the mountains, moss and ivy and the
other types of vegetation that seem to regard it as their
duty to cover up human errors don't seem able to take
hold on fallen masonry; there were a few patches of
wispy grass growing in the cracks of the exposed
mortar, two young rowan saplings perversely trying to
make a living in the gap between the wall and the hard
earth, and this fine, mature ash tree he had chosen to

cut down, standing tall in what should have been the middle of the floor. If he was a superstitious man and one given to reflecting on past horror and glories, he might be tempted to make a connection between the fall of the house and the rise of the tree. But he wasn't, and it was the only piece of straight timber he'd seen in two days.

Beside him on the cart's box, the boy shifted impatiently.

'That's ash, isn't it?' he said. 'I thought we were after yew or osage.'

'It'll do,' Loredan repeated.

The boy jumped down from the cart and saw to the horses while Loredan walked round the base of the tree, peering up into its branches and mumbling calculations under his breath. The boy watched him with his head on one side.

'I thought you said this stuff was rubbish,' he commented. 'More trouble than it's worth, you told me.'

Loredan frowned. 'Maybe I exaggerated,' he replied. 'Get a fire going, then come and give me a hand.'

He lifted the big axe down from the cart and tested its edge with his thumb. It felt dull, and he licked it over with the stone before slipping off his coat and squaring his shoulders for the first stroke.

'I can't get this fire to light,' the boy complained. 'Everything's damp.'

Loredan sighed. 'Forget it,' he said. 'I'll do it after we've done this. Got your axe? Right, you go round the other side and try and match me cut for cut, try and keep it even. And for pity's sake watch what you're doing with that thing. Take it steady, don't go wild.'

He adjusted the position of his hands on the axe, left hand at the bottom of the handle, right hand just under the axe-head, then fixed his eyes on where he wanted the blow to fall and swung. The shock of impact jarred his shoulders and he felt an uncomfortable twinge in his back, warning him to ease off a little.

'Don't just stand there,' he grunted. 'Your turn.'

The boy swung; typical boy with a big axe, wanting to show how strong he was. It was a wild, flailing swing, and he missed, hitting the tree with the handle of the axe rather than the blade. Needless to say, the head snapped off, whistled past disconcertingly close to Loredan's elbow and landed in a patch of nettles.

'Idiot,' Loredan said indulgently. He remembered doing exactly the same thing himself when he was just a kid; younger than this boy, of course – by the time he was the boy's age he really had known everything there is to know about felling a tree, instead of merely thinking that he did. 'Go and find the axe-head.'

'It went in the nettles,' the boy replied.

'I know.'

He carried on cutting, swinging the axe in a slow, economical rhythm, letting the weight of the head do all the work. After twenty or so strokes he moved round to the other side and evened up the cut; then he started again a quarter-circumference round, until he'd cut through to the core on three sides. He paused and leant on the axe-handle.

'Found it yet?'

'No.'

'Gods, you're slow, it'll be dark soon,' he said. 'Come on, leave that and fetch the ropes.'

Together they roped the upper branches and made fast to what was left of the cottage's doorframe. 'Keep back,' Loredan warned. 'And don't get under my feet.'

He finished the job then; and when he was all but through, the weight of the tree ripped away the last few splinters of heartwood and the trunk jerked sideways, came up against the restraint of the rope and slid off the stump, coming to rest more or less where Loredan wanted it to be.

'That,' he said, stepping back, 'is the proper way to fell a tree. If you'd been paying attention, you might have learnt something useful.'

'You told me to look for the axe-head,' the boy replied. 'Anyway, what's the big deal about cutting down trees? You just hit them till they fall over.'

Loredan breathed out slowly. 'Absolutely,' he said. 'Get the saw. There's still just about enough light left to make a start.'

The boy yawned and fetched the long two-man bow-saw, and together they trimmed off the axe-cut point of the log, leaving a flat circle with the growth rings clearly visible.

'That'll do for today,' Loredan said. 'We'll leave the next stage till tomorrow; that's the important bit. Now find that axe-head while I light the fire.'

'My arms are all stung,' the boy pointed out mournfully.

'Use the hook to cut back the nettles,' Loredan said patiently. 'Then you'll be able to find the axe, and you won't sting yourself.'

The boy grunted. 'You might have told me that earlier,' he said.

Loredan looked up from the pile of kindling and smiled. 'I was hoping you might have worked that one out for yourself,' he replied. 'Get a move on, we haven't got all night.'

They came an hour after sunset; five long black ships with their masts down, making almost no sound as they slipped through the two rocks that stood in the mouth of the cove. It was a fine piece of seamanship, bringing five warships through a narrow gap at twilight, and it was done with confidence and efficiency.

They disembarked quickly and quietly, every man knowing what to do, then their officers marshalled them into two parties and led them up the beach. There was nothing to hear, no clinking of armour or weapons or creaking of straps, no talking or careless footfalls. From where he lay, Gorgas couldn't see well enough to count them, but he put the number at over two hundred, possibly as many as two hundred and fifty. A substantial force for a simple foreclosure, except that no foreclosures were simple any more.

'There's more than we expected,' whispered the man at his side. He sounded frightened, which was how it should be.

'We can handle them,' Gorgas replied softly. 'Now shut up and keep still.'

Brave words, he said to himself; odds of nearly three to one aren't good business. He glanced up the hill towards the farmhouse; there was a light burning in the tower, as he'd ordered, and the path from the beach led straight up to the front gate. Logically they'd follow the path until they were maybe a hundred yards from the stockade and then split up, one party to the front, the other round the back. That's what he'd have done. There weren't that many options; it was a relatively simple job.

The raiders were hard to see against the rocks that crowded the sides of the path, and Gorgas could make them out only because he knew what he was looking for. It would have been much simpler to have taken them there, with the rocks for cover, but the line would have been too extended; he couldn't have engaged all of them at once and the rearguard might have made things unpleasant for him if they kept their heads and didn't run. Besides, if they were expecting an ambush, that was the obvious place for one.

The leader of the first party was passing the stone Gorgas had measured off as his fifty-yard mark. He could see them rather more clearly now, there were recognisable arms and legs and heads instead of a dark moving blur. It was, he realised, all rather like still-hunting deer in the forest when he was a boy. The trick was to be patient, to wait for the last possible moment before standing up and shooting, but with the proviso that the longer you waited, the greater the risk of spoiling the whole thing with a careless sound or movement. There

was a small, fine irony there: he'd always been the impatient one, anxious to get it over with and shoot as soon
as the animal was within range. Just as well he'd learnt
his lesson.

The last man was clear of the rocks, and they were
still moving at a smooth, unhurried pace, unaware that
there was anything wrong. Probably, if they were experienced men, they were feeling a little surge of relief now
that they were clear of the rocks, where an ambush
might have been waiting. Between them and their objective, the ground was open and level. They'd be reckoning
they were as good as home and dry.

Gorgas stood up and called, 'Loose!' at the top of his
voice.

He'd chosen his ground well. The path ran along the
crest of a slight ridge, so slight that you'd hardly notice it,
but just enough to give his men sufficient angle to shoot
up towards the path without the risk of dropping arrows
among their own people on the other side. At fifty yards,
even in this light, there was no excuse for missing, and
he'd seen to it that his men could shoot. The first volley
was gratifyingly effective.

The enemy leader was down, so there was no one to
give the immediate orders that might have made a difference. Instead, most of the raiders froze, not knowing
what to do, plenty long enough for a second volley.
Gorgas realised his own first arrow was still on the string.
He picked a man at random, looking at him down the
arrowshaft as he drew back with his right hand, pushed
forward with his left; then, as his right forefinger brushed
the corner of his mouth he relaxed his right hand and let
the arrow fly. He didn't stop to see where it went; the
enemy was still holding, but he could hear their officers
shouting – *Left wheel, about face, keep the ranks together!*
– and there was no time to lose if he wanted to keep the
initiative. They were one volley ahead of the game
already, which had probably gone some way towards
reducing the numbers problem. He shouted, 'Go!'

It was an awkward business, that clash of arms in the darkness. The man he came up against must have taken him for one of his own, because he turned to meet him with his shield lowered, started to say something but never got the chance to finish. Gorgas shot him from about four feet away, and he could hear the arrowshaft snap under the force of such a close impact. The man went down without a sound, and Gorgas looked around quickly. He could no longer tell friend from enemy himself, which was disconcerting. He quickly nocked another arrow and started to flex the bow, ready to make the last pull and push to full draw as soon as a target presented itself. In the event, he didn't have long to wait. Someone barged towards him, presumably an enemy, certainly too close to take risk. He opened his chest into the strain of the bow, and something snapped.

For a moment he wasn't sure what had happened. Something had hit him hard, in the face and the pit of the stomach simultaneously, and his fear told him the enemy had taken him and he was done for. But the man he'd been about to shoot had brushed past him, gone on a few paces and suddenly fallen; and then Gorgas realised that his own bow had broken at full draw, and the two ferocious blows he'd taken were the two limbs of the bow striking him. He swore joyfully, at the same time gloriously happy to be alive and furious that his favourite bow was broken. *Why would it do that after all these years?* he demanded angrily as he let go of the handle and fumbled for his sword. *Of all the rotten luck . . .*

Someone was standing directly in front of him, no more than a foot or so away. Gorgas pulled out his knife – the damned thing snagged in the sheath, nearly didn't come out – and stabbed quickly. The other man gave a little sigh and folded up, his own weight pulling him off the knife. As he slid to the ground, Gorgas saw that he was an enemy.

When he looked round again, he realised it was over. There were men with torches running down the slope from the stockade – his reserves, too late and not needed. Just in time he remembered to give the order to disengage, before anybody mistook anybody else for an enemy. That, he realised as he stepped over the body of the man he'd just killed, had probably happened a few times in the course of the evening's events; but in the dark nobody else would know, there'd be no point worrying about it. These things happen.

The torchlight showed him a sight he could be well satisfied with. About seventy of the enemy had dropped their weapons and sat down as soon as they'd realised they'd been had; the rest of the raiders were dead, most of them taken out in the first two volleys. He'd lost seven killed and a score or so injured, only a handful seriously. There was one man with an arrow through his lung; he wasn't going to make it and that was unfortunate, since none of the raiders had carried bows. He noticed another man whose face had been cut open from the cheekbone to the lip, so that his cheek was peeled back to show his teeth and jaw. There were enemy wounded too, but the Bank's policy was quite clear there and saved him the trouble of making a decision.

'All right,' he said in a loud voice, 'looks like we're all through here. We'll get some sleep and bury the bodies in the morning.' He looked round and found the young clerk he'd been next to before the ambush. 'Get the wounded up to the farm, organise some clean water and bandages. You'd better put them in the main house. The rest of us can go in the long barn.'

The young man nodded and hurried away. He looked very shaken, appropriately enough for a kid after his first taste of combat, and having something to do would help take his mind off things. Gorgas knelt down and picked up two pieces of stick joined by a waxy string.

'That's your bow,' said a voice above his head. He nodded.

'That's right,' he said. 'The bitch snapped on me right in the middle of things. Pity, I'd had it years.'

The other man, a senior clerk who worked in his office, sat down on the ground beside him. 'It went off all right,' he said.

'Can't grumble,' Gorgas replied. 'Except for this. I'd better go and talk to the farmer. After all, that's what we're here for.'

He stood up and walked away, taking the broken bow with him. Somehow he couldn't bring himself just to throw it away.

The farmer and his family were in the main house, the man piling up wood on the fire, his wife fussing round another man with a slight but messy scalp wound, while the children scampered about the place with jugs of water, blankets and strips of linen torn for bandages. Gorgas suddenly found he wasn't in the mood for being praised and thanked, but the whole point of the exercise had been to show these people that he could protect them, so he had to go through the motions, say the right things - *it was nothing, a pleasure, that's what we're here for, time we showed those bastards they can't do that kind of stuff any more.* He was good at it, usually. Tonight, though, he just wanted to wash and go to sleep, and in the morning go home to his own house and family.

'We owe you everything,' the farmer's wife was saying, 'everything. We'll never forget what you've done for us, risking your lives and ...'

'That's all right,' he replied, perhaps a trifle curtly. 'Like we told you at the beginning, it's all part of the service. You just be sure and tell your neighbours.' He remembered something. 'Now then,' he went on, 'we're going to need some ground to bury the bodies. If it's all right by you, we'll dig the grave there, where the fighting was. My men want to be on their way, we'd rather not spend time in the morning ferrying corpses about.'

The farmer clearly didn't like the sound of that, and Gorgas could see his point; it was fallow right now, but the battlefield was a good flat strip of land that probably yielded a decent crop, far too valuable to waste. He suppressed a grin, thinking of what his father would have said if someone had suggested burying a couple of hundred bodies in their back two-acre. 'That's settled, then,' he said. 'We'll see to it in the morning. No need for you to bother.'

The farmer looked at him and said nothing. He could read the man's eyes, the thought of having to go back and dig up two hundred graves, load the mouldy remains into a boat and tip them out in the sea. Days, even weeks of work before the patch would be ready for the plough, when they should be harrowing for the winter barley. He was right, it wasn't fair. 'On second thoughts,' he said, 'why don't we cart them down to the sea for you? It'll be no trouble.'

The farmer's face brightened and he nodded; a man of few words, clearly. His wife made up the balance with a further gush of gratitude. Gorgas stifled a yawn and went out to the barn.

Maybe they're used to this sort of thing, he thought, as he walked across the courtyard. The place was recognisably a farm – every inch of space used for something, nothing for show, everything for a purpose – but it wasn't like the farms among which he'd grown up. The stockade of twelve-foot stakes, the thick walls and massive gates, a fortified tower instead of a farmhouse; as if the life wasn't hard enough already. Why *did* people do this sort of thing to each other? Pointless question; it's the way things are here. They must like it like this. He suggested as much to his friend the senior clerk.

'I don't think so,' the clerk replied. 'They're just used to it, that's all. Amazing what you can grow up not noticing, just because it's always been there. Our farm wasn't much different from this. A lot bigger, of course,' he added quickly, 'we were a good family. But the same basic shape – perimeter, except ours was stone, and we had a gatehouse as well as a tower. Once, back in my great-grandfather's time, we were besieged for six days.' He sounded proud of that; Gorgas didn't follow it up.

'Stupid way to live,' Gorgas replied, snuggling his back into a heap of straw. 'Wouldn't suit me, anyway.'

'What, the farming or the fighting?' The clerk smiled. 'Can't be the fighting, because that's what you do. And didn't you tell me once you were raised on a farm?'

Gorgas yawned. 'Either is fine,' he replied. 'It's the two together that'd get to me. I mean, how can you face ploughing and harrowing and planting every year when you know there's a good chance some bastard'll come along and set fire to it before you can bring it in? You'd go crazy thinking about it.'

The clerk shrugged. 'Pests are pests,' he replied amiably. 'You get mice, rabbits, rooks and pigeons, and you get soldiers. You bring in what's left. You make allowances and budget accordingly. And if you lose the lot one year, you increase your borrowing and start again.' He frowned and looked away. 'That's how it all started,' he said quietly, 'and how it's gone on. Just as well there's people like us who're prepared to do something about it.'

'Quite,' Gorgas replied, rolling onto his side. 'And now I think I'd like to get some sleep, if it's all the same to you.'

The clerk grinned. 'You're upset because you bust your nice bow,' he said. 'Which is fine,' he added. 'I can understand that.'

Gorgas thought for a moment. 'You're right,' he said, 'I am. Like I said, I've had the thing for years, ever since I was a boy. My brother made it for me, as a matter of fact.'

'Which one? You've got so many.'

Gorgas smiled. 'I've made some good shots with this bow in my time,' he said. 'Got me out of trouble more often than I care to think. And in it, too; but that wasn't the bow's fault, just mine.' He collected the broken limbs and held them up to the yellow light of the oil-lamp. 'Went in the belly, would you believe,' he said. 'There, in the layer of horn, that's where the crack started, right up through the wood into the sinew.'

'Really,' said the clerk, bored. 'Well, that's just ...' He

didn't bother to finish the sentence. Gorgas put the remains down beside him and tucked his hands behind his
head.

'I shall have to get him to make me another one,' he
said.

'The Director will send for you presently,' the man said.
He nodded at a cold, hard-looking stone bench, and
walked away.

Alexius thought of his piles, groaned inside and sat
down on the bench, which was just as cold and hard as
he imagined. Perhaps it'd be better to stand; but he
thought of his rheumatism and decided against it. All in
all, he reflected, he was too old to hang around in stark,
miserable waiting rooms outside the offices of people
with titles like Director. Come to that, he'd been too old
for that game on the day he was born.

Which was not to suggest that the place didn't have a
certain grandeur about it. The anteroom was wide and
high, with a hammer-beam roof and thick ornamental
pillars of roughly finished pink granite; no decoration,
not even whitewash, but everything built in a way that
suggested money and resources were no problem. That
impression, he reckoned, was true enough. The Director
(whoever that turned out to be) had enough of both
effectively to buy him from the Islanders and have him
whisked away on a big, fast ship before his rich and
powerful friends on the Island had been able to do anything about it. But who these people were, let alone what
they could possibly want him for, was beyond him
entirely. This didn't look like the establishment of someone who collected philosophers as a hobby.

The bench wasn't getting any more comfortable with
the passage of time, so he made the effort to stand up
and hobble on his protesting legs as far as the doorway
he'd just come through. That at least was vaguely familiar. It was an attempt to copy the grand Perimadeian
style, done by somebody who'd never been to the City or

seen anything like what he was being asked to copy. It looked bizarre and ever so slightly ridiculous.

Most of all, he realised, what offended and disconcerted him most about this place was the fact that it was obviously all so new. He was no expert, but if the clean, neat, sharp lines and unfaded colours were anything to go by, this whole building was no more than five years old. It even still had a faint residual smell of new building, the slight musty dampness of new plaster and the unmistakable scene of stone-dust. *That tells me something*, he said to himself. *Not only rich, but suddenly taken rich.* He tried not to let the thought worry him, but he couldn't help it. Being a Perimadeian, he was uncomfortable in new buildings; even the outside privies in the City had been four hundred years old and made of polished basalt.

Suddenly taken rich; well, that could be honest trade – a newly discovered seam of silver or a better sea-route to the South – or piracy, or revolution and civil war. It could be a new dynasty or a usurping warlord, except in that case he'd be waiting to see a king, not a director. Director suggested trade, and he felt marginally more comfortable with the idea of a merchant prince of some kind. But didn't newly wealthy merchants fill their palaces with gorgeous and vulgar splendour, the skimmings of five continents jumbled up together in a casserole, statues in every niche and pictures jostling each other for wall-space? This austerity suggested something else, something that was ever so slightly familiar – a contemplative order, perhaps, as it might be some newly schismatic and successful heresy. The combination of sparseness, discomfort and unlimited expenditure put him in mind of some of the establishments of his own Foundation back home, while the lack of ornament might suggest some taboo against pictorial images. Or it could just be a monumental lack of imagination, again not incompatible with contemplation and scholarship.

The far door opened and a man came out; not the one

who'd brought him here, but very similar. He was gone before Alexius could even clear his throat. A busy man, then, which suggested trade or administration – but where were the sumptuous robes and round stomach of the clerk? Could it have been the Director? The man had looked more like a soldier, stiff-backed and quick-moving, and his drab dark-brown clothes could easily have been the sort of thing a fighting man puts on under his armour. Alexius shook his head and sat down again. He was cold, hungry and confused, and his bladder needed emptying as a medium-term priority. He decided he didn't like this place very much.

I'm a philosopher, I should be sitting here contemplating the infinite, not the pain in my backside. What I wouldn't give for something to read. But the only writing in the place was a single line of unfamiliar letters cut into the stone above the Director's door, and he didn't need to be a linguist to recognise NO ENTRY EXCEPT ON OFFICIAL BUSINESS when he saw it. He folded his hands, closed his eyes and wished he could go to sleep.

Curiously enough, he managed it; because somehow the place changed around him, and he was standing in a workshop of some kind, looking at the back of a man's head. It was dark where he was; the man stood in the middle of a shaft of light that flooded in through the open door. He was standing over a workbench, planing a long, narrow piece of wood. The air was full of floating specks of dust, clearly visible in the limited beam of sunlight.

The man was Colonel Bardas Loredan, the fencer-at-law. What was he doing here?

Alexius tried to speak, but his voice didn't seem to work properly here. *Oh dear, this must be the future again. I thought I was done with all that.* He noticed streaks of grey in the hair above Loredan's ears; well, it had been two years, and Alexius was only too aware of how much he'd aged over that time. He tried to move to see

Loredan's face, but his feet appeared to be stuck, so he tried craning his neck instead. That didn't help either. There was a horrible smell, which he recognised as burning bone, and he looked back over his shoulder and saw an iron pot simmering over a charcoal fire, the smoke drifting slowly up and out through a hole in the thatch.

A boy appeared in the doorway, briefly interfering with the light, until Loredan told him to shift.

'Sorry,' the boy replied, offended. 'But you said ...'

'All right,' Loredan grunted. 'Put it down on the bench.'

The boy crossed the floor and put down what he'd been carrying: a tray covered in little bundles of some kind of thread or fibre, each bunch about a finger's length and breadth. 'Did I do them all right?' he asked hopefully.

'Fine,' Loredan muttered without looking up. 'Now lay them out where I can reach them. Got to work quickly while the glue's still warm.'

The boy did as he was told, arranging the little bundles in a row down the side of the bench, while Loredan put down his plane and ran his fingers over the surface of the wood. Then he turned round, and Alexius caught sight of his face—

—And felt his head jerk sideways, as the shoulder it had been resting on was taken away. He opened his eyes and grunted.

'I'm sorry,' said a voice beside him, 'I didn't mean to startle you.'

Sitting beside him on the cold stone bench was a woman, the owner of the shoulder he'd been using as a headrest. She studied the embarrassment in Alexius' eyes for a moment, then smiled.

'I do apologise,' Alexius said, still groggy with sleep and a headache that presumably had something to do with the angle of his head while he'd been asleep. 'I didn't realise—' 'That's all right, really.' The woman was still smiling. She was probably taller than she looked; but she was plump, with a round face, a little knob of a chin crowning the space where her fat, smooth cheeks met at the bottom. Her hair was grey and looked as if it had gone that colour five or so years earlier than it should have. She wore it in a neat round bun secured with an undecorated whalebone comb; it was pulled in tight, like a prisoner's arm twisted behind his back. She was wearing a plain grey smock, with a moth-hole skilfully darned on the point of the right shoulder. 'You know, my grandfather was just the same; he'd fall asleep in the evenings and whoever was next to him on the settle had to stay exactly where they were till he woke up.' She peered at him and frowned a little. 'Actually, you do look tired,' she said. 'Are you all right?'

'Fine,' Alexius replied, straightening his back a little.

'You don't need to go for a wee or anything?'

'No,' Alexius said firmly, 'thank you. Excuse me,' he went on, 'but you wouldn't happen to know if the Director's actually in his office, would you? You see, I've been sitting here for hours, and I don't believe he's really there.'

The woman nodded. 'I was in there a moment ago,' she said. 'There's nobody in there.'

Alexius sighed. 'Then do you think it'll be all right if I go now?' he said. 'It must be getting late, and I've still got to find somewhere to stay the night. The soldiers who brought me here didn't tell me much, but I gathered that the Director's summons didn't include anything about a place to stay. I don't know,' he went on, 'maybe they're going to give me a guest room, or throw me in the cells.'

'You're here to see the Director,' the woman said. Odd, the way she said it; not a question, not quite a statement. 'You're right, it is late. And you look as if you should be in bed.' She stood up and went across to the door of the office. 'Would you like something to eat or drink?' she said.

Alexius considered for a moment. 'Yes,' he said, 'if it's no trouble I'd quite like a long drink of water.'

'No trouble,' the woman said. 'And something to eat?'

'Maybe later. I suppose it depends how much longer I've got to sit here.'

The woman tilted her shoulders a little. 'That's fine,' she said. 'In that case, we'd better make a start. Let's go through into the office. It's more comfortable in there.'

Fine clairvoyant you are. 'You're the Director?' Alexius said, stupidly. The woman didn't reply immediately; she pushed open the door, strode across to a big, solid chair behind a big, solid desk – the roof could fall in, and when they dug it out of the rubble the furniture would be as good as new – flumped down and wriggled a little to get herself comfortable. Alexius followed. There was another chair, also monumentally built but smaller and straighter, on the other side of the desk. It was quite dark, and the woman fiddled briefly with a tinder-box to light a plain pottery lamp.

'That's better,' she said, as the light began to spread. Just the one lamp, in a big, spare, empty room. He was used to corridors, pantries and closed-file stores being better lit than this. 'Now then.' She smiled, pinching little birds'-footprints-in-the-snow dimples in the corners of her cheeks. 'Welcome to Scona.'

'Thank you,' Alexius replied. His head was hurting badly now, and even the pale yellow light of the lamp was painful. 'I'm sorry,' he went on, knowing as he spoke that he could only make things worse, 'I didn't think you were the Director. I thought ...'

'Not to worry,' the woman said briskly. 'I'm Niessa Loredan. I own the Bank.'

Alexius nodded, unable to think of anything intelligent to say. He noticed little dots in the lobes of her ears, where they'd been pierced for earrings long ago and left to heal over. 'I think I know your brother,' he said. 'Bardas Loredan?'

She nodded, with no perceptible change in expression. 'And I think you've also met another of my brothers, Gorgas,' she said. 'He's mentioned you.'

'Yes,' Alexius said. 'Yes, I met him once. Briefly.'

She looked at him thoughtfully, as if he was a fairly expensive cut of meat she'd bought for a dinner party, and she was trying to decide which was the best way to cook him. 'And of course, I've got two other brothers back in the Mesoge, but you haven't met them. Oh,' she added, 'I forgot. Your drink of water.'

Before Alexius could say anything she was on her feet and pouring water from a huge embossed brass jug into a wooden cup. The jug looked like a trophy of war or a gift from a neighbouring ruler on a state visit. The cup was home-made, laboriously hollowed out with a gouge rather than turned out on a lathe. There was a tiny split in the rim. Alexius took it and held it in the palm of his left hand, not quite knowing what to do next. Would it be rude to gulp it down while she was talking to him, or offensive not to drink it now that she'd been to the trouble of pouring it with her own hands? *This is a very sparse, tidy room*, he noticed, irrelevantly. *And she acts as if she's just rented it for the week and doesn't want to touch any of the fixtures and fittings in case she breaks something and has to pay for it. That jug's Southern, there ought to be porcelain cups to go with it. I wonder if she keeps them for special visitors?* A strange picture floated into his mind, of this woman busily tidying and dusting the room, just as his mother used to do when company was expected, while he waited miserably outside on a cold, hard bench. He raised the cup to his lips and took a little sip of water. 'So,' he said, 'what can I do for you?'

She smiled again. Her face reminded him of a cooking apple. 'You mean,' she said, 'why did I have you dragged halfway round the world to a place you've probably only heard of two or three times, and then dump you in the waiting room for hours? It's a fair question. The answer to the second part is, I was busy. You will tell me when you want something to eat, won't you?'

Alexius nodded and took a deep breath. He had no idea whether he was frightened of her or not. She was thirty years younger than he was, but she reminded him of his grandmother. 'And the first part?' he asked.

'Oh, I'd assumed you'd already guessed,' she replied. Without taking her eyes off him, she reached out and helped herself to a handful of raisins from a shallow unglazed pottery dish. 'I want you to do some magic for me, please.'

Alexius took a deep breath. Not so long ago, he'd had a set speech for these occasions, one that neatly and concisely explained the difference between an abstract philosopher and a conjurer. It had been composed for the benefit of students and the wives of civic dignitaries making small talk at official receptions. Since the Director fitted neither category, he decided to improvise.

'I'm sorry,' he said, 'but I'm not a magician. I couldn't do magic even if I wanted to. I don't think anybody can. What I do is study a half-scientific, half-metaphysical concept which we call the Principle, which is all about the structure of Time. Over the years, our studies have occasionally had bizarre and uncontrollable side-effects which could be confused with magic, but since none of us really knows the first thing about these phenomena—'

'Of course,' Niessa Loredan said, with a touch of impatience. 'That's the aggravating thing. You don't know much about it.' She laced her plump fingers together, and in that gesture Alexius could see the woman who'd founded and built up a highly successful bank. 'You don't understand magic, but you can do it. I understand it all right, but I can't do it – well, not as much as I want to. So here's the deal: I teach you, and you help me. Fair?'

A long time ago, Alexius had had an uncle who ran a sawmill. Now his uncle was very good at sawing wood, and not much else; but his wife (his second wife, fifteen years his junior) had a positive genius for business, and she'd taught the young Alexius a trick or two about negotiation. One: if they talk a lot, summarise and simplify. Two: as soon as possible, get to the deal. Three:

let them know some of your weaknesses. Four: make them think you know all about them. Five: never try and strike a deal that doesn't have at least some small benefit for the other side. Coincidentally, his aunt-by-marriage had been short and substantial.

'You know about magic,' he said. 'That's very interesting. We – the scholars of my Foundation – recognise the kind of person who has a natural ability to understand and even manipulate the workings of the Principle; we call them "naturals", in fact. Usually they don't seem to realise what they can do. You're saying you're one of them?'

Niessa Loredan clicked her tongue. 'You haven't been listening, have you?' she scolded. Your "naturals" don't understand, but they can do it. I'm the opposite. I'm not the natural in this room, Master Patriarch; you are.'

Alexius had already opened his mouth to reply when what she'd said sunk in. He sat quite still for two or three seconds without speaking.

'And like you said,' Niessa Loredan went on, 'you've never realised what you can do. Come on, think about it. That business with my daughter and my brother Bardas; you did some fairly strong magic there, and I'll bet you couldn't tell me how you did it. Well?'

Again Alexius opened his mouth, then hesitated. 'No,' he said, 'I can't. Well, in very general terms, yes; but a step-by-step description of the procedure, no.' He narrowed his eyebrows. 'You're telling me that you can?'

Niessa stifled a yawn. 'Oh, yes,' she said. 'It's what you might call simple but difficult. Like it's a fairly simple operation to lift a huge boulder, but impossible to do unless you're very strong. I know how to lift things, but I'm not strong enough to go humping boulders around. It's the same with magic.' She looked him in the eye for a moment, then continued, 'I can see you're uncomfortable with that word, but I can't think of a better one. I suppose you'd call it "anomalous physical phenomena associated with manipulation of the Principle", but that's too much of a mouthful for me. Well? Do you want to learn, or don't you?'

Alexius thought of his uncle's wife. 'You're asking me to buy goods I haven't seen,' he said.

'No,' Niessa replied. 'The deal is this. We agree the terms, then you get the goods, then you pay for them. After all, you can't do what I want you to until you've learnt what I've got to teach you.'

'All right,' Alexius said cautiously. 'Tell me what you want me to do first.'

Again, Niessa looked him in the eyes before answering. It was meant to be unnerving, and it worked. 'It's no more than you did for my daughter,' she said.

Alexius shook his head. 'I can't be certain because I don't know enough about it,' he replied, 'but I have an idea that what I did at the very least contributed to the fall of the City. It certainly caused an awful lot of trouble, and also made me very ill. I don't think I want to get involved in anything like that, even if it means not learning what you know about magic. After all,' he added, with a slight shrug that his aunt-by-marriage would have approved of, 'it isn't actually what I'm interested in.'

'Very well,' Niessa said. 'Now let me tell you a little bit about my family. As you know, when we were younger and still living in the Mesoge, my brother Gorgas set me up to be raped by two rich young men from the City, and then murdered my father and my husband and tried to kill me and our brother Bardas, in an attempt to cover up what he'd done. When he got away, my brothers all blamed me for what happened - and yes, I'd been making eyes at the two City boys, hoping they'd take me with them to Perimadeia. Gorgas killed them too, which means he killed the father of my daughter. In spite of that,' she went on, with a little shake of her head, 'Gorgas and I are quite good friends; at least, we're all the family each of us has got, since Bardas and Clefas and Zonaras all refuse to have anything to do with us.

'Now Gorgas really believes in family; I'm not so bothered, I can take it or leave it alone. I've had to lock my daughter up in the guard house, because she's not right in the head and keeps making threats and saying all sorts of dreadful things. Gorgas thinks I'm horrible for doing that, but since most of the threats are against Bardas – he dotes on Bardas, always has – he agrees it's the right thing to do. But you see, Gorgas and I are business people; we know when to cut our losses, when to put the past behind us, we knew that together we could make a future for ourselves, and we did.'

Niessa paused for a moment, letting Alexius digest what she'd told him. 'I suppose you could say that above all else, we're single-minded, and practical. We're practical about life and death, love and hate, right and wrong; and we're practical about this thing you call lots of long, difficult words and we call magic. And that's the sort of people we are. And if you think you have any choice about whether or not you help us,' she added, with a slight smile, 'then all I can say is, for an old man you're pretty naïve.'

Alexius nodded. 'You want me to kill someone,' he said. 'Lots of people, because one man wouldn't need magic.'

'Oh, no,' Niessa said. 'Again, you haven't been listening. Now this time, listen and use your brain. We don't want anybody killed; quite the reverse. You were the one who wanted to kill Bardas, remember, and we stopped you. And now,' she went on pleasantly, 'we want you to make Bardas love us again. It's for Gorgas' sake more than mine, really, but it'd please me too. It's time we were a family again, what's left of us. And besides,' she added, 'we could use him in the business. You're his friend; don't you want to see him reconciled with his nearest and dearest?'

Alexius smoothed his beard with the palm of his hand. 'I see,' he said. 'You want to give your brother your other brother as a birthday present?'

Niessa smiled. 'Why not?' she said. 'After all, it's something he wants.'

The boy looked up. His face was glowing in the light of the fire.

'Why do we have to do this at this time of year, when it's cold and dark?' he said. 'We could have finished in a single day back in the summer.'

Loredan didn't turn his head; he was staring into the fire. 'It's better to cut the staves when the sap's down,' he said. 'That way, they're easier to season. When I was your age, we'd wait till the snow was a foot thick on the ground before we'd even think of cutting timber.'

The boy looked at him. 'You're not from the City, are you?' he asked. 'Originally, I mean.'

Loredan shook his head. 'You haven't heard of where I'm from,' he said, without expression. 'It really snows there. This is what spring's like where I was brought up.'

The boy shivered. 'Sounds horrid,' he said. 'This is bad enough. I suppose I'll get used to it,' he added forlornly. Loredan smiled.

'Amazing what you can get used to if you have to,' he said. 'Try putting on more clothes, for a start. You shouldn't have to be told that, at your age.'

The boy stared into the fire, as if trying to see what Loredan was looking at. 'Is this what you used to do,' he said, 'before you came to the City?'

'Not really, no. We were farmers, just like everybody else. But that meant you had to know all sorts of things. We never bought anything we could possibly make ourselves. I learnt this trade along with a couple of dozen others, and thought no more of it. I mean,' he added with a grin, 'it's not exactly difficult, is it?'

The boy pulled a face. '*I* think it's difficult,' he said.

'You would,' Loredan replied pleasantly. 'I don't suppose you can shoe horses, either. Or build a house, or make nails, or cast pots, or weave rope. I can. Not well, mind you,' he added, 'but well enough. But I'll admit, I was always better at this line of work than most people. And it's light work and by no means disagreeable. Not a bad living, either, in these parts. This is a remarkably cack-handed race we've found ourselves among.'

'Farmers,' said the boy. 'Oh, sorry, no offence.'

Loredan shook his head. 'Not farmers,' he said, 'peasants. There's a difference. I didn't use to think so, but it's true. Still, that's none of our business. Thank the gods for the military, that's what I say. All the work we can handle and they pay on delivery.'

The boy sucked his teeth. 'I thought they specified yew or osage,' he said. 'Why're we cutting ash?'

Loredan chuckled. 'My friend,' he said, 'that lot couldn't tell the difference between a yew tree and a stick of celery. They just said yew or osage because that's what they read in some book. Ash'll do just fine, so long as we back it with rawhide.'

He threw another lump of dead wood on the fire and lay back, his hands behind his head. Far away, down in the valley, a wolf howled. The boy sat up with a start.

'Calm down,' Loredan said, with a grin.

The boy looked at him nervously. 'That was a wolf,' he said.

'Sure. Now go to sleep.'

'But surely ...' The boy looked round, as if expecting to see the glint of eyes at the edge of the firelight. 'Shouldn't we climb a tree or something?'

Loredan yawned. ' You're welcome to climb a tree if you really want to,' he said. 'Assuming you can find one, of course. I think we just cut down the last one. On the whole, though, I think you'd be better off getting some sleep. We've got a lot of work to do in the morning.'

The boy was clearly not convinced. 'Well, at least one of us should keep watch,' he said. 'Just in case, you know.'

'Please yourself.' Loredan sat up, reached out for his toolbag, pulled it under his head and lay back again, closing his eyes. 'Good night.'

Almost at once, he was asleep. He knew he was asleep, because he was standing on the ramparts of the great gatehouse of Perimadeia (which wasn't there any more) and he was looking past the tents of the plainsmen towards the east, where the river seemed to flow upwards into the sky. Beside him on the walkway was his brother Gorgas; and in this dream they were on speaking terms, almost friendly, because Gorgas was telling him about the war in Scona, and he wasn't really listening. Other people's war stories are usually very boring.

'You should come out to Scona,' Gorgas was saying. 'This city's had its time. They're going to win, and you don't want to be here when that happens. I could use you back in Scona, a man with your experience.'

Loredan saw himself shaking his head. 'No thanks,' the dream-Loredan said. 'What's the point in sailing halfway round the world to fight a war when I've got one right here? Besides, I'm not a mercenary.'

Gorgas frowned at him, as if offended. 'It wouldn't be like that,' he said. 'You're family. We should stick together.'

'I'd steer clear of that subject if I were you,' this other Loredan replied. 'If I ever do leave the City, I'll go somewhere I can earn an honest living without people trying to kill me all the time.' He shrugged. 'I might even go back to farming. Hey,' he added, 'did I just say something funny?'

Gorgas grinned at him. 'Sorry,' he said, 'didn't mean to be rude. It's just the thought of you back on the farm, that's all. It's enough to make a cat laugh.'

'All right,' Loredan said, 'then I'll set up in a trade. There's all sorts of things I could do.'

'Name three.'

Loredan thought before answering. 'I could set up as a wheelwright,' he said. 'Or coopering. I used to mend all our barrels, remember.'

'They leaked,' Gorgas said. 'You could never quite get the new staves to fit flush. Remember that year the damp got into the seedcorn, and when we took the lids off, it'd all sprouted?'

'All right, not coopering. There's still plenty of other things. I could be a coppersmith. I'd be good at that.'

Gorgas bit his lip and smiled. 'I can see you now,' he said, 'with your pack on your back, trudging round the villages mending pots. Admit it, brother, for anything that doesn't involve spilling blood, you're useless. You should stick to what you're good at, like I've done. That's what I'm for; it's all a question of the right tool for the job. I was designed for making money. You were designed for killing people. There's nothing *wrong* with that.'

'The hell with you,' the other Loredan said in disgust; and the Loredan who was watching all this was heartily grateful that no such conversation had ever taken place, or ever would now that the City was in ruins. 'That's a nasty thing to say, and I don't think it's true, either. You make me sound like the knacker's cart, with a swarm of crows always hovering around it just out of stone's throw. And I don't know where you get this idea of yourself as a straight-up businessman from,' he added irritably. 'If there's anyone in this family who's made his way in the world by cutting throats, it's you.'

Gorgas leant his elbows on the parapet and studied the distant tents for a while. 'I won't deny that,' he said. 'I've done a lot of things I'd have preferred not to, over the years. But it was always as a means to an end; I never made a career of it. And if we're going to be brutally honest here,' he added, turning slowly and looking this other Loredan in the eyes, 'then I'll just make the point that at least I *have* made my way in the world, as you put it. You've spent your life simply floundering along, and every day some new fight to the death; you always win, of course, and the other poor bastard always dies, but where the hell has it ever got you? At least when I've shed blood, it's always been for a purpose, and nearly always unavoidable.' He sighed and looked away. 'I'll be straight with you,' he said. 'If I were in your shoes, I'd have trouble sleeping at night.'

—Which was apparently some sort of cue, because Bardas woke up and saw that it was first light, and a cold, weak sun was swimming in thin grey clouds. The boy was fast asleep a few feet away; Bardas smiled and prodded his shoulder with his toe.

'Wake up,' he said. 'The good news is, the wolves didn't get you after all.'

The boy grunted and turned over, tugging at the blanket. Loredan pulled it away. The boy grunted and sat up, rubbing his eyes with his knuckles.

'Get the wedges,' Loredan said. 'Come on, we've got work to do. You'd better pay attention, because this is important.'

The boy mumbled something as he dragged himself up off the ground, but it was too indistinct to make out and Loredan was pretty sure he didn't need to hear the words in order to get the general idea. He sat down opposite the log-end and examined the growth rings.

'What do you want me to do?' the boy asked.

'Fetch the saw,' Loredan replied. 'We've got to trim off the branches before we do anything else.'

The sun was high by the time they'd finished dressing up the log. There was no wind, and even a slight suggestion of warmth. 'We'll get four good staves out of this one,' he said. 'Maybe even five if we go steady. A lot depends on how cleanly it splits. Right, you sit on the log, I'll drive in the first wedge.'

He placed the blade of the wedge on the line he'd chosen and tapped it gently but firmly with the back of the axe-head, one-handed, until he was sure it had bitten into the wood. Then he stepped back with the axe in both hands, left hand in the curve at the end of the handle, right hand just below the head. He fixed his eye on the head of the wedge, concentrated and swung. The back of the axe-head hit the wedge pretty square, and the first signs of a split began to show along the line he'd hoped he'd seen.

'Got that?' he said, straightening up.

'No,' the boy replied. 'I can't see anything from here, remember.'

Loredan sighed. 'Come round here and take a look,' he replied. 'See how it's just beginning to go?'

Ten or twelve hard blows opened the split up to just on five inches; long enough to admit the next wedge, which Loredan drove in from above with another dozen carefully weighed blows, each of them being nothing more or less than the weight of the axe-head falling from the top of his swing. 'That's really important,' he said, stopping to catch his breath – was he really short of breath after a few swings with an axe? Getting lazy, or old. 'Remember what I told you. Just let the weight of the axe do the work.'

'You said.'

Two more blows were sufficient to widen the crack far enough for the first wedge to fall out. Loredan picked it up and pressed the blade a quarter of an inch into the top of the crack. 'And so on,' he said. 'Are you paying attention?'

'Sure,' the boy replied guiltily. 'I was watching, honest.'

Loredan grunted. 'You ought to be watching this carefully,' he said reproachfully. 'There's a lot more to it than you'd think. It's not just a case of splitting it any old how, it's got to be clean and straight or we'll have wasted our time and a perfectly good tree. Did you find that axe-head you broke off, by the way?'

'I'll look for it later, I promise. Go on with what you were doing. I'm watching.'

'You better had be. You're going to be doing the next one.'

Loredan was pleased with how it went, each wedge in turn opening the crack a little further, splitting the wood along his chosen line and releasing the previous wedge until it could be lifted free without effort. *Curious*, he mused, *the way my life's become a sort of celebration of mechanical advantage. It's enough to fool a man into thinking he's in control of things.* The final wedge, driven in diagonally, split the last couple of inches and the two halves of the log rolled apart on either side of his synthetic line, as neat and consistent as a proposition in algebra. He nodded, and handed the axe to the boy. 'Your turn,' he said. 'Split the halves into quarters. And if you cock it up, you're walking home.'

The boy looked at him resentfully, then stooped down to gather the wedges. 'I'll bet you didn't get it right the first time you did it,' he said.

Loredan laughed. 'As a matter of fact, I did,' he said, as the boy knelt down and studied the timber. 'It was the second time when I wrecked the stave, chipped the wedge and broke the axe. It was two days before I dared show my face in the house again. So think on.'

'Huh.' Loredan watched the boy scrutinising the grain with all the fierce, brief concentration of youth, and suppressed a grin. It was like stepping back and watching himself, as if in a dream. He could remember that same furious indecision, the frustration of not allowing himself to ask advice. *Look for the flaw,* he wanted to say, *there's always a weak spot in every billet, it's just a matter of knowing where to look.* But he managed not to; let the boy work it out for himself, and then he'd know it for ever.

'Got it,' the boy said. He looked up and saw the stump of the tree, then slid the billet along the ground until it was jammed against it. Loredan nodded his approval, but the boy wasn't looking. That was a good sign, too.

'This time,' he said, 'for crying out loud don't bust the axe. We'll be here all week if we've got to stop and make new handles.'

'All *right*,' the boy replied, annoyed. 'I'm trying to concentrate, you know,' he added.

'Sorry,' Loredan said meekly. 'You carry on.'

The boy took a deep breath and started tapping the

wedge. The axe was too big and heavy for him to be able to manage it single-handed with any degree of comfort, and the wedge refused to bite. At the third attempt, the boy rapped his knuckles and swore.

'Want me to start it for you?' Loredan asked.

'It's all right,' the boy said angrily. 'I can manage.'

Loredan kept quiet. In the back of his mind he could see his father showing him the other way of starting the split, standing up straight with one foot bracing the wedge, holding the axe by the end of the handle and letting it swing gently like a pendulum to apply the small, measured degree of force necessary for the first bite. He could remember himself, raw-knuckled, red-faced and close to tears after he'd tried so many times and failed, and been told to get out of the way. On the other hand, this was a job of work, not an Academy seminar. 'Stand up and brace the wedge with your foot,' he said. 'You might find it easier that way.'

As the boy straightened his back, Loredan looked away and then down at his hands, noticing the calluses that fringed his palms, the thick pads of skin between the first and middle joints of his first three fingers, the shaven patch on his left arm just above the wide purple bruise across the inside of his wrist, the characteristic and unavoidable injuries of his trade, that had become part of him over the last two years; because every human occupation leaves its own very specific disfigurements, and these were at least preferable to many. An observant man would know at once from these who he was and what he did, or at least what he did now.

The crisp chime of the axe-head on the wedge made him look up. 'It's starting to go,' the boy said proudly. Loredan nodded. 'Steady does it,' he replied, 'don't go mad.' The boy didn't reply, he was concentrating on what he was doing, and without having to be told. Loredan turned his back. He could tell if the boy was doing it right by the sound of the axe-head. It didn't sound too bad.

'There, all done,' the boy said. 'Come and tell me if that'll do.'

Loredan examined the work gravely, like a colonel inspecting his troops. 'Not bad,' he said. 'Now you can do the other one, while I make a start on stripping the bark off.'

'Oh.' The boy picked up the axe again, a little less enthusiastically this time, while Loredan walked over to the cart and took the drawknife out of the box. The sky was clouding over. It'd be a good idea to get a move on if they didn't want to have to finish the job off in the pouring rain. He felt the edge with his thumb; it was sharp enough for sloughing off bark, for which purpose a slightly dull blade is marginally preferable. As he turned to walk back, he heard the sound of the axe pecking the wedge.

'That's the ticket,' he called out. 'You never know, we might make a bowyer of you yet.'

CHAPTER TWO

It was late afternoon by the time Gorgas Loredan's ship dropped anchor in Scona Bay, and he decided to put off making his report until the next morning. There was, after all, no hurry; the enemy would still be dead tomorrow, and quite probably the day after as well, and he could see no pressing reason why he should toil all the way up the steep hill to the Director's office and hang about there for an hour or so until his sister condescended to see him when he could be at home, with his boots off and his feet up on a footstool, watching the sun set over Shastel with a mug of hot spiced wine in his hand.

From the Quay he strolled down the long sweep of the Traders' Dock, making a mental note of the ships that had arrived since he left and checking them against his comprehensive mental register: two more ore-freighters from Colleon (Why all this activity in the copper trade? Was someone trying to corner the market?); a huge timber-ship from the South Coast with thirty enormous cedar logs stacked pyramid-fashion the whole length of the ship; a handful of light, fast cutters from the Island, three of which he'd never seen before. It was good to see the dock this busy; it suggested confidence.

As usual at this time of day, the Dock was crowded with people taking the pre-dinner stroll around which the life of Scona seemed to revolve. This was the time of

38

day when the shops and stalls did their best business,
while merchants gathered under the white awnings of
the taverns to put deals together and deplore whatever it
was that was threatening them all with penury and ruin
that week. Craftsmen and shop owners walked slowly
with their families along the curve of the sea-wall at the
top end of the Dock, husbands and wives arm in arm,
their eyes fixed straight ahead in case they caught sight
of someone they didn't want to have to stop and talk to,
while the children ambushed each other from behind the
barrels and bales that stood outside the warehouses of
the Bank. The deep hum of voices in pleasant conversation that pervaded the place always reminded
Gorgas of sleepy bees on a hot day, and put him in mind
of the seven hives that used to stand at the top of their
home orchard, a perpetual terror to him when he was a
boy; perhaps it was that association that always made
him uneasy here on the Dock in the early evening. He
preferred to take his walk in the Square, and let his
children play round the base of the grand fountain, with
its three sad-looking bronze lions.

   He left the Dock and walked uphill along the Promenade into the Square, passing the vast bulk of the
Bank's new offices on his left. Half the façade was still
covered in scaffolding, masking its outline like three
hundred years' growth of ivy, so that he still didn't really
know what the building was going to look like. Given the
awesome scale of the thing it was almost self-effacing; a
stranger could quite conceivably walk past it and not
notice. Partly this was because it had been chipped out
of the side of the great rocky outcrop that dominated the
town, so that the frontage was just a small panel cut into
the side of the hill, like the worked face of a quarry.
Mostly, though, it was because they couldn't be bothered
with grandiose columns and porticoes and all the other
clutter of which builders were so fond. There was no
need to tell the people of Scona that this was an important building. They knew that already.

There is something almost arrogant about the lack of ostentation displayed by the Directors of Scona; a hectoring determination to prove that they have nothing to prove. Gorgas smiled as he savoured the words in his mind; the Dean of Shastel at his supercilious best, in a letter they'd intercepted a month or so back. On balance, he had to admit, he preferred the bewildering and vulgar complexity of Shastel architecture to the slab-sided four-walls-and-a-roof approach his sister had chosen, but he wasn't sure that he liked himself for liking it. When his sister got going on the subject, as she often did, and started talking about every cornice and architrave on Shastel being stained with the blood of forced labour, he tended to keep his head down and his mouth shut. As he passed the fountain he converted the smile into a wry grin and went left into Three Lions Street, where he lived.

He had only just turned the corner when a small, incredibly fast object hurtled down the paved street towards him yelling, 'Daddy! Daddy!' and collided sharply with his midriff, knocking the wind out of him. He stepped back, put down his kitbag and lifted the object up, so that her eyes were level with his.

'Hello,' he said.

'I banged my head on your belt,' his daughter said reproachfully, 'and now it hurts.'

Gorgas solemnly examined the slight red mark on her temple. 'We'll have to post you as wounded in action,' he said. 'We'll ask Mummy if you deserve a medal.'

The little girl smiled at him with a mercenary glint in her eyes. 'Please can I have a medal?' she said. 'I'd really like one. You get medals for being brave.'

'That's right,' Gorgas replied, putting her down and taking her hand. 'And you're going to be very brave and not cry just because you bumped your head.'

'All right. Then will I get a medal?'

'If you eat all your dinner.'

'Oh.' The little girl frowned thoughtfully. 'I don't think

I really want a medal, actually,' she said. 'I'm not very hungry.'

'Oh, really?' Gorgas made a pantomime of ferocious scowling. 'You mean you've been stuffing yourself with nuts and honeycomb all afternoon, so you haven't got any room left for proper food. I know you too well, my girl. Now run indoors and tell Mummy I'm home.'

He watched her scuttle into the house, and not for the first time wished he hadn't agreed to call her Niessa, after her aunt. It had been a bad omen, in his opinion; far better to have named her after her mother, or picked a name that had no connotations at all. I wouldn't mind her having her aunt's brains, he told himself, or her strength of will, or even that clarity of thinking that's so easy to mistake for callousness and cruelty; but that's about all I'd want for her out of that particular package. Let's all hope she takes after her mother.

Though comparatively modest for one of his position and means, Gorgas' house was large by the standards of Scona and reflected the tastes and experiences of its owner. The central courtyard with its surrounding covered cloister was in the approved local style, but whereas nearly all the houses on Scona were entirely inward-looking, offering nothing to the outside view except four dour walls with narrow slits for windows, Gorgas had built a verandah on the side that faced the sea, Island-fashion, where he could sit and look out across the channel to Shastel and the mountain ranges of the mainland. The builders who'd executed his design hadn't known what to make of it; they'd insisted on calling it the look-out, on the assumption that it must have something to do with his position in the Bank. Presumably they imagined him sitting there with wax tablets and stylus, jotting down details of the ships arriving at the Dock, or brooding over maps and military textbooks as he planned the next phase of the war. Fortunately the verandah was hardly overlooked at all, and so only a few of his neighbours ever got to see the scandalous sight of the Chief Executive sitting idly in a huge cedarwood chair with his wife on a pile of cushions beside him and his offspring playing with wooden bricks at his feet.

As if that wasn't bad enough, the interiors all betrayed more than a hint of Perimadeian decadence; there were frescoes painted on the walls, bushy and inedible plants in pots dotted round the edge of the cloister and, in the middle of the courtyard, a fountain supplied by a natural hot spring in which the members of the household were rumoured to wash themselves at regular intervals. Infuriatingly for the neighbours, Gorgas' servants were all foreigners and depressingly reticent about their master's eccentricities, and (since they also formed his personal bodyguard) it was deemed unwise to press them too closely for information they weren't prepared to give. One consequence of this tantalising shortage of hard data was the quite bewildering cloud of rumour and speculation that had settled around the man, which included such bizarre and improbable tales as the one that held that he'd fled from his native country after prostituting his sister and murdering his father and half his family. Needless to say, nobody actually believed that particular fantasy. But there were plenty of quite sensible people who felt there was no smoke without fire, and that there might well be secrets in Gorgas' past that would be better left undisturbed for everybody's sake.

He dumped his kitbag in the lodge and went straight through into the courtyard, which was the likeliest place to find his wife at this time of day. She had set up her desk in the shade of the cloister, just clear of the ring of sparkling fallout from the fountain, and he kept back in the shadows for a minute or so watching her as she painstakingly copied a long legal document. At the end of each line she carefully read through what she'd written, comparing it a word at a time with the original. A strand of her long black hair had worked loose from the tight bun on the back of her head, and was dangling perilously close to the ink pot.

'Watch out, Heris,' he said softly. 'You'll get ink on the page.'

She twitched, almost knocking over the ink. 'Idiot,' she replied, with a smile. 'Don't make me jump like that. So you're not dead, then.'

'Not so as you'd notice,' he replied, strolling across the courtyard and kissing her gently on the cheek. 'All well?'

She nodded. 'A couple of men came looking for you, middle-aged merchant types, yesterday, and an old boy this morning. They both said it wasn't important and they'd come back. Vido sent the North Coast papers down, and I'm copying them now. Luha got sent home from school for fighting,' she continued with a frown. 'Again. Oh, and She wants us to go round for dinner tomorrow.'

Between the two of them, there was no need to specify who She was. By and large, Heris managed to cope remarkably well with the all-pervading presence of her sister-in-law. She'd known before she married Gorgas that there was no way in which she could compete with Niessa Loredan in any department of her life. When Niessa spoke, Gorgas listened, and when she gave an order, he obeyed. Dimly Heris was aware that it had something to do with various disagreeable things in the past, and she had the common sense to keep out of it. Common sense was, in fact, the cornerstone of her existence. If she had been the princess in the fairytale who was forbidden to go into the one locked and secret room in the castle, then into that locked and secret room she would never ever have gone, and the happy ending would have happened for her years earlier than scheduled. So, instead of making difficulties and trying to intervene between Gorgas and Niessa, she made sure that the things that mattered to her were areas in which Niessa had no interest or involvement.

The compromise was simple and effective, and only failed to be completely viable when Gorgas had to go away on business, most specifically the sort of business that made it necessary for him to wear his mailshirt under his coat and pack three days' rations in his kitbag. There had been a time when she'd been able to keep her mind off those, too; but ever since his last trip to Perimadeia, when he'd barely managed to get out of there alive when the plainsmen sacked the place, she found she had difficulty in being properly detached about it all. That aside, she represented the part of his life that took place here inside the enclosed area of the house, where nothing too disagreeable was ever allowed to enter. Anything he did outside, be it his work, his relationship with his sister or even his occasional infidelities (and they were very occasional; or at least she had no reason to think otherwise) might have been the acts of some other man who by coincidence shared the same name. They were neither interesting nor relevant to her, just as the management of the house and the buying of vegetables for the evening meal were of no interest to him.

'Tomorrow,' Gorgas repeated, sliding into the chair beside her and peering over her shoulder at the mortgage deed she was copying. 'That's a nuisance. I was going to spend tomorrow evening catching up on the work that'll have piled up while I was away. You know, I wish she'd think about things like that sometimes.'

Heris kept her eyes on the page and didn't answer. Years ago she'd worked out that while Gorgas frequently said all sorts of unpleasant things about his sister, that prerogative was reserved for him alone. For what it was worth, she got the impression that Niessa liked her, or at least approved of her, in the same way a chess-player approves of one of his pieces when it stays where it's been put and doesn't go wandering off all over the board.

'Have you got much more of that to do?' Gorgas said. 'I'd like to take a walk around the Square before dinner.'

Heris shook her head. 'At least,' she added, 'I wasn't planning on finishing it today. There's miles of it. The parcels clause alone is two sides.' She hesitated and wrinkled her nose. 'This is a big place,' she said. 'Since when did we have clients among the landed gentry?'

Gorgas laughed. 'You should see it,' he said. 'Three square miles of rock and scrub, no useful timber and about the only thing you'd ever grow there is old before your time. The two brothers – they're both in their late sixties – gave up trying to make a living farming it years ago; they just net the weirs for salmon and pootle about in that little toy quarry they've got on the western edge. We'll be lucky if we see a bent quarter out of that one while they're still alive. But two old boys living on their own – call it a long-term investment.'

'I see,' Heris replied. 'I expect you know what you're doing. There,' she added, drawing a line under a finished clause with her ebony ruler and putting the stopper back in the ink bottle. 'That's enough of that for one day. I'll get Luha and Niessa ready while you put the desk away for me.'

It was almost dark by the time they arrived in the Square, and the evening promenade was nearly over. Around the steps of the fountain the stallholders were gradually packing up for the night; fortunately, they all knew Gorgas Loredan by sight and quickly unfolded their trestles, spread their cloths and started laying out their goods again. Heris bought a honey-cake each for Niessa and Luha, cheese and sausages for the evening meal and a quarter of cinnamon to flavour the wine, while Gorgas amused himself by haggling with an old friend and sparring partner for a new penknife and set of writing tablets he didn't really want, and ended up striking such a good bargain that he was obliged to buy them.

'Heris,' he called out across the Square, 'I've come out without any money. Have you got seven quarters?'

The stallholder grinned and assured him that his credit was good, but Gorgas looked suitably shamefaced and promised faithfully to send his boy out first thing in the morning with the money. The stallholder insisted on making a show of wrapping the things carefully in a square of waxed silk tied up with red cord, packed up his stall with a flourish and departed with his trestle and pack over his shoulder, whistling cheerfully.

'Not another penknife,' Heris sighed. 'You've got a whole box of them you never even look at, and you insist on using that old thing you made out of a pan handle that you've had ever since I've known you.'

Gorgas shrugged. 'I'm afraid that if I take the good ones out of the house I'll lose them somewhere. You know what I'm like. But if I leave the old home-made one somewhere or it falls out of my pocket, then it's no great loss. Besides,' he added, 'it gets the job done. You can sharpen pens with it. What more do you want from a penknife?'

'Rubbish,' his wife replied. 'You just prefer using things that are old and tatty.'

'Old, tatty and *functional*,' Gorgas said gravely. Heris laughed, but with just the trace of an edge; *and that's why you're still with me, and not one of those girls you pick up when you're away ...* She called to the children. 'Come on,' she said. 'Time we were getting back.'

Niessa protested, needless to say, and made a specious but basically ill-founded case for being allowed to go paddling in the fountain, which her parents wisely ignored. Luha swallowed the last of his honey-cake and licked honey and the last flake of almond off his thumb. They were just about to go back when Gorgas stopped dead in his tracks.

'Just a moment,' he said. 'You go on, I'll catch you up. There's someone I haven't seen in a long while.'

Heris nodded and led the children away. Gorgas stood motionless for a while under the shadow of the fountain, hard to see in the dim light, studying an old man who was buying the last loaf of bread from the last remaining stall. It was two years since Gorgas had seen him last, in the city of Perimadeia, on the night before it was stormed by the plainsmen. He'd heard since that the old man had escaped and was still alive, but the rumours had placed him on the Island, where he was said to be living off the thinly disguised charity of a young merchant and his sister. Gorgas frowned. He knew without understanding why that the former Patriarch Alexius was a very important man, important enough to have come to the attention of his sister. If he was here in Scona, it followed that she had had him brought here; and if that was the case, what was he doing pottering about in the Square buying stale bread at a discount?

He crossed the Square quickly and quietly, keeping in the shadows more from force of habit than for any conscious reason; but the old man saw him and recognised him before he spoke.

'Gorgas Loredan,' he said.

'Patriarch,' Gorgas replied, with a polite nod. 'You're looking well.'

Alexius smiled. 'I can say the same of you,' he said, 'and with the added advantage of telling the truth.' He hesitated, having nothing else to say; he remembered their last conversation, in his lodgings at the Academy.

'Would you like to join us for dinner?' Gorgas said. 'We're having lentil soup and a leg of lamb, and my wife's just bought some rather fine-looking sausages. It's not far, just around the corner.'

Alexius looked at him, and Gorgas was reminded of the expression in the stationer's eyes as they argued over the price of the penknife. A bargain was being struck here, compromise traded for compromise. 'That's very kind of you,' Alexius said, and he glanced down at the lump of hard barley bread he was holding in his hands. 'But your wife won't thank me for rolling up for dinner at a moment's notice, I'm sure.'

'Not at all,' Gorgas replied. 'We enjoy having people for dinner, and there's plenty to go round. Our cook always makes at least one helping more than we need, and then eats it himself. He could do with losing weight, before he ends up getting hopelessly wedged in the scullery doorway.'

'In that case,' Alexius replied, 'I'd be delighted.'

In the short time he'd been on Scona, Alexius had seen rather more than he'd wanted to of a couple of large, apparently official buildings and slightly less of the very cheap inn where he'd deposited his second-best coat and shoes. So far, he hadn't seen inside a real house, and he had to admit to himself that he was curious. Why this should be, he didn't know. Since he left home and joined the Foundation, he'd spent most of his life in dormitories, cells and lodgings, and the only ordinary dwellings he'd ever got to know properly were his family home and the house of Venart and his sister Vetriz, the merchants from the Island who'd rescued him from the sack of Perimadeia. The two establishments had been so unlike each other that any scientific attempt to extrapolate a model of an Ordinary House was clearly futile. Nevertheless, he wanted to see inside Gorgas Loredan's house, and that was all there was to it.

If he'd been hoping to find anything in common between the Loredan house and either of his two previous samples, he was disappointed. It was as if his old home had been cut open and turned inside out, like a rabbit's skin; instead of the house being surrounded by the garden, what passed for a garden was in the middle of the house. A more inconvenient arrangement, he couldn't help thinking, would be hard to devise. If you wanted to go from one room to another that happened to be on the opposite side of the square, you'd either have to traipse all through the intervening rooms or else walk across the grass - aggravating if it was dark or raining. Also, because the little patch of open space was surrounded by high walls, it was overshadowed at all times of day, which meant there was no chance of growing vegetables or fruit, and surely that defeated the whole object. He could only guess that this style of building was forced on these people by the needs of defence and security, so that each house was enclosed by high walls like a little city. A strange way to live, he reflected, and not to his taste.

On the other hand, it was better than the inn, although since the same could be said of virtually any building with a roof, that wasn't a supreme compliment. Loredan's wife, a pleasant-faced woman in her late thirties, seemed genuinely pleased to have company, and the little girl immediately understood, with that special sense that small children have, that here was an old man not particularly used to children who could be charmed to death. All in all, it seemed like a fine specimen of a family, the sort of household you might show students round as a field exercise for the part of the course dealing with human relationships. It was almost as if it had been designed that way, and the accessory family members carefully selected for the purpose; or was that just his knowledge of Gorgas' past life colouring his judgement? Quite possibly. After all, he had about as much hard data on families as he had on dwelling-houses, and for all he really knew, the Loredan household might easily be as typical as it seemed.

There was one thing about normal family life that he was fairly sure of, however: in unhappy homes the cooking is usually lousy, and vice versa. On that basis, Gorgas Loredan and his family were as happy and contented as they looked. And, since he had no idea where his next good meal was coming from, he made the most of this one with all the professional thoroughness of the lifelong student. If his hosts were offended or amused, they showed no sign of it. If Loredan was deliberately trying to create images of normality about him, then as far as keeping a good table as befitted a man of his position went, he'd done a good job.

When the last plate had been cleaned off and taken away, the wife and children discreetly withdrew in the approved manner and left the two men alone. There was a well-laid fire in the hearth, with a kettle simmering over it to provide hot water for the spiced wine, the chairs were deep and comfortable and a fine chessboard stood conveniently at hand on a rosewood pedestal, though Alexius somehow had the feeling that it had never been used. Normally a heavy meal and a warm fire would have sent him straight to sleep, but he wasn't even feeling drowsy. He nodded his thanks as Gorgas handed him a cup, and took a careful sip. The stuff was quite hot, almost black, highly aromatic and extremely sweet.

'Welcome to Scona,' Gorgas said with a grin.

'Thank you.' Alexius took another sip. The aftertaste was ever so slightly stale. 'You're the second person to say that to me. Maybe you know why I'm here.'

'Me? Sorry.'

'Oh, well. I thought, since your sister had me brought here—'

Gorgas' mouth set in a dry imitation of a smile. 'I'm afraid I don't know the half of what my sister does. All I can say is, if she fetched you here, it'll be for a good reason. Good for her, of course, and for the Bank. But I'll do my best to see to it that your stay here's as pleasant as possible. Which reminds me, where are you staying? Has Niessa had you installed in one of the lodges at the Bank, or have you been slung out to make your own arrangements? Actually,' he added, 'if it's the latter it's a good sign, if you see what I mean. From your point of view, that is.'

Alexius' mouth twitched. 'I asked one of the clerks at the place I was taken to if he could recommend a good, cheap inn. To be fair to him, it's cheap.'

Gorgas laughed. 'If it's the Wildcat in Cat Street, it'd be cheap at half the price. It is the Cat, isn't it? Well, in that case, I'd like it if you'd stay with us here. No, really,' he added, as Alexius made polite noises. 'The Cat's one of the Bank's inns and really, you don't want to stay there. I'll send my boy round there in the morning for your luggage.'

Alexius decided not to protest. True, there was something he could not quite fathom about this house that made him feel uncomfortable. On the other hand, he had no difficulty whatsoever in isolating any number of things about the inn that made him feel very uncomfortable indeed, ranging from the fleas to the certain knowledge that he wouldn't have enough money to pay the bill after the first week. Mental discomfort, he decided, may be a cruel thing, but sharing one's bed with half the bugs on Scona was just as bad and rather more immediate. 'Thank you,' he said. 'You're being extremely kind.'

'That's all right,' Gorgas replied, meticulously sprinkling cinnamon powder into his cup from a small pointed spoon. 'Sadly I'm in no position to say that any friend of my brother's is a friend of mine, though not from any lack of goodwill on my part. How's the fire doing? Are you warm enough?'

'I'm fine, honestly,' Alexius answered. Just fine, he added to himself. And thank you for not pointing out that I keep shivering, because it'd be embarrassing to have to explain that these shivers have nothing at all to do with how cold it is. 'Please excuse me if this is a rude question,' he went on, 'but haven't you put on a little weight since I saw you last?'

Gorgas pulled a mock scowl. 'You're a horribly perceptive man, Patriarch,' he sighed. 'The truth is, I'm getting to the age when men start to slow down and thicken out. I'm told the condition is incurable. You, on the other hand, are obviously pickled in wisdom and likely to keep good almost indefinitely. They do say scholars only come in two sizes, short and round or long and thin, and the latter category's like the strips of dried beef you take on long journeys.'

Alexius smiled from the neck up. 'Your sister's just taken me on a long journey,' he said pleasantly. 'I do hope she doesn't mean to eat me.'

'Not in the sense you mean,' Gorgas replied, straight-faced. Then he leant forward, resting the points of his elbows on his knees, his hands cupped under his chin.

This man has the biggest hands I've ever seen, Alexius noticed. 'If you want to know why you're here, my guess is that those two merchant friends of yours – Venart and something or other, I forget the girl's name – have been dining out on stories of their friend the great wizard, and my sister's heard about it. She's very fond of collecting things she believes may come in useful at an unspecified future date, and I imagine you fall into that category.'

Alexius' expression stayed fixed. 'But I'm not a wizard,' he said. 'There's no such thing as wizards. I'm sure a – a businesswoman like your sister must know—'

Gorgas shrugged. 'Niessa knows all sorts of obscure things,' he said. 'Quite possibly – and no offence intended – she knows rather more about what you are and what you aren't than you do. Or maybe she just wants someone who's widely believed to be a wizard, which is probably every bit as useful as the real thing, looked at from the practical point of view. In any event,' he added, rubbing his broad cheeks with his fingertips, 'if I know Niessa the worst she'll do to you is keep you hanging around and maybe be a few weeks late paying your expenses. After all, she's a banker, not a wicked queen.'

Alexius nodded. 'Thank you for the reassurance,' he said. 'I'll admit I was worried. But tell me, I'm never ashamed to admit my ignorance: I really know next to nothing about Scona and this Bank of yours. Your sister said something about being at war. I didn't realise that banks fought wars.'

Gorgas leant back and folded his hands behind his head. 'That,' he said, 'is by way of being a very long story. I'll be happy to tell it to you now, but it'll keep till morning if you'd rather.'

'Now will do fine,' Alexius replied. 'If it's no trouble.'

'A pleasure.' Gorgas smiled. 'But first, my guess is that you'd be very interested indeed to know if I've got any news of my brother, but you didn't like to ask, in case – well. Am I right?'

Alexius dipped his head. 'Understandably enough, I think. But yes, I'd dearly love to know what's become of him. I only knew him for a short time, but—' Alexius hesitated, then closed his mouth. Gorgas nodded.

'Quite so,' he said. 'Well, you'll be pleased to hear that my brother's very much alive, disgustingly healthy and, as far as I can tell, as happy as a lamb in his new profession, which is making bows, of all things.'

'Making bows?' Alexius repeated.

'Making bows. You know, as in bows and arrows. Apparently he's very good at it and earning a comfortable living, up to his ankles in shavings and his wrists in glue, in the mountains here on Scona and ostentatiously having nothing to do with his sister or myself. I expect he'd like to see you, though, so I'll see about having a message sent to him. Or better still, perhaps you'd best write him a letter. Otherwise he might assume a message from me is some kind of game and refuse to hear it.'

'Thank you,' Alexius said. 'If you don't mind doing that, I'd be very grateful.'

'My pleasure. Now, I was about to start the history lesson. A drop more wine before class? Good idea, I think I'll join you. Now then, I think the best place to start would be the beginning.'

In the beginning (according to Gorgas Loredan) there was a large triangular spit of land jutting into the sea. The distance across the base of the triangle, which was reasonably flat, is ten days' ride; but that's virtually the only flat land on the peninsula; the rest of it's taken up with mountains of varying degrees of bleakness, and nobody in their right mind would want to live there if they didn't have to. Unfortunately, however, the ancestors of the people who now occupy the Shastel peninsula didn't have the choice. They were thrown out of their own country by some wild and woolly tribe or other - second cousins of your own plainsmen, so I believe - and settled in the mountains because horsemen couldn't go there. By the time the horsemen had gone away, they'd been there over a century, and so they stayed.

Now, it's in the way of things that some people do better in life than others, and after a few generations there were a few families who'd done well, and a great many more who hadn't, and there's nothing unusual in that. What made the settlers in Shastel different was the fact that over the years they'd become – what's the word I'm looking for? Not superstitious. Religious, perhaps? No, that's got the wrong associations. Pious, maybe, or at least they were all very moral people, terribly concerned about right and wrong and thinking deep thoughts about spiritual matters when they weren't killing themselves trying to scratch a living. In any event, those families who'd become better off than their fellows came together and decided that it wasn't right that they should have more than they needed while others didn't have enough; not only was it rather terrible and wicked, it also offended against what their philosophy saw as the fundamental principle of balance and equilibrium – I don't know why I'm telling you this, because of course you know all about it. Isn't that where your own system of philosophy originated, and the study of the Principle? Anyway, that's all rather above my head. The upshot as far as this story's concerned was that they decided to pool all their surplus resources and endow a great and good Foundation, which was to last for all time and devote itself to the two things they held to be most worthwhile: helping the poor and working out a coherent code of morality and ethics.

This Foundation was given the name of the Grand Foundation of Charity and Contemplation, and its development and management were entrusted in perpetuity to the twenty leading families of Shastel. They built a magnificent place called the Hospital in the valley at the foot of Mount Shastel itself; it was big enough to house up to five thousand needy people and five thousand scholars, and it was open to everybody. People who couldn't make

a living, or who wanted to devote their lives to philosophy and learning, could just turn up at the gates and
have board and lodgings for as long as they wanted, with
nothing to pay and no obligations.

('It sounds like a good idea,' Alexius murmured.

'It was a splendid idea,' Gorgas replied. 'They always
are.')

Anyway (Gorgas continued) the Foundation's endow-
ments flourished, and the noble houses carried on adding
to them, and soon there were no more poor and destitute
families to be taken in and looked after; but the ones
who were already there were starting to get restive,
cooped up in the Hospital with nobody but the scholars
to talk to. They said they were very grateful for everything the Foundation had done for them, but they didn't
want charity, they wanted the chance to work and make
something of themselves, and everyone agreed that that
sounded like a very good idea, too.

So the Foundation decided that the best thing would
be to lend the poor people enough supplies and equipment to allow them to go back outside the walls and
support themselves. It was generally agreed that if a
family was given enough food to last them five years, and
the basic tools and equipment, it was perfectly possible
for them to turn the wilderness into good, productive
farmland, by building terraces, clearing forests, draining
marshes and diverting rivers. That was how the peninsula had been settled in the first place, with hope and
goodwill and a great deal of hard work. That sounded
like a perfectly splendid idea, and so that's what they did.
The Foundation became a bank and lent the pioneers
everything they needed – it couldn't be an outright gift,
everybody agreed, because if they gave away their
endowment to this generation of the poor, who would
provide for the next generation, and the one after that? –
and the loans were secured on the allotments of land
that the pioneers were given.

Of course, it was understood from the outset that it

would be a very long time before they'd be able to pay
back the capital of the loans, but that was fine, nobody
was in a hurry provided that the Foundation still got
enough resources to continue its work in both its fields of
endeavour, charity and contemplation. So it was decided
that repayment of the capital would be postponed
indefinitely, and all the pioneers would be expected to
pay would be interest; and to make it fairer still, the
interest wouldn't be calculated in the normal way, as a
percentage of the capital, because that might prove more
than the pioneers could afford. Instead it was agreed that
after the first five years, by which time the land ought to
be ready and in production, they should pay back a set
proportion of everything they produced – so much grain,
so much wine and wool and what have you. In the end
they settled on a seventh part, because it seemed reasonable to expect surpluses of that order from half-decently
run holdings. And everybody concerned felt that that
was an extremely good idea; quite possibly the best yet.

(Gorgas Loredan paused and took a long drink; then
he wiped his mouth and continued.)

A hundred years later, of course, the full extent of the
disaster was obvious to everyone. Three generations had
gone by and none of the pioneer families had even made
a start on paying back the capital; the one-seventh share
they had to pay the Foundation Bank exactly cancelled
out their surpluses, and no matter how hard they worked
they were still stuck at subsistence level with no prospect
of ever being able to improve their position. Meanwhile,
there was a constant stream of produce flowing in
through the gates of the Hospital which couldn't just be
left to moulder away in the jar; it had to be lent out to the
poor, or else the whole charter of the Foundation would
become meaningless. So lend it out they did; and anyone
who didn't want a loan was reasoned with until he did,
because the books had to balance and the good works
had to be done. And what with the new loans and the
general effect all this was having on the people who

weren't debtors to the Foundation, who had to buy their seed corn in bad years out of their own pockets and pay for their own ploughs and do their ditching and terracing at their own expense, it wasn't long before the Foundation Bank had mortgage stones in nearly every boundary wall in the peninsula, and more and more funds coming in each year to be invested in charity, or else.

That was when the first debtors' revolt broke out, and the Foundation couldn't understand it. So they asked their scholars and moral philosophers, who'd had plenty of time to think about these things and came back with the reply that human nature is basically rotten, being prey to ingratitude and envy and sheer abstract malice, and the more you help people, the more resentful and ungrateful they get. And when that happens, the philosophers said, all you can do is treat them as you'd treat spoilt and spiteful children, and give them a good thrashing for their own good. Otherwise, they argued, the Foundation would be failing in its quasi-parental duty towards the people it had adopted, and for whose welfare it was entirely responsible.

Now the debtors (by this time they'd started being known as heptemores, which is the word for 'seventh-parters' in the old language) had plenty of men and idealism, but no weapons or resources to sustain a war; and when they showed up outside the Hospital gates they found that the Foundation, which by this state was calling itself the Grand Foundation of Poverty and Learning, or the Grand Foundation for short – although people always seem to refer to it as the Foundation – had somehow come by a pretty substantial supply of weaponry and the like; it turned out that the upper echelons of scholars had suspected for some time that this sort of thing might happen and had been getting ready. They'd bought or made large stocks of weapons and armour – ever such a lot of armour, all to improved and scientific designs – and it turned out that they'd been drilling the Poor (that's the people who still lived in the Hospital, five thousand families) into a kind of standing army. So when the heptemores refused to disband and go quietly home, they were able to give them a very substantial thrashing and do them a world of good; according to the best sources, about a thousand killed and three thousand more wounded or taken prisoner, while the Foundation's losses were negligible. It seems like you can't keep a good idea down, at least not once it's started to take hold.

After that, of course, things had to change a little. The old Hospital was pulled down and the stones put towards building a huge castle right up on the top of Mount Shastel, big enough for a garrison of ten thousand men and the treasury of the Foundation; and since works of that kind do tend to cost a lot of money, they had to increase the share they took from a seventh to a sixth, and the debtors stopped being known as heptemores and became the hectemores, which means 'sixth-parters' and is really rather easier to say. Of course, these measures did solve the problem of what to do with the surplus income in future years, once the castle was paid for, because instead of being obliged to find poor and needy people to lend it to, they now had a standing army to feed, pay and quarter, as a legitimate expense of the Foundation incurred in carrying out its work. For a long time, in fact, it was undoubtedly the finest army in the world; the best trained, the best equipped, made up of people brought up from childhood to be soldiers for the Foundation. Until, that is (and here Gorgas' face creased into a big, fierce grin) my sister came to Scona and changed all that.

Alexius sat up, startled.

'Your sister?' he queried.

'My sister,' Gorgas replied. 'All on her own, to begin with; and then I joined her, and we carried on from there. But she was the one who started it all; credit where credit's due.'

'I see,' Alexius said. 'And what did she do?'

'Simple.' Gorgas stifled a yawn. 'She founded another bank.'

'Another bank?'

Gorgas nodded. 'The Loredan Bank, which she established here on Scona fifteen years ago, when this was an uninhabited island with only the ruins of the farmsteads the Foundation had cleared out after a minor revolt. Actually, she was clever; she *bought* the island from the Foundation, and a trading franchise which she never intended to operate. But it gave her a reason for being here while she was setting up the Bank and starting to put out feelers among the hectemores, planting the idea in their heads. Then, when the time came, she anticipated the Foundation's first strike and formed a business alliance with some long-term trading associates who also conveniently happened to be pirates: safe haven on Scona in return for stopping the Foundation from crossing the straits. They did a wonderful job, proper warships against the barges and tenders which were all the Foundation had available; I believe about seven hundred of Shastel's finest went to the bottom that day, heavy armour and all. They've never tried it since, and as soon as Niessa had put together her own army she soon got rid of the pirates—'

'Your sister has an army?' Alexius asked mildly.

'Yes indeed. Well,' Gorgas said, 'I'm in charge of it; that's mostly what I do. But it's her army, just as it's her Bank. Let's say it's all in the family.'

Alexius took a deep breath and let it go. 'So what exactly did she do? I mean, how does this Bank of yours work?'

'It's all very straightforward,' Gorgas replied. 'The hectemores borrow from us to pay off the capital of their loans to the Foundation. Then they pay us. But we only take a seventh, just like in the original deal. And we don't throw our weight about quite so much as they do, in the parts of Shastel we now run. Of course,' he went on, 'the

Foundation doesn't just sit there and take it; when a family remortgages, they send a raiding party to burn down the house and kill the people. And we send a raiding party to stop them; or, if we don't happen to get there in time, to stop them doing it again. We're very popular with the hectemores, of course; and we're gradually opening up more and more territory where they can join us if they want to. They always do. You might say,' he added with a wry grin, 'that we're a benevolent institution, just like the Foundation used to be.'

'I see,' Alexius said. 'It sounds like a good idea.'

'Oh, quite,' said Gorgas Loredan. 'It always does.'

CHAPTER THREE

From her window on the fifteenth floor of the east wing of the Citadel of Mount Shastel, on a clear day, Machaera could see across the lagoon to the small, rocky island of Scona. It wasn't an impressive sight. At best, she could make out a brown hump on the skyline with no particular features, and when the sky was grey and grainy with snow-clouds there was nothing to see except a slight variation in colour and texture. But she often sat for hours at a time at her window, looking out and wondering why the Scona people hated her, and her family, and the wonderful Foundation she had worked all her life to belong to.

This afternoon there was a slight flurry of snow on the sea and the island was indistinguishable from the slate-coloured water of the lagoon, which made it hard for her to focus her thoughts and send them there. She sat with her elbows on the stone window ledge and let her eyelids droop; she'd be able to see better with her eyes closed (there was a paradox for Doctor Nila's collection) and her mind open. A little snow drifted in through the open window and flecked her face with moisture, like tears.

As a lifelong student of the Principle, Machaera had been taught various techniques for focusing her mind. Most of them were more tricks than anything else, ways of fooling herself into believing that she was in a heightened state of awareness and thereby more closely attuned to the Principle than usual; she found them annoying, because surely it was stupid to try and trick oneself. But there was one, a simple mental exercise, that she did sometimes find useful. It was basically just a way of clearing her mind of irrelevant thoughts, a room-tidying procedure, mental housework, but the fact that it was prosaic didn't make it any less effective.

She screwed her eyes shut, as if forcing her eyelids together could somehow wring out the recollection of what she'd been looking at and make them lightproof, then allowed the muscles of her face to relax. That part of the exercise alone always made her feel more at ease, less concerned with success or failure. She took a couple of deep breaths and began the job of locating the various parts of her body and relaxing them. After a few minutes she yawned, which was a sign that she was doing the exercise properly.

One by one she examined the thoughts and memories she found cluttering up the floor of her mind. She imagined that she was in a library, and that the floor and tables were covered with books, left open and abandoned. She imagined herself picking up each book in turn, dusting it off, winding it tightly and sliding it into its tube, slotting it back into its proper place on the shelf. Here, for example, was the book of trivial distractions, containing such things as the pair of sandals that had to be collected from the cobbler, the raw patch of skin on her elbow where she'd grazed it on the chipped rim of the well, the slight headache that always bothered her when there was snow in the air. All those she solemnly rolled up and filed away, then turned to the book of intrusive preoccupations—

(*Choose a place at random and read before rolling it up: the war, the enemy; why must there be a war now, in my lifetime? Why now, it isn't fair; I have so much to do, so much to learn, I'm only young for such a short time, why must the war descend on me like an obnoxious relative who comes visiting when you want to be alone and refuses to* leave? So many things impractical, impossible because of the war – the chance to travel, to visit great libraries in other cities, to learn; Mazeus on active service, instead of here, to talk to and listen to when there's something I've read or thought of that has to be discussed; roll up this book, it's fatally distracting.)

One by one she rolled them up and put them back, even the bewitchingly tempting book of speculations, in which was written all her thoughts on theories and interpretations, everything she wanted the truth to be (that one especially; roll it up and put it on the top shelf) until the desk was clear and her mind was ready to receive a new book. She visualised it, lying on the polished wood in front of her. She imagined the burnished brass tube with the label pasted on it; pushing her first and middle fingers into the top and opening them, pulling back to slide out the rolled-up book, taking the slender wooden batten to which the top edge of the roll was pasted in one hand, easing back the rest of the roll with the other, nudging across her heavy wooden ruler to stop it coiling back, reading the first section, which was always the same—

The one Principle that pervades all things – the concept is nebulous and vague enough to deter all but the most determined. Sometimes the thread is so wide and clear that it seems mundane and obvious, therefore not worthy of study. At other times, the stream dwindles down into so slight a trickle that it appears to be a figment of the imagination, something one deludes oneself into perceiving because one desires it so urgently. Between the general and trite, the doubtful and the self-made evidence, there is a dangerous temptation to steer a middle course, to assume that the truth must be the average of the available alternatives; which is like trying to write history by taking a vote from a convention of historians, assuming that the majority opinion must be the truth. But in the pursuit of the Principle, there is no place for common sense, belief or democracy. The Principle cannot be amended or *simplified or improved. The Principle is that which it is.*

Dry, uncompromising words that all students were required to know by heart; not something to believe, since belief presupposes scope for doubt – rather something to accept, in the same way one accepts the fact of death, which does not need to be believed in. So much for the preface; she pictured herself bobbing an awkward curtsey before a stone image standing in front of an archway, waiting uncomfortably for a moment before being allowed to proceed.

And then she was through the gate and into the open air, with no roof or walls crowding around her; she always pictured the contemplation of the Principle as a garden (how foreigners laugh at the Shastel people for their obsession with little patches of organised nature, regimented grass and troops of well-drilled flowers that stand to attention and present petals at the word of command!) where she was free to sit or walk, to work for the benefit of the garden or to cut whatever she wanted without fear of spoiling the display. Sometimes she came here to weed out errors and false conclusions, to dig and mulch and flick out stones, to mow and prune and break off the dead heads of redundant enquiries. At other times she came with a basket over her arm to gather what she wanted and take it home, although it wasn't quite as straightforward as that – the garden gave her what it wanted her to have …

She opened her eyes and saw a workshop. It reminded her of the cooper's yard where her father used to work, because she could see a long bench with a heavy wooden vice clamped to it, and on the wall hung familiar-looking tools, the drawknife and the spokeshave and the boxwood plane, the H-framed bowsaw, the heavy rasp and the wooden blocks inset with pads of sandstone, the bundle of horsetail rushes, the chisels, the gouges, the hickory mallet and the small copper hammer. The floor was carpeted with curled white shavings, and on the crossbeams that braced the rafters of the roof rested billets of rough-sawn green timber, adding the sweet smell of sap to the more delicate scent of newly sawn cedarwood. Light slanted into the shop through an open shutter, and fell across the back of a man crouched over a billet clamped in the vice, which he was working down with a large block plane, his arms and shoulders moving with an oarsman's rhythm. She could only see the back of his head; but the old man who was sitting just outside the light was facing her, although the shadows masked his features.

'And then what happened?' he said.

The other man stopped working and straightened his back with a little grunt of discomfort. 'Oh, it was all anticlimax after that,' he said. 'It turned out that my confounded sister had sent the ship to pick me up – if I'd known that, I'd have taken my chances swimming. But I didn't, and they delivered me here like a parcel, FOB as per the bill of lading, and I was marched up the hill to pay my respects and be properly grateful.' The man picked up his plane and fiddled with the set of the blade for a few moments. 'Kept me hanging about in her damned waiting room for best part of an hour, which didn't improve my attitude.'

'And were you?' the old man asked. 'Properly grateful, I mean.'

'I don't think our old friend the City Prefect would have approved of my manners,' the craftsman replied. 'I can't say that I behaved terribly well. And no, I wasn't. On the other hand, I did manage to get out of there without hitting anybody, which was probably just as well. There was an awful lot of professional muscle lounging about in there along with the pen-pushers. I have the feeling that if I'd lost my temper, I'd have left there in a sack.'

'It didn't strike me as a particularly friendly place,' the old man said. 'So then what did you do?'

'I wandered down to the harbour, that place where everybody takes their evening stroll, and sold my mailshirt. Got a reasonable price for it, too; enough to buy some tools and have enough left over for the makings of a fine hangover the next morning, which was when I started walking. When I got tired, I stopped, and here I am.'

The old man nodded and lifted a wooden cup to his lips. When he put it down again, the craftsman topped it up from a tall terracotta tub that stood on the floor in a pail of water to keep it cool. 'And the boy,' the old man went on. 'What about him?'

The craftsman laughed. 'I'll be honest with you,' he said, 'once we'd reached Scona and I'd made my duty-call on my sister, I'd more or less forgotten about him. Pets, waifs and strays, charity cases – I've never had much time for that sort of thing. I'd gladly dump my loose change in some poor devil's hat if I felt sorry for him, but my rule was always that charity ended at home, and if a stray dog follows me in the street, it's asking for trouble. No, I reckoned I'd done enough for the kid pulling him out of the bonfire, and the rest was up to him.' He sighed. 'No such luck.'

'No?'

He shook his head. 'He turned up one morning looking all lost and sorry for himself, and as luck would have it I was trying to put in a gatepost, which is an awkward job to do single-handed; so without thinking I said, "Grab hold of that," and he held the post while I knocked it in, and then he held the crowbar while I dug the hole for the other post, and then he helped me get the lintel up and held one end while I closed up the dovetails. And then, when the job was done and I realised he'd been helping me and never said a word except, "Like this?" and, "Where d'you want this to go?" I hadn't got the heart to tell him to get lost, so he's been here ever since. I'm teaching him the trade, and on balance he's more help than hindrance. It's funny, though,' the craftsman went on with a chuckle. 'When I'm trying to teach him something and for some reason he just can't or won't get it, and I stop and listen to myself, all patient and reasonable to start with and finally losing my temper and bawling the poor kid out – it's like I'm the kid and I'm listening to my father, back in the long barn at home. And that makes me stop shouting, at any rate. I remember it all too well myself.'

'Ah,' the old man said with a grin. 'The son you never had, then.'

'Never had and never wanted,' the craftsman replied with a grunt. 'Company doesn't bother me, but it's never been something I need, the way some people can't live without it. And give the lad his due, he works hard and tries his best, even if he does chatter away all the time. The hell with it, I'm not complaining.'

'I can see that,' the old man said with a smile. 'If you ask me, you're beginning to mellow.'

'I'd rather call it seasoning, like that wood up there. Which is just a way of saying I'm beginning to act my age. One thing about killing people for a living, it kept me from getting middle-aged. This is a different way of life entirely.'

'Better?'

The craftsman gave that some serious thought before answering. 'It's bloody hard work,' he replied. 'But yes, much better. I wouldn't go back now, not if they made me the Emperor and gave me the whole upper city to live in. It's possible that this is what I've always wanted to do; in which case, I must remember to buy young Temrai a large drink next time I see him.'

The old man laughed. 'I'm sure he had your well-being at heart all along,' he said.

'What's a burnt city among friends so long as you're happy? Quite.' The craftsman lifted the plane and slid it across the face of the billet, producing a clean slicing noise. 'I tend not to think about that side of things very much,' he said. 'It's amazing how much better life can be if you manage to lay off the thinking.'

The old man drank some more, put the cup down and

covered it with his hat to stop the sawdust getting in it. 'Business is good?' he asked.

'Can't complain,' the craftsman replied. 'It's quite remarkable how little these people know about bow-making. I could get technical and bore you rigid, but that'd be unkind, so let's just say that for a nation who're supposed to depend for their survival on their skill as archers, the people of Scona don't know spit about the tools of their trade. The idea that there's more to a bow than a bent stick and some string has come to them like some divine revelation. In fact,' he added, stopping to wipe his forehead on his arm, 'business is a bit too good, as you'd be able to work out for yourself if you took a walk around here looking for a reasonably straight ash tree. Which you won't,' he added, 'because they're all up there.' He pointed up at the billets stacked between the rafters. 'That lot won't keep me going for very long,' he continued, 'and I've got an order for six dozen sinew-backed recurves for the military that I'd loose sleep over if I stopped to think about it. If ever you meet anybody whose doctor's ordered him six weeks of total and utter boredom, send him to me and I'll put him on carding sinew.'

The old man smiled. 'That's a very good sign,' he said. 'You must be doing well if you're grumbling like that. You sound like a farmer complaining of too much rain.'

'I think they call it reverting to type. There now,' he said, putting the plane to one side and picking up a pair of calipers, 'that's not looking too bad. Let's see whether we've got that ...' he stood up and turned, and just as Machaera was about to see his face, she lifted her head and blinked, and saw Scona across the lagoon, and herring-gulls circling in the snowy air, and a single ship with a blue sail dragging itself across the wind into the arms of Scona harbour.

Now what was all that about? She tried to imagine the library table again, but when she found the image in her mind, all she could see was an untidy heap of brass tubes, some empty, some with the ends of badly rolled books squashed into them. She shut her eyes and did her best to think, but a savage headache had taken hold about an inch behind her eyes, and thinking was like trying to see through thick fog and driving rain. *Which of them was I supposed to see? The old man or the man he was talking to?* She made an effort to force the pictures back into her mind, but there weren't enough of them left to get a grip on. Rationalising, it ought to be the old man. When she'd looked into his eyes, it was as if she'd recognised something there; it was like looking at your friend's grandfather and saying to yourself, *Ah, yes, that's where the nose comes from.* She guessed that what she'd seen was some kind of mark or scar left behind after looking at the Principle, just as she'd been doing, the same kind of flare or burn as if she'd looked too long at the sun and it had left a permanent mark visible whenever she closed her eyes. But he hadn't said anything; he'd just sat there asking questions, so surely it was the other one who was important, the one she'd been given this special privilege of seeing. But he was just some kind of artisan, a worker in wood like her father. How could anything concerning a man like that be of any relevance to the Principle, or the survival of Shastel and the Foundation? A great warrior might just possibly have some significance; conceivably a mighty engineer, destined to design some fabulous new engine of war that could overthrow the enemy at a stroke. But a tradesman – a *small-time* tradesman, one who was struggling to meet an order for six dozen (six dozen, that's five twelves are sixty plus twelve makes seventy-two) seventy-two bows – why, the Foundation's arsenal probably made that many in a single day. If she didn't know better, she'd be tempted to think that the Principle was making fun of her.

Remember, Doctor Gannadius had told them last year, just before the written exam, *don't look for what you want to see, or you think you should see, or even what you expect to see. Don't look* for *anything. Look at what's there, and mark it well. What you see is always the truth; the distortions and errors come afterwards, when you think about what you've seen.*

She frowned. Nobody in the whole world knew more about the Principle than Doctor Gannadius; after all, he was the last surviving member of the Foundation of Perimadeia, designated to succeed the old Patriarch if only the City hadn't fallen. The mere fact of his coming to Shastel had done more for the morale of the Foundation than a hundred victories against the enemy could have achieved. It was Doctor Gannadius, after all, who'd recognised her special gifts and brought her here to the Cloister, among the top ten per cent of the novices, and taught her the very technique she'd just been using. In which case, she realised, the sensible thing would be to stop trying to puzzle it out for herself – all she'd do would be to muddy the image in her mind and corrupt it – and take it to him for interpretation, so that he could make proper use of this important piece of intelligence, maybe something so important it could win them the war ...

And maybe that was going a bit too far. The whole point was, she didn't *know*. For all she knew, embedded in the conversation somewhere was some tiny detail that gave the key to understanding some major intelligence issue – invasion plans, a fatal problem with material procurement, an opportunity to recruit a spy who would come across with the vital secret of something or other she simply couldn't imagine. But wasn't history crammed with recorded instances of morsels of apparent trivia, overheard in dockside taverns or mumbled by lovers in their sleep, that had resulted in the fall of great empires and the deaths of untold thousands? One thing was for sure; if she kept it to herself and tried to figure it out all on her own, the momentous turning point in history could be the failure of Shastel to pick up on the vital clue that might just have saved them from the deadly and hitherto unforeseen danger ... She jumped up, slammed the shutters closed and had to make a great effort to stop herself running along the corridor and down the spiral staircase to Doctor Gannadius' office; which, when she reached it, turned out to be empty.

'Apparently,' muttered the sergeant, 'she's the Director's niece.'

The corporal stooped and took another peep through the hole in the door. 'I heard tell she was her daughter,' he replied.

'You don't want to go hearing things like that,' the sergeant said. 'Stunts your growth, listening to that kind of talk.' He drew his hand across his throat. 'Anyway,' he went on, 'she's some sort of family, which means she's none of our business. Just watch her when you take in her food. She can only scratch left-handed, but she knows how to kick.'

The corporal nodded gravely. True, the girl in the cell didn't look like she was capable of hurting anybody, not with that mangled hand; it was as much as she could do to get the food into her mouth and change her clothes. But it was different when she started cursing and screaming; having to listen to that was enough to sour a man's beer, even through two inches of oak door, and there wasn't much anyone dared do to shut her up, what with her being some kind of family of the Director's. You never knew whether she'd be out the next day and sitting behind a desk in an office putting her seal to transfer orders that'd send a poor soldier to his death. Best to be on the safe side, and keep well clear.

'Makes you wonder, though,' the sergeant said. 'Carved up like that and shoved away in a cell, and she's one of them. Gods only know what they do to their enemies.'

Away down the passage a key scraped in a lock; someone was giving orders. The sergeant twisted the cover back over the peephole and gestured to the corporal to get back to his station quickly. When the newcomers reached the end of the line of cells, the sergeant stood to attention, saluted and crunched the heels of his boots down with parade-ground precision. The newcomers didn't notice.

'She's in here,' said a captain of the guard, a rare and exotic creature to find in the cellars. 'We've kept her apart from the other prisoners, just as you said.'

The other visitor, a big bald man in a dark non-regulation coat, grunted. 'She's not a prisoner, she's a detainee. You want to learn the difference. Right, open it up. I'll bang on the door when I'm done.'

The sergeant jumped forward like the automaton in a mechanical clock and turned the key; then he stood well back from the door, as if there was a risk of infection. The captain gave him a sour look and sat down in his chair.

'Uncle Gorgas,' the girl said.

'Don't start, Iseutz,' Gorgas Loredan sighed. He slumped down on the bed and slouched forward, his elbows on his knees.

'You look worn out,' Iseutz went on, sitting on the floor beside him. He moved a few inches away.

'I'm tired,' Gorgas said. 'And I'm not in a very good mood. And as far as I'm concerned, you can damn well stay here until you learn how to behave yourself. But your mother—' Iseutz made a hissing noise, like an angry cat. Gorgas sighed. 'Your mother,' he repeated, 'keeps insisting that I reason with you. Which is all very well for her to say,' he added, 'since she doesn't have to come down here to this shithole and put up with your performances. Obviously she believes I've got nothing better to occupy my time with.'

'Well,' muttered Iseutz. 'And have you?'

Gorgas scowled at her. 'I've got plenty that needs doing, thank you very much,' he said. 'I've got a wife and children I don't see for weeks at a time. I've got a sister who treats me like an errand boy, I've got a brother up in the hills making grand gestures at me, and in my spare time I've got a war to run. And of course I've got you. Gods, it must be wonderful to have a really dull, boring life. I'd love to be bored just once, just to say I've tried it.'

Iseutz looked at him. 'Save it,' she said. 'In fact, why don't you just go away? You're wasting your precious time here.'

Gorgas yawned and stretched out on the bed, his fingers laced behind his head. 'Other people,' he said, 'have nieces who're pleased to see them. Favourite nieces they spoil with little presents, who ask to stay up late when their uncles come to dinner.'

'Other people don't murder their brothers,' Iseutz replied sweetly. 'You could have had lots of nieces if you hadn't killed off most of your family.'

Gorgas breathed out heavily through his nose. 'Very true,' he said. 'Although as a matter of cold fact, I've never murdered any of my brothers, just my father and my brother-in-law. As it is, I have to make the best of what I've got. For gods' sakes, what's the point of doing this to yourself? Aren't there enough martyrs in this family already?'

Iseutz smiled at him. 'You should know, Uncle Gorgas. And please don't say I'm doing this to myself. I didn't exactly drag myself down here and turn the key, you know.'

'And you know you could be out of here in two minutes flat, if only you'd give up this ridiculous posturing. If there's one thing that's the curse of this family, it's melodrama.'

She studied him, her head slightly on one side. 'Are you sure about that, Uncle?' she said. 'I always thought the curse on this family was you.'

Gorgas sighed. 'All right,' he said. 'I'll say it again. When I was young I did some terrible things, and so did your mother. We behaved appallingly. We were *bad*. But now we're different, we're trying to make up for what we did. We're trying to help a whole lot of people who've had a really bad deal, and we're trying really hard to make it up to the rest of the family. And before you start again, please remember that you're the one who's sworn to kill your Uncle Bardas, and he's probably the only half-decent one out of the whole lot of us.'

'Half decent?' Iseutz squawked. 'He made his living killing people. People he didn't even know.'

'True,' Gorgas replied. 'But compared with the rest of us ...'

The girl was about to reply; then suddenly she giggled. 'You know,' she said, resting her elbows on the foot of the bed, 'when you come to think of it, we're a pretty sick bunch. I think that's probably why I hate Mother more than you or even Uncle Bardas. At least you two are just murderers. What I can't forgive her for is making me the way I am.'

'Oh, please yourself,' Gorgas grunted, sliding off the bed and standing up. 'Maybe you're right, at that. But that's not the way I see things; I don't believe in this idea that evil people are evil and can't ever be anything else. I mean, do you confine that to individuals, or does it go for whole nations as well? Just because our ancestors massacred some other city or tribe a thousand years ago, does that mean we're going to carry on being bastards for the rest of time? There wouldn't be anybody left. And think about it: doesn't it work both ways? Take Temrai and the plainsmen. They sacked the City and killed all the people; all right, they're evil, they're bastards. But they did it because the City people used to go around killing them—'

'My Uncle Bardas used to go around killing them.'

For the first time, there was something in Gorgas' expression that suggested he might be getting angry. 'Yes,' he said, 'and he also saved your life. He spared your life when you were trying to kill him, and then he got you out of the City when he should have been thinking about himself. And you still say no, he's got to die. All right, so if you'd killed him, what'd that have made you?'

She thought for a moment. 'A chip off the old block, presumably.' She held up her truncated hand. 'Look at me, for pity's sake. I'm as bad as the rest of you, *and* I'm incompetent. I'm a murderer who can't even get the job done. You've no idea how proud it makes me feel, knowing I'm useless as well as rotten.'

Gorgas reached out and banged twice on the door with his fist. 'Melodrama,' he repeated. 'High tragedy. Family curses, poisoned blood and the downfall of the gods. Give me a shout when you've had enough and maybe I'll show you round the real world some time. In the meantime you can stay here and write your lines. I'll just make sure that nobody else gets to hear them.'

The key turned in the lock and he barged the door open, pushing the sergeant out of the way. The door rolled shut and the key turned again.

'All right,' Gorgas said, 'get me out of here. And for pity's sake get that cell cleaned up. I wouldn't keep a pig in that state. I don't care how it got that way, but there's no excuse for not clearing up a mess.'

He felt better as soon as he was above ground again, and by the time he was clear of the guard house and out into the fresh air of the courtyard, the feelings of frustration and anger were back to manageable levels, which was just as well. Gorgas Loredan had built his life around the principle that positive thinking gets things done; he found monolithic negatives impossible to understand and therefore hard to deal with, and so he'd always managed to find a way to go round the immovable object. One of his favourite stories was about two generals in command of an army who found themselves faced with the prospect of laying siege to an impregnable city. As they sat in their tent, staring wretchedly at the massive walls before them, the old general sighed and declared, 'We'll never find a way of taking that city.' The younger general smiled at him and said, 'In that case, we'd better find a way of not having to take that city.' Whereupon he explained how it might be possible to lead the army round another way, bypassing the city entirely, and fall upon the enemy's unprotected homeland, thereby winning the war and rendering the insurmountable obstacle irrelevant. For the moment, he couldn't yet see how to apply this lesson to dealing with his intransigent niece, or his equally intransigent brother; but he knew there must be a way, simply because there always is.

Another gift that had helped him greatly over the years was the ability to put a difficult problem out of his mind entirely, leaving him free to tackle something he could manage. Solving the soluble problem, he'd generally found, often gave him the confidence and the sheer momentum to overwhelm the apparently insoluble one. Fortunately, the next job on his list was eminently soluble, and he found that he was looking forward to it.

He walked briskly down the hill to the Quay and took the boat to the small island at the mouth of the harbour where the refugees from Shastel were housed in a large sprawl of wood and canvas structures, a sort of hybrid of huts and tents, while they were waiting to be permanently resettled. To someone without Gorgas' attitude to problem-solving, the Camp would have been a depressing place, full of uncomfortable reminders of failure. Here, after all, was the place where people ended up when the Bank had failed to make good its promise to protect them from the vindictiveness of the Foundation. The families crowded in here had all seen their houses burnt down, their cattle driven off, their crops trampled; by definition, they were here because they had nowhere else to go, and the people who'd said it was all going to be all right had let them down and were now faced with the burden of looking after them and finding them somewhere else to live and work.

To Gorgas Loredan, however, they were the answer to a prayer. At first he'd looked here for recruits for his army, because at first that was what he needed most; but there were women and children and old men here too, and they constituted a resource that it would be wasteful to neglect; almost as bad as leaving a good field fallow for want of a bucket of seedcorn and the effort of ploughing.

He'd taken charge of the running of the Camp, made an inventory of what was available, and worked out the best way to make use of what he'd got.

Thanks to his imagination and hard work, the Camp was now an inspiring place to visit. As he walked through the gates (permanently open, now that there was no need to keep starving malcontents penned up out of harm's way) he passed the training ground on the left, where his hand-picked corps of instructors were turning the adult males into an efficient and disciplined force of archers, and carried on down the narrow lane that ran between the long sheds where the women and children were employed making the things the Bank so badly needed. Each shed housed a different manufacture. First he passed the door of the clothing shop, where they produced uniforms and boots for the army, all to the best specifications. Next to that was the mailshirt factory, where several hundred women sat on benches at long tables twisting together the thousands of steel rings that went to make up each issue-pattern mailshirt; each worker was equipped with two pairs of pliers to grip and twist the rings, which were brought to them by the ten thousand in closely woven wicker baskets by porters who spent all day going backwards and forwards between this shed and the wire foundry, where a hundred anvils were grouped in a circle around one enormous central furnace; at each anvil, one worker hammered and drew the red-hot billets of steel into wire, while another wound the wire around a mandrel before slitting the coil down its length to produce another bucketful of rings.

Next to the foundry was the fletching shed, where he had four hundred women and children occupied sorting feathers by sizes, splitting them down the middle with sharp knives and peeling them apart, trimming them and serving them to the finished arrowshafts with sinew dipped in glue. The shafts themselves were produced in the next shed down the row, where the workers sat in front of tables with three-foot-long grooves scored into them; in these grooves they laid the dogwood and river-cane shoots the arrows were made from, planing each surface flat and then turning them a few degrees until eventually they were left with a perfectly round, straight shaft, each one of uniform length and diameter. All told, there were sixty sheds in the Camp, each one producing the Bank's entire requirement of some essential military commodity, and all at a fraction of what it would have cost to buy them on the open market. As for the workers, they were fed, clothed and occupied instead of aimless and starving. It was, Gorgas couldn't help feeling, a remarkable achievement; and all the result of looking at a problem and seeing an opportunity.

His business today was with the superintendent of the nock factory. Each arrow was fitted with a bone nock, which was carved to shape, drilled at one end to accept the shaft and sawn at the other to fit the string. The problem he was here to deal with concerned the supply of bone. The raw materials came from the slaughter-house on the other side of the island; the slaughtermen stripped the bones out of the carcasses, bleached them and loaded them on carts (six carts a day, every day, were needed to satisfy the demand from the factory); when they arrived here, they were sorted by type and size and passed on to the sawbenches where they were cut to size, and the stench of sawn bone could be smelt right across the Camp. The last few consignments had apparently not been satisfactorily cleaned. The superintendent of the factory had registered an official complaint with the slaughtermaster, who had taken offence and filed a counter-complaint about erratic collections by the factory carters and a number of other issues about the work of the factory which were really none of his concern. Neither official was now on speaking terms with the other, deliveries to the factory were down to a mere trickle, and production was almost at a standstill, which in turn affected production in four other sheds. As

Gorgas saw it, it was another example of attitude and melodrama making a mess of things; the difference was that this mess was going to be cleared up, or he'd know the reason why.

As it turned out, the mere announcement that Gorgas Loredan was on his way to sort things out had had a remarkable effect on the officials concerned; they'd had a very productive meeting and dealt with all the outstanding issues, and three enormous cartloads of immaculately bleached bones were even now trundling their way down the narrow backstreets from the slaughterhouse to the Camp, while both parties were unreservedly withdrawing their complaints and thanking each other, with an almost frantic display of mutual goodwill, for their co-operation. Gorgas was extremely pleased, congratulated everyone for doing a splendid job, and took the opportunity to make an unscheduled tour of inspection; very much an unexpected honour, as the superintendent hastily admitted.

'There's still going to be a shortfall, though,' Gorgas said, as he walked between the rows of benches. On either side of him sat twenty or so children, each one diligently filing slots in half-finished nocks. 'Can't we do something about the lighting in here, by the way? It's a bit dark for fine work.'

The superintendent snapped at his secretary to make a note – *Investigate ways to improve lighting in shed.* The secretary scribbled hastily, the waxed tablet braced against the spread palm of his left hand – you could tell a scribe by the calluses on his fingertips and the way he sat flexing his fingers when he wasn't writing.

'I suppose we'll have to make up the difference from civilian contractors,' Gorgas went on. 'Place an order with the usual suppliers and have the invoices sent through to my office. I'll deal with them myself.' He didn't need to look round to know what kind of expression was on the superintendent's face; an outside order was one of the few opportunities he got to make a few quarters on the side, provided that the invoices could be processed in-house. The stipulation was intended as a reprimand, and the way it was made constituted a strong hint that the superintendent had got off lightly. 'And if you get any more problems with supply, just let me know instead of going through channels. After all, we're all on the same side.'

The superintendent thanked him politely for his help, and Gorgas urged him to think nothing of it. 'Actually,' he added, turning round and facing the man, 'there was just one thing. When you do the requisitions, would you mind placing an order for – what, twelve dozen? Yes, call it that – with a man called Bardas Loredan. He lives up in the hills; one of my people can tell you where to find him. He's my brother.'

The superintendent nodded twice, and relayed the order to his secretary, who'd already written it down. 'Of course,' he said. 'No trouble at all. Shall I add him to the usual list of suppliers?'

Gorgas thought for a moment. 'Better have a look at the quality of his work first,' he replied. 'It's all very well helping out family now and again, but we aren't doing this for the good of our souls. I expect they'll be all right, though; he's a good worker.'

If the superintendent was curious to know why a brother of the Chief Executive (and also, by implication, of the Director herself) made his living working with his hands up in the hill country, he certainly didn't show it. It wasn't all that long ago that the superintendent had arrived on Scona in a small leaky boat from Shastel with nothing more than a coat and a pair of shoes. As far as he was concerned, the Chief Executive stood fair and square at the centre of his universe; it was Gorgas Loredan who'd personally signed the deed that allowed him to pay off his debt to the Foundation, and when he'd stumbled off the boat onto the Dock, one of Gorgas' clerks had been there to meet him and his family and take them out of the mob of refugees being herded into the Camp. Instead, they'd gone up the hill and been greeted by Gorgas himself in his own private office, where he'd been told there was a good job waiting for him if he wanted it. He had no idea why he'd been chosen, or what might one day be expected of him in return; all he could think of was that he'd been one of the Chief's own personal clients, and that when he'd been burnt out, the Chief somehow felt responsible for not preventing it. But the reason didn't matter; what mattered was that he spent his days in an office at a desk, while men every bit as good as him, or better, coughed up their lungs in the dust and stench of the sawbenches.

'Right,' Gorgas said. 'I think we're all sorted out here. If there's any other problems, you know where I am.' He paused for a moment, looking out over the rows of workbenches, listening to the scritching of blades and files on bone coming from every side. 'You know,' he said, 'this is all looking very good. You've done a fine job.'

'Thank you,' the superintendent said.

'Let us consider,' Gannadius said, 'the two Opposites that combine to make up this thing we call the Principle. Let's call them' - he paused for effect - 'let's call them The Same, and Different. About The Same, there is nothing to be said; it's always the same, it has only one nature. It can't be changed, or improved, or made worse. You may find it hard to imagine this Opposite; think of a granite cliff, and sooner or later you'll imagine the sea grinding it down, or men quarrying it and hauling it away in carts. You could try to imagine death, I suppose, but death is only one stage in a cycle. If a thing is dead now, it must once have been alive. The Same is very hard to imagine; so you must take it on trust and think of it largely as what it is, an Opposite.'

He paused again and looked round the hall, pleased to see that he could still grab the attention of a hundred or so young people with something he knew was as trite as sunrise. 'Now consider Different,' he went on. 'Different is easy. Different is so easy that it's easy to let yourself believe that Different is somehow more important, more real than The Same. That would be very foolish, because The Same is the world, but Different is the Principle. Does that make any sort of sense? Or am I going too fast?'

Rhetorical pause. Needless to say, none of them understood; not yet. 'Let me refine that a little,' he said. 'I want you to consider the concept of Product. Take heat, for example. Heat is the Product of fuel and fire. Take a tree and burn it; the fire turns the wood to ash and smoke. It's easy to see Different in that, because where there was once a tree there's now only charcoal and a smell of burning – there has been an act of Difference. But look again, and try and see the operation of the other Opposite. Has the tree disappeared? No, it's still there, in the ash and the smoke and the heat of the fire. In other words, there has also been an act of Sameness, but achieved through the agency of Product. The Same and Different have collided, have been at war, Different has come and gone, The Same remains behind in the Product of the act – which in the case of burning a tree is ash and smoke and heat.

'That's a very simple example, of course, but it might help you to see that Different might not be as important as you thought it was. It might even occur to you to ask yourselves if The Same is always the same, and Different is always different. Confused? Try it again, now that you're a little bit better educated. Every time you burn a tree, you get ash, smoke and heat; you get the same difference, the difference is always the same. Now you might ask yourselves, is there really such a thing as Different, or is it just The Same in some other configuration, the tree becoming ash in the same way as life becomes death or night becomes day? Can you burn a tree and get flowers and milk? Now that *would* be Different.'

Sure enough, every single face in the hall was a study in bewilderment; mostly, he knew, they were frantically trying to work out whether Doctor Gannadius was immensely wise or a raving lunatic. Very good.

'Now then,' he resumed, 'by the looks of you, you've all had about as much education as you can take for one day, so I'll leave you with one last subject for your consideration. Let's assume that The Same is always the same, and Different is always different; the key to this riddle must be something to do with the nature of this elusive third factor, Product. Where there's a Product, there must be a Process. In our example with the tree, the Process is burning. We've seen that Product can be both an act of difference and an act of sameness. The ash and smoke and heat are different from the tree, but they're still the tree, they're the Product of the Process of burning. This may lead you to believe that it's the Process that makes the difference, except that the Product of the burning Process is always the same. So now, instead of just two incomprehensible abstracts, we have four. Are they really all the same? Or are they different? I'd like you to think about that before we meet again; and if by then any of you can answer the riddle, please feel free to come up here and take over the class; provided, of course, that you can prove you understand it by burning a tree and producing flowers and milk.' He paused and grinned. 'Dismissed.'

As he walked back to his lodgings, he felt a little guilty, as if he'd been doing something dishonest; as if he'd sought to convince his audience of some abstruse point of philosophy by pulling a rabbit out of his hat, and had succeeded. *I'm trying to make it sound like magic*, he confessed to himself, *which it isn't, of course. It's just that occasionally, if things go wrong, it can do the same things as magic. And that's like saying that a sack of flour is a sword, because if it falls on you out of a high loft it can kill you.* He wondered why he was worrying about it. Perhaps the guilt came from trying to make the subject sound interesting, which was certainly an act of deception.

'Doctor Gannadius!' That voice. Oh, *hell*!

'It's Machaera, isn't it?' he said as he turned, trying his unsuccessful best to look frail and confused. 'Ah, yes, of course it is. How can I help you?'

The dreadful child was beaming at him, her small oval face a study in humility and devotion. *Idiotic*, he said to himself as he resisted the urge to shudder. *The child's got twenty times more ability than I'll ever have, she really is a magician. Which is why she should be killed immediately, for the public good.*

'Could you possibly spare me just a few minutes?' she was saying – she was skipping backwards so as to be able to face him and keep up with him at the same time. He really didn't want to stop and get bogged down in theoretical debate in the middle of the courtyard; the girl might be a natural genius, but she was simply too young to be able to grasp even the most basic implications of the word *rheumatism*. Escape, he knew, was impossible, but back in his lodgings he would at least be able to sit down. There was even a possibility of getting rid of her by feigning sleep.

'Certainly, certainly,' Gannadius replied. 'Follow me.' Not for the first time he envied his old friend and colleague Alexius his years and infirmities, for which people were always so ready to make allowances. Gannadius was that much younger and obviously spry, and so not entitled to mercy. 'I mustn't be too long, though,' he added in forlorn hope. 'Paperwork to catch up with, that sort of thing.'

The girl Machaera was getting better, give her her due; she didn't start up until after he'd sat down and kicked off one boot.

'I thought what you said in the lecture was *fascinating*,' she was saying. 'And so *true*. Except,' she went on, with a little glint of far-away in her eyes, 'I always seem to think of it as a massive great tree fallen and lying endways, and if you find a crack and hammer in a wedge, it suddenly splits open, just like that.'

'Sorry,' Gannadius interrupted. 'Think of what?'

'Sorry?'

'What is it,' Gannadius said carefully, 'that you always seem to think of as a log?'

'What? Oh I *see*. Well, Sameness, I suppose. Or whatever the Principle isn't – I'm a bit muddled about that bit. But the Principle's like the wedge; you find the crack and the rest of it's so easy. What's the proper technical term? Mechanical advantage, that's it.'

Oh, so that's how it's done. Assuming you can spot the crack, I suppose. 'You could put it like that,' he replied guardedly. 'In fact, it's not a bad comparison. But surely that's a bit far removed from what the lecture was about.'

The girl looked puzzled. 'Oh, surely not,' she said. 'Surely the whole point is that the Principle is what you use to turn The Same into Different. When it doesn't want to, I mean.'

You may well be right; how the hell would I know, though? 'In a sense,' he replied. 'Though that's oversimplifying things rather, if you don't mind my saying so.' He devoutly, earnestly wished she'd go away, this little cute-faced bubble of a creature who talked so blithely about using the Principle; it was like listening to a mouse chattering on about harnessing a team of cats to a cheese-wagon, except for the horrible knowledge that she could do it. *Break the world in half?* he could imagine her saying. *Oh, that's easy. You just press here, and then put your thumbnail here, like this* ...

'Sorry,' she said. 'I'm gushing again, aren't I? And running before I can walk. You see, I'd never thought of it in those terms before, but it's so obviously the right way of seeing it – well, of course, you know that,' she added, with a self-deprecating little grin. 'No, what I really wanted to do was tell you about this projection I did, using that special formula you taught me.'

Blood and thunder, not another one. It's a miracle we're

all still alive. 'You've managed another projection?' was what he actually said. 'That's really very - well, I'm impressed. Was it—?'

She smiled at him. 'Why don't I just show you?' she said.

—And, before he could say anything, suddenly he was standing beside her in a workshop of some sort, next to a long bench with a heavy wooden vice clamped to it, and lots of peculiar-looking tools hanging on the walls (except that, because she was there too, he realised that at least for the time being he knew that that was a draw-knife and that was an adze and that was a boxwood plane, and those green twiggy things were horsetail rushes, which are rough and abrasive enough to be used for smoothing toolmarks out of wood). Light slanted into the shop through an open shutter and fell across the back of a man crouching over the bench - dear gods, that's Colonel Bardas Loredan, the fencer-at-law - and an old man sitting talking to him, who turned out to be someone he knew very well indeed.

'Alexius?' he said.

The Patriarch looked up and saw him. 'Excuse me a moment,' he said to Loredan, who nodded and carried on with his work. 'Hello, Gannadius,' he went on. 'I was thinking about you only the other day. I didn't even know if you were alive.'

'Me neither. I mean,' Gannadius corrected, 'I didn't know if *you* were alive. I'd heard a few rumours, but nothing I was prepared to believe. Dear gods, but it's good to see you again.'

Alexius smiled warmly. 'I agree,' he said. 'Though the circumstances—'

'I know,' Gannadius agreed hastily. 'Hardly ideal. Look, I'm sorry if this is an idiotic question, but when is this? Are we in the present, or is this the future, or what?'

Alexius thought for a moment. 'I don't think this is for a while yet; I mean, I haven't been to see Bardas yet in real life, I haven't even found out properly where he lives,

just something vague about "in the mountains", which
could mean anything. I think this must be the future.'

'I see,' Gannadius said. 'Well, in a way that's reassuring.
At least it suggests we're going to have one. Are you
well?'

Alexius nodded. 'I believe so. It seems that discomfort
and uncertainty and being chivvied about tend to agree
with me, rather more so than comfort and tranquillity. I'd
say I felt ten years younger if I knew when this is meant
to be. And you?'

'Oh, well, not so bad. Average, I suppose. Except, of
course,' he added, 'for this problem I've got.'

'Oh, yes? What's that?'

Hellfire, he doesn't realise. 'Well,' Gannadius said edgily,
'it's not the sort of thing I like to talk about with, er, this
young lady present. Another time, perhaps.'

'What? Oh, right, yes. We'll have to try and make sure
it's after this one, then. Otherwise I won't have a clue
what you're talking about.'

'Alexius!'

'I'm sorry. I don't mean to be flippant, it's just - well,
it's all a bit ridiculous, isn't it? Normal people write
letters. I'm sorry; I'd better—'

—And Gannadius' hands closed around the arms of
his chair. His head felt as if someone had taken it for a
fencepost and nailed a rail to it. 'I say,' he muttered, 'that
was really rather good. Did you, er, work out how to do
that all by yourself?'

Machaera nodded happily. 'It just sort of came to me,'
she said. 'Only I got it wrong, of course,' she added,
suddenly remembering, and her face fell. 'Perhaps it was
because you were there this time—'

'I see,' Gannadius said, managing to keep his voice
calm at least. 'So the first time, the words were different.'

'It was that old man and the other one talking,'
Machaera said, and she briefly summarised the conversation. 'Sorry, does that mean I've - well, changed
something?'

'Nothing important, I'm sure,' replied Gannadius, who was sure of no such thing. 'That man I was talking to is called Alexius; he was my friend and superior back in Perimadeia. He was the Patriarch of the Foundation there.' The girl looked suitably awed. 'And,' he went on without knowing why, 'also probably the greatest authority in the world on, um, projections. We did a lot of research into the subject together.'

(*And nearly got ourselves killed, and maybe actually caused the fall of the City in some ghastly way we don't understand, and did who knows what other damage . . .*)

'That's *wonderful*,' the girl said. 'Oh, do you think he'd mind terribly if I - well, talked to him? Myself, I mean. Just to ask him a few questions?'

Gannadius felt as if he'd just been kicked in the stomach. 'Perhaps it'd be better if you didn't,' he managed to say. 'He's, well, a very private sort of man, and—'

'Of course. I shouldn't have suggested it.' The girl looked down at her shoes. 'I'm afraid I get a bit carried away sometimes,' she added. 'That's very wrong, isn't it?'

'Let's just say these things ought to be treated with respect,' Gannadius heard himself saying. 'And caution, too, of course. I don't want to alarm you in any way, naturally, but it can be - well, I'll be absolutely straight with you, it can be rather dangerous. Bad for you, I mean. If you go too fast without knowing the proper procedures and everything.'

'I see,' the girl said. 'Oh, I'm really sorry. I just don't think, that's my trouble.'

Gannadius took a deep breath. Was that a tiny glimmer of light he could see, he wondered? Or just a hole in the sky through which Disaster was about to come cascading down? 'It's all right, really,' he said. 'And you're making satisfactory progress. Very satisfactory progress. But since you *are* so far advanced, maybe you really ought to stop doing projections on your own for a while. What do you think?'

'Oh, absolutely,' Machaera replied quickly; she looked like a child who's just been told her favourite toy's about to be taken away, and then hears the merciful word *unless*. 'Obviously, the last thing I want to be is irresponsible. I wonder – would you mind helping me? Being there when I do projections, I mean? If it's no trouble, of course. If it's any trouble—'

Gannadius smiled thinly. 'That's what I'm here for, isn't it?' he said.

CHAPTER FOUR

I hope I won't die today, Master Juifrez muttered to himself as he took his place in the landing barge. He looked at his shipmates, fifty halberdiers of the Foundation's Fifth Company, and wondered how many of their minds were occupied with variations on that theme. At the bow, a thin, nervous young corporal was clutching the banner of the Fifth: *Austerity and Diligence*. Scarcely the kind of inspiring concepts that men willingly die for, which was probably all to the good. Master Juifrez didn't want his men to die for anything.

To divert his thoughts from such depressing topics he undid the straps on his pack and peeled open the linen parcel that contained his three days' rations. He couldn't help smiling; Alescia had put in a thick wedge of his favourite cheese, some peppered sausage (rock-hard and bright red, the way he liked it), a block of mature rye bread, six onions, a leg of cold chicken – he looked up and saw that the men were watching him. He folded the parcel up again and strapped up the pack.

He wanted to say something – *So what've you got in yours?* – but of course he couldn't. A Master of the Foundation, twelfth-generation Poor, with a doctorate in metaphysics and a master's degree in philology, doesn't ask his troops what their wives have put in their lunch-boxes. Obviously not. For some reason. He smiled vaguely, and the men looked away. *Strange*, he reflected. *We're off to fight together, possibly die in each others' company, and yet we seem to have so little in common.* On reflection, that wasn't so strange. What *do* ordinary people talk about? Not about textual variants in the early manuscripts of Mazia's *Epiphany*, or the fallacy of moral duality, or modern developments in the art of counter-sapping during long-term sieges, or aspects of the problems of extended lines of supply during protracted foreign campaigns, or Dio Kezma's early instrumental music, or the likelihood of a fall in interest rates among the federated banks of the Island, or who was likely to succeed Master Biehan as Chief Executive of the Department of Public Health and Waterways. And if you discounted that sort of thing, what *was* there to talk about? The weather?

A heavy wave shoved against the barge like a rude man in a hurry, and Juifrez grabbed at his helmet just in time to stop it toppling off his head into the sea. *Organised sport,* he remembered, *and shared experiences in the workplace, known as 'shop'.* But he knew nothing about organised sport, except that in theory it was forbidden, and he had an idea that enlisted men weren't likely to want to talk shop with their commanding officer. As for the weather – *There's a light drizzle. Yes, isn't there?* He frowned and picked at a loose end of binding-cord on the handle of his halberd. It was a pity; because he was there, the men seemed to feel that they couldn't talk among themselves – presumably because what they wanted to say was how crazy the mission was and what little confidence they had in the judgement of their commander. Absolutely no way of knowing. The nearest he'd ever been to their situation was when he'd been a very young freshman, and he and six or so of his classmates had found themselves sharing a ferryboat with their class tutor. Of course they'd all sat there in stony silence, all the way from Shastel Pier to Scona Point, but that was because they were all terrified of dour, humourless, miserable old Doctor Nihal ... Juifrez frowned, not liking the implications. *Me dour, humourless, miserable? Maybe Doctor Nihal wasn't any of those things either, and we all assumed he was just because he was Them. Am I Them? When did that happen, I wonder?*

Not long after that, the condition of the sea and the bad manners of the wind and waves helped clear his mind of all thoughts except, *I hate going on boats*, and just when the steady drizzle was leading him to the conclusion that four coats of wool grease on a military cape aren't quite enough to make it waterproof, the pilot sang out, 'Roha Point!' and he snapped out of his personal thoughts and became an officer again.

First, he looked behind, but the drizzle and the sea-fret were so thick that he couldn't see the other two barges. That didn't mean anything. Visibility was down to twenty yards, if that. He narrowed his eyes, trying to blink away the raindrops, and peered ahead, but there was nothing to see. *How in hell's name does he know we're at Roha Point? We could be anywhere.* Master Juifrez reflected that one of the things he knew least about in the whole wide world was boat-handling. There were bound to be ways of knowing where you are in the middle of a thick fog, or else how did anyone ever get anywhere?

He heard the splash of the anchor and stood up, at first swaying helplessly until his hand connected with the rail. Tradition and honour demanded that he should be the first to jump off the boat into the cold water of unknown depth that separated him from the beach. He scrambled awkwardly over the bench, sat astride the rail, swung his other leg over, dropped off the side of the barge and ended up sitting in nine inches of water. *Marvellous*, he muttered to himself as he hoisted himself back to his feet using the shaft of his halberd, *leadership by example*. Behind him, the men were disembarking in a rather more orderly, scientific manner (*because they're trained to do this and I'm not; after all, I'm just the damn commanding officer*). He raised his left arm and waved the men on, giving the sign to fall in. Behind his boatload, he could see two other similar bodies of men, blurred dark shapes forming a vague platoon-shaped mass. All present and correct, then; time to go.

Up the hill, the scouts had told him, back in the relative warmth and comfort of the Fifth Company's barracks in Shastel; up the hill, follow the track until you come to a cluster of derelict buildings; that's the abandoned tin mine, the Weal Erec. From there, you want to march for about an hour due north, that's carrying on uphill, until you find yourself just under the hog's back; then you turn east and follow the line of the crest until you come to a sudden deep combe, a fold in the ground. The village is down there, in the dip.

Simple enough directions, easy to remember. Master Juifrez led the way, his boots squelching abominably, the rain trickling down the gutter formed by the rolled-over seam between the fluted plates of his helmet and straight down the back of his neck. Did it always rain here? The ground was sodden, and great clumps of mud stuck to his feet, making them impossibly heavy to lift. The further uphill he went, the thicker the low cloud seemed to get, so that by the time he stumbled and tripped over a block of fallen masonry from the wheelhouse of the abandoned mine, he had convinced himself they'd come the wrong way and was on the point of giving the order to turn back.

We're where we're supposed to be; fancy that. He called a halt, and watched the men fall out and perch on the broken-down walls of the mine buildings, bedraggled and gloomy-looking as a flock of rooks roosting in the bare branches of winter trees on a rainy day. Some of them were emptying water out of their boots, others were wringing out hoods and capes, while the majority just sat with the absolute stillness unique to exhausted, demoralised men. He reflected for a moment on how heavy rain makes cloth, and wondered whether there was any realistic chance of getting these sad, sorry people to exhibit any degree of aggression whatsoever, as and when they finally came upon the enemy. *If they've*

*got any sense, they'll invite us inside for a hot drink and a
seat by the fire; they'd be safe as houses if they did that.*

He could feel the urge to snuggle down inside his cape
and go to sleep becoming steadily more insistent; time to
start moving again, or he'd never get them to budge. He
stood up, waved them on, and they formed up in line of
march like so many sleepwalkers, without so much as a
grumble. Looking at them, the expression 'raiding-party'
seemed so incongruous as to be absurd. Raiders pounce
and swoop; they don't squelch, or trudge along with their
heads down like a work detail on their way to the peat
diggings. Maybe he ought to address the men, say a few
inspiring words that'd stir up their military ardour. He
remembered reading something to that effect, but
decided against it. In all the years of their history the
armies of the Foundation had never once mutinied, but
there's always a first time.

From the Weal Erec, march due north for an hour
until you find yourself just underneath the hog's back.
Master Juifrez looked round for a landmark. Stupid: he
couldn't remember which direction they'd come from. He
did know that due north was uphill, but there was an
awful lot of uphill in front of him; which way were they
supposed to go now? Absolutely no chance of fixing due
north by the position of the sun (what sun?). Utterly
ridiculous, the idea that a hundred and fifty grown men,
supposedly professional soldiers, could lose their way on
an open hillside, just because it was raining and there
was a touch of low cloud. He concentrated, trying to
visualise the ruined site as he'd first seen it.

*Well now, if we keep going uphill, sooner or later we'll
find the hog's back, and then we just turn right. As simple as
that. You couldn't get lost if you really tried.* He signalled
the advance, and felt his stiff legs protesting as he
trudged and slithered through the unspeakable mud. Not
for the first time, it struck him as ludicrous that anybody
should be willing to die for the right to own this loathsome place. So far he'd seen no cultivation, no cattle or

sheep, nothing to indicate that this sloppy, squelchy mess was of any interest to anybody – quite understandably. You couldn't plough this mud or plant anything, it'd simply rot in the ground. Livestock wouldn't last a season before footrot and starvation decimated them. Nothing but waste and an abandoned, flogged-out mine. You'd have to be mad.

They came up onto the hog's back almost without knowing it. One moment they were dragging themselves up a steadily increasing gradient, having to use halberd-shafts to pole themselves up the hill; the next, the ground seemed to fall away under their feet, and Juifrez found himself staggering, waving his arms to try and keep his balance. He signalled a halt, wiped the rain out of his eyes yet again, and tried to make sense of the landscape.

They were on the top of the ridge all right, but directly to the west he could see the hillside tumbling down in just such a combe as the scouts had described – which was bewildering, since the combe where the village lay should be to the east, and about three miles further along. Either this was a different combe entirely, or else they'd taken a diagonal course up the hill, overshot the combe and come up on the other side. The combe itself, of course, was full of cloud, which billowed up onto the sides of the crest like the head on a mug of beer. Ridiculous; but here he was, and he had to do something. He could send scouts to see if the village really was down there, but somehow he didn't feel that was wise. The thought of any of his bedraggled, unhappy-looking force being able to descend that steep slope quietly enough to avoid detection was, he felt, fairly remote. Nothing for it but to order the advance, lead his men down the hill and hope he'd got the right combe. Ridiculous. Ah, hell ...

He raised his halberd and pointed down into the mist. The question wasn't so much whether they'd be able to get down the slope quickly enough to be onto the enemy before they had a chance to get ready. It was more a matter of whether, in all this filthy, slippery mud, they'd be able to stop at all. A vision of a hundred and fifty heavy infantrymen tobogganing into battle on their backsides, frantically trying to steer with the butt-ends of their halberds, flitted through his mind and made him cringe. *Austerity and Diligence*, he muttered to himself, *victory or death. Does it count as a victory if the enemy can't fight back because they're laughing so much?*

With severe misgivings and a general sense of being in the wrong place, he led the way. Their best, or only, chance lay in zigzagging their way back and forth across the slope, slowly working their way down until he felt the risk of detection was too great; then he'd have no alternative but to charge down the rest of the slope and trust to luck that there really was a village in the bottom of the valley. Wouldn't the scouts have mentioned it if there were two basically identical combes right next to each other? Maybe they had, and he hadn't been listening. And assuming, just for fun, that there really is a village down there, what are we supposed to do about it, exactly? Burn it to the ground? In this rain?

Maybe they're already waiting for us; bows strung, arrows nocked, just waiting for the command, 'Loose!' Maybe we're all about to die, any minute, here in the rain and the mud. No way of knowing, of course. I hope I don't die today.

It took a very long time to work their way down the side of the combe, maybe more in subjective than objective time, but it's the time you feel that matters. No signs of any life whatsoever, which was reasonable enough. Either this was the wrong combe and there wasn't a village down here at all, or else it was the right combe and everyone was safe and warm indoors, where any sensible person would be on a day like this. Only idiots and raiding parties go slobbering about in the rain and the mud. Idiots, raiding parties and people who are hopelessly lost ...

Juifrez stopped dead, digging his heels in to keep himself upright. Below, through a curling wisp of cloud, he could see a thatched roof, no more than a hundred yards away. *Damn it*, he thought, holding up his arm for the halt. He stood for a moment, trying to see or hear something, anything at all apart from the patter of rain on his helmet, like the drumming of a bored child's fingers on a desktop. Around him he could see the fuzzy outlines of his men, blurred by rain and mist, standing the way he'd seen herds of wild ponies, still and aimless in the rain, just standing and dripping. *Here goes nothing*, he muttered under his breath, and gave the signal for rapid advance.

The next moment he had more than enough to occupy his mind. Rapid advance was one way of describing it. The general philosophy behind it all seemed to be that if you ran fast enough you had a chance of keeping from falling over, as if instability was a pursuer hot on your heels. The three platoons of the Fifth Company (*Austerity and Diligence*) scampered down the hill like reckless, over-excited children, skipping and bouncing, sliding and careering, and all amid a dead, eerie silence that was quite unnerving. The danger they were in was very real indeed; if a man stopped suddenly (assuming such a thing was possible) it was virtually certain that someone'd go charging into the back of him and spit him clean through with the spike of his halberd. Being aware of this, everyone was trying to run faster still, so that the whole unit was accelerating, racing ahead like falling rocks bouncing down a mountainside, a hundred and fifty men all terrified of each other, running away from their own men directly towards the enemy. By the time the ground under their feet started to level out and the first houses loomed up at them out of the mist they were covering the ground at speeds most athletes would never aspire to, skimming over the mud like flat stones spun over still water. *Ludicrous*, Juifrez told himself, *ludicrous* ...

Then a shape reared up at him like a hostile animal – a log-built house, almost a shack, and he was heading

straight for it. He did the best he could to avoid it and
ended up colliding with the corner, feeling the impact
bumping all the air out of his body. His feet shot out from
under him and he slammed down onto his back, trying to
cry out as his head hit the ground but entirely lacking the
breath to cry out with. Somewhere in the mist in front of
him he heard a woman screaming, and he could see his
men streaming past, halberds levelled, completely out of
control. More screams followed, and crashes like someone dropping an armful of scrap metal, and then the first
scream that was pain, not terror. An accident, probably; a
halberdier blundering into somebody with his weapon at
the level, a collision like two carts crunching into each
other at a street corner on a foggy day. As he fought for
breath he could make out the voice of one of his
sergeants, bellowing orders – he couldn't hear the words
but he recognised the inflections – *form ranks, dress
ranks, present arms.* Another scream, quite close. Contact
with the enemy established.

He dragged himself into a sitting position and forced
himself to breathe; the instinct to do so seemed to have
been buffeted out of him, he had to issue commands to
his body to fill and empty his lungs. His halberd must be
somewhere; there it was, slippery with mud and unpleasant to hold, like something dead fished out of a river. He
trawled it towards him and levered himself up with it;
knees weak, body still winded, no pain yet but only
because of the shock. As he took a deliberate breath of
air, a shape materialised near him out of the fog, a tall
man, not a soldier, not a member of the Fifth Company.
Instinct, which had abdicated responsibility for getting
him to breathe, made him level the halberd and lunge.
The man just stood there. The spike went clean through,
until the blade obstructed it.

*He looks surprised. Why does he look surprised?
Doesn't he know there's a war on?*

The man put both hands round the halberd shaft,
opened his mouth to speak, died and fell down, sliding

neatly off the halberd spike. He didn't appear to have a weapon of any kind. It was then that the thought occurred to Juifrez: *maybe this is the wrong village. Maybe this isn't the village where, according to our spies, a platoon of Scona archers has been stationed for an attack on Bryzis. Oh, wouldn't that be ... ?*

A woman was running past, she hadn't seen him. He reached out and grabbed her by the arm, so that she swung round and thumped against his shoulder. She looked utterly bewildered.

'This village,' he said. 'What's it called?'

She looked at him as if he was some kind of weird mythical beast. 'Primen,' she said. 'This is Primen.'

Juifrez winced. 'You're sure?'

'Of course I'm sure. I live here.'

'Damn,' Juifrez replied, and let her go; no rabbit ever ran faster.

Fuck, he muttered under his breath. *Wrong village. These are our people, loyal subjects of the Foundation. This is absurd.* He took a moment to pull himself together, make sure he was breathing properly, stable on his feet; then he took a deep breath to shout out orders, call off the attack. That was when a man darted out of the mist and hit him over the head with a stool.

When he came round, he could hear voices; screaming and shouting and swearing, but different. These were battle-noises. *That can't be right, we hit the wrong village*, he told himself; then he recognised a voice with the low, rolling accent of Scona, someone trying to make orders heard over the noise. *Right village?* he asked himself. *No, can't be.* It took him several seconds to work out what had happened; that somehow someone had got through to the next village down the line and called out the Scona archers to come and save them. *Wonderful*, Master Juifrez lamented, shaking his head in disbelief. *Not only have I massacred the wrong village. I've managed to turn them over to the enemy. How the hell am I going to explain this when I get home?*

There were men coming. Boosting himself sideways
like a scuttling crab, Master Juifrez managed to scramble
under the dead body of the man he'd killed, just as a
dozen or so men walked out of the mist. He couldn't see
them clearly, peeping out from under the arm of a dead
man, but they were wearing mailshirts and helmets and
carrying bows; all he really needed to know, under the
circumstances. He lay as still as he could and prayed he
wouldn't sneeze.

'. . . Hiding to nothing,' one of the men said, in a voice
that was all Scona. 'We're outnumbered four to one and
we can't see to shoot. We aren't even supposed to be
here, for crying out loud. We want to get out of here
while we still can.'

'Can't see a bloody thing,' replied another. 'Definitely
wasting our time. Where'd you get that four-to-one stuff
from, anyway?'

'Someone said,' the first voice replied. 'They said it
was four platoons of heavy infantry, just sort of appeared
out of nowhere. I don't mind an even fight, but four
platoons—'

'Not up to us,' a third voice interrupted. 'The obvious
thing'd be to space out, surround the village, pick 'em off
as they come out.'

'And let 'em burn down the village?'

'Do they look like they're burning down the village?
Get real.'

The voices receded. When he was certain they'd gone,
Juifrez pushed the body aside and staggered to his feet;
he had cramp, and pins and needles in both legs, so there
was no way he was going anywhere quickly. Absurd, he
thought, if I get killed because I can't run because I've got
pins and needles.

It was time to get a grip, he reflected, as he stood on
one leg, leaning against the doorframe of the hut. After
all, he was meant to be the officer commanding this
situation, the man in control, or at least wrestling for
control with his opposite number, the enemy captain. As

it was, all he'd done since they'd charged down into the valley was collide with a wall, kill a loyal civilian, get bashed silly and hide from the enemy. He found that he wasn't too worried about that; but he did have a responsibility to a hundred and fifty men under his command, and it was time he did something about that.

Assuming he could find them, of course. If anything, the fog was thicker than ever. He tried to call his mind to order, but his mental parliament was a confused racket of shouting and screaming. All he could think of to do was to wander into the fog and try and find some of his men. It sounded like a fairly foolproof way to get killed, but he was aware of no other options. An extended scrabble on his hands and knees eventually revealed his halberd. He punted himself upright, muttered something under his breath and headed into the fog.

It was a case of fortune favouring the brave, or fool's luck, or at the very least serendipity of an extravagantly high order; but the first men he met were a dozen halberdiers. They'd formed a loose and unwieldy hedge-hog formation, a slightly bent oval with everybody facing outwards, so that the men at the rear were walking backwards. Because nobody was navigating and the fog was so thick, they lurched from side to side like a party of drunks, or a boatload of inexperienced oarsmen trying to paddle a longboat against a stiff current. One lurch carried them up against the side of a barn, and the three men on the end were squeezed into the wall and nearly crushed before the formation changed course and staggered the other way. It didn't help, of course, that the men had their helmets down with the cheekplates fastened, which made it virtually impossible for them to hear a thing.

It was a start, nevertheless, and Juifrez hurried towards them, waving his arms. At once the formation came to a rapid, disorganised halt, shuddering like a flimsy cart hitting a tree. Someone shouted at him. 'Go away!' or something like that. 'It's me,' he yelled back,

'Master Juifrez. Halt and hold your line. Stop!'

Somehow he got the impression they weren't terribly pleased to see him. They stood where they were, halberds still resolutely extended as if he were a squadron of heavy cavalry bearing down on them from all directions. 'Who goes there?' somebody called out nervously. 'Advance and be recognised.'

'Oh, for ...' said Juifrez. 'It's *me*. Master Juifrez. Don't you recognise me?'

'*Sir!*' The man who'd challenged him snapped to attention and - yes - actually saluted.

'Cut that out and let me through,' Juifrez growled, and he shouldered his way into the front edge of the formation. 'Right,' he called out, 'with me. Let's move. And for pity's sake, keep up.'

In the event, of course, he proved to be much more of a hindrance than a help. Now that there was an officer present, the men immediately stopped trying to navigate the formation themselves and kept going along the most recent straight line they'd been following until they heard the officer give a command. That was, of course, the way it should be, according to drills and regulations; but Juifrez couldn't see any more than anyone else, and the idea of him giving clear, precise, simultaneous orders to a dozen men, half of whom were facing the other way, was clearly absurd. It occurred to him, *Do we actually need to huddle up like this? Nobody's attacked us. Why don't we just form a column and march out of here?*

Another body of men walked out of the mist, almost colliding with them before either party knew what was going on. The meeting was so sudden that no one even had time to raise their halberds; just as well, since both parties were armed with halberds ... *They're Us*, Juifrez realised with a start. 'It's all right,' he shouted, before anybody got hurt, 'it's us. Shastel. It's all right.'

From somewhere in the thick of the other party, Juifrez heard a voice he recognised yelling orders, one of the sergeants. 'Conort,' he shouted, 'it's me, Juifrez.'

'Sir!' the sergeant barked back.

Juifrez closed his eyes for a moment; he was shocked to realise that the emotion washing over him was relief at the end of a period of great fear, which he hadn't been allowing himself to recognise. *I was terrified; and now I've found some more men and an experienced NCO, apparently it's all going to be all right.* 'Sergeant, form the men into column. How many have you got with you?'

It turned out that Conort had reassembled the most part of the second platoon; together, they were now about fifty strong, a force large enough to be able to deal with anything they were likely to bump into. 'All right,' Juifrez said, 'what we've got to do now is find the rest of us and get out of here. Their lot don't want to fight here, and neither do we. Sergeant, form the men into a double line. We're going to take this village through like a partridge drive.'

For the first time, Sergeant Conort understood what the officer was talking about; he was a farmer's son and had been out after partridges with the long net many times. He grinned as he acknowledged the order, and with a few brisk commands organised the men into the double-ply formation (*Why can't I do that?* Juifrez asked himself) necessary for the manoeuvre, which would consist of beating through the village in an ever-diminishing spiral. As they went they'd collect their own men and drive the enemy and the villagers before them, until they had them penned up in the notional net in the middle of the village. If they had any sense at all, they'd surrender without a fight, and then they could all go home.

Actually, that's rather brilliant, Juifrez realised, as the line advanced. *Maybe I'm not so bad at this, after all.* It seemed to be working just fine as they pushed forward, keeping it slow and steady, with the sergeant shouting out at regular intervals and the point men shouting back, to make sure the line stayed straight and together; it was just like a partridge drive, or maybe more like a boar flush, because of the danger. Yes, better comparison. There was the sense of controlled tension you got when you were driving wild boar through thick woodland, the knowledge that if you did it right you wouldn't get hurt making you concentrate rather than panic (because of course you knew what you were doing; nobody's allowed to join the flushing line unless they know what to do; any bloody fool can play at soldiers, but boar flushing's a serious business).

Every time someone appeared before the line, the sergeant shouted out the challenge: 'Who goes there? Advance and be recognised.' Their own men called back, name, rank and number; the enemy had plenty of time to run away, which was how they wanted it to be; plenty of time to deal with them later, when they'd all been flushed into the net. In fairly short order, they'd regained two-thirds of their strength. So long as they took it nice and steady, kept the line, stayed calm, then it was bound to work. It was all going to be all right.

And then a line of men appeared out of the mist in front of them, and someone shouted something. Juifrez frowned - he didn't know what this meant - and an arrow hit the man next to him, stopping him in his tracks. Another arrow hit Juifrez on the right side of his chest, just between his armpit and his collar-bone; he felt the impact, like a hard shove, but couldn't feel any pain, except that all his strength seemed to drain out of him, like water out of a hole in a bucket. Sergeant Conort was yelling words of command - *front rank present arms, make ready* - and then suddenly stopped, at which point Juifrez realised that they were no more than thirty yards from two platoons of archers who were making a fight of it. Oh, hell, what had to be done now? Take cover? No cover, can't stay here, only one place to go. 'Front rank present arms, at the double forward march' - someone was yelling that; me. He saw the men on either side of him surge forward, felt someone pressing against his back, pushing him forward. *I suppose I'd better go too, though I ought to be excused this, after all, I'm wounded. Yes, that's a point. I wonder how bad this is? Doesn't hurt much, but I just want to fall over. Better not to, though; not now.* He shuffled towards the vague line in front of him, aware that they were edging back and that arrows were still pitching all round. Still, only a few yards and we'll be on them, they won't stand, they'll break and run. He took another step and saw the ground rushing up to meet him, felt somebody's boot crash into his ribs, sharp pain as the arrow twisted in the wound as he landed. Then something heavy fell across him, knocking all the air out of his lungs. It twitched and struggled (dying man, probably) but he couldn't move to shrug it off him. He didn't have a clue what was happening. Probably not relevant now. *So this is it, then. Oh, well.*

As far as he knew he didn't lose consciousness at any point. Rather, he lay still, eyes closed, not listening to the noises, letting his mind drift. That was just pragmatism on his part; if he didn't try to focus but just let it all slide and blur, then the wound didn't hurt. It was still there, of course; he pictured it as a mattress of nails, and if he lay perfectly still and relaxed, the nails didn't hurt. At first he made the effort to breathe, self-consciously filling and emptying his lungs, but that was starting to be more trouble than it was worth. *Death, he reflected woozily, is a perfectly natural thing. Nothing to be afraid of. It'll probably do you good if only you'd let it.*

Then something landed on his chest, and the fragile truce with pain was abruptly broken. Now it all hurt like hell, and he didn't like it. *Some bastard just trod on me,* he realised, and for the first time he felt angry. He opened his eyes and saw two men standing over him, staring down at him with terror of almost comic intensity in their eyes; then they reached down and grabbed him, hauling him up – *ah shit, that hurts, let me go!* – and mauling him about like a big sack of wool. He tried to protest but none of the right bits worked, so he closed his eyes, let it happen and tried to concentrate on dealing with pain. He could feel his feet dragging on the ground, every jolt and bump sending blue lightning up his legs. It all lasted a very long time, until it became no time at all.

At one point they appeared to have stopped moving. He opened his eyes, let the weight of his head swing sideways until his face was a few inches away from that of the man on his right. He didn't know who he was.

'I think it's all gone wrong,' he said. The man opened his lips to reply, but he didn't catch any of it; his eyelids flopped back down and the pain washed back in like the sea. *Hey*, he heard himself thinking, *if it hurts I must still be alive. That's good.* Then the waves of tortured feeling broke over his head, and there wasn't anything else.

'Well, what do you expect,' said Gorgas Loredan, grinning as he knelt down to retrieve a perfectly good arrow from a body, 'from an army where you get to be an officer by passing an exam?'

'What's an exam?' asked his colleague.

'It's where you sit down in a big open hall with a couple of long tables,' Gorgas replied, 'and they give you a piece of paper with questions written on it, and you write answers to the questions on another piece of paper. And whoever writes the best answer, wins.'

Gorgas' colleague frowned. 'They must have a lot of paper,' he said.

'They make it out of reed-pulp,' Gorgas said. 'They ship in the reeds from the Salinarus delta. It's a big thing in Shastel, something we ought to be looking at one of these days.'

'There isn't the demand, surely,' the colleague said. 'I mean, apart from them, who uses it?'

Gorgas folded a corner of the dead man's sleeve round the arrowhead and wiped off the blood, then dropped the arrow into his quiver. 'Like I said,' he replied, 'it needs looking into.' He stood up, groaning a little at the stiffness in his knees. 'I think we probably got most of them,' he said. 'I still don't know what all that was about, but it didn't turn out too badly in the end.'

'They helped,' said the colleague with a wry grin. 'They helped a lot.'

'Couldn't have done it without them,' Gorgas agreed. 'You know, whenever I start having my doubts about this war, wondering if we've taken on more than we can handle, I just think about the stupidity of the enemy in all its many and wonderful forms, and then I know it's all going to be all right. I mean,' he went on, as they continued their stroll through the dead and dying, 'one of these days I'd really like to win a battle, rather than just stand quiet while they lose it at me. You know, just to be able to say I'd done it. But I'm not complaining. I mean, it works.'

They completed their tour of inspection and made their way back to the longhouse in the middle of the village, where the orderlies were patching up the wounded. Mostly civilians, Gorgas noted; and once again he found himself asking what on earth had possessed these idiots to attack a loyal village, killing sixteen of their own people and injuring twice as many again, in a thick fog, just when his expeditionary force was arriving to open negotiations with the villagers? It was wonderful – this whole district would come over now, no question about that – but the sheer stupidity of it offended him. It was messy, and he hated mess.

'Look what we found.' Sergeant Harzio was waving at him, calling him over. He grunted. He ought to be in the longhouse, talking comfortably to the village worthies and discussing the articles of transfer, but he didn't feel like doing that. 'Coming,' he said. He turned to his colleague. 'Would you mind doing the pep talk?' he asked. 'I'm not in the mood. You know the drill.'

His colleague nodded. 'I don't mind being fawned on,' he said. 'I'll catch up with you later.'

Gorgas walked over to where Harzio was standing. At his feet were three men, sitting up against the side of a barn, their hands and feet tied. One of them was well out of it, his head slumped forward on his chest. 'What've you got, Sergeant?' he asked.

'Their CO,' Harzio replied, grinning. 'Goes by the name of Master Juifrez Bovert. Ring any bells?'

Gorgas raised both eyebrows. The Boverts were a leading family among the Poor of Shastel. 'You've got a collector's item there, Sergeant,' he said. 'Which one?'

The sergeant pointed. 'He'll make it all right,' he said. 'Diagonal hit through the muscle, lost some blood but nothing serious. We found them staggering about up yonder; they'd wandered into a closed sheepfold and couldn't find their way out again.' Sergeant Harzio grinned. 'What d'you reckon he's worth, then?'

Gorgas shrugged. 'Couldn't say offhand,' he replied. 'Not the sort of thing that comes on the market every day. Must be into four figures, though. Easily.'

Harzio whistled. 'That's not bad,' he said. 'The boys'll be pleased. It was worth coming on this trip, then.'

'That's assuming we ransom him,' Gorgas went on, and the sergeant's face fell sharply. 'Oh, don't worry, if we decide to keep him I'll make sure we see you right, the lads won't lose out. Better for you, in fact; I'll see to that.'

The sergeant's grin broadened into a beautiful smile. 'Always a pleasure doing business with you, Chief,' he said. 'What do you want us to do with him? We stopped the bleeding and he looks like he'll be all right, but – well, now we know he's worth money ...'

Gorgas nodded. 'I'll send him out first thing in the morning.' He knelt down beside the slumped body and had a look for himself. 'He's asleep,' he said, 'which is a good sign. He'll do. Throw a blanket over him and get him under cover before it rains again. And set a guard, just in case.'

He stood up and yawned. It'd be wonderful to be able to go to bed now, but no such luck; too much to do. As he turned to head back to the longhouse, someone behind him tugged his sleeve.

'Casualty figures,' the soldier said, 'as near as we can make them. We got a hundred and seventeen dead, thirty-one prisoners. We lost four killed, two seriously wounded.' Gorgas asked for the names; nobody he knew, but still, it was a pity. It had been an unnecessary battle, for all that it had turned out well. The fact that they'd killed a hundred and seventeen men gave him no satisfaction at all, quite the reverse. A sharp and total defeat of this order of magnitude would represent a substantial loss of face for the Foundation, which meant there would have to be reprisals, quite possibly directed against Scona itself. No fun for anybody. He sighed, and wished, not for the first time, that people wouldn't keep interfering in his business. True, the whole district was now pretty sure to come over to Scona, but there was every chance they'd have done so anyway, in the normal course of events, simply because Scona's interest rates were lower and their attitude less overtly tyrannical. The whole idea of coming here with a relatively small expeditionary force was to avoid starting fights. Now he was going to have to bring in more men, probably as a long-term garrison, just to stop the Foundation from killing every living thing in the district by way of making an example. Not, he reflected as he pushed open the long-house door, the way he liked to run his business; and he had the unpleasant feeling that his sister would see it the same way.

'Magic,' Alexius said.

Niessa Loredan nodded briskly. 'Not philosophy,' she replied, without looking up. 'Not metaphysically enhanced non-verbal communication. Not drug-induced hallucinatory trances in which the participant's subconscious mind assembles and analyses already-known data with exceptional but nevertheless entirely natural insight and then disguises the result as a mystic experience. Magic.' She yawned, and reached for a tiny pair of bronze scissors. 'Magic is just science we don't understand yet.

Probably there was once a time when people thought
the bow and arrow was magic, because it did something
new and unexpected and not many people knew how.
But the bow and arrow works because it works. The
arrow flies through the air and hits the target. And magic
works, too.'

Alexius waited for her to look up, but she didn't. Whatever it was that she was making, it seemed to occupy her
full attention. It looked like a patchwork quilt.

'I'm not saying it doesn't,' he said. 'All I'm saying is
that I've studied these things for sixty years and never
once seen any direct proof—'

'Ah.' This time she did look up, to give him a patron-
ising smile. '*These things*, you say. But what you've been
studying all these years is science and philosophy and
mathematics and all that kind of stuff. You haven't been
studying *magic*. The very most you could have done was
just nudge into the edge of it while you were off studying
something else. It's like a plumber has to know a bit
about carpentry, but he doesn't need to know how to
make mortice and tenon joints. You're saying you don't
think mortice and tenon joints could ever possibly work,
since you've been studying plumbing since you were a
boy and never came across them.'

Alexius thought for a moment, while the Director bit
off a length of thread and fed it through the eye of her
plain bone needle; then he said, 'Tell me, do you always
negotiate with the truth? When you come up against a
fact, a plain and simple and straightforward fact, do you
always try and beat it down, wheedle it into making
concessions?'

Niessa lifted her head and smiled. 'Always,' she said.
'In the City, when I first went there, they had a saying:
truth is what you know is true when you can afford fresh
fish every day of the week. Now then,' she went on,
looking down at her work, 'these days I can afford anything I want, and all sorts of things I could never even
imagine myself wanting. Truth is what I know is true, and

everything else is a matter of bargaining.'

Alexius laughed. 'I haven't heard that one in a long time,' he said. 'Only we used to say, truth is what you know is true when you sit in the front three rows.'

'At Chapter,' Niessa interrupted, 'meaning you've reached the fourth grade or above. I *hated* that.' Her eyes met his, and he saw in them a fire he hadn't noticed before. 'I hated the Foundation, you know. Because they thought they were better than the rest of us because of what they knew. And they didn't know *anything*. Oh, the City was full of people who knew things, useful things: how to make machines, how to extract nitre from urine, how to cure toothache without pulling out the tooth, how to case-harden steel, how to make clear, coloured glass, how to do long division without counters – you name it, somewhere in Perimadeia there was someone who knew how to do it, and who was looked up to and respected for their knowledge and wisdom. The Foundation couldn't get a stopper out of a stone bottle without a book of instructions, three commentaries and a scale diagram. Let me tell you something, Patriarch Alexius. I know more about magic than you'll ever know if you live to be twice as old as you are now; practice *and* theory. But I didn't learn it in Perimadeia, and I didn't learn it here, and you aren't going to learn it unless you do what I ask, however hard you try and trick me into showing off just to disprove your scepticism.' She sniffed, and rubbed her nose on the back of her left hand. 'It was a good try, though,' she said. 'You're the only scholar I ever met who might just have made a living in the markets.'

Alexius nodded, accepting the compliment, and as he did so he wondered, *How much of any of this is real, and how much is just negotiation? This woman could be anything, anything at all, for the purposes of striking a more favourable bargain. Look at her now, painstakingly stitching together scraps of cloth to make a piece of patchwork; she's being the plain, shrewd no-nonsense countrywoman, so as to undermine me, the soft-fingered City scholar. Tomorrow she'll be the Director of the Bank when she's telling a delegation of peasants why the mortgage rate's gone up, and the day after that she'll be something else again; and they're all her, and she's all of them, and none of them are real. Nevertheless; we've been cooped up in here for an hour and a half and still I haven't even started doing what she's told me to, and she was the one with the crowded schedule. Not bad, for an other-worldly old bookworm.* 'And you're the only banker I've ever met who can quote three of Acadius' hypotheses in one sentence,' he replied. 'Though "metaphysically enhanced non-verbal communication" is rather over-simplifying the second book of *Axioms*, don't you think?'

Niessa shrugged, eyes on her work. 'The whole second book is based on a false premise anyway,' she replied, 'as you well know. Mometas proved that a hundred years ago. And,' she added casually, holding the seam up to the light, 'his refutation is basically a circular argument, so the whole thing's a waste of time.'

Alexius wasn't expecting that. In spite of himself, he couldn't help asking for details.

'Oh, it's quite simple,' Niessa replied. 'He takes the analogy of light refracted in a rainbow, and then knocks down the hypothesis he's just built up by saying it's just an analogy. It's very well argued, of course, but it's still as obvious as a bull in a chicken-run. He'd have starved to death if he'd been in the linen trade.'

She's right, Alexius thought angrily. *Either she's read something none of the rest of us ever saw, or she figured it out for herself. She's right. Dear gods, if I were thirty years younger I'd give up philosophy and get myself indentured to a sack-maker.* 'It's an interesting theory,' he heard himself say, 'but what about Berennius and the irregular flux theory? I think you'll find that for the last fifty years, Mometas' theorem has only ever been regarded as a starting point, not an end in itself.'

'Whatever.' Niessa Loredan dismissed the whole topic

with one small wave of her needle. She'd won that round, they both knew it, she had nothing to gain by continuing the battle on that front. 'Obviously you know far more about the subject than I do. Frankly, I'd be appalled if you didn't. Now then.' She carefully folded her work and laid it in her lap. 'Let's get down to business. It's time we did some magic.'

'Well?' asked the boy anxiously.

Bardas Loredan pursed his lips. This was awkward.

On the one hand, his father had never been tactful with him. When he'd been learning this particular skill, the old man's way of indicating that he'd got it wrong was pulling it out of the vice and snapping it across his knee, while adding a few short, pithy remarks about wasting good timber. (As far as Bardas could remember, he'd never actually said that good wood doesn't grow on trees, but he'd been close to it on several occasions.) On the other hand, Bardas Loredan wasn't his father.

'It's terrible,' he said. 'Do it again.'

The boy looked at him as if he'd just killed his pet sparrow by crushing it in his fist. 'Oh,' he said. 'What's wrong with it?'

Bardas sighed. 'You really need to be told?' he said. 'I knew you weren't listening. All right, here we go. First, the belly should be flat, and it isn't. Second, when you're shaping the back you should follow one growth ring, otherwise you're wasting your time, and you haven't. Look,' he went on, pointing to where the boy had shaved through three years' worth of growth, 'it's a mess. Third, you've got to leave knots and pins standing proud, or else they'll form weak spots and the bow'll snap. You've just planed right through them. Fourth—'

'All right,' said the boy. 'I'm sorry.'

Bardas breathed out sharply. 'It's not a matter of being *sorry*,' he said wearily. 'It's not as if you've done something wicked. You've just not done it right, that's all. True, you've wrecked a perfectly good piece of wood, but we

all do that. Just ...' He sighed again, not really knowing
what to say. 'Just go away and do it again, and this time
do it right. You think you can manage that? Or would
you rather watch me do one, and this time—'

'I'll try again,' the boy interrupted swiftly. 'This time I'll
do it right, I promise.'

'Sure,' Bardas replied. 'Well, do your best, anyway. And
when you've done that, get this mess swept up, we're
knee-deep in shavings again.'

The boy made himself scarce, and Bardas sat down on
the bench, his chin cupped in his left hand. In the vice in
front of him was another mess; a banjax, a really lousy,
crummy piece of work, an abortion, garbage, trash, junk.
It also represented several weeks' work and about
twenty quarters' worth of bought-in material. He'd
already tried swearing at it, but it hadn't helped.

'My own bloody stupid fault for listening,' he grumbled, opening the vice and lifting out the wreck. It had all
started with a chance remark made by a man who called
in occasionally to sell him timber, the rare and exotic
stuff that came from the South Coast, types of wood he
didn't know the names of from trees he'd never seen. The
man had said that once he'd seen a bow made out of
buffalo ribs—

'You mean horn,' he'd interrupted. 'Buffalo horn. You
slice it thin and glue it—'

'Ribs,' the man had repeated firmly. 'Lovely thing, it
was; no more than a yard long, a thumb wide at the
handle, fingertip wide at the ends. Bloke who showed it
to me said it drew fifty pounds and shot an arrow two
hundred and twenty yards.'

'He can't have said ribs,' Bardas maintained. 'He
meant horn.'

'Ribs,' the man repeated. 'Buffalo ribs.'

And there the matter would have rested if it hadn't
been for his own stupid pride and a chance encounter
with a dealer in hides who'd said yes, well, there was no
call for them, not *ribs*, but as a special favour ... And a

month later they'd arrived, greasy, smelly and expensive; and once he'd paid out all that good money, he was obliged to continue.

'Stupid,' he muttered under his breath as he turned the horrid thing over in his hands. 'Should know better at my age.'

There followed hours of work with the drawknife and the spokeshave, whittling the bones down into flat, even strips, checking with the calipers after every dozen or so strokes to make sure the strips matched exactly at four-inch intervals, identical in width, depth and profile. When the strips were precisely three sixteenths of an inch thick, he'd set them aside and made a wooden core out of a choice billet of imported red cedar, which he'd pain-stakingly heated over a steaming cauldron, draping a thick hide over the top to keep the steam in, until the wood could be bent into broad, flowing recurves at the tips so that it looked like a crawling snake, or the upper lip of a smiling girl. Then he'd set to work to make up a specially strong pot of glue, flaking small crumbs of hide into the pot, adding the boiling water and simmering the mess until it was the consistency of year-old honey. Clamping the bone to the core had been a special night-mare; he'd used every clamp in the shop, and improvised a dozen more out of wood and rawhide, and the glue oozing out of the joint had slopped everywhere, making the thing almost impossible to hold. Then it had taken forever to dry – just his luck to be doing the job during a rainy spell, when the damp got into the glue and stopped it hardening – and he'd needed the clamps for other work but didn't dare take them off because the glue-drips were still sticky and he was terrified of the heavily stressed bone pulling off the core.

Finally, when at last the glue was hard enough and he'd got the use of his clamps back and the thing was actually holding together and not peeling itself apart like the skin of a grape, he'd spent a day with a full glue-pot and an extravagant amount of his best deer-leg sinew, laying the glue on the bow's back and smoothing the bundles of sinew into it with the handle of a wooden spoon, making sure that every bundle overlapped and the thickness of the backing was consistent. That too seemed to take a lifetime to dry; but at last the day came when the glue was as hard and brittle as glass, and he'd chipped away the excess, scraped the back smooth, rubbed the whole thing down with abrasive reed and bent it for the first time, just enough to get the string on it. That had been first thing this morning.

'Useless bloody thing,' he growled, his fingers following the flowing curve of the mid-limb section, feeling how perfectly smooth he'd made the back and belly. To look at it was an absolute delight, quite possibly the most graceful and elegant bow he'd ever seen, let alone made. The proportions were perfect, the recurves immaculately balanced; with the string on, it had the classic double-juxtaposed-S shape of the thoroughbred composite bow. The trouble was, it didn't work.

When he'd first set it up on the tiller and drawn it a tentative inch, it had felt wonderful, the indescribable combination of yielding and resistance that only comes with the bonding together of sinew, wood and horn. But this wasn't horn, it was bone, and (as he now knew extremely well) bone will bend so far and no further; in this case, seventeen inches, at which point it jammed solid and refused to budge any further. The wood and sinew stopped it breaking, but nothing he could do would induce it to flex another inch; which left him with a forty-two-pound bow with a seventeen-inch draw, not much use for shooting a thirty-inch arrow. Oh, it propelled the arrow, sure enough – if you were prepared to contort your arms and shoulders into a knot, like crawling through a hole not much wider than your head, but trying to aim with it was the next best thing to impossible. For all practical purposes it was completely useless, unless he ever came across a rich tiny man with very short arms who was looking for a lightweight bow for shooting squirrels with. Stone-deaf squirrels, at that; the thing made a horrible creaking noise every time he drew it that'd frighten away every living creature within a square mile.

He looked it over one more time, then laid it on the bench and went back to rubbing the big sore yellow patch on his left wrist where the string had hit him. *Useless*, he reflected, *and it bites, too. Well, we all make mistakes. I just hate it when it's me.*

It had started raining again, and he crossed the shop and pulled the shutter closed. If it got any darker he'd have to light a lamp, even though it was still only early afternoon. The pattering of water on the thatch soothed him a little, as it always did; it reminded him of days when it was too wet to do anything outdoors, and his father ushered them all into the long barn to learn a new skill at the workbench. Back then he'd assumed that his father knew how to do everything, that there was nothing he couldn't make or mend if only he could be talked into it and the rain kept on long enough. It annoyed him, then and now, that there had never been quite enough time, what with the real work that always needed to be done outside, and the way his father had to slow down so that the others, who weren't nearly so quick or so keen when it came to making things, could follow too. He'd always been the impatient one, who'd already worked the next stage out for himself while the old man was trying to get it across to Gorgas or Clefas; Clefas was the slowest, he remembered, Gorgas was perfectly capable of understanding but simply couldn't be bothered, Niessa could grasp some things almost instinctively and then completely fail to understand the next step, and Zonaras – well, the old man had stopped wasting his time and patience on Zonaras by the time he was ten. No doubt about it: he'd always been the very best at making things, just as Gorgas had been the best at using the things that other people made. Nobody could lay a hedge like Gorgas, not even the old man;

nobody could handle a net or lay a wire like he could, or spear fish at the weir or shoot a bow ...

Bardas thought about that for a long time, and then smiled. Odd, that of all of them he should be the one who ended up making a living out of his manual dexterity; he, not Gorgas, had been one of the most successful fencers-at-law in the history of Perimadeia, fighting and killing with the sword, a tool notoriously awkward to manipulate. Odd that he, not Gorgas, had ended up making a living out of killing people. It only goes to show, we're given talents but don't always use them.

He put the thought of his brother Gorgas carefully to one side, stowed the useless bone bow under the bench and looked around for something to do. No shortage of that; the billets of that ash they'd cut in the mountains needed to be drawn down into staves, preferably before the boy turned them all into firewood for the benefit of his education. He climbed up onto the bench and pulled one out of the stack stowed between the rafters, then got down again, picked up his drawknife and tested the edge with his thumb. Blunt, of course; his diligent young apprentice had been using it, and as usual had left it as sharp as a tomato. Bardas growled softly and looked round for the stone.

'I think I left the stone out by the back gate,' Bardas said, 'when we were cutting back the brambles. Go and see if it's there, would you?'

'It's raining,' the boy pointed out.

'So? You weren't made of salt last time I looked.'

The boy muttered something under his breath about justice and the fair division of labour, and slouched very slowly towards the door. 'You sure it's not under the bench?' he asked, as he reached for the latch.

'Sure,' Bardas replied. 'I looked there just now.'

'There's all sorts of places it could be.'

'Very true. Now get down to the gate and fetch it.'

While he was gone, Bardas tidied away some of the tools he'd been using that morning. Under the heap he found the stone. *Damn*, he said to himself, and set about putting an edge on the drawknife. He'd just about got it right when the boy came hurrying in, his hair plastered round his head like seaweed on a wet rock.

'Sorry about that,' Bardas said, 'it was here all the—'

'There's two boats down below in the cove,' the boy interrupted, the words spilling out of his mouth.

Bardas frowned. 'That's odd,' he said. 'Who's dumb enough to be out fishing in this weather?'

'They aren't fishing boats,' the boy went on in a sort of terrified glee. 'They're barges. They were just coming in past the Horn Rock.'

'Barges,' Bardas Loredan repeated, as if the word was meaningless.

'Two of them, full of men. I think they're soldiers, from Shastel.'

Barges. Soldiers from Shastel. That doesn't make any kind of sense. 'Are you sure about that?' he said. 'Damn it, why am I asking?' He straightened up, stopped and hesitated. 'You're sure?' he repeated.

'Of course I'm sure,' the boy replied angrily. 'Really, it was two barges, I stopped and looked. They didn't see me, because as soon as I saw them I ducked down behind a rock, but I saw them and they were both full of men. I couldn't see them properly because they wore all wearing hoods because of the rain, but what else would two barges full of men be?'

Fair point. 'All right,' Bardas said. 'Here's what you do. Run down to the village as fast as you can, go to the smithy and tell Leijo you've seen what looks like a raiding party; he'll tell you what to do.'

'All right,' the boy said. 'What about you? Are you coming?'

Bardas shook his head. 'I'll probably join you later, but I suppose I ought to go and have a look first. Here,' he added, 'take the four flatbows we finished yesterday and the big sheaf of bodkinheads. Can you manage them by yourself?'

'Of course,' the boy replied. 'Are we going to fight them, then?'

'Don't be stupid,' Bardas said. 'Anyway, not if we can possibly help it. That's what the army's for. Go on, get a move on. You'd better go through the lower copse, just in case. And be careful.'

He helped load up the boy's arms with the bows and arrows and watched him run off. Then he shut the workshop door and walked quickly over to the house. He had to go down on his hands and knees to get it; a long greasy bundle of cloth he'd stowed under his bed some time ago, put away out of sight and largely out of mind. *Damn*, he thought again, as he shook off the wrapping and lifted out the two-handed Guelan broadsword his brother Gorgas had given him, just before the City fell. There was a touch of mildew on the shoulder-strap, a slight fog of rust on the pommel, like the mist left behind when you breathe on glass. He put the strap over his shoulder, then took his bow and quiver off the hooks on the wall. *Absolutely not*, he told himself as he shut the house door behind him; *it's just that it'd be stupid to leave the sword lying about, it's worth a fortune. And I wouldn't want to lose the bow, either.* He looked back at the house and then across at his workshop, as if he was leaving on a long journey, then set off up the hill at a brisk walk.

CHAPTER FIVE

From the gate at the top of the track, there was a clear view across the narrow ribbon of cliff-top grazing land to the cove. Bardas crossed the green strip and pushed his way through the tangle of briars that overlooked the neck of the cove. It was a good place to see without being seen.

The men on the shingle beach below didn't seem to be in any particular hurry. They had hauled the long, heavy barges up out of the water and were unloading their gear – armour and halberds in waxed-cotton covers, kitbags and satchels, all sodden and glistening in the rain. They looked bone-weary – reasonably enough: it was no easy run from Shastel round the back of Scona Island in this sort of weather even in a proper boat, let alone the primitive, cack-handed punts that were the best the Shastel people could do in the way of seafaring transport. *You wouldn't get me out in one of those things*, Bardas assured himself with a true landsman's shudder. *Only idiots choose to be surrounded on all sides by water.*

He counted them; seventy-five heavy infantry, the celebrated Shastel halberdiers. He'd never seen any of them before, and, he had to admit, they looked just like any other soldiers: awkward, brutal and alien, out of place in any landscape. *Maybe all soldiers look alike in the rain*, he reflected. *And it always rains, sooner or later. I'm just glad I'm not down there with them. Rotten job, and nobody really has to do it.*

A sergeant started shouting orders and the men shuffled across the grinding shingle to form a column, while another man, the officer presumably, huddled over an increasingly waterlogged and useless parchment map. From the way he kept glancing down at it and then up at the surrounding wall of cliffs, it was either the wrong map, upside-down or not particularly accurate; in the end the officer stuffed it like an old rag into his satchel and stumped across the shingle, sliding a little over the loose stones – *he looks just like a duck,* Loredan observed, *waddling down to the river with her chicks.* He took one last look round, as if hoping for inspiration, then led the column towards the one track that wound up the side of the cliff towards Loredan's house and the village beyond.

My house, Loredan thought gloomily. *Well, it's too wet for a fire to burn properly.* Just for fun he considered the tactical position. There was only one track up from the beach, and five men could hold it all day against any army, provided you could find five lunatics with a death wish at such short notice. More realistically, a dozen or so trained City archers could pin this lot down almost indefinitely on the straight stretch of track that led up to the downs; and if he had two dozen spearmen to circle round behind this fuzz-patch and take the goat track that led down onto the beach from the other side – but he didn't, and that was probably just as well. It was, after all, none of his business; they might trash his house, but then again they might not, if their mission was to burn the village. The point was that he didn't belong here, and so he didn't have to join in when this sort of thing happened. That was the whole point of not belonging.

He kept still and quiet, waiting for the soldiers to go away. Thinking about it logically, there was no reason for them to go anywhere near his place if they were heading for the village; it'd waste time, possibly enough time for word to get to the village or even the nearest guard post. (Bardas knew that the village had already been warned and there wasn't a guard post nearer than Scona Town itself, but maybe they didn't.) And even if they did go snooping round his place, what harm could they actually do? The thatch would be too wet to burn, they weren't going to waste time pulling the buildings down with ropes and bars, and who in their right mind would want to plunder a woodworker's shop? Planes, drawknives and spokeshaves aren't high on an experienced looter's list of priority items. No, as soon as they'd satisfied themselves that there was nobody about, they'd push off and get on with their work.

Even when he was fairly certain that they were long gone, he stayed put – if they're gone now, they'll be even more gone in fifteen minutes – and lay snuggled in his coat under the surprisingly effective shelter of a big, fat briar-bush. If anything, the rain was getting heavier; a bit of wind had got up, coming in off the sea. There was no reason, in fact, why he couldn't stay here all day. It'd probably be the most sensible thing to do, in the circumstances. On the other hand, it was very boring. He stood up, picked trailing shoots of bramble off his arms and legs, and cautiously made his way out of the fuzz.

The first thing he saw was a satisfying absence of smoke rising from the direction of his property. *The beer-barrel*, he remembered; a nearly new barrel of quite reasonable beer in the middle house, they'd fined and tapped it two days ago. Soldiers can smell beer across vast distances, even when the wind's in the other direction; in fact, it probably wasn't smell but something far more abstruse, closer to the sort of metaphysical stuff his old friend Alexius was so deeply into. Chances were, he could kiss that goodbye. Still, if they'd been busy drinking his beer, they wouldn't have had time to damage anything else.

A combination of rain, mud and issue boots results in a trail a blind man could follow. Bardas picked it up at the top of the cliff path and followed it to his gate, where (oh, joy) it carried on without deviating, down the slope towards the village. Perhaps the officer had made sense of his map after all, or maybe they hadn't even realised there were any buildings here; come to think of it, they were pretty well hidden by the outcrop and the rank growth of nettles he'd been meaning to do something about for the last month. Just as well he hadn't. Three cheers for bad husbandry.

I ought to go home now, he thought. *True, they'll presumably be back later, returning the way they came; but they aren't likely to stop on the way back, they'll have done the job and be in a hurry to get away. I should go home, maybe even get on with some work. Me, I'm no bother to anybody, so why should anybody bother me?*

Instead, he took the narrow rough track over the rocks that made an uncomfortable and hazardous shortcut to the village. It was a while since he'd been along here, and there was a season's obstructive growth to tread down or wriggle under. *Damn you, Nature, why can't you leave things alone?* he thought savagely, clambering through a notional gap in the branches of a rowan tree that had fallen across the path. (Rowan? No good for bows. Waste of everybody's time it being there in the first place.) At least he could be sure nobody had been this way today, and since the path ran along the top line of the crest, he was out of sight of the main track. Not as sensible as staying home, perhaps, but sensible enough for a sensible man.

As he came round the sharp bend at the bottom of the Chapel Rock, the big outcrop that overlooked the seaward end of the village, he found a dead body. It was one of the halberdiers, lying face down in a patch of mud with an arrow sticking out of one ear – *one of mine,* he noticed, *that batch I made with those sub-standard white goose quills and sold off cheap in the village.* The man's halberd was gone; he'd been stabbed several times in the back as well, but there was no blood – someone making sure, or just taking it out on dead meat, which would imply something to be angry about. No helmet either, but that figured. If he'd been wearing his helmet, he wouldn't have got shot.

So someone was making a fight of it down in the village. Bardas frowned. They'd never struck him as war-like types, the sort who dream of tackling burglars and rustlers or marching down to the beach to ambush marauding pirates. Very few people were, in his experience; back along, when he'd been the one raiding and burning the encampments of the plainspeople to uphold the security of the City, he'd learnt pretty well all he'd ever want to know about how people react to this sort of thing. Generally, they ran; sometimes away, quite often round and round in circles, like ducks in a pen when the fox breaks in. Those that didn't run, hid, and sometimes that was the right thing to do and sometimes it wasn't. Sometimes they just stood there and watched, some-times they shouted and screamed, sometimes they tried to talk to you and persuade you to go away. But one thing they very rarely did was fight; probably because human beings are not, at a fundamental level, that stupid. And when they did, some basic survival instinct made them give up short of actually killing one of the enemy, because if there's one thing guaranteed to make a party of raiders mad at you, it's killing one of their friends.

I don't know, Loredan said to himself, as he stepped over the body, *maybe these people just don't know about these things*. The sensible thing to do now, at any rate, would be to go home, put some food and some dry clothes in a bag, and head off into the mountains, maybe hide up for a day or so in one of the derelict farmhouses he'd seen there. That'd be the sensible thing.

Instead, he walked round the corner and down the track towards the village. It was a mess. There were a few bodies, but mostly it was just ordinary damage, the sort of thing a flood or a freak storm does so much better than human beings ever could. Perhaps

understandably, given their recent experiences, the
raiders seemed to have vented most of their rage on the
village boats, the small ash-framed hide-covered
curraghs that could cope with the worst tantrums the
sea threw. As luck would have it, most of them had been
drawn up in the square to have their hides regreased
with the thick, foul-smelling dubbin that the Scona
people made from newly shorn fleeces. The grease had
been curing all summer and was now ready, and at this
time of year the smell of lanolin and tanning fluid hung
over the island like a cloud of midges. Now there wasn't a
single boat left intact, and bits of spar and scraps of hide
were scattered everywhere, trodden into the mud like
fallen leaves.

Maybe half a dozen fishermen lay among the smashed
boats, draped and flopped in positions no living body
ever lay in, and here and there Loredan found arrows -
someone had lost his temper, perhaps, run indoors,
grabbed his bow and started shooting out of the window.
Here was a middle-aged woman with half a sack of flour
under her and an arrow in her back, and an old man with
his head cracked open like a walnut. Here was a fat
young woman with a halberd still sticking in her, and a
man's arm, crudely severed at the elbow, a few feet away;
it had taken two, maybe three cuts, and Loredan could
picture him warding off the blows with an expendable
part of his body, until presumably the attacker had
decided he'd done enough and let him run. Here was a
dead chicken, chopped nearly in half, and a dog with its
belly ripped open, and here was a goat with a long rip in
its side running across the line of its ribs from front
shoulder to back; it lifted its head as Loredan came up to
it, and went on chewing. Here was a dead halberdier -
extremely dead - by the look of it two or three men had
got hold of him and attacked him with knives and
cleavers; and here was one of those attackers, presumably, lying on his back in a big mucky puddle with a
small hatchet in one hand and a red palm-sized patch

caked on the front of his shirt. More like a brawl than a
battle, Loredan reflected disapprovingly; the officer's
fault for letting things get out of hand. We managed
these things better in my day; though of course the
plainsmen were used to being raided, they knew the drill
as well as we did.

Here they'd tried to get a fire going, several times by
the look of it, and failure hadn't improved their temper.
Neither had one of their men getting shot, because
they'd made a fair mess of the house they hadn't managed
to set light to, and the two men who'd been in it as well.
A little further down the street he found a live one,
though only just; he recognised the sergeant who'd been
giving the orders on the beach by the rather splendid
gilded ridge round the crown of his helmet. He had managed to prop himself up against the side of a house and
get the arrow out of his chest, but someone had had a go
at cutting his throat, made a bad job of it and gone away.
He tried to say something while Loredan looked at him
and decided there wasn't anything much that could be
done; he shook his head and walked away, as if passing
by an unconvincing beggar on a street corner. That
brought him to the end of the main thoroughfare. It was
very quiet, except for the pattering and dripping of the
rain. His shoes were waterlogged, and he wriggled his
wet toes with distaste. The sensible thing now would be
to go home and change into dry clothes, before he
caught his death of pneumonia.

Instead, he followed the trail the raiders had left, down
the hill towards the next village.

Not a good day for making the short but troublesome
crossing from Shastel to Scona. Gorgas Loredan, usually
a good sailor, had to admit to being a trifle wobbly and
green as he walked down the plank from the sloop
Butterfly and gratefully set foot on the Traders' Dock.

Gorgas Loredan was always glad to be home, but on
this occasion he could feel the relief rushing through him,

the way blood starts to flow again through a numb leg
when you wake up and find you've been lying on it. He'd
spent a more than usually unpleasant couple of days in
the hectemore country, fought an unanticipated battle
and brought back with him a couple of problems that he
suspected would turn out to be awkward.

One of these problems had tried his best to die on him
during the night. Master Juifrez' relatively straightforward wound had turned bad, and the wretched man
was in the grip of a thoroughly melodramatic fever. Field
surgery with a hot knife, raw spirit and a bread-mould
poultice had kept him alive, but he still looked awful, and
he appeared to have about as much interest in staying
alive as Gorgas had in Colleon religious poetry. He could
understand that, in a way – a man who'd managed to
make such a comprehensive mess of his life and his
nation's affairs might be forgiven for deciding to call it a
day. But no businessman likes having the stock die on
him; so as soon as the *Butterfly* tied up, a runner was
sent off to fetch a doctor. Death was a luxury not permitted to the prisoners of the Bank of Scona.

As the patient was carried off on a door by the
doctor's orderlies, Gorgas shouldered his kitbag and
started to walk up the Promenade. He hadn't got far
when a runner skittered to a halt beside him and tugged
on his sleeve.

'Urgent message,' the boy panted, without waiting to
catch his breath. 'There's an enemy raiding party loose in
the hills around Horn Point. They burnt down a village
and killed all the people. The Director wants you to get out
there as quick—'

'Horn Point,' Gorgas repeated. 'You're sure about
that?'

The boy nodded. 'My cousins live up there,' he said, as
if this was somehow definitive proof. 'Sounds like the
village they burnt was Briora; that's just on the Point,
straight down the hill from Horn Rock. I'd say they must
have landed in the cove.'

Gorgas frowned. 'Never been there,' he said. 'Who did you get this from?'

'A kid ran in from there, he'd seen it happening. I talked to him before I came here. They were about to send someone else when your ship was spotted.'

'That's just as well, then. Did the boy say how many men?'

The runner shook his head. 'Just that there were a lot of them, probably more than a hundred.' He stopped to wipe away the rain that was running from his plastered-down fringe into his eyes. 'Proper soldiers, he said, in armour. Some of the village men tried to fight them, and then they got really nasty and started smashing up everything in sight.'

Gorgas took a deep breath. 'All right,' he said, 'here's what you're going to do. Run up to the Bank, get a message sent to the Director that I'm on my way and I'm taking the five platoons of the Tenth that're on standby down here at the Dock. Say that I want the whole of the Seventh called in and sent after me as soon as possible. Then meet me back at the Dock barracks gate – you know where that is?' The boy nodded. 'I'll need a guide, and you sound like you know the way. Are you on for that?'

'You bet.' The boy was grinning.

'That's good, then. You get on, and make sure you get the message straight.'

Fortunately, Gorgas' staff who'd come back with him on the *Butterfly* were mostly still hanging round the Dock. He caught hold of one of his runners and sent him to round them up, and dispatched another runner to the barracks with the mobilisation orders and the message that he'd be following straight away.

Briora village, near Horn Point; as he forced his pace along the Dock towards the barracks, he tried not to think about it. *I knew I shouldn't have let him go swanning off like that; if anything's happened to him . . .* The rational part of his mind suggested that this was sheer folly.

There had never been any reason to assume that the back country around Horn Point was a dangerous place to be; and besides, if Bardas Loredan could survive the sack of Perimadeia, there was a fair chance he'd be able to cope with a Shastel raiding party. There had never been any question of keeping Bardas cooped up in Scona Town; he wasn't a prisoner, he'd only have fretted and made trouble. He'd done everything he could for the man. It was pointless blaming himself. Yes. But. When it's family, you can't help blaming yourself.

The guard captain met him at the gate. 'We can be ready in an hour,' he said, fumbling with the hooks of his mailshirt. His hair was uncombed, and under his armour he was wearing an old shirt with frayed cuffs – *probably caught him in the middle of his dinner*, Gorgas thought with a smile. *Food; gods, yes, I remember food. It's something that happens to other people.* 'But I haven't got a ship. What about the one you came in on?'

'The *Butterfly*,' Gorgas said. 'Good idea. Send a runner to find the captain, get him to round up the crew and be ready to leave in an hour. We can get three platoons on board at a push; choose who you want to take the other two and tell him to find himself some transport.' He looked up at the sky; foul weather for sailing round the island. He didn't know Horn Cove, but he guessed it'd be tricky work bringing a sloop in anywhere on that side. Still, the captain of the *Butterfly* had seemed like a reliable man. 'Right,' he said. 'Get me a map of the area while you're at it, and see if any of your men know the place. We don't know how many of them there are and we don't want to have to waste time pussyfooting about, so some local knowledge'll be very handy.'

Damn you, brother, he said to himself as he sat down in the porch to catch his breath and clear his head for a few precious minutes, *why must trouble keep following you like the cat and the farmer's wife?* But in some deep and rather unseemly way, he had to admit, what he was mostly feeling was excitement, almost pleasure at the thought of rushing to his brother's rescue. At very bad times, when he caught himself wondering what sort of a man he must be to have done some of the things he'd done, had to do, over the years, he always pulled himself out of it by reminding himself that someone who really cared about family, as he did, couldn't really be a bad man. After all, what else was there, when you came right down to it? Pulling Bardas out of the fire back in Perimadeia had been a good thing to do; and now here he was doing the same sort of thing all over again. Well, it had to count for something. Saving a brother was sort of like balancing the books.

Bardas can look after himself, insisted his rational voice. *He was a professional soldier, remember, one of Uncle Maxen's men, not to mention all those years of swordfighting for a living. You'd better hope he's left you a few of the enemy.* That'd be right, he reflected; and then he thought of what the boy had said, about some of the villagers trying to make a fight of it, and that was when the trouble had started. *Mess,* he thought bitterly, *and melodrama. Oh, why can't people stay where they're put and do as they're damn well told?*

Short, sharp and nasty, the Dean of Lay Works had said; a fast response, hitting them right between the shoulder blades where they least expect it, then out again and home before they know what's happening. It had sounded fair enough when the Dean was explaining it, but between there and here something would appear to have gone wrong.

Master Renvaut, officer commanding the Scona task force, sat down on a fallen tree and scraped some of the thick crust of mud off the sole of his boot with the blade of his halberd. Maybe it was the weather, or the fact that they'd scrambled into action the moment the news of the disaster at Primen reached Chapter, without time for proper preparations and planning. Maybe it was all his fault. Didn't matter, particularly. The only thing that mattered now was getting out of this mess, before he managed to make Juifrez Bovert look like a strategic genius in comparison.

'Nine dead,' the colour-sergeant reported, his voice completely neutral, 'four wounded, one of 'em's cut up pretty badly but the other three'll be all right.'

Renvaut nodded; it was better than he'd expected. He still had sixty-five men on their feet and presumed fit for duty. 'Fall them in,' he said, and he grunted with pain as he stood up. 'I've had enough of this. We're going back.'

It had stopped raining, and there were even a few scraps of blue scattered across the sky, like flotsam on a beach after a storm. A bit of warmth, to dry out their sodden clothes, maybe even dry up the mud so that every step they took wasn't quite such an effort; a bit of warmth and sunlight might make everything seem better. There was still a chance they'd get out of this mess in one piece, and be home in Shastel by this time tomorrow.

Assuming, of course, that the boats were still there, and that they didn't sink to the bottom of the sea on the way back. Ah, but all human life rests uncomfortably on a fragile bed of assumptions, interposed between hope and fear like the thin skin of a boat; or so they'd told him in Cloister. Out here it sounded both annoyingly glib and depressingly true. So much for the benefits of a first-class education.

Back the way they'd come? He didn't fancy the idea. He was all too aware that he was painfully behind on his schedule; the rain and the unexpected resistance had seen to that. The Scona armed forces were supposed to be mostly made up of light infantry and archers, quickly mobilised and able to move at speed. In theory, that oughtn't to be a problem, since two platoons of trained, disciplined heavy infantry should be capable of ramming its way through the sort of opposition they'd be likely to encounter. But somehow this didn't seem like a good day for fighting. Being an educated man and a member of a moderately good Poor family, he didn't believe in luck, but he'd been taught the basics of the operation of the Principle, which as far as he'd been able to make out was nothing more than luck in a fancy hat. So; the Principle wasn't running his way today, so perhaps it'd be a sensible idea to go back the other way, the one marked in red on his map and annotated as Alternative Route. Besides, the thought of trudging back through those dreary and now rather horrible villages was infinitely depressing. He fished in his rain-soaked satchel for the map, and found a clammy, sticky ball of rawhide, already starting to swell. As the men shuffled into their ranks he spread the map out on the tree-trunk and tried to make some sense of it.

As luck (or the Principle) would have it, the red ink was slightly more watertight than the black, and he was able to trace the line of Alternative Route with his fingertip. If he was where he thought he was (another assumption to add to the fragile bed), then the path lay above the main road they'd come along, under the brow of the mountain ridge, curling up and round through yet another poxy little village until it came back to the beachhead at the little cove. He nodded, dislodging drops of rainwater from the channel formed by the curled-over seam of his visor; they fell on the map and added a couple more red smudges. Just as well he didn't believe in omens, either.

His feet hurt, and his wet stockings were rubbing his heels into nagging blisters. The stitching of his left boot was just beginning to fray, and the impact of an arrow on the left cheek-piece of his helmet had creased the metal so that it grated just behind the ear, catching him every time he turned his head. The rain had raised the grain in the shaft of his halberd, and a splinter had lodged under one of his fingernails. Nothing about him felt comfortable or right. This wasn't the way it was meant to be. He gave the order to move on. For twenty minutes or so an old, crazy dog followed them, barking wildly, running

up and down the line and prancing away with its ears
back, as if cringing away from some anticipated attack;
but nobody had the energy or the enthusiasm to aim a
kick at it. Eventually it lost interest and lay down in a
pool of muddy water, its tongue lolling out and its tail
wagging furiously, giving the impression that it could see
something tremendously amusing.

The second village had looked much like the first, except
that there hadn't been any boats. Instead, the litter in the
main thoroughfare had been smashed-up wicker hurdles,
the wreckage of an old and decrepit dog-cart, a few sacks
of seedcorn ripped open, some storage jars smashed, a
few more bodies. They'd tried to break up a plough, but it
had proved too solid; there were a few blade-cuts in the
shafts and handles, and that was all. A wagonload of
sea-coal had been overturned, and the body of another
soldier lay a few yards away from it, helmetless and with
the mark of something like an axe or a mattock on the
crown of his skull.

At least it wasn't raining any more. Bardas Loredan
folded his hood back onto his shoulders and rolled his
wet sleeves up to the elbow. It made no sense to carry on
following the trail. He sat down on the boom of the
overturned wagon, reached in his pocket and found an
apple he'd picked up along the way.

No sign of the boy so far, at least, he hadn't been one
of the flotsam of corpses. Loredan frowned. He'd sent the
boy to raise the alarm so that people could get clear, but
people obviously hadn't. Well, if he wasn't among the
dead it was reasonable to assume he was still alive. He
took a few bites out of the apple, which was small and
sour, and then lobbed the rest over a wall.

There was something or someone moving about close
by. He stayed put and listened for a while, then hopped
off the boom, walked away a few paces, circled back
round behind the wagon, stooped quickly and grabbed.

'I was wondering where you'd got to,' he said. The boy

recognised him and stopped wriggling. 'Obviously it's my role in life to fish you out from under carts at the scenes of massacres.'

'I thought you were them,' the boy said, standing up. He was caked in mud. 'I tried to tell them but nobody'd listen.'

Bardas Loredan shook his head. 'Wonderful,' he said. 'Well, there doesn't seem to be any sign of them, but I don't think there's much to be gained by hanging around here. We can go home, or we can press on up into the hills, just to be on the safe side. What do you reckon?'

'Me?' The boy shrugged his shoulders. 'I don't know,' he said.

'You're a great help. All right, we'll head on home. Probably best to follow the road back to Briora and then take the short-cut from there, in case they double back in a hurry. Are you all right, by the way?'

'Fine,' the boy replied. 'I gave them the bows and arrows like you said—'

Loredan frowned. 'I shouldn't have done that,' he said. 'Bad idea. I expect the trouble only began when they started shooting.'

'More or less. I mean, they were smashing things up and hitting people, but once the villagers shot at them they went mad. They started killing people, and then some of the village men ran away and others tried to jump in and stop the soldiers; and they grabbed this little girl and threw her down the well in Briora, and then this woman tried to grab hold of the men who were doing it, and they cut her hands off, just like trimming a sapling. She just stood there then, and they went away and left her. It was as if they were more frightened of her than the other way about.'

'Get a move on,' Loredan said. 'Like I said, I don't want to stay on the road longer than we can help.'

'I expect the army will come soon,' the boy said, after they'd splashed half a mile down the road. 'And then there'll be a proper battle.'

Loredan shrugged. 'Maybe,' he said. 'More likely, if the army does get here in time, they'll try and surround them and make them surrender. And if they come by sea, they'll hole the barges so they can't get away.' He smiled. 'They made pretty sure of that themselves when they smashed up the boats in Briora.'

'If they surrender, what'll the army do to them? Will they hang them? That's what I'd do.'

Loredan shook his head. 'I doubt it,' he said. 'If you kill your prisoners, the enemy stop surrendering, and then you've got to fight it out to the last man every time, which is stupid. War isn't about killing people, it's about winning.'

The boy nodded. 'Did you kill many people when you were a soldier?' he asked.

'No, not many.'

'And did you win?'

'Not so as you'd notice.'

The boy thought about that. 'You won when you fought those men that night when the City fell,' he objected. 'I saw you.'

'True, but I was supposed to be defending the City, remember. You can't lose more conclusively than that.'

The boy thought some more. 'If you'd had more men and someone hadn't opened the gates, you'd have won,' he declared. 'So really it wasn't a fair contest.'

'Thank you,' Loredan said. 'That's taken a great weight off my mind.'

The rain started again as they rounded the bend into Briora. The boy didn't have a hood, so they stopped and found one that more or less fitted. 'That's stealing,' the boy pointed out, as he tied the string under his chin. 'Isn't it?'

'Looting, possibly,' Loredan replied. 'Though looting's more your gold and precious stones. When it's just useful things we used to call it requisitioning.'

'Oh. And that's all right, is it?'

'It is if nobody's watching. Look, if it bothers you, dump the wretched thing.'

'But then I'd get wet,' the boy objected.

They skirted round the village and picked up the track. The dead halberdier was still there; the rain had washed silt down off the mountainside, lightly covering his hair with grime, as if the mountain was in a hurry to bury him. The boy stepped over the body without saying anything.

It was harder going in this direction, of course, since the gradient was against them most of the time, and the extra few hours' rain had made the track slippery. After a mile they stopped and had a rest.

'Did they find the house?' the boy asked.

'Went straight past it,' Loredan replied. 'We were lucky.'

The boy nodded. 'If they'd tried to smash the house up, would you have fought them?' he said.

'No chance,' Bardas Loredan answered. 'Seventy-five of them and one of me.'

'Oh. Was that why you didn't go and try and help the village? You could have told them what to do.'

Loredan frowned. 'That'd have been a stupid thing to do,' he said. 'What they should have done is clear out until the soldiers had gone away. And besides, we aren't anything to do with these people, or this war. Only idiots get involved in other people's quarrels.'

The boy looked at him. 'You used to,' he said. 'When you were a lawyer back in the City. You used to fight people in the lawcourts.'

'That was different,' Loredan said. 'That was my job. And it wasn't seventy-five to one, either.'

'I see,' said the boy, doubtfully. 'So it's all right to get involved if you get paid and you're going to win.'

'I'd drop this subject if I were you,' Loredan said. 'In fact, if I were you I'd keep my face shut till we get home. That'd be the sensible thing to do.'

'All right,' the boy said. 'I didn't mean to be rude.'

'Let's get on,' Loredan said. 'No point sitting here in the wet when we could be back home.'

They struggled on up to the top of the rise, where the downs started to fall away from the rocky sides of Horn Point. Then Loredan told the boy to stay put while he went ahead and had a look around. He made his way carefully up to the edge of the briar-patch and pushed his way through, until he was looking down onto the beach.

There was a ship just inside the mouth of the cove. It looked like one of the military sloops, and it had crept in as far as it dared. There were two longboats on the water, both filled with men heading for the beach. The army had arrived.

Loredan stayed where he was and watched. The men in the boats were definitely Scona military; they had bow-cases and quivers, or shields and short, heavy pikes, not halberds, and their helmets were a different shape. One man, who was standing in the bow of the nearer of the two longboats, wasn't wearing a helmet, and the rain glistened on his bald head. Loredan's brows furrowed, and he crawled out of the briars and walked quickly back to where he'd left the boy.

'The army's here,' he said. 'They're landing men right now, and presumably they're going to follow on up the road and try and engage the enemy. Best thing we can do is head up the mountain and sit it out there till it's all over.'

'But shouldn't we go down and tell them what we've seen?' the boy queried. 'I mean, we know pretty well where they've been, it might help.'

'None of our business,' Loredan said firmly. 'We stay out of it and let them get on with it.'

'Because it's their job,' the boy said.

'Right. I say we carry on up the hill till we come to one of those old abandoned farms we passed when we were up there with the cart. Give it tonight and tomorrow morning; it should all be over by then.'

'All right,' the boy said. 'I'd have liked to have seen the battle, though.'

'That's because you're a sick little bugger,' Loredan said. 'Mind you, kids are like that at your age. Anyway, this time you're out of luck. Let's get moving before anything happens.'

The cart track up into the mountains broke away from the coast path about two miles beyond Horn Point and traced a series of zigzags up the face of the main escarpment, occasionally dodging behind one of the lesser formations. At first it was a steep climb, made even more disagreeable by the mud, but once they were on the slopes, the ground was harder and less muddy and the gradient was easier. There were several clumps of trees (no osage or yew, just stumps), and quite a few streams cut across the trail, all of them louder and more boisterous with the rainwater draining off the mountains. Low cloud was draped over the higher ground up above, but they weren't going up that far. They stopped at the foot of a farm tower that faced out to sea; unusually it still had most of its conical slate roof, although the rest of the farm buildings had been picked over for building stone a long time ago.

'This'll do,' Bardas announced. 'We can see right down the slope from up here, and we can cut some of this gorse to block the doorway with. From the track it'll just look overgrown.'

After an hour sitting in the middle of the floor with nothing to look at but the walls and the crumbling remains of the stairs, the boy was thoroughly bored. 'I'm cold,' he said. 'Can't we start a fire?'

'Don't be stupid,' Loredan replied.

'And I'm hungry,' the boy added. 'We could go out and lay wires for rabbits.'

Loredan frowned at him. 'We haven't got any wire,' he pointed out.

'What about the string off your bow? We could make wires out of that.'

Loredan wasn't amused. 'This bowstring,' he said icily, 'is made of twenty-four strands of the best-quality linen thread money can buy, woven into three plies, laid into a three-forked loop at both ends and served with three plies of silk. It took me four hours to make, not counting spinning the thread. Get lost, will you?'

'All right,' the boy said, 'why don't we take the bow and go and shoot something to eat?'

'Because we're supposed to be hiding,' Loredan replied irritably. 'Look, you're just going to have to stay hungry. It won't be for long.'

'I'm bored.'

'Of course you're bored. We're in a war. Four-fifths of any war is very, very boring. The other fifth makes you realise what a wonderful thing boredom is. And keep your voice down, will you? Just because we're in here doesn't make us inaudible.'

The boy thought for a while. 'Are you good at making string, then?'

'A bowyer's got to be. And we made all our own rope and twine on the farm when I was your age. You can make good string and cord out of almost anything that's got fibres in it.'

The boy nodded. 'If you can make string, you could pull some thread out of your coat and twist some string to make wires with.'

Loredan sighed. 'For the last time, we aren't going to set any wires. If the enemy see newly set wires all over the place, they'll know there's somebody about. We're staying here, and that's all there is to it. Got that?'

'All right.' The boy yawned. 'Will you teach me how to make string?'

'One of these days. Like I said, it's something you'll need to know how to do.'

'Why can't you teach me now?'

'Because.'

The roof of the abandoned tower was almost water-tight, but not quite. The dripping and gurgling of rain-water reminded Loredan of an apartment he'd had in a tenement block when he'd only just arrived in

Perimadeia. Like most of the 'islands', as the huge, spec-built blocks were called, it had belonged to one of the craft guilds, who used the income to provide for the needs of elderly and infirm members and their families. It had always struck him as odd, that organisations set up for such praiseworthy objectives should be the most notorious slum landlords in the City. But then, the whole business of owning property in the rabbit-warrens of Perimadeia was so complicated and arcane that nobody really understood it, and since legal disputes were settled by the swords of the fencers-at-law, nobody ever needed to. *There'd have been no trouble finding a tenant for this place, at twelve quarters a month*, he said to himself, looking up at the sky through the holes in the roof. *They'd have been queuing up.*

'Why did they build these towers?' the boy asked. 'I thought this place was an old farm.'

'It was,' Loredan replied. 'But they were difficult times back then. Gangs of soldiers roaming about the place were an everyday occurrence. So people lived out in the open instead of in villages, and every farm had a high wall round it, and a tower. Who knows, if things carry on the way they seem to be going, maybe it'll end up that way again.'

The boy considered the matter for a moment. 'Should we build one, then? Just in case, I mean.'

Loredan shook his head. 'If it starts getting bad, we'll be off out of it. I've got no intention of hanging about here on the edges of somebody's else's war.'

'Somebody else's?' The boy looked at him. 'I don't understand.'

Loredan didn't reply.

Thanks to the local knowledge of the messenger, Gorgas Loredan knew all about the top path. He decided to split his force into two. The larger part would press on up the main road, while he took forty men with him up the top path to try and overtake the raiding party and stop them getting any further. With luck he'd be able to hold them until the rest of his force came up behind them, and then they'd have them surrounded. That would make it much easier to contain them until the substantial reinforcements arrived overland from Scona Town.

He set the pace himself, clambering through the rocks and the mud at a rate he knew they wouldn't be able to keep up for long. With luck, they wouldn't have to; it all depended on how far the raiding party had got. According to the messenger, the top path was a substantial short-cut, forming the hypotenuse of a right-angle triangle whose other sides were formed by the road running due west to Briora, then a few miles north to Penna, the next village on, before angling sharply back to follow the slope down towards Scona Town.

When he blundered headlong into the enemy, coming down the path in the opposite direction, he was taken as much by surprise as they were. It didn't take him long to realise that he was in trouble, however; the enemy were right on top of them, far too close for comfort for a half-platoon of archers facing heavy infantry. It was also too late to fall back, and as the enemy lowered their halberds and charged, he didn't really know what to do. It was probably fortunate that his thinking time was reduced to a few seconds.

The halberdier officer gave the order to charge, but in the context of a narrow slippery path ground out of the side of a steep slope, it was meaningless. Instead, the halberdiers edged forward and a pantomime fight broke out, something like the mock combats at fairs where two men stand on a greasy plank and hit each other with sacks of feathers. There wasn't room for more than one man on the path at a time, and outflanking either above or below the path was out of the question because of the gradient. As the two parties pushed forward, Gorgas found himself squeezed up against his opponent, so that neither of them had any room to use their weapons; instead, the contest turned into a shoving-match, with the raiders' superior weight of numbers becoming a hindrance rather than a help because of the treacherous footing. After a very uncomfortable fifteen seconds, the halberdier slipped and fell forward, grabbing Gorgas to break his fall and pinning his arms to his sides. Gorgas did everything he could to stop himself going over, since the greatest danger was clearly getting trampled underfoot, but it was no use. At the last minute, though, he did manage to fall backwards onto the man behind him, who caught hold of him by the scruff of the neck as if he was a delinquent child in an apple-orchard, and kept him from going down, until the forward momentum of the men behind put him back on his feet again. He still couldn't get his arms free, however, and could do nothing except stare into the round, terrified eyes of the halberdier, only a few inches from his own. It was the closest he'd ever been to someone he was trying to harm in his life.

Then, quite suddenly, the shoving-match stopped, and Gorgas found himself falling forwards as the enemy stopped trying to force their way through and started to give ground. Unable to stop himself, he toppled over on top of the halberdier, who cracked his head against a rock as he went down and let go of Gorgas' arms. Gorgas tried to stand up, but the man behind him shoved him forward, and this time he landed with his knee in the halberdier's face; he heard a sharp crack as the man's nose broke. He had the presence of mind to grope for the dagger on his belt, but he couldn't reach it.

Somehow the halberdier managed to roll them both over, then scrambled to his feet, turned and ran. Gorgas tried to grab him, but all he managed to do was fall on his face in the mud, cutting his forehead on a stone. Somewhere behind him, he heard the sound of a bow being loosed, but the arrow went wide.

Someone caught hold of his arm and yanked him up; presumably whoever it was was trying to help, but he contrived to wrench a muscle in Gorgas' right shoulder, and he shouted with pain.

'Get off me, you clown,' he yelped. 'What the hell did you think you were doing?'

Since he knew the answer already he didn't wait for a reply; instead, he gave a rather superfluous order to stop the line, and looked to see what the enemy were doing.

They'd vanished out of sight past the bend in the track they'd just come round. *They're up to something,* Gorgas realised, *I just wish to hell I knew what it was.* He waved his men forward and they edged along the track until they came round the sharp corner and were able to see what the halberdiers were doing; they were following the bed of a stream up the hill, clambering as much as walking, heading for the top of the escarpment. It seemed a curious thing to do, and Gorgas didn't waste any time on trying to puzzle out their motivation any further. He gave the order to nock arrows and loose.

But it wasn't a good day for archery. The rain had saturated their bowstrings and soaked through into the wood of their bows, sapping the cast. The first volley fell short and, as the archers tried to compensate, the second volley mostly overshot. Two of the Shastel men went down, but both scrambled up again. There was the added complication of shooting up a steep slope, which threw out the archers' largely instinctive estimation of range. By the time they had drawn for the third volley, the halberdiers were among the large boulders halfway up the slope, a good hundred and twenty yards away, and the arrows from forty bows were spread fairly thin at such a range. Scowling, Gorgas led his men up the slope after them, but the Shastel men were moving so quickly that it was all he could do to keep pace with them; there was no time to form the line and loose another volley. *They aren't going anywhere,* Gorgas told himself, and slowed down the pursuit. The last thing he wanted to do was actually to catch up with them, and face sixty-five heavy infantry with forty bowmen hand to hand; that would be inviting the enemy to charge, with the gradient in their advantage. He sent back two men to try and find the relief parties and let them know what was going on. With luck, the main force from the city could be diverted round the other face of the escarpment, to come up on the enemy from the other side and complete the encirclement. It didn't look as if the Shastel men had any stomach for a fight. Quite probably they'd guessed that there weren't any boats waiting for them now. A reasonable show of force ought to be enough to prompt a surrender without any further significant bloodshed. Gorgas contented himself with keeping up with them, driving them steadily up the mountainside like a party of beaters flushing out game. *Wherever they end up, they've got no place to go,* he reminded himself. In fact, putting himself in the enemy commander's position, he couldn't think of anything that could be done, except to wait until there were enough of the enemy to justify an honourable surrender.

They'll have trashed the boats. That's the first thing they'll have done. And we're on an island.

At the head of his men (*when running away, always lead by example*), Renvaut dragged himself over the brow of the ridge only to find that it was no such thing; in front of him was a patch of dead ground, a dip leading up to a slightly more gradual slope that extended to the true brow, about a quarter of a mile further on. He signalled a halt; there was something in this dip that might solve his problems, at least in the short term.

Yet another poxy little village. This one, however, had much to recommend it. First, there was a seven-foot-high stone wall all round it, with two substantial-looking gates controlled by gatehouses. Second, there was no river or stream running through, which meant the water supply must come from a well-spring inside the village, something that couldn't easily be cut off or diverted. Third, it had the look of having been abandoned, thoroughly and in a hurry.

'Penna?' asked the sergeant.

'What?'

'On the map,' the sergeant said, 'there was a village called Penna.'

'Yes, but that was miles away. Over there somewhere.' Renvaut waved vaguely in the direction they'd come from. 'It could be Penna, I suppose. Or was that one of the ones we trashed? Anyway, doesn't matter. Take an advance party and look around.'

But the name Penna tugged at his memory, and he remembered; the priory of Penna, founded early in the Foundation's history, abandoned about seventy years ago and turned into a village; the hermit crab in the limpet shell. That would account for stone walls and gatehouses, and the handful of rather fine stone-built houses he could just see beyond the wall. Better and better. Defence had always been the first priority of the Foundation's architects. Quite by chance, they'd stumbled on a purpose-built fortress just when they needed one. *Luck*, he mused, *is having us and eating us.*

'Nobody home,' the sergeant reported a little later. 'And there's water, flour and bacon lying around, geese and chickens running about everywhere, even a couple of carp-ponds and a dovecote. So, what are we going to do?'

Good question. They could load up with supplies and try struggling on to the coast, or they could dig in and be besieged. The courageous, military thing to do would be to press on, make the most of their small lead and trust that the barges would still be there waiting for them. Holing up in a village on a hostile island might make them feel safer for a day or so, but in the long term it was suicide. Once inside, they'd never find a way of getting out again; their only hope would be a relief party from Shastel, and as a patriot and a staunch believer in the Foundation, Renvaut devoutly hoped they wouldn't try anything so stupid.

'So, what do we do?' the sergeant repeated. 'Whatever, we'd better hurry.'

Renvaut took a deep breath. One day, the whole of Shastel could end up looking like this, and the Foundation would be dead and gone.

'We're staying here and digging in,' Renvaut said.

CHAPTER SIX

'I seem to have this knack,' the young merchant muttered, 'of stumbling into other people's wars. It's a bad habit and I think I'll try and break it.'

His sister sat down on a coil of rope and opened her writing tablet. 'I wouldn't,' she said without looking up. 'Wars have always been good for business. Think of yourself as a pig with a talent for sniffing out truffles.'

'That's not really— Look out, he's coming back.' The merchant, whose name was Venart, straightened his back and tried to look bored as the soldier came stomping down the deck towards him. 'Finished?' he asked. 'Because we do have work to do, you know. This lot isn't going to unload itself, and—'

The soldier looked at him, and he subsided. 'All seems to be in order,' the soldier said grudgingly. He opened the small wooden box he was holding and produced a strip of clay, stamped with three columns of small writing and kept wet between two layers of damp cloth. From his satchel he took a signet ring on a length of flax string and pressed it into the clay; then he closed the box and handed it over. 'Here's your docking clearance and licence to trade,' he said. 'You should be prepared to offer it for examination whenever required to do so by an officer of the Bank, and you'll need to produce it when changing money or sealing any bill or document with a Scona resident. It must also be endorsed with an excise stamp indicating that all duty has been paid before you'll be permitted to leave Scona. Is that clear?'

Venart nodded wearily. 'Perfectly,' he said. 'Now can we please start unloading?'

'Go ahead,' the soldier replied. He called out an order to his three subordinates and led them down the gang-plank and off the ship.

'You realise,' said the merchant's sister, whose name was Vetriz, 'that if you'd been even half polite to that man, we'd have been spared all that poking about in sacks and opening of barrels. Honestly, why do you always insist on carrying on as if you were an Imperial envoy?'

'I wasn't,' Venart replied, stung. 'I just resent it when some lout in a uniform—'

'Of course you do,' Vetriz said soothingly. 'You don't see why some horrid little man should push you around when all you're doing is carrying on an honest trade. And that's why we spend so much time sitting at the dock having our cargo ransacked. You're a merchant, you're supposed to cringe and fawn and kiss their smelly boots. It's called business, or hadn't you heard?'

Venart sighed. 'I don't like this place,' he said. 'Never have. It's sort of—' He paused while he carefully sorted through the resources of his vocabulary. 'Sort of creepy,' he went on. 'There's a bad feeling about this island, I don't know what it is.'

'You don't? How extremely unperceptive you are. Come on, let's make a start, or it'll be dark before we're finished.'

Vetriz got up and walked away briskly, leaving her brother to trot after her. 'All right,' he said, 'if you're so clever, what *is* it about this place?'

'What do you expect in a country run by an ex-slave trader?' Vetriz said casually. 'Oh, don't say you didn't know. Everybody knows that.'

'I didn't.'

'Well, now you do. That's how the Director of the Bank made her money, back in Perimadeia. She ran a chain of brothels.' She stopped and smiled sweetly. 'You *do* know what a brothel is, don't you?'

'Don't be aggravating,' Venart said irritably. 'But isn't she supposed to be related to that man we met, the one who killed people for a living?'

'That's right,' Vetriz replied. 'Her name's Niessa Loredan. Anyway, she made her fortune buying women and children from the South Coast pirates and selling and hiring them in the City. At least, that's how she started. And now she runs Scona. Which probably has something to do with why it's not a particularly nice place.'

Venart thought for a moment. 'Well, she's done all right for herself, at any rate,' he said. 'You get the bill of lading sorted out while I go and see the warehouse people.'

Most of the cargo was made up of barrels of raisins and sacks of pepper and cloves, none of which were likely to be improved by being left standing out in the rain for any length of time. The warehouseman wasn't in his office, but Venart eventually ran him to ground in the harbourmaster's office, where he was playing knuckle-bones with three of the clerks. He didn't seem to be in any great hurry to leave the game, but eventually Venart was able to persuade him to open up the warehouse and take his money.

'And the porters' fees,' the warehouseman added.

'That's all right,' Venart replied. 'We do our own unloading.'

'Not on Scona you don't,' the warehouseman said with a grin. 'Not unless you want all your stuff pulled out of store and dumped in the sea.'

'But that's outrageous,' Venart protested. 'You can't do that.'

'Custom and practice,' the warehouseman said with a shrug. 'Nothing to do with me.'

'It isn't custom and practice,' Venart insisted. 'Or at least it wasn't three years ago, when I was here last.'

'It's a new custom,' the warehouseman said. 'I mean, customs have got to start somewhere. Sixty quarters, and you won't have any trouble.'

Venart looked him in the eye. 'How about if I take this up with the harbourmaster?' he said sternly.

'Can if you like,' the warehouseman replied in a bored voice. 'But he's a busy man, and by the time you get to see him, all your gear'll be being washed up on Shastel. The choice is yours.'

Venart paid him the sixty quarters and went back to the ship. There was no sign of any porters, but that didn't surprise him in the least. He told his men to start unloading.

'I've been through the list and everything's fine,' Vetriz said, sitting next to him on the sea wall. 'Oh, and by the way, don't let them sucker you into paying porters' fees. Apparently they try it on with newcomers, but it's all a scam.'

'Do I look like I was born yesterday?' her brother answered. 'I've told Marin and Olas to take first turn watching the cargo. Let's go and find somewhere out of this rain and get something to eat.'

'The Unicorn, just off the Strangers' Quay,' Vetriz said. 'It's not too expensive, for Scona, and if we're lucky we might get out again without having our throats cut.'

There was no point asking how she knew that; there were just some things that Vetriz knew, and that was that. Venart guessed that she asked people.

'We'll leave making a start till the morning,' he announced, dumping his kitbag in the corner of the room. 'I don't suppose anybody does any business around here in the evenings.'

'Actually, the time to do business is the evening promenade,' Vetriz corrected him. 'There's three or four taverns where the provisioners hang around, over on the other side of the Dock. We'll need to take samples along, and it's customary not to start talking business until after the second drink. Once we've told them what we've got, we leave it to them to have a sort of informal auction, and whatever we do, we don't name a price ourselves, because that's a sign of weakness. They make the offer, and we take it or leave it. They don't haggle much.'

'How the hell do you know? Never mind.' Venart shook his head. 'You'd better lead the way, then.'

'I don't know where to go,' Vetriz replied. 'I've never been here before in my life.'

The provisioners' pitches turned out not to be hard to find. The fifth tavern they looked in smelt overpoweringly of cardamom and cumin, and they saw ten or twelve men sitting on cushions on the floor passing round a pewter jug, while all about them were open bags and sacks of fine-grade produce. When the two Islanders joined them, they were greeted with cheerful curiosity, more cushions and more cups were called for, and a space appeared in the ring. Two boys hurried up with the cushions, the cups, another quart jug and two wide copper plates of raisins, dates and dried figs. To Venart's surprise, three of the men in the circle turned out to be women, dressed in the same heavy brocaded coats and trousers, embroidered slippers and big shapeless felt hats as the men.

After the barest minimum of small talk, the circle got down to business. Venart produced his samples, handed them to the man next to him to pass round, fixed a pleasant smile on his face and resolved to say nothing, while Vetriz (who was hungry) kept herself occupied with the plate of dried fruit. As predicted the merchants started haggling and arguing among themselves, for all the world as if the two strangers weren't there. It was only when one man opted out of the negotiations after a good deal of arm-waving and furious language that he leant forward with a warm, friendly smile on his face and said, 'Welcome to Scona.'

'It's a pleasure to be here,' Venart replied inaccurately. The provisioner acknowledged the formula with a slight bow from the neck. He was an elderly man with a round face, pale brown eyes and four hairless chins. 'I can see you're familiar with our way of doing business,' he said, 'so presumably this isn't your first trip here.'

'Not for me, no,' Venart said. 'But my sister, who's learning the business from me, hasn't been here before.'

The provisioner nodded two or three times. 'It can be a very offputting place when you're new here,' he said. 'But once you're used to it, and you know better than to be taken in by the dockers' scams and the excisemen's bluster, you find it's more or less the same as any market place anywhere. If people want to buy what you're selling, it's easy enough; if you're not carrying the right lines, you have to work harder.'

'And what about the war?' Venart asked. 'Is that making much difference?'

The provisioner grinned at him like a tired dog. 'War?' he said. 'What war? Oh, I know what you mean, but it's like an unspoken rule, you don't call it that. You say "the state of tension existing between the Foundation and ourselves", or "the intense rivalry between the Scona Bank and its local competitors".'

Vetriz frowned. 'Not meaning to be rude,' she said, 'but why not call it a war when it is one? It seems – well, a bit silly.'

Venart scowled ferociously at her, but both Vetriz and the provisioner ignored him. 'I'm afraid I don't know the answer to your eminently reasonable question,' the provisioner said. 'That's just what's been decided, and so we do it. To give you an example, our forces have just wiped out a larger enemy unit right in the heart of the Foundation's territory, which effectively gives us control of the area. Now what'll happen is that the accredited Scona representatives in Shastel will call at the offices of the Foundation and hand over a letter of credit – drawn on Scona, needless to say – for the value of the mortgages held by the Foundation in the territory we've just taken, and the Foundation will seal receipts on the mortgage deeds acknowledging that all sums due have been paid in full. Then as soon as they're able, they'll send a larger army to chase us off again, and if they succeed, their agents will call on us and give us a letter of credit (drawn on Shastel, needless to say) and we'll receipt our mortgage deeds back again, and so it'll go on. Neither side can actually cash the letters, obviously, but I know for a fact that we solemnly enter them in our accounts as fixed assets, and I wouldn't be at all surprised if they do the same.'

Vetriz bit her lip. 'I see,' she said. 'It still seems a funny way to do business.'

The provisioner shrugged his shoulders. 'It is; but, to use our favourite phrase, it's custom and practice. And it does make a sort of sense, in a way; we treat warfare as one of the many forms that commercial activity can take. And if you ask me, running commerce and warfare in parallel is no sillier than simultaneously waging war and playing diplomacy, which is what all governments do.'

The rest of the circle had stopped arguing and gone back to talking pleasantly among themselves – *except when they're negotiating* Venart noticed, *they're a very soft-spoken lot* – and a middle-aged woman on the opposite side of the ring got up, sat down next to Venart and started talking terms. Vetriz tried to follow the conversation for a while, but it wasn't particularly interesting stuff, and for all her determination to learn the business she still found it hard to get enthusiastic about warranties of actual state and condition. Instead she turned to the man they'd been talking to.

'I was wondering,' she said. 'Do you happen to know a man called Bardas Loredan? I think he's the Director's brother.'

The provisioner raised both eyebrows. 'Not personally,' he said. 'I know of him, naturally. If I may ask, why?'

'Oh, I met him once in Perimadeia,' she said, with

slightly exaggerated lack of concern. 'We did some business with him just before the City fell.'

'Really,' said the provisioner softly.

'Oh, yes. We bought a lot of rope from him.'

The provisioner nodded slowly. 'Well,' he said, 'Colonel
Loredan - that was his official rank, wasn't it? - he's
something of a mystery to us, if the truth be told. He
came here immediately after the City fell, but as far as
anybody knows he's having nothing to do with either the
Director or his brother—'

'His brother,' Vetriz repeated. 'Gorgas Loredan?'

'That's right. Our Chief Executive. Do I take it you
know him as well?'

'We've met,' Vetriz replied, looking past him rather
than at him. 'I gather he works for his sister.'

'Gorgas Loredan's a very important man here on
Scona,' the provisioner said, deadpan. 'If you know him
personally, that could be a great help to your business
dealings here. For one thing, he's in charge of all the
buying for the military.'

'Oh, I don't suppose he remembers me,' Vetriz said
quickly. 'Does anyone know why there's bad feeling
between Bar— between Colonel Loredan and his brother?'

The provisioner shook his head. 'Rumour and speculation,' he said, 'and no two stories agree. It's not all that
uncommon for brothers to fall out, you know.' He
paused, apparently thinking something over, and then
went on, 'If you knew the Colonel in Perimadeia during
the siege, did you ever come across a man called Alexius,
the Patriarch?'

Vetriz blinked several times and then nodded. 'I did, as
a matter of fact. He was a friend of Colonel Loredan's,
and we also did business with him. In fact, it was our ship
that brought him out when the City fell, and he stayed
with us for a while on the Island afterwards.'

'That's interesting. I only asked because he's here on
Scona too; he arrived not long ago, and I did hear
somewhere that he was anxious to find where Colonel

Loredan's living now. If you want to see the Colonel, he may well be the person to ask.'

'I see,' Vetriz said. 'Well, I don't suppose we'll have the time to go looking up old friends, because we're on quite a tight schedule. But if we do, I'll certainly bear that in mind. I don't suppose you have any idea where Patriarch Alexius is staying, do you?'

The provisioner smiled. 'As a matter of fact, I do. He's the guest of Gorgas Loredan. I can show you where he lives if you'd like.'

'Oh, I wouldn't want to put you to any trouble,' Vetriz said immediately.

'It wouldn't be any trouble,' the provisioner insisted, and if there was an edge of wickedness in his voice he concealed it very well. 'It's on my way home, in fact, and since it doesn't look like I'm going to do much business this evening, I might just as well walk so far with you.'

'Well, I really ought to wait for my brother, you see,' Vetriz replied with a slight tinge of desperation. 'And I really have no idea how long his business will take.'

'I'm in no great hurry,' the provisioner said. 'I don't mind waiting.'

Vetriz shifted a little on her pile of cushions. 'I expect you're just being polite,' she said. 'And really, I'd hate to hold you up.'

'No trouble, no trouble,' the man said firmly. 'While we're waiting, perhaps you'd indulge my curiosity just a little further. You see, I'm terribly interested in what actually happened in the last days of the City, and meeting someone who was actually there - if you don't mind my asking, that is.'

'Oh, no, not in the least,' Vetriz answered unenthusiastically. 'But really, we didn't see very much, and I wasn't actually there at the end, it was my brother—'

'Only,' the provisioner went on, 'the story is that the City fell because somebody actually opened the gates and let the plainsmen in. I find that extremely hard to believe, and I wondered if you knew anything.'

Vetriz shook her head. 'I expect I've just heard the same rumours as you,' she said. 'I mean yes, I've heard that story, but to me it just sounds like rationalising; you know, Perimadeia couldn't possibly have fallen to the plainsmen unless it was treason, and then that turns into speculation and the speculation becomes a rumour—'

'Quite so,' the provisioner agreed. 'That's how tales get about, as my father used to say. But I've heard this story from several quite different sources, and they all seem to agree on so many details that maybe there really is something to it after all.' He smiled, and appeared to relax slightly, like a hunter slowly easing his bow when he's decided that the animal he's just drawn on is actually too small to be worth shooting. 'So what was it *really* like?' he went on. 'I used to visit the City quite regularly at one time, but that must be, oh, ten years ago now, so the truth is, I really have no idea what it was like towards the end. Is it true, do you know, that Chief Temrai actually built scores and scores of siege engines from scratch, just from what he remembered seeing in the Arsenal? If so, I'd say we've all been underestimating the plainsmen for far too long. The potential for trade . . .'

As Vetriz listened and tried her best to reply intelligently to the provisioner's questions, she had the distinct feeling that she'd been deliberately let off the hook; no, it wasn't even that, more a case of having been saved till later, like the best of a batch of honey-cakes. Whatever the reason, he didn't insist on walking with them once Venart had struck his deal, and they were able to escape.

'This isn't bad at all, you know,' Venart said as soon as they were back out in the open air. 'I've got rid of all the raisins at twenty-five per cent profit, and she's going to take half the cloves at thirty per cent. They don't seem particularly keen on pepper, though; she offered me fifteen quarters a quart, so I turned her down on that. I've got this feeling we can get it up to seventeen if we stick at it; I mean, they must use mountains of the stuff, and I can't really believe they're getting it cheaper from the Colleon boats.'

Vetriz made some sort of show of listening to her brother's blow-by-blow account, but her mind was preoccupied with other things. The thought that Alexius was here, on Scona, was somehow vaguely alarming, as well as extremely mystifying. If she'd been told he was on Shastel, that would at least have made better sense, because Shastel was heavily into all the mystic stuff and magic that Alexius knew about; they weren't the same denomination as the City magicians had been, but they talked a lot about this peculiar thing called the Principle, so they might well be expected to invite one of the greatest living authorities on the subject to come and join them. But for him to go and join their enemy—

Unless that was it, and what was being planned was some kind of wizards' war, with Alexius and the Shastel scholars trading fiery spells with each other across the Scona Straits. That would make just a little sense, if it wasn't for the fact that Alexius couldn't do anything remotely resembling magic (and nor could anybody else, for that matter) and even if he could, he wouldn't offer himself for hire like a cotton-picker at the start of the season. She was so preoccupied that she forgot to keep saying, 'That's nice,' at regular intervals, and Venart stopped talking and looked at her.

'What's the matter?' he asked. 'You look like you're miles away.'

'What? Oh, it doesn't matter. Go on with what you were saying.'

'I will if you can tell me what I was talking about. Is it something that merchant told you?'

Vetriz nodded. 'He was asking me if I knew Patriarch Alexius. Apparently he's here. On Scona.'

Venart raised an eyebrow. 'Well, everybody's got to be somewhere. Maybe he got offered a job. Don't look at me like that. For all practical purposes he's just another City refugee, he's got to earn a living the same as everyone else.'

Vetriz gave him one of her patient looks. 'I don't think it works like that in his line of business,' she said. 'I mean, I haven't heard of any annual hiring fairs for abstract philosophers, have you? I think . . .'

'Well?'

'I don't know,' Vetriz confessed. 'I just have this feeling, that's all. You'd probably best ignore me.'

Venart sighed. 'The last time you had a feeling,' he said, 'I had to pull him out of the fall of Perimadeia. This time, can whatever it is you've got a feeling about please be something a little less strenuous and exciting? Maybe even something where we can turn a few quarters? You want to try and get rid of this idea that we're princes and princesses out of a kids' story.'

'Huh.' Vetriz pushed her hair back behind her ears. 'If it wasn't for me you'd lead ever such a boring life. You should be grateful.'

'I'm sure I know you from somewhere,' the man said for the third time, raising his voice so as to be heard above the background noise in the inn. At the other end of the room, ten or so soldiers were having a heated discussion about something technical, to do with fletchings for arrows. 'you're Perimadeian, aren't you?'

Alexius nodded slowly. 'Actually, I was born in Macyra, but I lived most of my life in the City.' He smiled, as if at some private joke.

'I've got it,' the man said, pouring himself another mug of cider. 'You see, I studied in Shastel, years ago, of course, before the Bank was ever founded, when I was a student, and I was sent to the City as one of Doctor Raudel's pages. There, I thought you'd recognise the name.'

Temper, Alexius commanded himself. *Bear in mind, this nuisance is much less of a nuisance than some of the nuisances you've managed to be perfectly civil to in the past. And he did buy you a meal.*

'Oh, I remember Doctor Raudel Bovert; I met him a

number of times.' Alexius turned his head slightly and stared up at the smoke-grimed rafters. 'Rather pompous, very opinionated, like so many of the scholars of the Foundation. He had a few very brilliant insights which he'd completely failed to understand, but his manner was so offputting that nobody in the Academy could be bothered with them. A typical Foundation scholar, in fact.'

The man wasn't quite sure what to make of that. 'Anyway,' he said, 'now I know who you are. You're one of the Perimadeian Foundation, something quite high up.'

'The Patriarch, actually,' Alexius replied casually. 'Last of the line, of course, there won't be any more of us after I'm gone.' He made the effort to frown. 'No great loss, really,' he added, to himself as much as to the man. 'When I think of all the talent and resources we had at our disposal, and then of what we actually achieved— But that's probably just as well. It'd be rather distressing to die knowing that something valuable was dying with me.'

'Oh, I don't know,' the man said. He was still rather vexed at hearing Raudel dismissed so trivially, but obviously the thought of having an opportunity to talk to the greatest living authority on the Principle was worth the aggravation. Alexius could visualise the expression on the man's face as he bored all his friends with the story that evening. 'Anyway,' he said, 'first things first, how about another drink?' He turned his head and called out, 'You there! Wake up, there's people dying of thirst.'

The last thing Alexius wanted was another drink; his head was already foggy from the two mugs of strong cider the man had practically forced down him already. But it would have been easier to stand off the whole of Temrai's army single-handed than resist such grimly determined hospitality. Fortunately, after half a mug, he fell asleep—

—And then he was sitting on a bed in a room in an

inn, quite like this one but slightly less depressingly sparse; and there on the other bed, lying on his back with his boots off, was Venart, the young Islander he'd known back in the City and afterwards. He was asleep, snoring softly, and on the floor where it had fallen from his hands was a fat ledger. *Small world*, Alexius thought, and then the door opened and Vetriz came in, cautiously, furtively even, holding a bundle of sailcloth. She closed the door quietly, walked over to the small table and unwrapped her bundle, which turned out to contain a roll of expensive-looking fabric. Vetriz made sure her brother was still asleep, then spread the roll out and held it up against herself, craning her neck to peer down and see what it looked like. *So she's bought some cloth that probably cost more than she's allowed to spend, and she doesn't want her brother to know*, he thought. *For a final revelatory vision granted to an eminent sage on his death-bed, it's a bit prosaic. I thought these things were meant to show you the crucial cusps of the future, the point of balance where momentous trends can go one way or the other. I had no idea the future of women's fashions was so important.*

After striking various poses and leaning over backwards to look at them, Vetriz rolled up the cloth and put it away under the bed, just behind Alexius' feet; she was so close that he could see the individual hairs on her head, and the tiny white line of scalp where she'd parted it to form her rather appealing fringe. In fact, the quality of the vision was markedly better than any he'd had before in terms of clarity and realism, and he suddenly realised that he was indeed actually there—

This is ridiculous. Of course I'm not there, although it'd be wonderful if I was. But I'm here, stuck in a horrible inn with a boring man, dying. This is starting to annoy me.

Then the door opened again, and a man came in; slowly, painfully, leaning on a stick. *But that's me, and that's ridiculous, because I'm already here.* He opened his mouth to protest, but no sound came out, and the other

Alexius hobbled over to the bed and sat down beside himself, while Vetriz closed the door and woke up her brother with a brutal shove.

'Wake up,' she said, 'look who's here. Patriarch Alexius, this is—'

'Please,' the other Alexius interrupted, 'I want you to help me. There's no earthly reason why you should, and it might well get you into serious trouble, but can you please get me off this island on your ship? You see—'

—And he opened his eyes, blinked twice at the round face of the hospitable pest, who was asking him if he was feeling all right, and tried to reply; but he was feeling drowsy again, so he closed his eyes, then opened them again—

—There was someone sitting on the bed; a stranger, a young girl. She was wearing a coarse dark-brown woollen robe, and her hair was tied back in a tight knot at the nape of her neck. She looked about eighteen, pretty in a slightly awkward sort of way.

'Hello,' she said, 'my name's Machaera. Can you see me?'

Alexius nodded. 'Are you here?' he asked softly. The girl frowned.

'I'm not sure,' she said. 'It feels exactly as if I am, but I know for a fact I'm in my cell at the lodgings doing a projection. Who are you?'

'My name's Alexius. When you say you're doing a projection, do you mean you're somehow using some latent mental ability to harness the Principle and use it to show you this vision? Come to that, can you understand what I'm talking about or is it a complete mystery to you?'

'Oh, I know about the Principle,' the girl replied. 'And so do you, obviously. You don't look at all well, by the way.'

'You're too kind. Now then, by the way you're taking it all in your stride, I'd say this isn't the first time you've done one of these, what did you call them, projections. Am I right?'

'Yes indeed. I've done heaps of them now.' *Oh, for pity's sake, another natural. What harm have I ever done anybody to deserve this?* 'But this is the first time I've ever been able to talk to anybody. Usually I just stand there and listen.'

Alexius made an effort and gathered up the few scraps of strength he had left. 'There could be several reasons for that,' he said. 'We may be sharing a vision - it's happened to me a few times, though never like this. I may be able to talk to you because of my experience with, ah, projections. There's also the possibility that I'm hallucinating because of this fever I've got, and you aren't really there at all.'

'Oh, I'm here all right,' the girl said, and she reached out to touch Alexius' hand. Somehow she couldn't quite reach, even when she shifted up very close. 'Oh. Well, I think I'm here and so do you. Isn't that proof?'

Alexius shook his head. 'Not really,' he said, and he realised that he was using the voice he'd always used when taking a tutorial. 'You see, I could be hallucinating you, or you could be hallucinating me. It'd be quite possible for me to imagine you saying you could see me.'

The girl looked disappointed. 'So you think I'm not really here at all?' she said. 'Really, I honestly think I am. But you can't take my word for that, can you?'

'I believe you,' Alexius said. 'And I can only assume you're here because this is some sort of cusp in the curve of history which—'

'Sorry. Do go on.'

'No, you were about to say something. I want to know what it was.'

The girl hesitated. 'Well, it was just when you called it a cusp. That's the word my tutor uses, Doctor Gannadius. He says—'

'*Gannadius!*'

'My tutor,' the girl repeated. 'Why, have you heard of him?'

'Gannadius,' Alexius repeated. 'Shortish round-faced

man with very pale blue eyes, just the right side of sixty, dark brown hair starting to get thin on top? He used to be Archimandrite of the City Academy of Perimadeia.'

'That's right,' said the girl. 'You do know him, don't you?'

'And he's your tutor. Where?' He felt something fall into place in his mind. 'On Shastel,' he said. 'You're a member of the Foundation, and Gannadius is working there. I'm right, aren't I?'

The girl dipped her head. 'He's the senior tutor in Applied Metaphysics,' she said. 'He taught me how to do this - well, how to do it properly, at any rate. Are you from Perimadeia too?'

Alexius smiled. 'Why does everybody keep asking me that? Yes. Listen to me; will you go at once and find Gannadius and tell him what you've seen? Please? It might be quite important.'

'Of course,' the girl said. 'Excuse me, but are you the Alexius who used to be the Patriarch? Doctor Gannadius talks about you all the time. He said you were the most brilliant—'

'He's wrong. Very gullible man. Now, please, will you do what I asked you?'

'I'll do my very best, I promise,' the girl said. 'And really, you shouldn't say such things about Doctor Gannadius. He's very highly respected in the Foundation.'

'Really? Extraordinary. Well. Look, I'm sorry if this sounds rude but I'd be really grateful if you could go and see Doctor Gannadius now. It's been very ... interesting talking to you like this, but I would just like to—'

—Someone was leaning over him, that damned hospitable fool with his earthenware jug of cider and his big fat face. 'Time for another one before you go?' he said cheerfully. 'Now then, say when.'

Alexius looked back at the girl. 'Please,' he said. She nodded. The hospitable nuisance looked straight through her, then at Alexius, and shook his head. 'I'm not hallucinating,' Alexius said. 'She wasn't actually here, you see, and ...'

'Of course you're not,' said the man, putting the jug down. 'You were just talking in your sleep, that's all. But maybe another one wouldn't be such a good idea after all.' He stood up, just a little too quickly to be convincing. 'Well, it's been a real treat talking to you, but time's getting on, so I'd best be on my way. Goodbye, Patriarch.'

Alexius sat quite still for a few minutes, making sure that the hospitable nuisance had actually gone, and hoping (rather optimistically) that his headache would go away. When it didn't he hauled himself to his feet and was nearly out through the door when the innkeeper called him back and told him that his friend, the one who left in such a hurry, had forgotten to pay for the drinks.

'What can you see?' the boy called out.

'There's people moving about,' Bardas Loredan replied, 'but I can't make out whether it's them or us.' He shifted carefully and put more weight on his elbows, painfully aware that his perch up among the rafters by the hole in the roof was unstable at best; if the roof-ties realised he was there, they'd be well within their rights to collapse under his weight and let him drop to the ground. 'They seem to be heading for that other ruin down in the dip there, but it's too far for me to be able to see clearly in this rain.'

'Why don't I creep out and see if I can get close enough to take a proper look?'

'Be quiet,' Loredan replied.

The boy muttered something, and went back to whittling a bit of stick. Loredan shifted a little more, trying to get out from under the persistent drip that was landing square on the back of his neck. His left hand had gone to sleep.

'If it's us,' the boy said, 'we should go down and tell them what we've seen. And if it's them, they'll be too busy to bother with us. We might even be able to gather useful intelligence.'

'I don't think you could spare any, even if you managed to get hold of some. Now shut up and let me concentrate.'

The boy abandoned his bit of stick, which he'd reduced to a thin shaving, and started sharpening the arrowheads on a piece of broken whetstone he'd found in his pocket. The slow scraping of steel on stone is, of course, one of the most irritating noises in the world.

'Pack that in,' Loredan snapped. 'They're perfectly sharp as it is, you'll only take the edge off.'

'I'm bored.'

'Then consider yourself extremely lucky. Now for gods' sakes keep still and quiet, before I lose my temper.'

'I still think—'

'*Quiet!*' Loredan peered down, trying to see past the rafter end that was blocking his view. He'd caught just a glimpse of two men coming round the side of the slope towards the base of the tower. 'Get over there in the shadows,' he called out softly, 'and keep absolutely still. I'm coming down, if I can get out of this—'

He wriggled, bumped his head and dropped and slithered back to the footholds he'd found in the wall, taking skin off the palms of his hands in the process. He landed awkwardly on the ground and shuffled across to where the boy was crouching, picking up his sword on the way. He had pins and needles badly in his left leg; not what you want if you're likely to have to fight at any moment. 'Where's the bow?' he whispered.

'I thought you'd got it.'

'Oh, for— Well, we'll just have to make do. Now shut up and stay still, and pray they'll go away.'

There was a shuffling and a squelching in the doorway, and something obscured the light that shone weakly through it. 'Hello?' someone called out. 'Is there anybody there? Colonel Loredan?'

Bardas Loredan held his breath; but the boy stood up

and called out, 'Over here! It's all right,' he added, 'they're us, it's archers. We're over here,' he repeated, as the two strangers peered round, their eyes not yet accustomed to the darkness. 'By the back wall.'

Wearily Loredan tried to stand up, but his leg refused to co-operate. 'Are you hurt?' said one of the strangers, seeing him wobble and sink back. 'There's a surgeon coming with the relief force, he won't be long.'

'It's all right,' Loredan replied, 'just a touch of cramp. You were looking for me.'

The two men came closer. One of them stopped by the window and pulled open the shutter. 'Chief Executive Loredan's orders,' the other one said. 'We've been searching for you for hours.'

'Well, now you've found me,' Loredan replied. 'What's going on?'

'We've got the raiding party pinned down,' the soldier said; he was a sergeant, quite a senior man by the look of him. 'Over the hill a way, at Penna, you know it? They aren't going anywhere in a hurry. Are you fit to move?'

Loredan shook his head. 'We're fine,' he said, 'don't you worry about us. You get back and rejoin your men, we can take care of ourselves.'

The sergeant shook his head. 'Chief Executive Loredan's orders,' he repeated. 'He wants to be sure you're all right.'

'Well, you can set his mind at rest. Thank you for your trouble, but we're going home now. We'll be fine.'

The sergeant took a deep breath, and Loredan felt sorry for the man, a good soldier trying to deal tactfully with difficult civilians. 'If you'll please just come with us,' he said. 'Chief Executive Loredan's orders.'

Loredan closed his eyes for a moment. It was a ludicrous situation; they'd come to rescue him and here he was refusing to be rescued, and he got the distinct impression that they weren't going to take no for an answer. He had no wish to see his brother; the question was whether it was worth fighting two men over. He thought about that for a moment.

'I'm very sorry,' he said, 'but I can't come with you right now.'

The boy was looking at him as if he'd gone mad. Loredan took a step forward, so as to be between the soldiers and the boy. He realised that he had the broadsword, still in its case, in his hands, and that that might be taken as an aggressive gesture.

'I'm sorry,' the sergeant said. 'But you've got to come with us.'

'Oh, all right, then,' Loredan said. He carefully put the sword down, swung fast and drove his fist into the sergeant's face; then he stepped over him, kicked the other soldier in the groin and punched him hard on the jaw as his head came down. He felt the skin on his knuckles tear against the sharp edge of the man's helmet.

'What the hell are you doing?' the boy asked.

'Don't swear,' Loredan replied. 'Come on, let's go home.'

CHAPTER SEVEN

The Scona chargé d'affaires was called to the offices of the Foundation and asked politely what the Bank thought it was playing at. The chargé d'affaires replied that as far as he knew (and all he'd heard was the official Shastel version), his people were simply defending themselves against an act of unprovoked aggression, just as the Bank's team of advisers had done here on Shastel when the Foundation's armed forces had attacked them for no readily apparent reason when doing whatever it was they were doing in that village. In fact, he went on, he was prepared to say that the Bank took a grave view of recent developments. The Shastel spokesmen replied that the Foundation also took a very grave view of the whole situation and deplored the recent violence and loss of life. The chargé d'affaires replied that the Bank always deplored violence and loss of life, whatever the circumstances.

Having reached agreement on the fundamentals, the two sides became more specific. The Bank, said the chargé d'affaires, was a purely commercial organisation and had no military or political agenda whatsoever; all it wanted was to be able to go about its business, which was primarily the lending of money on the security of agricultural property, without fear of violence being offered to its staff or customers. The spokesmen for the Foundation replied that they too represented an organisation that, although not wholly commercial in its

outlook, had substantial financial interests to protect and
mortgagors who looked to it to safeguard them against
such unsupportable burdens as raiders, brigands, pirates
and other lawless elements; that was why the Foundation felt it necessary to maintain security forces on a
permanent basis. That, surely, was something that the
Bank ought to be able to understand better than
anybody.

The chargé d'affaires thought for a moment and said
that although, clearly, there were some issues on which
they would find it hard to reach consensus in the short
term, surely they were both agreed that armed conflict
was in the interests of neither party, and the first priority
ought to be an immediate halt to hostile activity on both
sides, followed by a period of restructuring and general
negotiation which might in time lead to a more fundamental settlement between the two sides.

'In other words,' the spokesman reported back to his
superior, 'they're planning to make us pay through the
nose for the hostages and they're going to take their own
sweet time about it. It's a disaster.'

'The hell with that,' the superior agreed. He was one
of the five deputy wardens of the Poor, a member of the
Soef family and the holder of two doctorates, in
Linguistics and Applied Mathematics, and the thought of
being held to ransom by a Perimadeian whoremonger
wasn't something he was very comfortable with. But he
was also an intelligent man, and one of the hostages was
a Bovert. 'We've got to get the hostages back,' he said,
'and we've also got to get out of this without sending a
message to the hectemores that we've lost our grip and
given up. I'm going to have to take this to Chapter and
see what they want to do, while we've still got a few
options.'

Just before this meeting, he'd been talking to Doctor
Gannadius, another of these Perimadeians who seemed
to be getting into everything these days, but for once the
Doctor had had something interesting to say. Of course,

he'd be a complete fool to base policy decisions on the word of a foreign mystic; on the other hand, he was enough of a scientist and a philosopher himself to be able to keep an open mind when it came to things he didn't understand. The obvious priority here was to keep a sense of balance and neither rush into anything nor dismiss anything out of hand. As for the hostages, well, he hoped they were somewhere warm and dry in this foul weather, because whichever option was eventually chosen, it was likely to take some time.

'It'd depress me to think I was going to be stuck here for the rest of my life,' muttered the young soldier, peering up at the drops of water falling from the leak in the roof, 'if it wasn't for the moderate certainty that the rest of my life won't take very long.' He shuddered and threw another piece of wood on the fire. 'Looked at from that angle, a man could get to like it here.'

Master Renvaut nodded. 'Well, by my calculations I'm dead already,' he said. 'Or at least, I ought to be. But the medicine that butcher of an orderly gave me was so foul, I think it made me too ill to die.'

The young soldier nodded. 'Blue bread mould in garlic juice,' he said. 'It certainly adds a new dimension of horror to serious illness. I mean, nobody's saying death is a barrel of fun, but it's got to taste nicer than *that.*' He grinned. 'I take it you're feeling better,' he said.

Renvaut nodded. 'I think I sweated out the fever in my sleep. I still feel a bit shaky and not the least bit hungry; which is fortunate, from what I can gather.'

'That's true,' the young soldier agreed gloomily. 'We've got enough for a week, maybe two if we really torture ourselves, and that's about it. At least drinking water isn't a problem,' he added, as a raindrop fell in his eye.

'Marvellous,' Renvaut sighed. He rolled over on his back and stared at the black patches in the thatch where the water was seeping through. 'Your first mission, is it?'

The young soldier laughed. 'I'm afraid so,' he said. 'I'm in the third year of my degree course, and like a fool I chose to do my six months in the ranks early, so as to get the feel of what soldiering's really all about.'

'You got lucky,' Renvaut grunted. 'This is pure concentrated essence of soldiering, as far as I'm concerned. Now, when I was your age, I pulled every string I possibly could and got assigned to the secretariat.'

The young soldier grinned. 'Actually,' he said, 'I reckon it's a good rule. After all, if you're going to command men in combat, it helps to know what makes them tick.'

'Absolutely,' Renvaut said. 'And what is it you're studying?'

'Oh, mostly the usual, Ethical and Economic Theory, with a bit of Literature and Metaphysics thrown in. After that I'm going to specialise, but I haven't quite made up my mind yet. I'll probably go for Ethics because that's what I'm good at, but secretly I'd rather have a go at the Philosophy of Commerce course. After all, that must be the key to understanding what the Foundation's all about.'

'Well, yes,' Renvaut said, straight-faced. 'Mind you, it's a big subject.'

'Well, of course,' the young soldier replied. 'But since all the leading texts are written in the Shastel dialect, it'll save me three months learning Old Perimadeian and Southern and Bathue; I was always useless at languages. About the only subjects you can take where there isn't a whole lot of language work are Phil. Comm. and Military Theory, and,' he added with a wry smile, 'I reckon if I get out of this alive, I'll have had all the Military Theory I can take.'

'Mil. Theory graduates usually go straight into teaching,' Renvaut said with a yawn. 'Which explains a lot, don't you think?'

The young soldier shook his head 'Our society is run on unique and original lines,' he said. 'Arguably, it should tend to produce the ideal: the altruist, the scholar, the soldier and the practical man of business all rolled into one. I'd feel rather more sanguine about the concept if we weren't in this shed surrounded by the enemy.'

Renvaut shrugged. 'You only really start to get problems when you can't control all the human elements in the equation. It's pointless trying to apply scientific method to something as completely random and perverse as human nature, particularly human nature *en masse.*'

'People are a nuisance, you mean?' the young soldier suggested.

'That puts it rather well,' Renvaut agreed. He yawned, stretched until he felt something twang painfully in his back, and stood up. He'd lost the best part of a day because of the fever, and there was a great deal to do and nobody else really competent to do it. A professional soldier, he reflected, is someone who's not quite good enough at a range of administrative and managerial skills to earn a living at them (or else that'd be what he was doing for a living) and ends up exercising those skills for lives rather than money.

'Any sign?' he asked the sergeant in charge of the sentries, who shook his head. 'They've been prowling around on the top of the ridge,' the sergeant went on, 'but just scouts, nothing serious. My guess is, they're waiting for something.'

'Reinforcements.'

'Or siege gear,' the sergeant replied. 'Catapults and rams and stuff like that. Only they'd have a job getting anything too heavy up into these mountains; they'd have to take 'em to bits and put 'em back together again when they got here. Too much like work.'

Renvaut pulled a face. 'Reinforcements are more likely,' he said. 'It all depends on what they're planning. Myself, I don't see them trying an assault. After all, why bother? If they bring up enough men to invest this place properly, they can starve us out in a week or so and never risk a man. Plus,' he added with a wry grin, 'we're worth more to them alive – as hostages, or plain and simple commodities for sale.'

The sergeant shrugged his shoulders. 'Sounds good to me,' he said.

'Me too.' Renvaut peered through the crack between the window frame and the hastily improvised and purportedly arrow-proof shutter at the steady and relentless rain outside. 'Unfortunately, one thing they don't teach you in any of the classes I took is how long you've got to hold a besieged position before it's polite to surrender and you don't have to worry about being court-martialled and killed by your own side. I think it's safe to assume that once the food runs out, it's all right. I mean, that'd be logical, wouldn't it?'

The sergeant wasn't prepared to venture an opinion on that, and Renvaut left him to his duties and got on with his own list of things to do. *Civilised commercial warfare*, he reflected; *buying and selling, trading and negotiating; it's just a pity we have to be stuck in this dump for a fortnight while they sort it all out. But it should be all right*, he insisted, *provided everybody keeps calm and nobody does anything stupid, like send another expedition to rescue us. And even we're not idiotic enough for that.*

There was nothing to eat apart from slightly stale rye bread and the last of the red cheese, which neither of them liked particularly much. The boy started to say, 'Looks like I'll have to go down to the village tomorrow and buy—' He fell silent, and Loredan said nothing, went on chewing the disgusting food.

'Do you think there'll be any trouble?' the boy asked after a long time. 'About hitting those two soldiers, I mean?'

'Doubt it,' Loredan replied with his mouth full. 'If you think about it, I don't suppose my brother'd go to all the trouble of sending men to rescue me on the one hand, and then have me slung in jail for assault on the other.' He paused, and frowned. 'Although that doesn't actually follow,' he said thoughtfully. 'In fact, that's just the sort of thing he would do. Then, after he'd left me to stew in the prison for six months, he'd petition the judge for a free pardon and make a great show of pulling strings and using his influence to get me out again. And then he'd expect me to be grateful. He's a strange man, my brother. I don't like him much.'

The boy took a moment to consider. 'Why not?' he said. 'Or is that a rude question?'

'Because,' Loredan replied. 'And yes. If you don't want that last bit of cheese, give it here.'

'You're welcome. I had a brother, back in the City. Did I ever tell you that?'

'No, you didn't.'

The boy looked down at the wooden bowl in front of him, lifted up one side, put it down again. 'Sometimes,' he said, 'I have this fantasy that he'll just turn up one day; you know, walk in through the door without saying anything, just to surprise me. Oh, I'm sure he's almost certainly dead, but I don't actually *know* that. Like, I know my mother and father are dead, because I saw them getting killed, but my brother got left behind when we were running down the street, so it's just possible—' The boy picked up the crust of his bread and dropped it in the bowl. 'I mean, it's something to dream about; you know, suddenly finding him again, years later, when I'd been sure all that time he was dead.' He stood up and collected the bowls and the breadboard. 'Is he your only brother?' he went on.

Loredan shook his head. 'I've got two other brothers still living, or at least as far as I know they are, back in the Mesoge where I was born. Haven't seen them in - oh, I can't remember how long. Anyway, to the best of my knowledge there they still are, still scratching a living out of the same patch of dirt we all scrabbled about in when I was a kid.'

'You don't like them either, then?'

'I don't dislike them,' Loredan replied. 'In a way, I

suppose I care about them. But they're all right, they've got the farm. I guess you could say they're having the life I should have had.'

'Is it the life you'd have wanted?'

Loredan frowned. 'I'm not sure,' he said. 'Let's put it this way. If I'd carried on and never left the farm, never left the Mesoge, I wouldn't have been able to imagine any other kind of life; so I suppose I'd have been happy, or satisfied, whatever. The thought of anything different probably wouldn't ever have occurred to me. That's the thing about farming, you're completely taken up with the job in hand, you never have time to think beyond the next stage in the working year. Some people would say it means your mind gets cramped up and atrophied, but I'm not so sure about that. For a farmer, the only thing that matters is working the farm; nothing else really interests him, because it isn't really anything to do with him. People make fun of us because all we ever talk about is how bad the weather is, too much rain or too much sun, it's too wet to turn the cows out and too dry for the sheep to find enough to eat – well, fair enough, I suppose. But the pay-off is, if you do your work and then a bit more, and the weather's not too horrible and the rooks don't go down on the flat patches in the wheat, then basically it'll all be all right and you can look forward to going through it all again next year, and the year after that. It's the feeling that if you keep your side of the bargain, then, cosmic bastardry permitting, you'll get a fair return and the system will work, you can rely on it working.' Loredan shook his head. 'Dear gods, if I could have had a life like that, I don't think I'd have very much to complain about.'

The boy, who hadn't really followed much of all that, rubbed his jaw thoughtfully. 'So why don't you go back to it?' he said. 'Why don't you buy some land and be a farmer, if you think it's so wonderful?'

Loredan smiled. 'I don't know,' he admitted. 'Maybe it's because I know it isn't really like that, so I'd never be able to rely on the system working. I know too much about it all, you see; I know that one day you can be leaning on your scythe, touching up the edge with a stone, and a dozen horsemen will suddenly appear, riding towards you through the corn with spears levelled. I know that five bad years will send you begging at someone's door, and they'll say yes, take all the seedcorn you need, but first put your mark on this paper. I know that one day the recruiting sergeant will come and take your sons, and the bailiff will come and take your surplus for arrears of tithes, and the tax-collector will come and take what's left for the Great King's wars, and then the ploughshare snaps and the smith wants paying, and your daughter gets ill and the doctor has to be called, and one thing and another; and you walk past the cooper's shop and see him sitting in the shade tapping away with a small hammer and you think, half your luck, you smug bastard, I wish to gods I'd been a tradesman's son, just exactly the same way he wishes he'd been born to the land, and the Crown Prince in his tower dreams of running away to sea and becoming a pirate.' Loredan grinned. 'The whole thing's garbage, if you ask me. Fetch me the forty-pound recurve and let's go and shoot something decent to eat.'

As they let themselves out of the back door, they realised that it had stopped raining. The air smelt sweet, and the evening sun was already pulling a faint haze of mist out of the wet earth. 'When you said something decent to eat, you meant rabbits,' said the boy accusingly. Loredan shrugged.

'I know how to shoot rabbits,' he said.

'But I'm sick of rabbit,' the boy protested. 'And even when you stew it up with tons of spices and stuff, it still tastes of bones.'

'True. But nothing else that's edible is stupid enough to let me get up close. Actually, roasted and with just a touch of rosemary—'

'We haven't got any rosemary.'

'That's not all we haven't got. Rabbit or go hungry, right?'

Before the boy could reply, a big, fat cock pheasant scuttled out of the long grass under their feet and exploded into flight, clucking frantically. Loredan had an arrow on the string; he fixed his eyes on the bird, drew to the corner of his mouth and loosed, all in one fluid movement. The arrow sailed off to the left and vanished in a clump of tall nettles.

'Another thing I like about rabbits,' Loredan said after a moment, as he drew the nock of another arrow smoothly onto the string, 'is that they can't fly. Forget the arrow, it'll be all smashed up.'

'Shall I have a go?' the boy asked hopefully.

'Get lost,' Loredan replied. 'Now then, let's take a look at that warren by the oak stump.'

They walked quietly down into a shallow dip where there were several patches of brambles and fuzz. 'There's one,' the boy whispered. 'You can get him from here.'

'Quiet,' Loredan replied. 'I'm not wasting any more arrows. Now stay put.'

He moved forward carefully, taking small steps, keeping the rest of his body still and straight. When he was forty yards away, the rabbit stopped grazing and sat up; Loredan stopped where he was and waited until the rabbit's head went down again before continuing at the same slow, breathless pace. At thirty yards the rabbit looked up again; he halted, balanced uncomfortably on one leg, but the rabbit scampered five yards towards the mouth of its hole, then stopped, as they always do. Loredan waited. The rabbit dropped down on all fours but didn't graze, just sat looking at safety as if wondering whether it was a good idea. Loredan walked on another five yards, making sure he put his foot down flat each time, gradually easing his weight onto it just in case there was a twig or a thistle-stalk he hadn't seen.

At twenty-five yards he raised the bow and started to draw, looking along the arrow with the bow canted at forty-five degrees; as the base of his thumb brushed the corner of his mouth he dropped the arrowhead a yard below and a yard to the right, then continued the draw until he felt the tip of his finger against his lip, at which point he relaxed his hand and watched the arrow all the way to the target. As he'd expected, the rabbit saw the arrow and started towards home, but he'd allowed for that; the slender bodkinhead passed through the rabbit's back, pinning it to the ground. It was struggling against the shaft, kicking frantically with all four legs, as Loredan ran in, letting the bow fall. By the time he reached it, the rabbit was dead, its eyes wide open, and the last few twitches were just reflexes. Loredan, who had killed more men than rabbits in his time, waited until it was completely still before he pulled out the arrow, wiped the head and dropped it back in the quiver at his belt. Then he picked up the rabbit by its back legs and hocked it, passing the blade of his knife between the tendon of the right leg and the bone, cutting the tendon of the left leg and passing the left foot through the slit. He looked round for a bit of stick and hung the rabbit on it, then walked back and retrieved his bow.

'Enough for two meals on that,' he said.

The boy nodded unenthusiastically. 'And I expect you'll make broth with the carcass, too,' he said gloomily.

'Well, you don't go wasting good food,' Loredan replied. 'Or nasty food, for that matter.' He undid the hock, lying the rabbit along the palm of his left hand, with the head lolling back over his wrist, gently squeezed the piss out of its bladder with his thumb, then pricked the point of the knife carefully into the skin of the belly until he'd penetrated it; then he turned the knife round so that the blade pointed upwards, and slit an opening in the belly up as far as the ribcage. The boy looked away. Loredan put a finger round the rabbit's neck, another round the back legs and turned it upside down, shaking it till the guts dropped out through the slit, then jerked with his wrists to flick them away. With his index finger he hooked out the heart and what was left of the intestines, but left the liver and the kidneys, then picked up his knife again and cut the skin of the back leg from the belly slit to the leg joint. He put the knife down and pushed his finger carefully between the skin and the flesh, easing it away without tearing it until he had enough purchase to pull it away from the rabbit's back, then worked the other leg free and let the skin hang forward close to the ground. He put his foot on it and pulled up on the rabbit's hind legs until the whole body was pulled out of the skin up to the chest, then prised out the front legs and cut through the neck. Having folded the skin carefully with the fur on the outside, he twisted all four legs against the joint until they snapped, cut through the muscle and sinew just below the feet and tossed them away. The rabbit dangled from his fingers, naked and bloody as a new-born baby.

'What are you keeping the skin for?' the boy asked.

'Glue,' Loredan replied. 'You boil it up and it makes gesso; it's good enough for putting a rawhide backing on a lightweight bow. Actually, you can make glue out of almost anything living, but some things are better than others.' He picked up the little parcel of skin and fur, while the boy gathered up the bow and wiped the damp off it. 'Like I said,' Loredan went on, 'nothing's wasted.'

The boy grinned uncomfortably. 'We spend our lives making things out of bits of animal,' he said. 'Sinew and rawhide and horn and glue, and gut for strings, and all the fiddly bits we use bone for.'

'And blood,' Loredan added. 'Mix blood with sawdust and it makes a good sizing glue. I use it sometimes for sealing the grain.'

'Right,' said the boy, uncertainly. 'But don't you think it's a bit – well, gruesome, really?'

Loredan nodded. 'But very efficient, wouldn't you say? It'd be a shame to kill something and then just throw it away. It's only other people we do that to.'

*   *   *

Gannadius looked round uncomfortably, wishing (not for the first time in his life) that he'd kept his mouth shut. Just because you have something intelligent and useful to say doesn't always mean you should go ahead and say it. More often than not, in fact, the opposite is true, depending on circumstances, and the circumstances in which a fifty-nine-year-old professional philosopher is in a position to point out the painfully obvious to the ruling council of a military oligarchy are among those where keeping the mouth tightly shut and not getting involved are most highly recommended.

The chapter house was enormous, four or five times the size of Chapter back home and probably larger than the council chamber of Perimadeia, though he'd only seen that a few times and had no real recollection of it. As with most of the Foundation's public architecture, it was light and airy, with a high domed roof and five huge windows, all of them glazed with thousands of small panes of clear, slightly blue glass, whose colour showed that they'd come from Perimadeia, probably at some point in the last twenty years. That made them irreplaceable now, of course. Other people could make glass, sure enough, but nobody else knew the secret of the City formula, which the guild had fanatically guarded for centuries. As a boy, Gannadius had thrilled with delicious terror at the dark tales of the guild's assassins, who ruthlessly tracked down and exterminated any City glazier who tried to slip away and sell the secret to foreigners. Later he'd found out that the 'secret' was no such thing; Perimadeian glass was slightly blue because of something or other in the sand that they used to make it from that was unique to the City coastline. Still, it made a good story.

An usher touched him on the shoulder and pointed to an empty seat at the very back, directly opposite the rostrum and lectern where the council of faculty heads would be sitting. He thanked the man and set off on his long march across the marble floor, marvelling yet again at the extraordinary acoustics of the place. From the middle of the floor he could hear quite distinctly what two men were saying right in the distance, where he was going. He smiled, reflecting that a council chamber where the faintest of whispered conversations could be overheard from any part of the building must make for either very boring or very exciting politics.

He didn't know the man to his left, but on his right was one Haime Mogre, who lectured in Applied Metaphysics and Military Administration. They'd exchanged a few words at some faculty meeting or other; as far as he could tell, the Mogre were a powerful family among the Poor, their family name meaning 'thin' or 'starved' (not a hereditary characteristic), and Haime was the youngest son in his generation, which meant that he'd ended up with the lowliest post that his birth and position permitted him to accept – a profound nuisance, since he'd have been far better suited to one of the lowlier faculties, such as Accountancy or Poetry, both of which were too low-class for him to be allowed to work in. Haime was, by his own admission, a poor metaphysician and a dreadful administrator, but (as he pointed out on every possible occasion) not nearly as bad at either as his brother Huy, who was a year his senior and his immediate superior in both departments.

'This is terrible,' Haime muttered to him, leaning over and whispering in his ear so softly that Gannadius could hardly catch the words; those confounded acoustics, presumably. 'An absolute disaster.'

Gannadius nodded sympathetically. 'I suppose so,' he whispered back, though why it was necessary to be so secretive he didn't know. 'Two defeats in a row—'

Haime Mogre looked at him as if he was simple. 'I'm not talking about the military situation,' he replied. 'Damn it, the day we can't take the loss of a couple of hundred men in our stride is the day we start packing and looking for somewhere else to live. No, I mean the effect this is going to have on the balance of power. I really can't see how we're going to get out of it this time.'

'Ah,' Gannadius replied. 'I'm sorry, I'm not terribly well up on Foundation politics.'

'Well,' Mogre replied, drawing in a deep breath; and he started to explain. Gannadius was hampered by the extreme quietness of his voice, the quite incredible complexity of the situation, and the fact that in the key family of the Deporf, whose members were evenly divided between three out of the four warring factions, all the male children were traditionally given the forename Hain. Nevertheless, he managed to piece together enough snippets and scraps to know that Juifrez Bovert, the commander of the first lost unit and now a prisoner of the Bank, had belonged to the Redemptionist faction (which had once favoured allowing the hectemores to redeem the mortgages but now bitterly opposed the idea), which was why the Separatists (supporters of a separate committee on finance and general purposes) had insisted that Renvaut Soef lead the retaliatory strike, because the Separatists were at daggers-drawn with the Redemptionists over proposed revisions to the Military History syllabus, with the unfortunate consequence that the Dissenters (who had objected to the annexation of Doure seventy years ago) now had plenty of ammunition to use against the Separatists in their dispute over the vacant seat on the Minor Arts faculty council, in which dispute they were siding with the Traditionalists (advocates of the traditional, as opposed to the First, Second and Third Revised, wording of the Articles of Foundation) in exchange for their support on the vexed issue of the recognition of Medicine as a separate faculty, rather than a part of Minor Sciences. The situation was complicated by the irresponsible behaviour of Hain Doce Deporf, who had suddenly taken it into his head to change sides on the Annexation issue –

('Are they still arguing about that?' Gannadius interrupted. 'After seventy years?'

'Of course,' Mogre replied. 'In fact, the debate is just
starting to get interesting.')

- thereby tilting the balance on the Acquisitions committee dangerously in favour of the Traditionalists, who
didn't gave a damn about the Annexation, but who now
had a majority over the Redemptionists on the sub-
committee that was considering the issue.

'And now this has to happen,' Mogre continued.
(Gannadius still didn't have a clue which faction he supported.) 'You can see what's going to happen, can't you?
The Separatists are going to do their best to bury the
hostages and forget about the whole thing, since all this is
basically their fault, which means the Dissenters will
demand a rescue attempt to embarrass them *and* the
Redemptionists, so the Traditionalists'll be able to force
the Separatists to back down on condemning the Amended
Declaration if they want the Traditionalists to vote against
the Dissenters on the hostage crisis. All this,' he concluded, 'just when we thought we were getting somewhere
on the Standards issue. It's enough to make you weep.'

Before Gannadius could ask about the Amended
Declaration, let alone Standards, the chief usher banged
the floor of the rostrum with his ebony staff for silence,
and everybody stood up as the faculty heads filed in.
They were all old, old men, two of them so decrepit that
they had to be bustled along by a couple of ushers, like
drunks being helped home by their friends. But they all
wore flowing scarlet robes under sleeveless gilded mailshirts that reached below the knee and must have
weighed forty pounds, and each one gripped a cer-
emonial sword and a huge copy of the Articles in a long
silver tube the size of a standard Perimadeian drainpipe
section, which the ushers took from them before they sat
down and piled neatly in a stack behind the rostrum.
Clowns, Gannadius muttered to himself. *Even we were
never as bad as this, and look what happened to us.*

The debate started with a bang and carried on getting
hotter and hotter. There was a three-way shouting

match ('Who's that?' Gannadius asked, pointing at a tall man who was shaking his fist at the rostrum and yelling at the top of his voice. 'Hain Deporf,' Mogre replied) which went on for several minutes before one of the very old men on the rostrum staggered to his feet and joined in in one of the loudest voices Gannadius had ever heard. That shut up the three previous speakers, but then another very old man on the rostrum joined in, talking in a whispery croak that the remarkable acoustics made audible right back where Gannadius was sitting. Since he was making a savage personal attack on another council member (not the man he'd interrupted), being able to hear every word didn't help Gannadius terribly much; it struck him as ironic that, thanks to the truly exceptional design of this magnificent building, he should be able to hear so much and understand so little.

Just as he was on the point of drifting off into sleep, he heard his name mentioned and discovered that everybody in the place seemed to be looking at him. It was a terrifying moment, and at first he wasn't able to get his legs working and stand up.

'All I wanted to say,' he announced, and his voice curled and echoed round the huge chamber like thunder reverberating in a canyon, 'is that Alexius, former Patriarch of Perimadeia, is on Scona.'

He blinked and looked round again. Everybody was still staring, and he couldn't think of anything else to say. He forced himself, and went on.

'The reason why I think this may be important,' he said, 'is this. I've known Alexius for many years, and I can't imagine anything that'd make him go to Scona of his own free will. So my guess is that he was somehow induced to go there by someone in their government. Now then,' he went on, gradually getting into his stride, 'you're wondering what the Bank of Scona wants with a seventy-five-year-old philosopher. That puzzled me too, until I remembered something I'd heard about the Loredan family.'

He paused for effect; sure enough, the name Loredan had caught their attention. He took a deep breath and went on. 'As you may know, the brother of Niessa and Gorgas Loredan lived in Perimadeia; in fact, it was Bardas Loredan who conducted the defence of the City against the plainspeople. I should mention in passing that, contrary to what you may have heard, he made a splendid job of it in the face of quite dreadful odds, not only the overwhelming numbers and determination of the enemy but the run-down state of the City defences and a criminal lack of co-operation from the City authorities. Before that, he learnt his trade as a soldier under the City's most illustrious general, his uncle Maxen. Make no mistake: Bardas Loredan is a thoroughly accomplished and talented soldier, and I'd hate to be on the opposing side to him in a war.'

Gannadius paused again, then continued, 'Unfortunately, that might be about to happen. It's common knowledge, on Scona and here, that Bardas Loredan fell out with his brother and sister many years ago and wants nothing more to do with them, even though he's been living on Scona ever since the fall of the City. What you may not know is that one of Bardas' few close friends in the old days was the Patriarch Alexius; and if anybody could reconcile Bardas Loredan to his sister, it'd be Alexius. I'm talking, of course, about ordinary persuasion, because I know that not all of you really believe in the rather abstruse metaphysical side effects of the workings of the Principle by which it's supposedly possible to change the future and influence people's actions. For what it's worth, however, if you do believe in all that, then you'll be interested to know that Alexius – and I, come to that – were involved in a strange and rather baffling sequence of events which we believe concerned Bardas Loredan and some sort of manipulation of the Principle, and Alexius was, let's say, the main conduit of the Principle in all this. In any event, I put it to you that the prospect of Scona acquiring the services of a

soldier of Bardas Loredan's calibre ought to make you
think long and hard before getting into any kind of
military confrontation with them. I'm no student of warfare, the gods know, but even I can see that even without
him, war with Scona could do us a lot of harm if we lose
and not gain us anything much if we win. Bardas
Loredan could make a bad situation much worse; so, as
we used to say in the City, think on.'

The silence that followed this speech was somewhat
unnerving, enough to make Gannadius wish he'd expressed
himself a little less flippantly (but they'd annoyed him;
they'd been annoying him ever since he'd arrived, and he'd
wanted to annoy them back). For a moment, Gannadius
believed he'd made an utter fool of himself and that
nobody was going to pay the slightest attention to what
he'd said. But then someone stood up in the middle of
the third row, and said that surely that settled it, on no
condition should they send more men to Scona now that
they had this new commander – obviously he was working for them, it explained how they'd managed to score
two consecutive victories over the superior forces of the
Foundation. Before he'd finished, someone else jumped
up and said, on the contrary, that was precisely why
Shastel should act now and with *overwhelming force*, to
nip the threat in the bud before this new Loredan had
time to retrain their whole army and make it invincible.
Fairly soon, the magnificent acoustics of the chapter
house were pounding Gannadius with monstrous waves
of raised and querulous voices, each one crystal clear and
marvellously audible. He closed his eyes, slouched back
in his hard seat, and groaned.

He was standing over her looking down, a puzzled
expression on his face, as if he was trying to remember
who she was. A slight twitch of the eyebrows; he'd
remembered, and now he was trying to work out what
she was doing here. Wherever here was.

'It's me,' she tried to say, 'Vetriz. You remember, we

met in the City; first after that time you fought someone in the lawcourts and you weren't expected to win, and we were sitting behind you in a tavern discussing the fight and saying all sorts of tactless things; and then we sort of kept bumping into each other, and when you were in charge of defending the City you and Venart had that deal with the rope . . .' She could hear herself saying all that, and she knew perfectly well that the words weren't getting out, for some reason.

Because she was dead.

I don't like this dream. I think it's horrid.

'What makes you think it's a dream?' Without moving – she didn't seem able to move – she looked the other way and saw the other Loredan brother, Gorgas; another familiar face, but not one that was welcome in her dreams. There had been the time when, quite uncharacteristically, she'd allowed herself to be picked up by this attractive but repulsive man, while her brother was away . . . And now here he was telling her she was dead. *Go away.*

'I can't,' he replied with a grin. 'I'm not here. And, strictly speaking, neither are you. This is just your dead body. You drowned.'

Did I?

Gorgas Loredan nodded. 'Shipwreck,' he said; and she realised that his brother Bardas didn't seem to be aware of his presence. 'You were sailing home after you completed your business here, and your brother misjudged the currents and got hit by a strong north-easterly squall. You were blown onto Ustel Point. You never had a chance, among those rocks at night. Hell of a way to go,' he added sadly.

But Venart's a good navigator. Whatever else he may not be quite so good at, he can handle the ship. He'd never make a mistake like that.

'Not left to himself, perhaps.' Gorgas Loredan smiled sweetly. 'But you're not the only one who has strange dreams. And people are very vulnerable to suggestions when they're asleep. Well-known fact, that.'

Angrily, Vetriz tried to move. What she really wanted to do was give Gorgas Loredan a smack across the face he wouldn't forget in a hurry, but she'd have settled for any kind of violent reproach. Unfortunately, nothing seemed to work; it was like being on the wrong side of a locked door.

'It's all right,' Gorgas said, with a rather hateful grin, 'I couldn't do that sort of thing even if I wanted to. And I really have no idea why your brother's usually flawless navigation had such dire consequences on this occasion. I've only the vaguest idea how this stuff works.'

Inside whatever part of her mind that was still functional, Vetriz felt something slide into place, like the tongue of a rusty lock. *You're a – what was that word Alexius used? – a natural. You can do that stuff that isn't really magic but looks just like it.*

Gorgas nodded gravely. 'In very general terms,' he replied. 'Truth to tell, I'm not convinced it's really me at all; no, that's putting it very badly. Let's say the part of me that can do this is very much a minority, and a rather unpleasant and disruptive one at that. Whenever there's a big issue and the whole of Me in convocation gathers together to decide on something, it's the part that always gets voted down. If I were inclined to melodrama, which quite emphatically I'm not, I'd call it the devil in me, though that would also be hopelessly misleading – makes it sound like some external influence that somehow possesses me, and it's nothing like that at all. But yes, there is a part of me that's unnaturally attuned to the Principle to such an extent that it has this bizarre ability to exist for just a few seconds in the future as well as the present and the past. The only way I can explain it is that it's some sort of compensation for all the time I have to spend in my own past, which isn't a very nice place to be. Does that make any kind of sense to you?'

I don't know enough about it, to be honest.

Gorgas sighed. 'Nobody does, not even the experts.

Not even your friend Alexius, who knows more about the Principle than anyone else living – I asked him. And, more to the point, I asked him again when he wasn't looking.'

You mean you invaded—

'Invaded his thoughts?' Gorgas shrugged his shoulders; meanwhile Bardas had walked away; he was a few yards further down the beach, examining what looked like another body, but she couldn't see it very clearly – Gorgas' leg was in the way. 'You make me sound like some kind of metaphysical burglar. His view is that the Principle – hell, I couldn't make head nor tail of what he was telling me, it was all far too technical, but he did say that the most useful comparison he knew was a cup of water standing on a table when a heavy ox-cart or a procession of soldiers goes by outside. You can't see what's making the table move ever so slightly, but the surface of the water in the cup ripples over and you can't see your face in it any more. Alexius reckons that the Principle is the cart or the soldiers, and the cup is our minds, vaguely able to sense the existence of the Principle but unable to perceive it. I'd beg to differ; I think that the visions or whatever you call them that I get from time to time are moments when the traffic stops. I'd go further and say that the traffic only stops when it's waiting for something – I get to see what I see when the Principle reaches moments where a thing could go one way or the other, but at that precise moment the course that the future will take hasn't been decided, it's a balance see-sawing backwards and forwards, and if I seize my chance and put my foot on one of the scales ... But this is all pseudo-metaphysical trash. All I know is that one time, I saw Alexius seeing my brother fight in the lawcourts, and he tried to tip the scale against him, so I had to jump in and tip it the other way; and I have the feeling that, because I didn't really have a clue what I was doing, I tipped the scale for a whole lot of other things as well, things I didn't know about then, some of them I still don't know about. Now am I making any sense?'

About as much as you were before. But go on. If I'm dead I'm not in any hurry.

'No, you aren't, are you? Another strange thing,' Gorgas went on, 'is that in these strange and obscure visions I keep bumping into *you*. Remember?'

Vividly.

'Ah, well, it's not deliberate, I assure you. So I tried to find out a bit more about you – with great success,' he added with a smirk, 'and the curious thing is, you're such a commonplace, unremarkable little person, with absolutely nothing out of the ordinary about you at all.'

Thank you.

'You're welcome. Now, all the other people I've met on these peculiar excursions of mine are what you might term remarkable people. There's Alexius, of course, and my wretched and loathsome niece, and my sister – it was a shock meeting her, I can tell you, and she wasn't best pleased. Bardas as well, though he doesn't really belong, he just seems to get dragged in there, probably because of Niessa and me. And there's clever Doctor Gannadius, who's got far more insight and raw ability than Alexius, but not nearly as much intelligence, and just lately there's a new one, a girl student in the Shastel Foundation; she's a remarkable person all right, I've had a look at what she gets up to in the future and no doubt about it, she's really mustard. But you – well, I'm puzzled. And now here you are, dead, and never achieved a thing in all your short and shallow life. It beats me.'

I'm so sorry. Please may I wake up now?

'Oh, why not?' Gorgas said—

—and she sat up, the blanket a confused tangle around her shoulders, and shouted, 'Ven!'

In the other bed across the room, her brother grunted and stirred. 'Go 'sleep,' he mumbled.

'Ven, have you been dreaming?' she asked anxiously. 'Just now?'

Venart propped himself up on one elbow. 'What you talking about?' he asked woozily.

'Did you just have a dream with a bald man in it? Come on, it's important.'

'Dunno.' Venart scrubbed at his face with his balled fists. 'Can't remember, never remember my dreams. Look, pack it in, will you, Triz? It's the middle of the night.'

Vetriz sighed. Her head was splitting. She got up and poured some water into a cup, drank it and got back into bed. 'Sorry,' she said. 'I had a nightmare or something.'

'Too much blood sausage,' Venart said wearily. 'Doesn't agree with you late at night, you should know that by now. Go back to sleep.'

Vetriz lay back but she didn't want to close her eyes. It was like those horrible sleepless times when she was a little girl, convinced that there was something under the bed or crouched behind the curtains. She was also angry, a little bit ashamed, worried. And she could no more go back to sleep than deliberately not think of a monkey.

'Ven,' she said.

'Go away.'

'Ven, when we sail back home, you will be careful, won't you?'

'No, I'll deliberately run us aground on the first rock I come to, just for the hell of it. Definitely no more blood sausage for you, ever.'

'All right,' Vetriz said. 'But you *will* be careful? Promise?'

'Promise. Anything, just so long as you shut up and let me go to sleep.'

She heard the straps of the mattress creak as he turned over, and soon he was making his distinctive soft-snoring noise. She closed her eyes and conjured up a mental image of doves pitching in a tall tree, which usually worked as a soporific. *Dead*, she thought. *And I was there too, inside the dead body; what a repulsive notion. Except, I suppose, that's what we all are, a living thing in a body. But commonplace and unremarkable – oh, why not? So much less trouble than being a remarkable person, surely. Much better to live a boringly contented life and then die.*

She tried to watch the doves gliding down with their wings back, then spreading them like sails to slow down as they turned into the wind and stepped out of the air onto the tree-branch; but the vision seemed to ripple, like the surface of a pond when you've just dropped a stone in it. Maybe if they set sail a day earlier, or later; but the vision hadn't specified a particular day, had it? It was all very well trying to be cunning and circumventing the future she'd seen, but that was a storyteller's cliché; if they left a day later, then that's when the storm would be, not on the day they'd originally intended. So what if they stayed on Scona indefinitely? For the sake of argument, suppose they stayed here for the rest of their lives? For all she knew, that'd only trigger some other, nastier chain of circumstances that led to a far more unpleasant fate than drowning. Such as? Well, spending her entire life on Scona, to name but one.

Maybe (she thought drowsily) the whole thing was a fake, an image *he'd* put into her mind so as to stop her leaving. Why should he want to do that? Obvious reason? Not very probable. Some peculiar magical thing he was cooking up? No such thing as magic. No reason why he'd want anything from a commonplace and unremarkable person like herself. She began to doze, and gradually the doves began to drift cautiously back to the tree, put their wings back and pitch; and if she had any other dreams that night, she didn't remember anything about them in the morning.

CHAPTER EIGHT

Family, muttered Gorgas Loredan to himself. *Family's what life's all about, but at times it can be bloody aggravating.* He wriggled his shoulder blades against the back of the hard stone bench and sighed.

The door opened and a clerk came out, the tip of his nose just visible over the pile of brass document tubes cradled in his arms. 'Hey, you,' Gorgas called out. 'What exactly is she *doing* in there?'

The clerk stopped and turned towards him. 'The Director's in a meeting,' said a thin, harassed voice from behind the stack of tubes. 'She'll let you know when she's finished.'

'Marvellous,' Gorgas replied. 'I come charging back from Penna because she's got to see me urgently, life or death, and here I am taking root in the outer office as if I was some punter overdue on his payments. I'm supposed to be running a *war—*'

The clerk didn't say anything, just left, and after a minute or so Gorgas calmed down. He might be angry with his sister, but that was no reason to go bawling out clerks, something he wouldn't have done if his back didn't ache and his boots weren't still sodden wet from fording a river in spate. He shook his head sadly at his own loss of control, then stretched out with his feet propped up on the far arm of the bench, stuffed his rolled-up coat under his head, and tried to relax. Apart from anything else, it didn't pay to take an attitude in with you when you had a meeting with Niessa Loredan, no matter who you were.

He tried to turn his thoughts back to the camp outside Penna. By rights he should be using this valuable and unexpected free time to analyse the situation and plot his next moves in quiet and peace, without the endless distractions of leadership and administration; but for him, it never quite worked like that. He couldn't play chess, either. An abstract, two-dimensional view of the battlefield, with painted wooden blocks representing the various friendly and enemy units, contour lines for hills, green hatched squares for woods and grey ones for houses, emptied his mind in seconds, making him feel as if he was being asked to play a game whose rules he didn't know; unlike his sister who, he suspected, saw the whole world as a chequer-board, used both for playing chess and calculating with counters. She would have made a fine general, he'd always assumed, except that he somehow couldn't see her in the grey mud of a battlefield, stepping over dead men and huddling under the canopy of a burnt-out wagon for a little shelter from the rain to read despatches and scribble orders. No; as far as he was concerned, theirs was a good division of labour, given that in Niessa's view, military involvement of any sort was evidence that she hadn't handled things as well as she should have done. She despised fighting, and undoubtedly that coloured her opinion of him. But then, as far as she was concerned, hadn't he always been a necessary, and now indispensable, evil?

The door opened, and instinctively Gorgas swung his legs off the bench and sat up straight, just as he'd done as a boy when his mother came into the room and caught him sprawling on the furniture. The two men who came out he recognised as Shastel diplomats, not the residents who lived on Scona but an actual delegation from the mainland. They looked as tired as he felt, and their coats and trousers were almost as damp and muddy - new proposals hastily despatched, no wonder she'd kept him waiting.

A clerk led them out, and a moment later Niessa appeared at the door and beckoned to him.

'What was all that about?' he asked.

Niessa smiled faintly, and quite suddenly her face changed, from the strong, confident expression he'd immediately recognised as her negotiations mask into a portrait of a middle-aged woman with a headache who's had quite enough for one day. Years ago, Gorgas remembered his grandmother telling them stories about the Nixies, who had the ability to change their shape and become whatever animal, bird or human they wanted to; Niessa had something of that ability, to such an extent that even after knowing her all his life, he'd still be hard put to it to describe her accurately if he was looking for her in a crowd.

'Don't ask me,' she said. 'It's something to do with Foundation politics; and I've got so many of the faction bigwigs on the payroll that I'm practically running the place, and still I haven't a clue what goes on there. Come in,' she added, as if noticing his wet boots and grubby hands for the first time. 'I think we could both do with cider toddy and pancakes.'

Gorgas suppressed a smile. His sister handled stress by eating and forcing food on others; good starchy peasant food and lots of it, with a hot drink to wash it down. He'd watched her grimly working her way through a stack of death warrants once, pen in one hand and a folded-over pancake in the other, and a little napkin tucked in her sleeve to make sure she didn't get pangrease on the parchment. He followed her into her office and slumped in the visitor's chair while she rang for the clerk and gave him the catering order.

'What they *said*,' she continued, as she settled herself into her chair, 'was that in return for us releasing Juifrez Bovert and the other lot you've got tied up at – what's the name of the place?'

'Penna.'

'That's it, Penna. If we let them go, they'll formally recognise the existence of the Bank as a sovereign entity—'

'That's big of them,' Gorgas interrupted. 'They're doing that already.'

'—And officially allow the hectemores to remortgage with us,' Niessa went on, 'provided that we pay them commission on the remortgage advances, withdraw all our advisers on the mainland and restrict our activities to a strictly defined area.' She sighed, and let her weight go forward on her elbows. 'Well? What do you reckon to that?'

Gorgas thought for a moment. 'Basically, it's too good to be true,' he said. 'It'd be like surrendering their whole client base to us without a struggle. And the conditions are meaningless, because we both know we won't honour them. I mean, we can't.'

Niessa nodded thoughtfully. 'It's a faction thing,' she said. 'Faction B gets Chapter to agree to a military adventure that goes wrong. Faction A makes Faction B look bad by blowing the military situation up out of all proportion and then saying that only desperate measures will save them from the consequence of Faction B's blunder. Then, as soon as Faction A's got the upper hand, they tear up the accords and launch their own adventure, hoping that they'll pull it off. That's the really annoying thing about these people,' she added, a harsh and asymmetric scowl suddenly creasing her face, 'they make us fight a war, but winning or losing it isn't what they're interested in, the war's just another arena where the factions can beat up on each other. How in the gods' names am I meant to plan a war when I don't know what the other side wants out of it?'

Gorgas grinned. 'It's just as well that they always lose,' he said.

'That's beside the point,' Niessa answered angrily. 'They can afford to keep fighting and lose. We can't afford to keep fighting and win. Every time we smash up one of their expeditions, it costs me money and people I can't afford. How can I run a business that way? It's not as if I can gather up all the dead halberdiers and sell them. And I can't settle it, because the only way it'll ever settle is if we go away and never come back.'

'Or if we take Shastel,' Gorgas interrupted quietly. 'Ever thought of that?'

Niessa gave him a contemptuous look. 'Don't be stupid, Gorgas. Who do you think we are, the City? We've got hundreds of men, they've got thousands. The only reason we're still here is because they don't like getting in boats. And,' she added bitterly, 'because the war's so useful to them. We're a godsend to the factions. Besides,' she said, in a colder, harder voice, 'I can't afford the war as it is now, let alone going on the offensive. A victory like that would ruin us.'

Gorgas smiled pleasantly. 'It doesn't have to be expensive,' he murmured. 'Perimadeia didn't cost us a quarter.'

'That was different,' Niessa replied. 'That was a wonderful stroke of luck. As far as I know, there's no horde of savages planning to sweep down out of the mountains and besiege Shastel. Which is one thing we can be thankful for,' she added.

'All right,' Gorgas said. 'But let's look at what we have got. We've got a fat, lazy standing army run by a bunch of idiots who spend their lives reading books and playing politics. We've got thousands of peasants who pay for all this fun, and who're never going to do anything about it because they simply haven't got the imagination. And right now, we've got at least one faction, probably two, in pretty desperate trouble because of sixty or so halberdiers cooped up in a village surrounded by our troops. Does that suggest anything to you?'

Niessa shrugged. 'You're saying we should deal directly with the factions who sent the raiding party, agree to let them go on favourable terms in exchange for some real concessions. That puts them in the ascendant, the in-fighting steps up a gear or two and we're controlling the winning party.' She shook her head. 'Won't work. As soon as they've got what they want, they won't owe us anything. It'll be business as usual within a month.'

Gorgas shook his head. 'You're missing the point,' he said. 'What if we executed all the prisoners, publicly and with maximum prejudice, so as to do as much damage as possible to the factions that sent them? You know, bodies on gibbets and the heads of two Poor-family members on spikes on the Strangers' Quay, where everybody can see them. Those factions'll be so desperate they won't know what to do, they'll be finished. That's when we start negotiations: you open the gates to us one dark and stormy night, we'll sort out your enemies and hand you back your precious Foundation to play with however you want to, just so long as we can post a discreet and well-behaved garrison where it'll be on hand to look after you – your benefit as much as ours, we'll say. And of course, they can pay for it, too; quietly and via the second set of books. And that way everybody wins, or thinks they do.' He paused and tried to read his sister's face. 'What do you reckon?'

The door opened and a clerk brought in a tray with the cider and pancakes. 'About time,' Niessa said. 'All right, put them down on the table.' She stood up and started spooning honey over the pancakes and folding them neatly. The clerk left quickly.

'Well?' Gorgas said.

'Supposing we try it,' his sister replied, 'and it doesn't work. They kill or capture our soldiers, our factions are condemned as traitors and they immediately mount a proper invasion. They could hire ships from the Island or the pirates – they could have done it years ago, but they don't want to, like I just told you. That'd be the end of everything, finish.'

'True,' Gorgas conceded. 'But I wasn't planning on losing.'

'All right,' Niessa replied with her mouth full. 'Suppose it works. And, for a while, we have a garrison in Shastel and tell them how to run their country. What for? How's that supposed to help us? It's bad enough having to govern this island without taking over the running of a full-sized country.'

'And their revenues,' Gorgas pointed out.

Niessa shook her head. 'Hopeless,' she said. 'You may not know this, but taxes aren't for the government to spend as they please, they've got to pay for running the country; which is what you have to put up with if you're a government. We aren't a government, we're a business, and you'd do well to remember that. Oh, sure enough, we could skim off ten, even fifteen per cent of the gross, but I doubt if we'd break even. No, what you're suggesting would have us bankrupt inside a year.' She swallowed her mouthful and drank some cider, which burnt her tongue. 'If you want to be a king, Gorgas, you go and find yourself somewhere you can amuse yourself at your own expense. You're letting the Perimadeia business go to your head, that's your trouble. Sacking cities is a rich man's hobby. I suggest you remember your station in life and act accordingly.'

Gorgas nodded slowly. 'I suppose you're right,' he said. 'So, you didn't drag me back here to ask my advice. What do you want?'

'It's Bardas,' she replied, wiping her mouth on her sleeve. 'You obviously haven't thought of this, but if I was in their position, I know exactly what I'd do. I'd send twenty men – *good* men, professionals – to bundle him onto a boat and take him to Shastel, trade him for the hostages. So; I want him brought back here where we can look after him, like we should have done in the first place. I didn't send you to the City to indulge your taste for damaging things so he could go mooning about in the hills playing bows and arrows. He's our brother and he's a security risk, and it's high time we sorted things out. I've got that priest friend of his here, so that ought to be all right. All I need is for you to do as you're told for once and get him here. Do you think you can manage that, or would you rather I sent someone else?'

Gorgas looked at her for a long time, then chuckled insultingly. 'Mother Hen,' he said. 'You can't resist being mother, can you?'

For a moment he thought he might have gone too far; not that he'd have cared particularly much if he had, at that precise moment. But Niessa just looked at him. 'That reminds me,' she said. 'You told me you'd deal with that stupid daughter of mine, and you haven't. Gorgas, it's *embarrassing*, having my only child locked up in the city jail. I know she's difficult, but you'll just have to make an effort. You can go and see her before you go back to your war.'

The boy put down the drawknife and watched.

Bardas Loredan was working a bow on the tiller. He'd made quite a sophisticated tillering bench: a three-foot section of oak gatepost bolted to a heavy sawhorse, with a winch on one end and a slot cut in the other for the bow-handle, with clamps to hold it firm. The body of the oak post was polished smooth and precisely calibrated in half-inches.

'You'd do well to watch,' Loredan said without looking up. 'This is the only skilful part in the whole process; the rest is just basic carpentry, with some black magic thrown in to impress the customers.'

The boy sat down on a log and folded his arms. 'I'm watching,' he said.

'Right.' Loredan unwound the winch. 'You start off with the roughed-out stave, which is just a slice of tree cut down to *look* like a bow, but it goes without saying, that doesn't mean a thing. I mean, sitting there in an apron with the drawknife by your side and sawdust in your hair, you look like you know what you're doing.'

The boy didn't bother to rise to that one. Loredan brushed a few shavings off the tiller-post and went on.

'Tillering,' he said, 'is the art of teaching a bow to bend. The difference between a stick and a bow is, if you bend a stick it either breaks or distorts and stays bent. You bend a bow, it flexes and then reverts to its own proper shape, and with enough power to drive an arrow through sixteen-gauge steel two hundred yards away. Big difference?'

'Big difference.'

'I'm glad you're following.' He started to wind up the winch handle. 'Now, to tiller a bow you loop a string nice and loose round both ends of your whittled stick, and you draw it up on the winch, bending the bow just half an inch or an inch at a time, and gently let it go, then again and again - fifty times per inch, minimum. Seventy-five's better. That way it learns to bend; the outside, what we call the back, learns to stretch, and the inside, the belly, learns to be compressed; and it's the combination of that stretching and compression that creates the power. Try and bend a stave into a semicircle, and you'll get two bits of broken stick; the stretch will tear the fibres in the back apart, and the compression will crush and rupture the wood of the belly. Bend a *bow*, a thousand-times-flexed stick, and you get a weapon that can kill any living thing in the world.' He grinned, and wiped his forehead. 'Little bits of torture, over and over again, and just when the wood thinks it can't take any more you draw it back an extra half-inch, increasing the tension and the compression; and the bow finds it can take it after all, and now it's that little bit stronger and more powerful, until suddenly you realise you're there and you can draw the bow the length of the arrow. That's tillering.'

'Little bits of torture,' the boy repeated. 'That's a funny way of putting it.'

Loredan shrugged. 'That's what you're doing,' he said. 'You're teaching the bow to be unnatural, after all. Its nature is to break, or give up and take a set; but you've got to teach it, by stretching and crushing, to do something it would never have been able to do if it'd just been left to stand around in one place and grow leaves.' He grinned. 'Someone once told me to think of it as driving the bow mad; torturing it, he said – I guess that's where I got the word from – so as to make it *violent*; not passive, not weak, not natural, but full of violence.' He carried on turning the winch, slowly drawing up the bow, unwinding, letting it relax, like a patient executioner with a man on the rack. 'Sounded pretty melodramatic to me when I was your age, but there's a sort of point there, I think.'

'So you keep winding it up and winding it out again,' the boy said. 'Is that it?'

Loredan shook his head. 'Rather more to it than that,' he said. 'When you're making a bow, you want it to bend evenly in both limbs, not just at the tips but all the way down, in proportion, so when you draw it the bow comes compass.'

'What does that mean?'

'Depends,' Loredan said. 'Some bows should be a perfect semicircle when you draw them; others want to be more square, so that the wood a foot up from the handle on both limbs scarcely bends at all. So, when you're tillering you keep an eye on the curve, and if one limb bends less than the other you scrape a little wood away in the right place until it matches the other limb. That's the difficult part.'

'Ah,' the boy said, and for about an hour he sat and watched as Loredan worked, turning and relaxing the winch over and over again, occasionally stopping, locking the winch and leaning over the bow to scrape off a few shavings with a sharp knife held at a right angle to the wood. As he watched, he could see what Loredan had been talking about; at some point the stick had stopped being a stick and had become something quite different.

'Of course,' Loredan went on, his eyes fixed on his work, 'there comes a point when it won't bend any further, it'll just snap; and just before that point, it's finished and ready to shoot. Ironic, I guess; when it's at its most fragile, where just that bit more tension and compression will break it in half, that's when it's at its most powerful, when it can reach furthest and hardest. That's the time when the fibres in the belly are crushed up so tight they simply won't go any further; we call that stacking. Generally the back will stretch further than the belly will compress, because we glue hide or sinew to the back to keep it together. In the very finest bows, we glue horn on the belly, because that'll take more compression before it collapses.' He rested for a moment and straightened his back. 'That's why the best bows are made out of bits of dead animal,' he said. 'Animals bend and squash much better than trees. When they're dead, of course.'

Well, quite, he thought suddenly. *And we're the back and the belly of the bow.* 'Here,' he said, 'you come and take a turn on the winch. I want to study the profile.'

The bow was just reaching that stage he'd mentioned, the point where it stopped being an abused piece of lumber and became a weapon. Loredan watched as the two limbs, upper and lower, bent together to the same profile under the same stress, creeping nearer and nearer to the moment where mechanical advantage became breaking strain. Vital that the two limbs be as like each other as possible, as similar as two brothers, both experiencing the same force applied equally to each of them, both withstanding the same stretching and crushing in the same way, storing the torture and turning it into violence, as the bee turns pollen into honey.

'That's looking pretty good,' he said.

'Are you going to stick anything on the back of this one?' the boy asked. Loredan shook his head. 'This is just a piece of junk for the military,' he replied. 'Self ash – that means it's made out of one piece of ash wood, and it's a flatbow, which means it's just cut straight, rectangular section, with no recurves. Good enough for government work, no point in making it any better.'

'A recurve's where you heat it, isn't it?' the boy said.

'That's right. You steam it till the wood softens, and it takes a permanent curve, away from the string.' Loredan yawned. 'All that does is increase the amount of tension you're putting the wood under, and that makes it more efficient. The best bows, sinew-backed and horn-bellied, are so heavily recurved that when they're unstrung they're like horseshoes, and when you string and bend them they pretty well turn inside out.'

'I see,' the boy said. 'Did you ever make any like that?'

Loredan nodded. 'I made a real beauty once, long ago. It pulled close on a hundred pounds, but it shot like it was twice as strong. And you'd never be able to pull it far enough to break it; it'd just keep on bending and bending. I've never made one that good since,' he added. 'Pity, really.'

'Have you still got it?'

'No, I made it for my brother. When I tried to make a better one for myself it just snapped, and I'd run out of that particular grade of horn, so I stopped bothering. Not that it matters. I make good bows but I'm only a fair-average shot, while my brother's a high-class archer. Now then, where are we? Another two inches and we're there.'

When the tillering was finished, Loredan fitted the bow with a proper three ply hemp string of the right length, and they went out into the yard to shoot it in. The boy dived into the woodshed and came out staggering under the weight of the heavy straw target boss, which he hung by a chain from a spike driven into the lowest branch of the apple tree beside the well. He got out of the way and Loredan, standing twenty yards or so back, drew and loosed in one steady movement. The arrowhead, a slim bodkinhead shaped like a narrow leaf, passed through the straw as if it was nothing but a patch of low cloud up in the hills, ripping the fletching feathers off until only the end of the nock was visible in the straw.

'Not bad,' Loredan said. 'It kicks a bit in the handle,

but I can't help that. After I've shot it in we'll slap some beeswax on it and call it done.'

He paced out fifty yards and shot the rest of the dozen arrows, ending up with a group about eighteen inches wide, about a foot low and a foot to the left of the middle of the target. His next group was fairly central but more open, and the third dozen was distinctly ragged, with two arrows missing the outer painted ring and only just clipping the outer edge of the straw.

'Can I have a go?' the boy asked.

Loredan shook his head. 'This is an eighty-five-pound bow,' he said, 'you'd do yourself an injury trying to draw it. And even this is on the light side for a military bow. Fetch the arrows for me while I go back to seventy-five.'

At seventy-five yards the group was fuzzy verging on non-existent, and one arrow missed the target completely and went sailing through the branches of the tree and over the hedge into the orchard. Loredan swore.

'We'd better go and find that one,' he said, stepping between the bow and the string and bending the bow against his knee until he could slip the loop off the top nock. 'Let's just see how much of a set this thing's taken.' He laid the bow on the ground and stepped back. 'Half an inch,' he said, 'could be worse.' The boy looked again, and this time noticed that the bow was no longer straight; it had followed the string just a little. 'That'll be more like three-quarters of an inch by the time it's properly shot in,' Loredan said, 'which'll bring the weight down to nearer eighty. Nothing you can do about that.'

They found the lost arrow about a hundred yards down the orchard; it had hit a tree and splintered. Loredan studied the break for a moment, decided that it was beyond repair and flexed it over his thumbs against the break, snapping off the head. 'Job for you tomorrow,' he said. 'Drill the broken shaft out of the socket and salvage the flights and the nock. I'll get the beeswax and the oil, you get the stove lit, we'll put a couple of coats of wax on the bow and it can cure overnight.'

The boy noticed the beginnings of a big purple bruise on the inside of Loredan's left arm, three inches or so above the wrist; he also had a raw patch on his left forefinger, where the fletchings had ridden over it as the arrow was released, ripping the skin. Loredan didn't seem to have noticed; he ignored the marks the way a woman takes no notice of the scratches left by her cat's ever-open claws, and if challenged replies that it's just the cat's way of being friendly. *If I become a master bowyer I suppose I'll end up all scraped and battered too*, he reflected.

They finished the bow with hot wax mixed with a little oil, wrapped the handle in cord and hung it horizontally on a rack to dry; then the boy went back to slicing the bark off a rough stave with the drawknife, and Loredan started roughing out another billet. Neither of them spoke for about an hour, until the boy had finished the stave he was working on and brought the drawknife over to be sharpened.

'Does it ever bother you,' he asked, 'making weapons that people kill each other with?'

Loredan shook his head. 'Not in the least,' he said. 'Compared with what I used to do for a living, it's blissfully innocent. And what I used to do never really bothered me all that much, or at least not in that way. Most of the time I was too busy worrying about whether I'd be alive at the end of the next fight.'

'And before that,' the boy persisted. 'When you were in the army. Did it bother you then?'

'Sometimes. But not very often, for the same reason.' He picked up the drawknife and tested the edge on the ball of his thumb. 'And every time, it bothered me a little less. Besides, it isn't really like that in the army. Most of it's very, very boring; boredom enlivened by rare interludes of extreme terror. But the more you do something, the easier it gets, and the easier it becomes to do something a little bit worse – it's gradual, you see, half an inch at a time, and you don't realise it's happening to you until it's done and you reach the point where quite suddenly you can't go any further without snapping.'

'Uncle Gorgas, what a surprise. I thought you weren't going to bother with me any more.'

Gorgas sat down on the bed and tried to keep from gagging. He'd been in some foul places in his time, but the smell here was unbearable. 'I never said that,' he replied. 'Or if I did, it was only because you'd annoyed me and made me lose my temper. Do you like living like this, by the way?'

Iseutz smiled. 'No,' she replied. 'I think it's disgusting. Don't you?'

Gorgas sighed. 'I'm going to tell the warders to get this place cleaned up, whether you like it or not. It can't be healthy, for one thing.'

'But Uncle,' she replied with a hurt note in her voice, 'that's why I want it like this. So I can catch some horrible disease and die, and then I'll be out of the way. You see? I'm just trying to be nice.'

Gorgas held up his hand. 'Not today,' he said, 'I'm not in the mood. I've been chasing Shastel halberdiers up and down the mountains, I've had your mother on at me, I can't remember offhand the last time I had any sleep, and as soon as I'm through here I've got to go back to the mountains to collect your uncle Bardas and bring him back here, whether he likes it or not. So don't start, all right?'

'Or?' Iseutz sat down on the floor opposite him and studied him. 'Or what? Come on, let's have the threat.'

'Just - don't start.' Gorgas closed his eyes and breathed out deeply through his nose. 'Another little job your mother gave me was to deal with you. You're an embarrassment to her, apparently. As is your uncle. And I'm not sure she approves of me, either.'

'Oh? Why not?'

'She reckons I'm not businesslike enough.'

The girl nodded. 'She's right,' she said. 'You don't know

when to cut your losses. You throw good money after bad, or good time at any rate. You can't see when the game's not worth the candle. You—'

Gorgas opened his eyes. 'All right, that'll do,' he sighed. 'You've made your point. Actually, I don't mind you saying that. It's just another way of saying that I don't give up on things that matter to me.'

She looked at him, her head slightly on one side. 'That's true,' she said. 'Oh, I don't know about the things-that-matter-to-you part, because I don't know what you mean by "things that matter". But it's true, you don't give up easily.'

'Thank you.'

'I'm not sure I meant it nicely. And you certainly don't let little things like guilt or ordinary common decency stand in your way, I'll say that for you.'

Gorgas yawned. 'You know, this is the first real chance I've had to relax since that damned raiding party landed. I could probably get to like it in here; no hassles, no worries, nobody depending on me for anything. Perhaps next time Niessa tells me to do something, I'll just refuse. If you take away the smell and the filth, it's not a bad little place you've got here. Better than a muddy ditch under a wall, anyway.'

'My heart bleeds,' said Iseutz. 'And you're changing the subject.'

'So what? You were insulting me.'

She shook her head. 'No, I was trying to understand you. I want to understand you, you see. If I can understand you, and my mother, and the rest of the family, it might give me some clues about how I managed to turn out such a mess.'

Gorgas nodded. 'That's possible,' he said. 'So, what's your point?'

'Well.' Iseutz thought for a moment. 'Let's see, we were talking about not knowing when to quit. Now then, I'd say that a man who's killed his father and brother-in-law and tried to kill his sister and his brother because he was afraid of what they'd do to him if they realised he'd arranged for someone to rape his sister – I haven't left anything out, have I? Only it's quite a lot to have to remember.'

'Go on,' Gorgas said.

'You'd have thought a man like that would give up on his family; you know, he'd come to the conclusion that probably the survivors wouldn't want to have very much to do with him any more, and so he'd just go away and do something else. But not you. Not Gorgas Loredan. You brush all that stuff magnificently away. Stop cribbing, you say, you're still on your feet, aren't you? Let's be friends.' She grinned. 'You know, in spite of everything, I can't help admiring that.'

'Like I said,' Gorgas replied, looking away, 'I don't give up easily when it comes to things that matter to me. Like family. I keep going, I don't listen till I'm hearing the answer I want to hear. You see, I've proved that people can change, and they can forgive, too. Look at your mother and me. And if we can do it, so can you. For pity's sake, you've only got one life. Why ruin it over something you can't do anything about?'

'Ah.' She shook her head. 'I'm like you, you see, persistent. When it comes to things that matter to me. Like killing Uncle Bardas. When it really matters to you, there's nothing you can't do something about.'

A mouse poked its head out from a crack between two stones in the wall, looked round and scuttled across the floor. With a quick, fluent movement Gorgas pulled his purse from his coat pocket and threw it hard, hitting the mouse's head and killing it instantly. The girl glowered at him.

'What did you do that for?' she demanded.

Gorgas shrugged. 'It was a mouse,' he said. 'What about it?'

'You don't kill things for no reason,' the girl replied angrily. 'You don't kill things just because of what they are. You just don't.'

'That's nice coming from you. You want to kill your own uncle.'

'Yes,' Iseutz replied, 'for a reason.' She got onto her hands and knees, crawled across the floor and picked the mouse up by its tail. 'A very good reason. Just killing things because they're there is a waste.'

Gorgas pulled a face. 'Big deal,' he said. 'So it's a waste of mice. There isn't exactly a shortage.'

'It's a waste of life,' she replied. 'That's bad. I was starting to think I understood you, but maybe I got you wrong.' She dangled the mouse above her head, reached up with her mouth, chewed off its head and swallowed it. 'Killing for food is all right,' she said.

Gorgas looked away. 'You're disgusting,' he said. 'You sit there talking like a rational person, and then you do something like that.'

'Look who's talking,' she replied. 'You're the one that killed it. What's more disgusting, killing or eating?'

Gorgas swallowed a couple of times; he badly wanted to be sick, but didn't allow himself the luxury. 'So when you kill Bardas, you're going to eat him, right?' he said. 'And what about the skin and the bones? You aren't going to waste those, surely? What are you going to make out of them?'

Iseutz considered for a moment. 'That's a good point,' she said. 'I'll have to give it careful thought. Of course,' she added, 'I'm not particularly good with my hands these days, but I might be able to manage something.' She held up the mouse again, but before she could eat any more, Gorgas jumped to his feet and slapped it out of her hand. She spat at him and recoiled, like a cat that's had its kill taken away.

'You're disgusting,' Gorgas repeated. 'You must take after your father.'

'I wouldn't know,' she answered sweetly. 'He died before I was born, remember?'

CHAPTER NINE

'Can we just go through it one more time?' Vetriz asked patiently. 'After all, this is an important part of my mercantile education. We're going to buy salted fish.'

'That's right.'

'We're going to buy salted fish,' Vetriz repeated, 'and take it halfway across the world to the island where we live, which sits in the middle of the sea—'

'That's right.'

'Which is stuffed so full of fish and fishermen that you can virtually walk across it from one fishing boat to the next on a *carpet* of premium-quality tuna, whiting, mackerel—'

Venart sighed. 'You're missing the point,' he said. 'Granted, the Island has a thriving fishing industry. Granted, fresh fish is plentiful and cheap. Now, if you've been listening to any of the things I've been telling you about trade, you'll have spotted the crucially important word I just used.'

'Plentiful? Cheap?'

'Fresh,' Venart replied. '*Fresh* fish you can hardly give away. Salted fish, however, is a different matter entirely.'

Vetriz stopped for a moment to look at a display of rugs. They were imported, but she wasn't quite sure where from; the patterns were unusual and the texture finer and thinner than the Mesoge rugs that fetched such good prices on the Island. Before she could ask the price,

212

however, Venart moved her on.

'All right,' she said, 'so there's not much salt fish sold on the Island. Maybe there's a reason for that.'

'You're being obtuse,' Venart said severely. 'Look, we've got an established market for fresh fish, everyone lives on the stuff, but it's so commonplace it's boring. People will always try something different, so long as it's not *too* different. Hey presto, salted fish. We could be on the verge of making a fortune.'

'Or complete idiots of ourselves. Have you thought of that?'

They left the main thoroughfare and passed under a low arch into a narrow street that went sharply uphill. Suddenly, it was dark under the low eaves of the house. 'Trust me,' Venart said calmly. 'I mean, it's not just the novelty aspect, there's also the practical side. Fresh fish you've got to eat immediately. You can't keep it.'

'You don't need to keep it. You just go out the next day and buy some more.'

'And,' Venart continued, as he dodged under a line of wet washing, 'there's the flavour. Entirely different flavour.'

'Yes, it's salty. Very salty.'

'And not forgetting,' Venart ground on, 'value for money. If we can buy it at the right price, we'll be able to make it so our salt fish won't cost any more than the fresh stuff. That's a very important consideration.'

Vetriz sighed. The infuriating thing was that Venart was quite probably right. She remembered the sun-dried-beef craze that had swept the Island a few years ago; sun-dried strips of prime beef steak, imported from Colleon, had been the only fashionable thing to serve your guests, in spite of the fact that it tasted like rawhide and broke your teeth, and the cattle-boats from the Mesoge were ploughing across the sea half empty. And then there was the imported-water craze, and Nean goat's milk cheese, and the live cuttlefish fetched all the way from Ria in huge terracotta vats, when you couldn't fall off Founders' Pier without coming up with three cuttlefish in your pocket.

The epicentre of the salt-fish trade on Scona was the inner courtyard of a small anonymous inn tucked away in an alley leading off the dark, narrow street they were walking up. They missed the turning the first time; it was little more than a doorway, in a street where most of the doors were open all the time, and it was only when Vetriz insisted on stopping and asking someone (much to her brother's disgust) that they found the right one. The alley was as narrow as a corridor, and they had to step over two or three old women who were sitting in the middle of it, completely blocking the way and appearing not to hear when politely asked to move; they were completely engrossed in their work, which was lacemaking. It was so dark in the alley that Vetriz could hardly see what they were doing, and the thought of them squatting in the shadows forming the tiny, intricate stitches made her feel sick – she had three beautiful lace collars back at the inn, which she'd bought in the market the previous day.

They found the inn, which also appeared to be entirely composed of corridors, and just when they were sure they'd taken another wrong turning and were about to head back, they stumbled through into the courtyard.

The first thing they noticed was the sunlight, and after that a beautiful cherry tree, which stood in the middle of the grass. Under it sat a very fat man, who appeared to be taking no notice whatsoever of the forty or so men and women who sat on stone benches on all four sides of the covered portico that surrounded the courtyard. They were mostly sitting still and staring vacantly at the sky or the ground, though a few were doing calculations on strings of tally-beads or writing laboriously on plain cedar-backed wax tablets. They showed no inclination to shift up and make room when asked to do so, and in the end Venart and Vetriz had to perch awkwardly on the end of a stone bench.

What little conversation there was seemed to have nothing to do with fish. An ancient and disturbingly thin woman whose forearms were encircled with massive gold bangles from wrist to elbow was telling a rambling story about her daughter's bad experiences in childbirth, which nobody was listening to. Two stocky bald men were playing checkers on a tiny board balanced on the points of their knees; the board was made of tiny tessarae of lapis lazuli and ivory, and the pieces were coral and amber. A bewildered-looking young man with long, tangled hair was working his way with dedicated efficiency through a tall brass jug of dark-red wine, which he held at arm's length and poured into his mouth, drenching his beard and tunic. A nice-looking old man with snowy white hair and a brand-new pair of red boots was softly playing a mandolin. The place looked like a cross between some versions of the earthly paradise and a lunatic asylum.

Then, quite unexpectedly, the fat man in the middle looked up from the book he was reading and started talking about cod. He said that because of the recent bad weather and the activities of pirates in the Belmar Straits, good salt cod would quite soon be at a premium. There was a moment of dead silence, almost as if the fat man had said something obscene, before a huge, ferocious-looking individual with a head like a skull replied that he had a warehouse full of barrels of the very finest salt cod, the best that money could buy, and fairly soon he was going to have to throw it all in the sea just to make room for something he might one day have a chance of selling. He was interrupted by a handsome middle-aged lady on the other side of the courtyard, who said in a very matter-of-fact voice that because of the vast quantities of unsaleable cod that were constipating her barn she was staring bankruptcy in the face and considering doing away with herself. A nondescript man with a short grey beard added that he'd invested his daughter's dowry in cod a short while back and accordingly was resigned to having the wretched girl on his hands for the rest of his life.

The fat man nodded, was silent for a while, and then announced that, owing to the unprecedented demand, he was afraid he would have to ration his customers to a maximum of fifty *elmirs* of cod apiece for the foreseeable future, and the price would henceforth be seventeen quarters an *elmir* –

('What's an elmir?' Vetriz whispered.

'I haven't the faintest idea,' Venart replied.)

– which was strictly non-negotiable, cash in advance, no notes of hand or letters of credit. A little wizened man in a corner, who was so tiny that Vetriz had to look quite hard before she managed to see him at all, called out, 'Fifteen quarters.' The fat man ignored him, repeated his price, and went back to his book. The dignified lady called out sixteen quarters, half on delivery, half in thirty days. Without looking up, the fat man said 'Sixteen, cash.' Everybody started to talk, and then shout, at once. Venart didn't hear the closing bid above the din, but apparently the bidding was over, because the fat man prised himself up off the ground, brushed off the seat of his trousers, waddled across to one of the checkers-players and started a lively but muffled conversation with him. A cheerful-looking woman with improbably red hair stood up, walked over to the tree, sat under it and produced an embroidery frame.

'Yes, but if we don't know what an *elmir* is,' Vetriz hissed, 'we won't have a clue how much we're buying.'

'Excuse me.' Venart looked over his shoulder. The man who'd just spoken was a tall, stern-looking individual with short grey hair and a magnificent beard that flowed down his chest like an iron waterfall. 'You aren't familiar with our weights and measures?'

'Not entirely,' Venart admitted.

'It's quite simple,' the man replied. 'We use the Colleon *elmir*, which is a volume measure, exclusively for cod; one *elmir* is roughly two Scona hogsheads, and the

Scona hogshead is more or less nineteen City gallons. For all other fish, except herring, we use the Shastel *elmir*, which is approximately two and a quarter Scona hogsheads, or when it's more convenient to deal by weight, we deal in Scona hundredweights, which are nine-tenths of the City standard, though for accounting purposes we convert that into Shastel hundredweights, which are eleven-tenths City. A Scona hogshead of cod is just over one Shastel hundredweight, if that's any help to you. Of course,' he added, 'it's all completely different for dealing in fresh fish, which is important to remember when you're buying fresh fish to salt down.'

Venart nodded helplessly and thanked the man for his advice, just as the cheerful woman under the tree announced, apparently to her embroidery, that she had four hundred *vezants* of prime tuna, but she was probably going to hang onto it until the price rose to something like the level she'd bought it at.

('*Vezants?*' Venart whispered.

'Four and an eighth Colleon *elmirs*,' his neighbour replied. 'Some people find it a more convenient measure for large quantities. She's lying, of course,' he went on, 'she's only got about a quarter as much; but if she manages to sell it all, she'll buy in the rest of what she needs later on in the day.')

Eventually, after an hour or so (it was hard keeping track of time) Venart managed to join in the bidding, and went away with a verbal agreement to buy twelve City hundredweights of salt mackerel at fourteen quarters the Colleon *elmir* from the young man with the brass jug. When they got up to leave, the whole assembly looked up and formally wished them long life and prosperity.

'I make that seventy-two quarters,' Venart said, as they found their way out of the alley back into the light and noise of the main street. 'Which is quite a good price, if you ask me.'

'Fifty-six,' Vetriz corrected him. 'Twelve City hundredweight is ten and four-fifths Shastel hundredweight, which is ten and four-fifths Scona hogsheads, or five and two-fifths *elmir*. Fifty-six quarters. From what I could gather, it's slightly on the high side of the going rate.'

'Oh,' Venart said. 'In that case, let's go back to the inn and have a drink to celebrate. I think we've earned one, don't you?'

There was nobody to be seen when they got back to the inn, and they gave up all hope of getting a drink and collapsed into two rickety chairs in the common room. Venart produced his tablets and was laboriously going over the calculations when he looked up and saw a man in military uniform standing over him.

'Venart Auzeil?' the man asked.

'That's me.'

'You're under arrest,' the soldier said.

CHAPTER TEN

'I think it's broken,' said Venart sorrowfully, dabbing at his nose with a scrap of bloodstained cloth he'd torn off his sleeve. 'In fact, I'm sure of it.'

'Don't be such a baby,' Vetriz replied scornfully. 'You'd know it all right if it really was broken. And anyway, it's all your own fault.'

Realising that he couldn't expect any sympathy from his sister, Venart turned away and looked round the room. It wasn't a dungeon cell or anything like that; as far as he'd been able to gather, they were in some kind of waiting room at the end of a couple of miles of corridors, somewhere in the head office of the Bank of Scona. But a room with four bleak stone walls, no window and a heavy closed door can call itself what it likes; if you happen to be in it, it's a cell.

'You really are an idiot, Ven,' Vetriz went on. 'What on earth possessed you to talk to that man like that?'

'How was I to know?' Venart protested bitterly. 'Ever since we arrived on this horrible island, all everybody's been telling me is, "Don't take any notice of what the scuffers say, they're just trying it on to get money." So, quite understandably—'

Vetriz sighed. 'If you can't tell the difference between a customs official and a palace guard, I'm amazed you've lasted this long in commerce. It was obvious he wasn't just an ordinary - what was that word you just used?'

'They all look the same to me,' Venart replied bitterly.

'Great big useless idiots in a uniform. And there was no need for him to hit me; all I did was say I wasn't coming.'

'That's not quite true,' Vetriz pointed out. 'You said – rather rudely – that you weren't coming, he tried to grab your arm, you shoved him—'

'I didn't shove him. He just sort of collided with my arm.'

Vetriz made a rude noise and folded her arms tightly around her chest. 'Have you been in places like this before?' she said. 'I mean, do you know what happens next?'

Venart shrugged. 'No idea,' he said. 'I suppose they'll have us up in front of a judge and we'll be fined a lot of money. That's what it's all about, I imagine, getting money out of us.'

Vetriz shuddered slightly. 'I only hope you're right,' she said. 'Assault on an officer of the state in the execution of his duties ... You don't think they'll hang us, do you? Or lock us up for years and years?'

Venart scowled. 'This is a bank,' he replied, trying to sound confident. 'How much business do you think they'd do if every time there was a misunderstanding with a foreign trader they slung him in jail? You just don't do that sort of thing if you want to deal with people.'

'There's that,' Vetriz replied, sounding thoroughly unconvinced. 'But of course, we don't know what it was they were arresting us for in the first place. That could be something *awful.*'

'Why? Have you done something awful without telling me?'

'No, of course not, but it could be something they think is awful.' Vetriz stared gloomily at the door. 'This is so stupid,' she said, 'being locked up like this and not knowing what's going on. How long have we been here?'

Venart shrugged. 'Three hours? I don't know. Too long, anyway. For one thing, I need to see a doctor.'

'Oh, shut up about your stupid nose. Don't you ever think about anybody beside yourself?'

'Well, if you hadn't kept on about how gullible I'd been giving that warehouseman all that money—'

Vetriz sighed. 'Oh, yes, do let's have a big argument and start calling each other names, it'll help pass the time. I'm frightened.'

'I'm not exactly having a wonderful time myself,' Venart admitted. 'If only we knew someone who could help us out of this.'

Vetriz opened her mouth and then closed it again; and a moment or so later, the door opened and a soldier appeared.

'Follow me,' he said.

So they followed him, along an endless corridor, up a flight of steps, down a flight of steps, up another flight of steps, along an endless corridor. There was nobody else to be seen, and the clopping of the soldier's boots echoed loudly off the stone walls and ceilings. Just when Venart was wondering if they were in fact going round in circles, the soldier stopped abruptly and pulled open a door. 'In there,' he said.

In there turned out to be another small, bare, window-less room, containing an almost identical set of two chairs and a table. Venart and Vetriz were bundled in, and the door closed.

'Wonderful,' Venart sighed. 'Maybe this is a special sort of punishment they reserve for people who do *awful* things. We could spend the rest of our lives—'

'Shut up, Ven.'

Ten minutes later, the door opened again and a different soldier led them out, down an endless corridor, up a flight of stairs and into another bare, miserable-looking room; but this one was wide and high, with a hammer-beam roof and thick granite pillars. That was it, apart from a wooden bench. They sat down and the door closed, but before they had a chance to get used to their relatively improved environment the door opened again and a clerk came in.

'The Director's ready for you,' he said. 'This way.'

Venart looked at his sister; she shrugged. They followed the clerk into the adjoining room, which was almost identical to the one they'd just left, except that in the very centre of it was a desk, and behind the desk was a woman. She was short, dumpy even, with a broad face and large eyes, greying brown hair pulled sharply back into a bun, and she wore a dark-green gown that was little more than a peasant's smock, with a plain cord belt. She sat in a large, old wooden chair without arms. There were no other chairs in the room.

The woman looked at them for a moment. 'Venart and Vetriz Auzeil,' she said, stating a fact.

'That's right,' Venart replied. The woman had a rather deep voice, with just a trace of an unfamiliar accent underneath the sing-song cadences of Received Perimadeian. 'Excuse me,' he went on, 'but why are we here?'

The woman looked at him.

'I mean,' Venart went on, 'I admit I did sort of shove that soldier back when he shoved me, but it was really just a reflex action, and he did shove first, and anyway, there was no call for him to go hitting me, so ...' He tailed off. The woman was still looking at him.

'So you assaulted an officer,' she said. 'I didn't know that.'

Venart opened his mouth and then closed it again. She stopped looking at him and turned her attention to Vetriz.

'You arranged the rescue of Patriarch Alexius from Perimadeia,' she said. Vetriz nodded. 'And then he lived with you for some considerable time before he came here.' Again it was a recapitulation of facts not in dispute, rather than an enquiry.

'That's right,' Vetriz said nevertheless; anything to break the silence. 'We got to know him when we were in the City just before the fall, and we became friends. He's a nice old man. We liked him.'

'I am Niessa Loredan,' the woman said. 'You know my brothers Gorgas and Bardas.'

Vetriz nodded.

'And you've heard of me.'

'Yes.' What Vetriz wanted to say was, *Yes, and haven't we met? Not here, but, well, somewhere else? And I'm frightened of you, but not nearly as much as you think I am.*

Niessa Loredan's mouth twitched a little at one corner. 'Do you know where Alexius is now?' she asked. 'Have you seen him at all since you've been on Scona?'

'No,' said Venart. 'We haven't seen him since he left the Island to come here. Didn't you invite him—?'

'I don't think so,' said Niessa Loredan. 'I think he came to see you and asked you to take him back to the Island with you. I think you know perfectly well where he is.'

Venart started off on a passionate denial, to which neither of the women listened. In fact, he wasn't there any more; Niessa and Vetriz faced each other across a hazy representation of a desk in a line drawing of a room.

'You know we haven't seen him,' Vetriz said.

'I know,' Niessa replied. 'Or at least, I do now. That's a pity, because I want to use him if I can to do something about this dreadful mess. Do you know about it?'

'Not really,' Vetriz replied. 'I've heard rumours, about a riding party—'

Niessa shrugged away the rest of the answer. 'But that's not why I wanted to see you. You're in love with my brother.'

'No!' Vetriz replied angrily. 'It was just one time, and I felt awful the next—'

Niessa smiled. 'Not Gorgas,' she said. 'Bardas. Well, aren't you?'

Vetriz frowned. 'Not that I'm aware of. And I think I'd have noticed something like that, don't you?

'Not necessarily. All right, let's say he fascinates you. You felt a strong attraction towards him the first time you saw him – fighting the lawcourts, wasn't it? And then by pure chance you met him again in a tavern immediately afterwards and talked to him, and you were – interested. Yes?'

Vetriz thought for a moment. There was obviously no point in lying.

'It's possible,' she said. 'But I often see men I like the look of, but for one reason or another I don't follow it up. It's not – nice.'

Niessa smiled again. Her smiles didn't mean the same thing as most people's. 'But you saved his life, didn't you? By using your gifts as a natural, using the Principle; you saw a moment in the future where he was killed, and you changed it. That's right, isn't it?'

Vetriz spread her hands. 'Honestly,' she said, 'I don't know. Gorgas said – well, I think somehow that Gorgas *communicated* to me that that's what happened, but if it did I wasn't aware of it. Isn't that the point about being a natural? I mean, apparently you should know that as well as I do.'

'Not quite,' Niessa replied, lacing her fingers together. 'I'm not a natural like you are, I found a way to use the Principle deliberately. I don't think anybody's ever been able to do that before. It means my abilities are limited, but I can use them, such as they are, whenever I want. I may not be a natural myself, but I can – now then, what would be the right word? Think of a cuckoo laying its eggs in another bird's nest, or a leech, even.'

'I think the word is "parasite",' Vetriz interrupted. 'You're a parasite on naturals.'

'Very well put,' replied Niessa, smiling. 'I wanted to find out about Alexius and that other man, Gannadius; I gather that they learnt or worked out for themselves how to do some of the things I can do without any natural ability at all, just acquired skill and knowledge. As far as they could tell, it was purely an accident in their case, something they stumbled on in the course of their academic research.' She made the pursuit sound utterly futile. 'Obviously I'd like to know what they know, which is why I brought Alexius here. Gannadius is a teacher with the Foundation, which is rather unfortunate, but I'll deal with that when I've got the time. Anyway, that's all beside the point. The point is your interest in my brother, and the fact that you seem to be able to – well, control him.'

'Oh, that's not true,' Vetriz protested. 'You make it sound like I can make him do things. And I'm sure I can't. I've never tried, but I'm sure—'

'You averted his death,' Niessa interrupted. 'Or you were used to achieve that end. Shall I let you into a secret? Yes, why not? Since you're not completely stupid, you'll work it out for yourself eventually. Your friend Alexius is a natural too, and the comic thing is, he didn't know. All those years reading books and yattering to old men in his stupid Academy, and all the time he had the ability to twist the Principle round his little finger. I don't suppose it ever occurred to him. Maybe he really wasn't interested. It's possible, isn't it? He told me that the practical use of the Principle – I was calling it "magic" at the time, to annoy him – is just an irrelevant side-effect of the true pursuit of philosophy. Can you imagine an attitude like that? All right, think of a charcoal-burner hundreds of years ago, devoting his whole life is getting the art of charcoal-burning just right. And one day he notices little bright shiny flecks in the ashes of his fire. He picks them up, decides they're not interesting and throws them away, and the next time he sees them, he takes no notice. Now, that man has just invented the smelting of iron, but since he's only interested in charcoal, he ignores it. Anyway, enough of that. Alexius is a natural, as sure as we're both here.'

Vetriz looked at her, but it was like looking at an arrow-slit high up in a castle wall. 'So what is it you want from us?' she said. 'You're in business, and so am I. What's the deal?'

'Ah,' Niessa said approvingly, 'you're beginning to sound like me. Actually, you've got a fine trader's mind, much more so than that buffoon of a brother of yours. It seems to be the way of things that women like us, with a keen commercial instinct, are hampered by our ne'er-do-well brothers. Count yourself lucky you've only got one. There, I knew I'd find the similarity between us if I looked hard enough. Well, I'll be absolutely straight with you. Sometimes I see a future, a moment in the future, where everything's gone wrong and everything I've worked for and built up has been wrecked, and in that moment I always see my brother Bardas; and don't ask me how I know but I just do, that if he wanted to he could step in and stop it happening. But he doesn't.' She paused for a moment, frowning, as if contemplating a ledger that was perversely refusing to balance. 'Obviously I've tried to avert it, but I can't. You see, I'm not actually *there* in that moment; it's part of some other strand of the rope that I can't get into, however hard I try. I think that strand has to do with my brother Bardas, and Alexius, and maybe even you as well.' She sighed. 'I won't hide it from you, it's becoming something of an obsession with me, getting in the way of the real work I ought to be doing. I don't like it; it niggles, if you know what I mean.'

'I can imagine,' Vetriz said, without expression.

'Can you really? How fascinating. Logically, I've got two courses of action open to me. I can make Alexius try and intervene, the way he did on behalf of my wretched daughter when she asked him to curse Bardas; but I haven't got much confidence in him for that. I suspect it was sheer luck that curse really worked, and setting it aside wasn't too hard. Alternatively, there's you. After all, you're also a natural, and my guess is a fairly substantial one. You're caught up in the strand yourself. And,' Niessa added quietly, 'you'll be so much easier to coerce than an old man who strikes me as tired of life. After all, you're young and attractive, you have a brother you care deeply about, you also care about Alexius, and Bardas too. There are so many ways to make you do what you're told, the only slight problem is deciding which string to pull first.' She folded her arms. 'Have I made myself clear?' she said.

—And Vetriz opened her mouth to reply, but Venart was still talking, finishing the sentence he'd just started when the strange interview began. Niessa Loredan let him finish, and then clicked her tongue. 'If you can't lie better than that,' she said abruptly, 'I suggest you quit commerce and find some other way of making a living. Anyway,' she went on, with a dismissive gesture, 'that's all very well. I think you, Master Venart Auzeil, would be well advised to get off this island within – oh, let's see, I don't want to make life too difficult for you, let's say forty-eight hours. Your sister will stay here, with me. We have other matters to discuss.'

For a moment, Vetriz was afraid that Venart would do something stupid, such as grab her and make a run for it, or hit Niessa. Instinctively she grabbed his arm. He shook it free.

'That's not acceptable,' he said, trying valiantly to sound firm. 'If you're trying to detain a citizen of the Island against her will—'

'It's all right,' Vetriz heard herself saying, 'I'll be fine. You go. Don't worry.'

Venart looked as if he'd just been bitten by a chair. 'No, it's *not* fine,' he said petulantly, struggling vainly with his bewilderment. 'You don't want to stay here, with her—'

'Yes, I do,' Vetriz said.

'You *don't*—'

'You can go,' Niessa interrupted, 'or you can both stay. But if you stay, Master Auzeil, you won't enjoy it. Now stop bickering with your sister, and go and conclude your business.'

Venart looked at her, then at Vetriz; he felt as if he was staring at two strange monsters in human disguise. He tried to think of something to say, but couldn't.

'Please,' Vetriz said. 'Really, I *will* be all right. There'll only be a problem if you make a fuss.'

Venart took a deep breath. 'I don't understand,' he said, with feeling.

'You amaze me,' Niessa said. 'The officer will show you out.'

What Gorgas really wanted to do was go home. Instead, he trudged through the corridors and up and down the stairs, and finally found himself in the hall with the hammer-beam roof and the tasteless pink pillars. He buttonholed a clerk, who told him that the Director was busy.

'No, she's not,' Gorgas replied. 'If there's anyone in there with her, tell her to get rid of them. This is important.'

The clerk gave him a long, hateful look and went into the Director's office. He came out again a moment later with an expression on his face that only just avoided being a smirk.

'I'm afraid the Director isn't here,' he said.

'Don't be stupid,' Gorgas replied. 'The Director lives here. If she isn't in her office she must be in her lodgings. Go and tell her – oh, the hell with that, I'll go myself. It's all right,' he added, as the horrified clerk tried to stop him, 'I know the way.'

He barged past the clerk, shouldering him out of the way, and closed the office door firmly behind him, then crossed the room to a small, almost invisible door in the wall. He banged on it once with his closed fist, then shoved. The door swung open sharply and Gorgas strode through.

'What the hell do you think you're doing?'

'Hello, Niessa,' Gorgas replied.

It was a tiny room, smaller than the cell her daughter was locked up in; cleaner, but rather more sparsely furnished. There was a stone shelf in the far corner which served as a bed, and a plain oak chest in the other corner, its lid padlocked shut. In a small crevice in the wall above the bed, an oil-lamp flickered on a short wick. There was no fireplace and no window, just a small grille under the low ceiling to provide ventilation. Niessa Loredan lay on the shelf, stark naked, darning the heel of a threadbare stocking that was already mostly composed of darning wool.

'Get out.'

'All right,' Gorgas said. 'I'll see you in the office in five minutes.'

Rather less than five minutes later, Niessa bundled out of her room. She was wearing a purple silk robe, and her feet were bare. 'If you ever do that again—' she started to say, but Gorgas interrupted her.

'There's a problem,' he said.

'Well?'

He sat down in the visitor's chair and drew one knee up onto the other. 'The hostages are dead,' he said, in a flat, expressionless voice. 'While I was here nattering with you, my men tried to smoke them out. They burnt down the village and,' he added, with a grimace, 'the Albiac plantation, which is a real blow. I thought you ought to know at once, so I came here straight away.'

Niessa stared at him for a moment as if she hadn't understood what he'd been saying, then started to swear. She swore well and fluently, like a man. When she'd finished, she swilled down what was left in her cider-mug and crammed a small cake in her mouth.

'Well?' Gorgas asked.

'You tell me,' Niessa replied with her mouth full. 'You were the one who *wanted* to kill them.'

Gorgas scowled impatiently. 'That's right, I did,' he said. 'And then you explained why it'd be a really stupid thing to do. Come on, pull yourself together. I really need to get some sleep soon,' he went on, reinforcing the point with a huge yawn.

Niessa rubbed her face briskly with the cupped palms of her hands. 'All right,' she said, 'let's try and think this through logically. First, what do you think the chances are of keeping it quiet? After all, there's no rule says we've got to tell them the hostages are dead; we can say they surrendered and we've put them somewhere safe in case of further rescue attempts. We could even say we've shipped them off Scona, quietly and without any fuss. It'd get us off the hook in the short term.'

Gorgas shook his head. 'First, we'd have to come clean sooner or later,' he said. 'Second, I don't reckon it'd be possible. The gods only know how many agents the Foundation's got among our people; I can name you thirty without even looking at my notes, and you can bet your life there's three we don't know about for every one we do. I say forget that option.'

'All right,' Niessa replied. 'Let's have another look at your original idea. As I see it, there's two ways we can play it. First, we could make a big thing of it – so perish all invaders – and hope the factions'll do the rest. But I don't think that's how these things work. The factions that were against the original expedition will be the ones calling for all-out retaliation, and the ones who were for it won't dare oppose that. My guess is, the factions'll end up holding an auction, and the side who proposes the biggest and most powerful expeditionary force will win.'

Gorgas nodded. 'That makes sense,' he said. 'So what's the other option?'

'Well,' Niessa said, pulling at the tip of her nose, 'there's your idea. The pro-raid factions really don't have anywhere to go. If they call for reprisals they're agreeing with the enemy. If they oppose them, they've lost their nerve and are weak and spineless. The question is whether they'd still be strong enough to ride it out, or whether we really could panic them into making a deal with us. What do you think?'

Gorgas thought for a moment. 'My instinct, bearing in mind what you said yesterday – gods, was it only yesterday? – is no, forget it. True enough, there's a few in the factions crazy enough to open the gates just to keep the enemy from winning, but not enough. I think we have to look longer term. They're going to have to go along with the retaliations, yes? So in that case, their only real hope is for the new expedition to do even worse than the original one; and that's where I see scope for talking to them.'

Niessa nodded. 'It's still a very big step for them to take,' she said. 'I grant you, it's covert treason rather than open treason, but they're still dead if they get caught and it doesn't work.'

'Fair point,' Gorgas conceded. 'But consider this. For the opening-the-gates thing, we'd need pretty well the whole of two factions to come in with us. For the revised version, we only need a handful of individuals – the real faction crazies, if you like – to pass us useful information and help out with sabotage on the supply and strategic fronts. I can almost guarantee you ten or so of those.'

Niessa shook her head. 'We're still both assuming there's got to be an invasion, and the best we can hope for is faction support to help us defeat it. I don't like those odds. I believe that even with inside information and our supporters doing their best to sabotage the raid, we're still just too damn small and weak to stand up to a full mobilisation of Shastel. In the end, numbers would win. And even suppose we did manage to defeat them heavily enough, short of wiping them out to the last man, isn't that just inviting an even bigger and better army the next time round?'

Gorgas yawned again. 'All right,' he said, 'what about trying the same thing from the other direction? Posit this. The hectemores suddenly realise that the Foundation's not invincible after all. The legendary Shastel halberdiers humiliated by the archers of Scona—'

Niessa laughed harshly. 'Romance,' she said dismissively. 'They're peasants, they aren't suddenly going to rise up and rebel. Or at least they might, but it'd be a fluke, a special combination of events that snowballs and gets everybody caught up in the excitement, until they're all a bit crazy and ready to do anything. These things happen, but you can't rely on it happening, and you can't make it happen. No, I was thinking of trying to make a deal.'

Gorgas raised his eyebrows. 'I can't see it myself,' he replied. 'We aren't talking about rational people, remember, basically we're dealing with faction members, hooligans. Even talking to us visibly would be suicide.'

'Maybe,' Niessa said. 'Unless we can put together a deal they can't resist. Try this. First, we say the deaths of the hostages was a tragic accident, the result of a forest fire. We sincerely and deeply regret the loss of life. Now obviously,' she went on, as Gorgas tried to interrupt, 'they won't go for that unless we make it worth their while. What we've got to do is think of what it'd take in the way of incentives to make them stop and think. And that's where we've got to be completely realistic. Let's face it: we're looking at complete annihilation here, unless we can come up with some way of avoiding a war.'

'I agree,' Gorgas said. 'So where do we pitch the offer?'

Niessa picked up a pen and fiddled with it. It was, Gorgas noticed, a typical Niessa object – a plain trimmed white goose quill fitted with a small gold nib. 'We can't start off too low,' she said, 'but we don't want to give them more than we have to, naturally.'

'Just plain money won't do it,' Gorgas said. 'Their capital reserves are so vast, money doesn't matter to them. It's got to be land, and probably something else on top.'

'Fine. I say we offer them all the mortgages we hold on the mainland. Every last one. After all, that's what they've really wanted all along, so why not give it to them? If they can have that without a fight, what the hell else could they possibly want from us?'

'Fine,' Gorgas replied calmly. 'And what do we do for a living after that?'

'Oh, we'll think of something. And I'll tell you this for nothing, we won't be doing anything for a living if we're dead.'

Gorgas nodded. 'All right,' he said. 'What you're saying makes sense. And as far as I'm concerned, the hectemore business wasn't getting us anywhere in the long run anyway. You know that for a long time now, I've been saying we should be looking at trade and manufacturing rather than just running the old racket. Mind you, I'm not saying we're ready, but—'

Niessa grinned. 'It's your big Scona-the-new-Perimadeia thing, isn't it?' she said. 'And I'm not trying to put that down, believe me; it's something we've been working towards and putting a lot of effort into. So, just as well, really.'

'That's right,' Gorgas said. 'And of course, we'll still have the ships.'

Niessa shook her head. 'Not so fast,' she said. 'I said land and something on top, remember. Look at it from their side: they can take the land for themselves if they take us out, and have all the fun of wiping out the shame of the defeat – and I reckon it'll take something quite special to make them pass up on that. Bear in mind, their whole culture's based on the notion that it's good to fight. We're asking them to pass up the chance of a good war, with a guaranteed victory at the end of it. If we're asking them to do that, we've got to make it worth their while.'

'So?' Gorgas shrugged. 'What's your idea?'

'We give them the fleet,' Niessa replied. 'It's the one thing they badly need which we've got and they haven't, which they can't just take by force of arms. We give them the ships, and we supply men to train their people and sail the ships in the meanwhile. Look at it from their point of view, and it makes sense. Of course, we'd have to make them force it out of us as a last desperate concession; but I think that's the way we should be looking to go.'

Gorgas scowled at her. 'It's also goodbye to any hope of making a living on this rock,' he said angrily. 'All right, perhaps *some* ships, *some* men. But why the hell should they want them all?'

'You're missing the point,' Niessa replied. 'It wasn't Perimadeian ships that built up City trade; it was quality goods at the best prices. The way I see us going is along the lines of those workshops of yours, where you make all the stuff for the army. Get all the people you've got making arrow-nocks and put them on making buttons. The same with your armourers; if they can make helmets and swords they can make brass pots and shovels and any damn thing, cheap and quick. Just think; if every button in the world is made on Scona, we'll bless the day we got out of the mortgage business. And we won't need an army and we won't have to fight any wars. We'll have Shastel to do that for us.'

Gorgas looked at her. 'Sorry,' he said. 'You lost me.'

'Think,' his sister replied. 'Shastel has a fleet of ships. Shastel has nothing to sell. So they carry our goods on their ships. Suddenly they need us, they start to rely on us for a lot of easy money.' She smiled broadly. 'We might just end up running Shastel, and without loosing a single arrow.'

Gorgas thought for a moment. 'It's a hell of a big step,' he said.

'So was coming here in the first place,' Niessa said equably. 'Compared with what we've already done, it's nothing; it's what you've been saying we should be looking towards doing anyway. And we don't fight a war and we don't get killed. That's the main thing. There's nothing, absolutely nothing, like a war for destroying money. Even if we had a signed contract with Death saying we'd win hands down I'd do anything rather than get us into a proper war. A little war for you to enjoy as a hobby is something I can put up with, but if you expect me to indulge you in a great big war, you're sadly mistaken.'

Gorgas sat still and quiet for a long time, thinking. 'All right,' he said. 'And suppose they just won't play? No deal, under any circumstances—'

'Which is a very real possibility,' Niessa interrupted, 'given the sort of people we're dealing with.'

'Well, quite. So what do we do then?'

Niessa pulled a wry face. 'Simple,' she said. 'We load as

much of the capital as we can on a couple of decent ships, go to the Island and let them get on with it, let them have their stupid invasion. After all,' she added with a sad smile, 'we've both cut our losses and run away from home in our time, we can handle it. And we'll be a damn sight better off than we were the last time.'

Gorgas stood up. 'I'm going home to bed,' he said. 'You think it over and let me know what you've decided in the morning. One thing, though.'

'What?'

'Bardas. How does he fit into all of this?'

Niessa shrugged. 'We take him with us, of course. Which reminds me, that job I gave you. I don't suppose you've even started it.'

'Niessa.' Gorgas frowned. 'I've been busy.'

'I'd noticed,' Niessa replied. 'Well, damn well make sure you get on with it, or I'll have to do it myself. And remember,' she added, 'I won't mess about trying to be like you.'

Gannadius?

No answer. Nothing. It was almost like being a small boy again, and standing in front of a door being towered over by someone's mother; *No, Gannadius can't come out to play today, he's helping his father with the chickens.* He sighed and opened his eyes. In theory, the headache should signify contact with the Principle. In reality, Alexius felt that it probably had more to do with sitting with his eyes screwed shut and his head at a funny angle. *Natural? Call yourself a natural? And the rest.*

It had been a long day, what with his first magic lesson with the Director and his complete and utter failure to get his newly acquired techniques to work. According to the Director, sitting cross-legged on the floor with your eyes shut and your head lolling on your shoulder like a dead man swinging from a gibbet was supposed to focus the mind, turn it into a sort of burning-glass to concentrate the stray wisps of Principle

that (apparently) waft around the place like dandelion
seeds. So far, however, he hadn't seen one shred of ev—

—He was sitting on a barrel on the deck of a ship, in
the middle of a calm, flat sea. Judging by the light and
the position of the sun, it was very early in the morning;
there were red streaks in the sky, and a pleasant fresh
smell, but he felt extremely tired, as if he'd sat up all
night to see the dawn. He appeared to be alone on the
deck of this ship, which suggested that the crew were all
still asleep.

He lifted his head and looked towards land. He recognised the island in front of him; it was the same view of
Scona he'd had from the ship that brought him here.
Seen from this angle, there was a passing resemblance to
Perimadeia, except that there was no upper city and no
dramatic backdrop; the mainland was a grey and green
blur daubed across the skyline in a hurry, and not
allowed to dry properly. Something was different, though.
Not hard to work out what it was.

Scona Town was in ruins. Smoke was rising from the
mess where the buildings had been. The harbour was
empty, and the warehouses that lined the quay weren't
there any more. Something prompted him to stand up
and peer over the side of the ship, and in the water a few
yards away he saw a dead body, floating on its face.
There were quite a few of them, in fact; too sodden and
deep in the water for him to be able to tell what nation-
ality they were, or even if they were men or women. Just
bodies; blood, bone and meat, with everything else taken
away. It's not often that we get to see our fellow humans
as things rather than people, as nothing more than the
sum of their organic parts. Even when they're dead,
humans are generally recognisable as having once been
individuals, but hide the face and the indications of
gender and the clothing and belongings that serve to
classify and distinguish, and all that's left is so much
blood, bone and meat, so much raw material.

There's been a battle, then, Alexius rationalised. *Bodies in the water ought to mean a sea-battle, or a bad storm. The burnt town suggests a battle, and the lack of ships in the harbour suggests they were launched to fight an enemy fleet or evacuate the town. Either there was a catastrophic fire followed by a terrible storm – and surely the storm would have put out the fire – or else there was a sea-battle followed by a successful attack on the Town. If that's the case, though, you'd think the attackers must have been Shastel, but Shastel doesn't have any ships.*

'Alexius,' said a voice behind him. 'What's going on?'

Gannadius. I've been trying to find you.

'Have you? I wasn't aware . . .'

Oh, thank you very much. So what's all this about you knowing more about the Principle than any man alive?

'You mean what Machaera said? She's just young, that's all. A bad case of hero-worship.'

I should say. And what's all this? And what are you doing here?

Gannadius sat down on the barrel and grinned feebly. 'Actually,' he said, 'I come here quite a lot. I find it soothing.'

Soothing? A burnt city and dead bodies? Are you out of your mind?

'Certainly not,' Gannadius replied, nettled. 'And compared with what I've been getting lately, it's wonderfully soothing. The end of the war, and all that. When you've been forced to live through graphic scenes of hand-to-hand combat and the massacre of unarmed civilians, a bit of calm sea and sunshine makes a pleasant change.'

You've seen the rest of the war?

Gannadius smiled sadly. 'Seen it? I've been writing it. Or whatever you do when you make up a different future out of your head. And before you ask why in blazes I should want to do such a thing, it isn't really me. Oh, I've orchestrated and choreographed it, but that's just me being professional. No, it's that confounded student of mine who dreamt all this up, in the rough, so to speak.'

That girl? She's managed to curse an entire island?

'It looks depressingly like it,' Gannadius replied. 'Quite unprompted, and certainly without any help from me. In fact, without being too obvious about it I've been trying to sabotage it, or at least tone down the nastiest bits. I don't think she's noticed, or at least not yet.' He scowled. 'You wouldn't want to see what it was like before; just scrambling and chopping and blood spurting everywhere. I suppose that's how someone that age who's read books and heard songs and never seen real fighting must visualise a battle; swords cleaving and men run through and heads rolling in the gutters or bounding down the streets like those stuffed leather balls we used to make when we were children. Quite ghastly, the whole thing.'

And you want this to happen, do you?

Gannadius shook his head vigorously. 'But what can I do about it?' he said. 'On my own, not a great deal. That's why I've been trying to find you.'

Sorry, but you'll have to leave me out of it. Taking a curse off just one man nearly killed me, if you remember. Taking a curse off a whole island would finish me off for sure. Gods, though, this Machaera must be a bloodthirsty little thing, something like that awful girl we had to deal with back home.

'Not a bit of it,' Gannadius sighed. 'Timid, meek, polite, mousy creature, the sort that gets panic attacks trying to summon up the courage to ask a question after a lecture. If anything, that makes it even scarier, don't you think?'

Alexius nodded slowly. *So tell me what happens,* he said. *Then we can start at the beginning and work out if there's any practicable way of stopping it.*

'Quite straightforward,' Gannadius said. 'The Shastel fleet sails round the blind side of Scona island—'

Just a moment, slow down. What Shastel fleet?

'My sentiments entirely. But apparently there's going to be one, and while it's ferrying the army across the straits, out come the Scona ships and the fun starts. They sink fifteen Shastel ships, all of them crammed with soldiers, all drowned, and they set fire to another six. That's before they're all sunk.'

Sunk. I see. Carry on.

'It's sheer weight of numbers, you see. It doesn't matter how vastly superior the Scona ships are, because at the end of the day there's just twenty-two of them, and any number of ours. Anyway, then the Shastel fleet forces a landing on the Strangers' Quay – horrible business, that, we lose a lot of men there, but again we push through because we outnumber them so much. The rest of it's just a great deal of killing. You can see the result over there.'

Gannadius, this is horrible. We've got to make sure it doesn't happen.

Gannadius gazed at him wearily. 'Fine,' he said. 'And how do we do that, exactly? You just spell it out in easy-to-follow stages and I'll help as much as I possibly can. Well?'

All right then, stop the girl. Make her see it's wrong. Tell her to stop doing it. You're her tutor, aren't you? You ought to be able to control one young, timid student.

'Oh, quite,' Gannadius replied angrily. 'Nothing simpler. And then she goes to the Dean and says, Doctor Gannadius saw I'd made up a victory for us in the war and told me to take it down again. They'd string me up from a lemon-tree and use me for javelin practice. No,' he went on, 'all I can think of that might work – and this is just guessing, mind – is killing her, and I can't do that. Sorry.'

Scona destroyed. Thousands dead on both sides. The Town burnt. Is there something in the life-cycle of towns and cities that makes a fiery death inevitable? Or is it more narrow than that? Say, just towns and cities I have anything to do with?

'Besides,' Gannadius went on, 'I don't think killing her would solve anything. No, if we want to head this off, it's not her we should be talking to, it's someone quite other.'

Such as?

'Such as the man behind the invasion, the man who leads the army and directs the fleet. And that's where you come in, I think.'

Me? Why?

A wild grin spread over Gannadius' face. 'You,' he said, 'because the general's name is Bardas Loredan.'

CHAPTER ELEVEN

Machaera woke up from the dream she could never remember, the one with the smoke and the killing and the man calling her name ... Gone again. She didn't mind in the least not being able to remember that one. It wasn't the sort of thing any sane person would want to carry about in her head.

She yawned and sat up. She hadn't meant to fall asleep; she still had a third of Heraud's *Responsibility and Volition* to prepare for Moderations, which were getting depressingly close. True, she was ahead of the rest of her year in Applied Science and Lesser Arts, but she'd spent so much time lately on projections and the like that she was weeks behind on her required reading, and Best Authors was the first test in Moderations. Even with all the practical work, she would have been able to cope if it wasn't for all the wretched headaches. According to the lodge Orderly, they might well be something to do with reading in a bad light, in which case she'd only be rid of them if she did her reading during the day. Maybe it would be best if she gave up the practical work for a while, at least until after Moderations. After all, Applied Science was only fifteen per cent of the marks.

She tilted the water jug towards her and saw it was empty. With a sigh she picked it up and trotted down the spiral staircase to the rainwater tank in the courtyard to fill it. She was just straightening up with a full jug in her arms when she heard a voice behind her.

'Hello,' it said. 'There you are. So where have you been hiding the last few weeks?'

She sighed. 'Hello, Cortoys,' she replied. 'I've been *working*. But you wouldn't know about that.'

'Very funny,' Cortoys Soef said. 'As it happens, I've been working very hard.'

'Really? Two-syllable words and everything?'

The young man's face became uncharacteristically serious. 'You bet,' he said. 'I've had this irresistible urge to study lately. Ever since,' he went on, 'I had my name pulled off the list for the Scona raiding party by Doc Gannadius because I was overdue on my Lesser Arts dissertation. It's that sort of thing that reminds me just what a bookish type I really am, deep down. As far as I'm concerned, you can lock me in a good library and chuck away the key.'

Machaera's eyes widened a little. 'You were supposed to be on the raiding party?' she said.

Cortoys nodded. 'Uncle Renvaut pulled some strings, arranged for me to go along as his adjutant or his page or something. Pleased as punch, I was, till Doc Gannadius interfered.' He looked away. 'They're saying the rebels have stuck Uncle Renvaut's head up on a pole on the Strangers' Quay. Apparently it's the first thing you see when you walk up the promenade towards the customs house.'

Machaera shuddered. 'It's probably not true,' she said gamely. 'Most of these rumours are nonsense. Ramo says they're deliberately put about by rebel spies, so as to worry us and make us think we'll lose the war.'

Cortoys shrugged. 'Well, if that's what they're trying to do, they're doing a pretty good job where I'm concerned. All those people, Machaera. There were friends of ours on that expedition. Hain Goche. Mihel Faim. Very nearly me, too. And Mihel was younger than me; damn it, I've been teasing him about being six weeks younger than me ever since we were in letters school together. How can someone younger than me possibly be *dead?*'

Machaera thought for a moment. 'Your cousin Hiro died when he was fifteen,' she said, and immediately wondered why she should want to say anything so mindlessly tactless; after all, reminding him of the death of a much-loved cousin wasn't going to make him feel better, was it?

'True,' Cortoys said dispassionately, 'but he was ill for six months, at least we all knew he was going to die, we had a chance to get used to the idea. But Hain and Mihel weren't ill. Damn it, Hain borrowed my Geometry notes only a few weeks ago to copy out the bits he'd missed. How the hell am I going to get them back in time for the test?'

Machaera was about to scold him for being so self-centred when he suddenly burst into tears. This was thoroughly disconcerting. Cortoys had *never* cried, not in all the years she'd known him; not even when he was just turned five and he'd fallen down the steps near the north cistern and taken all the skin off his knees. He'd wanted to cry; she'd stood there, watching him carefully as if observing an interesting astronomical phenomenon, waiting for him to cry, but he hadn't, not then and not ever. It was one of the things about him that irritated her most.

'Cortoys—' she said.

'Oh, damn all this to hell,' he muttered through a big sob. 'This is so *stupid*. And now you'll go around telling everybody—'

'Cortoys, I wouldn't.'

He shrugged. 'Doesn't matter whether you do or not,' he said, wiping his nose on his wrist. 'You know what really worries me?' he went on. 'I know, really *know*, that if I'd been there, like I was supposed to have been, I'd have been so terrified I'd either have run or else been so scared I'd have just stood there. I don't know, it's just the idea of it, being in a battle, all that anger and danger. You know what I've only just realised? I've been a coward all my life and never knew it.'

Machaera wanted very much to be somewhere else, but unfortunately she didn't have that option. Part of her hated Cortoys more than ever for choosing her to break down in front of. Part of her wanted to hug him tight and tell him it didn't matter; which was strange, because she really didn't like him, not one bit. 'Nonsense,' she said, as briskly as she could (a bit like Master Henteil when he got impatient in Metaphysics tutorials). 'You're no such thing. Everybody gets these ideas from time to time, imagines they won't be up to it when the moment comes. That doesn't make them cowards.'

Cortoys shook his head. 'From now on,' he said, staring at the fashionably pointed toes of his shoes, 'I'm going to make damned certain the situation never arises. And I don't care what anybody says; the further away I stay from the fighting, the happier I'll be.'

Machaera grinned in spite of herself. 'You could start a new faction. The Don't-Want-to-Fight faction. It'd be original, at any rate. I'm absolutely positive nobody's thought of *that* one before.'

'I'd be famous,' Cortoys answered, looking up at her with a tearful smile. 'The first all-new faction in Shastel for fifty years.'

'Doing your bit for the Soef family name,' Machaera added.

'Oh, quite,' Cortoys replied. 'Uncle Renvaut would have been so proud.'

Gorgas Loredan slipped off his horse and handed the reins to the sergeant of his escort. 'You lot had better make yourselves scarce,' he said in a low voice. 'Stay in earshot just in case I do need you for anything, but I don't think that's very likely.'

He approached the long barn from its blind side, stopping every now and then to look and listen, like an archer walking up a rabbit in long grass, just before the first cut of hay. He couldn't hear anything that suggested activity; no smooth *sshk* of plane-blade on wood, no sounds of sawing or rasping, no voices. He'd assumed, reasonably enough, that Bardas would be in his work-shop. After all, he was an artisan with a living to earn, so while the light was still good he ought to be at his place of work. That's where working men are during the day.

Unless he's out somewhere chopping down trees. Or dead. Or scared stiff by the raiders and run off into the hills somewhere. He frowned at this last speculation; men who have commanded armies and made their living as professional swordfighters don't scamper away into the bushes like bunnies at the first sight of a halberdier's greatcoat. *All right, then, he's out delivering, or buying materials. Or shopping, even.*

He walked slowly round the corner of the long barn into the yard and paused for a moment to look round. No signs of life anywhere, and he didn't have that nebulous but unmistakable feeling of being watched. Nobody home, his instincts told him, but there are several words to describe people who rely on their instincts in situations of this sort, most of them synonyms for 'dead'. Unlikely, of course, that Bardas would plop an arrow between his shoulders or jump out from behind the water-butt with a sword in his hand, but the whole object of the exercise was to stalk the quarry, not flush it out; the more notice he gave his brother of his arrival, the smaller his chances of scooping him up and taking him back to Town. Gorgas allowed himself a little smile, thinking back to the days when he and his brothers were regularly landed with the loathsome and near-impossible chore of rounding up the ducks off the pond, stuffing them in great big wicker baskets and bringing them back to the long poultry-shed. There are few things quicker moving or less predictable than a startled duck, and the fun usually began when there were only ten or so left. Gorgas had never worked so hard or sweated so much before or since.

Three stone steps up to the barn door, and he put his

head cautiously round the frame. The workshop was dark, shutters drawn. In theory, a man could hide behind the stacks of felled, trimmed timber, or behind the clay-pipe-and-brick contraption in the corner (Gorgas recognised it as a steamer, for steaming the limbs of a bow into a recurve; his father had tried to build one once and failed), but Gorgas only made a cursory inspection. At this range, he was prepared to go with his instincts. If Bardas was here he'd know it, and he wasn't.

Gorgas sighed and sat down for a moment on the bench. *Scruffy*, he noted. *Tools left lying about, shavings ankle-deep on the floorboards, whatever happened to Tidiness is the Mother of Efficiency?* He picked up a drawknife and held it up to the light. There were spots of rust like raindrops already starting to form on the polished blade. Father would have had a fit.

He put the drawknife carefully back where he'd found it and brushed away a little pile of shavings, resisting the urge to sneeze. There was a three-quarters-finished bow in the vice, a straight, flat self-bow intended for military use. Gorgas ran a finger along the belly and was impressed by the quality of the finish. Someone had been to a lot of trouble to get it feeling so smooth and glass-like. Why? Where was the point in exceeding the level of quality prescribed by the standard military specification? No one would ever notice or appreciate it – *correction, brother; nobody but you and me. Well, either you've shrivelled down into a perfectionist in your old age, or you've got an apprentice with not enough work to keep him fully occupied. Bad business, either way. Just as well you've got a brother who's in charge of military procurement who makes sure you get paid twice the going rate, or you'd never have lasted as long as you have.* Gorgas grinned at the thought of his brother's naïvety; no question but that Bardas hadn't yet realised that he was being secretly subsidised; he'd have a fit if he knew. A fine man, Bardas Lordan, but just a little bit unworldly.

He left the barn, closing the door behind him, and

crossed the yard to the house. That proved to be empty as well; not just of people, but of pretty well everything. It reminded Gorgas of his brother's sparse, horrible apartment in one of the 'island' blocks in Perimadeia. Obviously, Bardas had some sort of hang-up about accumulating possessions, which was a new development since they were children, but understandable in the light of what had happened in between. Still, he reflected as he surveyed the main room, it takes a special skill to be sparse and scruffy at the same time.

He poked about for a while until he found what he was looking for – a cloth bundle tied up with hemp cord and shoved under the mattress, containing a rare and extremely valuable Guelan broadsword. No chance whatsoever that Bardas would go away for good and leave that behind. Quite apart from its monetary worth, it was one of the finest swords ever made and no fencer who'd once owned such a thing could possibly bear to be parted from it by choice. If the sword was still here, Bardas would be back. Gorgas sat in the solitary and uncomfortable chair – *for a bowyer, brother, you're a piss-poor carpenter* – and settled down to wait.

What with one thing and another, Venart didn't really feel in the mood for conducting business. Still, he didn't have much choice; he had money to pay out and collect, loading to supervise, charter-parties and bills of lading to read through, provisions and chandlery to buy before he could leave Scona, and if he didn't do it, it wasn't going to get done.

It's one of the immutable laws of trading life that the busier a man is and the less time he has, the more complicated every simple thing becomes. The people who owed him money weren't at home; if he was quick he might just catch them at the Quay, or at the Golden Square, or on their way back from the Bank. His creditors, on the other hand, had no trouble at all in finding him, and he didn't seem to be able to make them

248 *The Belly of the Bow*

understand that the longer they kept him hanging about talking, the longer it would be before he'd be able to collect his money and pay them. Then he couldn't find any porters to load his cargo, and when he finally managed to round up a gang of dead-beats and loafers who belonged to the necessary guilds, he arrived at the customs house to find that the portmaster was away for the rest of the morning and might be back later, or not, depending on how things went generally. Then there was a mistake in the cargo manifest that meant the whole thing had to be written out again (but the clerk who'd done it wasn't in his office, and all the other clerks in Scona Town were all apparently too busy to take on a rush job), the provisioners were clean out of raisins, and the price of four-ply sailmaker's twine had somehow managed to shoot up overnight from three quarters a roll to ten. All in all, for a town that apparently didn't want him, it was making it very hard indeed for him to leave.

'Wool grease,' the last chandler in town muttered, stroking his chin thoughtfully. 'Wool grease. I might have some. There's not a lot of call for it.'

Venart waited long enough to count to ten. 'Then would you mind looking for it?' he suggested. 'I need two gallons, minimum. I'll take three if you've got it.'

The chandler shrugged. 'If I've got any, it'll be in the cellar,' he replied, and Venart couldn't tell from his tone of voice whether this was just a statement of fact or the chandler's roundabout way of saying that the cellar was blocked off or he didn't dare go in there because of the spiders.

'Would you mind going down into the cellar and looking, please?' Venart said.

'I could do,' the chandler conceded. 'Can you come back tomorrow, say about midday?'

Venart released a sigh that had been building up inside him for the last twenty minutes. 'It's all right,' he said, 'I'll try somewhere else.' He turned to go, but just as he was about to pass through the door, the chandler said, 'Wait there, I won't be long,' and disappeared, apparently straight down through a hole in the floorboards.

Half an hour later he came back empty handed. 'I've got olive butter,' he said, in a slightly awed voice, 'barrels and barrels of it. You can have as much of that as you like.'

Venart explained that he needed wool grease to proof his hull against shipworm, and olive butter would be not just useless but counter-productive. 'You sure you haven't got any?' he asked.

'I might have some in the roof,' the chandler replied.

Venart drew in a deep breath; but before he could say anything, he heard a familiar voice behind him.

'I can lend you some if you like,' said Athli. 'You can pay me back when I get home.'

For the first time in several days, Venart felt relatively happy. 'That's wonderful,' he said. 'What are you doing here?' he added.

'You're looking at the Zeuxis Commercial Bank,' Athli replied, smiling. 'All five foot three of it. Come on, I'll get you that wool grease. And you look like you could use a drink.'

'I didn't know your other name was Zeuxis,' Venart admitted as they walked together towards the Quay. 'Come to think of it, it never occurred to me to ask.'

Athli shrugged. 'I don't suppose the topic ever came up,' she said. 'You look harassed. Things not going well?'

Venart pulled a face. 'You could say that,' he said. 'But don't get me started on that subject. What's all this about a bank, then?'

'I've got the Island agency for Shastel,' Athli replied. 'Clinched it just the other day, in fact. And, since I was passing, I thought I'd stop off on Scona and see what the soft-furnishing market's like here. To tell you the truth, I don't reckon much to it. These people strike me as a miserable lot.'

Venart frowned. 'I don't know if you've noticed,' he

said, 'but there's something of a war going on between Scona and Shastel. I'm not sure that makes you being here such a terribly good idea.'

Athli shrugged. 'Nobody seems to mind,' she replied. 'As far as I can tell it doesn't seem to work like that. Actually, if we're going to be pedantic about it, there isn't actually a war, just a series of unfortunate incidents that are being actively reviewed by representatives of both parties in the hope of reaching a meaningful settlement in the short to medium term. Which,' she added, 'is just a way of saying "war" in gibberish, but it does open up interesting possibilities for an imaginative trader.'

Venart looked at her. 'Does it?'

'Oh, yes. Think about it, Ven. Without imaginative traders, with a war going on, how are they supposed to do business with each other?'

'I didn't think they wanted to.'

Athli grinned. 'It's hardly a matter of choice. There's at least five big merchant companies on Scona who're heavily involved in joint ventures with Shastel houses, and the Faims – that's one of the leading Poor families – have most of their working capital invested on Scona.'

'That's crazy,' Venart objected.

'True,' Athli agreed. 'But Niessa Loredan pays a better rate of interest. It's one of the things I like about this part of the world,' she added. 'They don't let war get in the way of sound commercial propositions.'

Venart couldn't think of anything to say to that, and while he was recovering Athli asked after Vetriz. He closed his eyes for a moment. One good thing about the endless aggravations of doing business on Scona was that they could be made to occupy his full attention and keep his mind off other things.

'She's in trouble,' he said. 'Very bad trouble.'

'Oh.' Athli stopped walking. 'What kind of trouble?'

Venart made a despairing gesture. 'That's the worst part of it, almost. I don't *know*. As far as I can tell, it's something to do with Patriarch Alexius, magic and

Colonel Loredan. But as for trying to make sense of it all—'

'Colonel Loredan,' Athli interrupted. 'You mean Gorgas Loredan.'

'No, Bardas. You know, *your* Bardas. Him you used to work for. If you remember, he's the Director's brother, but they don't get on. It's all mixed up with some stuff about Perimadeia, but I couldn't follow it.'

'What's Bardas Loredan got to do with it?' Athli asked quietly.

'Like I said,' Venart replied, 'it all went way above my head. At first, it looked like Triz and I had been arrested; then it seemed the Director wanted her help with something, and then Triz said it was all right, she wanted to stay and do whatever it is the Director wants her to. And here I am, worried out of my head about her – are you listening?'

'What? Yes, of course I'm listening. Look, let's get that drink and you can tell me all about it, right from the beginning. You never know, I might be able to help.'

Venart thought for a moment. 'All right,' he said. 'My mind's a complete blank, I'm afraid, so if you can suggest something, or make sense of what's going on, that'd be wonderful. Gods, I wish we'd never come here,' he added savagely. 'This is the most awful place I've ever been in my entire life. If only we can get away and make it safely back to the Island—'

'Yes,' Athli said impatiently, 'all *right*. Look, there's a wine shop on the corner, we'll go there. And for pity's sake, pull yourself together and start again at the *beginning*.'

'Six quarters,' the old man repeated. 'Take it or leave it.'

Bardas Loredan looked at the eel, then at the old man, then back at the eel. Pare off the man's limbs and there'd be a strong resemblance. 'Thanks,' he said, 'but on balance I think I'd rather starve. You can't get food poisoning from starvation.'

The old man blinked. 'Suit yourself,' he said. 'There's nothing else.'

'That's crazy,' Bardas replied. 'A bunch of Shastel soldiers roam about the island for a couple of days and smash up some villages, and suddenly there's nothing to eat on the whole of Scona?'

'Six quarters. Take it or leave it.'

'Four.'

The old man didn't say anything. He had a knack of sitting perfectly still, like a lizard.

'Five,' Bardas said. 'And that's just because if I don't buy it you might eat it yourself, and I don't want your death on my conscience.'

'Six quarters. Take it—'

'Oh, for gods' sakes.' Bardas fumbled in his pocket and produced the money. The old man tucked the eel under the crook of his knee while he held the coins up to the light. Five of them he reluctantly passed after a thorough inspection. The sixth he laid on a flat stone beside him, fished a chisel and a small hammer out of his pocket and cut into the coin on the edge of the rim. Then he held it up again and moved it about in the sunlight until the nick he'd just cut caught the light and sparkled. He clicked his tongue and handed it back.

'Plated,' he said.

Bardas looked for himself. 'You're right,' he said. 'How the hell did you spot that?'

The old man looked at him. Bardas produced another coin, which passed muster. The old man lifted his knee and handed over the eel.

'Pleasure doing business with you,' he croaked.

Bardas found the boy, who was sitting in the village square beside the well, eating an apple. 'Where did you get that?' he asked.

'Old woman gave it to me,' the boy replied with his mouth full. 'Want some?'

'What? Oh, no, you carry on,' Bardas said, looking wistfully at the apple. 'Never could stand the things.

Give me heartburn. Here's supper, look.'

The boy took one look at the eel and backed away a
little. 'I'm not eating that,' he said. 'It's gross.'

'Don't be stupid, it's a perfectly good eel. Delicacy where
I come from.'

'Bet you're glad you left, then.'

'It's this,' Bardas said with his last drop of patience, 'or
I give you a bow and one arrow and you can go bunny-
bashing. Your choice. No obligation.'

The boy looked at the eel and swallowed. 'It might be
all right,' he said, 'with some sage and chives and a lot of
pepper.'

'No sage. No chives. Certainly no pepper. If you'd
rather have rabbit,' he added, 'again,' he stressed, 'then be
my guest. We haven't had it stewed yet, have we?'

'Day before yesterday,' the boy replied sullenly. 'All
right, we'll have your rotten eel. But tomorrow we go into
Town and buy some bread, all right?'

Bardas shook his head. 'No. I've told you, I don't like it
there. We'll try up around Seusa, there's bound to be food
out that way. Remember the time we made a delivery up
there and had those doughnuts?'

The boy studied him carefully. 'Why don't you want to
go to Scona?' he said. 'It's much nearer than Seusa and
there really is food there. And we won't be ripped off like
we're being in the villages.'

'I don't like it there,' Bardas repeated.

'Why not?'

'Because. Now jump in the cart and let's go home
before it gets dark.'

Bardas was being over-optimistic. By the time they
got back it was pitch black and starless, and the boy had
to walk in front of the cart with a lantern for the last two
miles of the journey. When they reached the top of the
lane, the boy stopped dead.

'What's the matter?'

'There's a light in the house,' the boy called back.

Bardas thought for a moment, then jumped down and

handed the reins to the boy. 'Wait here,' he said. 'If you see anyone coming who isn't me, run for it back to that old tower we were in and wait there a day.' He reached in his pocket and pulled out a purse. 'Don't lose this, for gods' sakes. There's enough there to buy a passage to the Island. Find a woman called Athli Zeuxis and say I sent you. All right?'

The boy stared at him, his eyes wide with terror. 'What's happening?' he said. 'If it's something bad, why don't we both just go away and hide till they've gone?'

Bardas shrugged. 'You remember my brother sent some men to round us up and bring us in?' he said.

The boy nodded. 'You bashed them,' he said.

'That's right. Well, figure it out for yourself. Whoever that is waiting for us down there, he doesn't seem bothered about letting us know he's here. I think that rules out thieves, or the odd stray halberdier. I don't think it's more of my brother's soldiers, for the same reason. So, who else is left? A big party of halberdiers, possibly; and if so, I'll see the sentries and come right back. But I don't think so. If they're wandering about openly and lighting fires, we'd have heard about them by now, with all the travelling round we've been doing. I think I know who that is.'

'Your brother?'

Bardas nodded. 'Or it could be someone completely harmless, I don't know. Anyway, you wait here, and remember – Athli Zeuxis, on the Island. You got that?'

'Yes,' the boy replied. 'Can't I come with you?'

'No. Stay here. Pay attention.' He reached into the cart and took out the short heavily recurved ninety-pounder and the quiver of short reed arrows, looked at them and put them back. 'The hell with it,' he said, 'I can't shoot straight in broad daylight, let alone the pitch dark. Serves me right, I suppose.'

He walked quietly along the side of the barn as far as the woodshed. Fortunately, he knew everything there was to know about the woodshed door, including the precise way to lift it to stop the hinge squeaking. It was impossible to see anything in there, but he was able to find what he was looking for by feel: a hatchet-head fitted to a felling-axe handle, hanging from a strap from a hook in the centre beam. It was a weapon in the way rabbit was food; a significant improvement on nothing at all.

Why he felt so angry he didn't know. If it was Gorgas in there, he was glad he'd had some warning. The way he was feeling right now, he'd have gone for him straight away, without even thinking about it, and since Gorgas was most probably better armed than he was, that would have been a bad mistake. The advance notice hadn't changed how he felt; time to think about it had given him an opportunity to choose some semblance of a weapon, but it hadn't cooled his temper. And that was odd. He'd spent so many years killing for money that he couldn't imagine himself ever killing for free again. He hadn't felt this way when he first came to Scona and was confronted with Gorgas and Niessa. He'd even managed to be civil to them both while making it clear that he wanted to be as far away from them as the cramped geography of the island would permit. He hadn't enjoyed the interview and it had been hard work being in the same place with them, but he hadn't felt this terrific urge to see their blood.

Since then, nothing in particular had happened. They'd left him alone, just as he'd asked. Once he'd turned away a few messengers with gifts of money and clothes and the like, Gorgas had taken the hint and stopped trying. Recently Bardas had been able to go days at a time without feeling their presence in this enclosed space they owned. He'd worked hard, very hard, at shutting them out of his mind; and although he knew it was all entirely artificial, this pretence that he was a simple artisan making a satisfactory living by honest toil, that his bows were of such exceptional quality that the procurement officers paid a premium for them and took whatever he could produce, nevertheless it was an illusion that he believed he could maintain for a while yet (as his mind slowly took a set, like a bow left strung and put away, until the wood forgets the tension in the back and the belly and follows the string in a permanent bend), perhaps even indefinitely. He wondered about the physics of it, and considered the old saying in his trade that a bow at full draw is nine-tenths broken. He concluded that all he wanted to do now was break, and the hell with everything; but why this should be he couldn't quite grasp. Perhaps it was nothing more than this heavy-handed reminder of how shallow the illusion was, as simple as that; the act of walking into his home and lighting a fire. In Perimadeia, where houses quite often went without an owner (because someone had died childless and without family, or had gone abroad and not come back) it was the law that ownership was asserted by treating the property in some way as if one owned it – moving in furniture, whitewashing the walls, cleaning the curtains or even something as simple and ordinary as lighting a fire in the hearth. He'd have taken it without a word from a couple of stray Shastel halberdiers, even if they'd burnt the place down, because they'd have been passing through and wouldn't have been asserting ownership. Gorgas lighting a fire in his grate was another matter entirely; that made it a legal issue, and he'd spent long enough in the lawcourts of the City to know what to do about that.

Or it could just be a couple of burglars. Gods, I hope so.

He knew which shutter-bolt was loose, fastened into rotten timber; the axe-handle between shutter and window-frame was a lever, and a gentle but insistent application of pressure was enough to rip the bolts through the crumbling wood without making a noise. *I'd have made a good burglar myself; here I am, breaking in. Already I'm treating it as another man's house.* Once he'd got the shutter loose he paused and counted to twenty before slowly swinging it open, then another twenty before he carefully stepped though and into the pitch-dark back pantry. For all his care and attention to detail, he'd forgotten something; he remembered it just in time, when something dry and textured like skin batted him gently in the face. Two of those damned ubiquitous rabbits, skinned and hung to drain out the blood into a pudding-bowl placed under them on the flagstones; he let his breath out slowly, calmed himself down, and took a moment to remember exactly where the door-latch was, and where he'd put the bowls. Treading rabbit-blood footprints through his own house (*yes, my house, damn it*) would only serve to add another level of aggravation.

Another count of twenty after he opened the door an inch or so. The pale orange light was coming from the main hearth, no question about that. He was starting to feel horribly uncomfortable, as if the house had betrayed him somehow; as if it had been Gorgas' paid spy ever since he first came here, and he'd only just realised it. He felt as if he was sneaking up on his wife and her lover, listening to them as he edged down the dark passageway. No pretence of trying to make himself calm down, not now that he could practically smell his brother here, like unfamiliar hair-oil on a pillow. All he could feel was the urgent physical need to swing the little axe, to split bone like splitting a newly felled tree (*every tree will split if only you know where to hit, where to find the fault-line*); it was something he couldn't put away in his mind, insistent and distasteful like a full bladder or an upset stomach, something he'd rather not do but absolutely had to. *And then we'll be all square*, he reflected, *I'll finally be on the same level as him, though perhaps without his minor plea of expediency. Or he'll get me and be that much nearer the full set. Whatever. The outcome really doesn't bother me; it's getting it over with that matters.*

Indeed. He relaxed, stood up straight, took a deep breath. No earthly reason why he should skulk about in his own house. He put his left hand against the dividing door and pushed.

Gorgas was sitting on a stool in front of the fire, with his back to him; a pair of broad shoulders hunched a little and the back of a bald head. He turned round and stood up in the same movement – there had always been a sort of grace about the way Gorgas moved; he'd never been clumsy or awkward, even as a boy – and stepped a little to one side, so that the light of the fire shone in his face.

'Hello,' he said. 'I didn't hear you come in.'

'Gorgas,' Bardas said.

'I was passing,' Gorgas went on. 'I lit the fire, I hope you don't mind.'

Up till then, the axe in his hand had felt like an extension of his arm; now it was as if he'd been lying on it and it had gone to sleep. He could sense it was there, but he couldn't feel it. He looked at his brother and said nothing.

'I hope I didn't startle you,' Gorgas went on. 'I guess it's not a good time to be lurking about in someone else's house, though I'm pretty sure we got all of them. Even if there were one or two we didn't get, I wouldn't give much for their chances of getting this far.'

Bardas narrowed his eyes, puzzled, and then realised his brother was talking about survivors of the raiding party. He heard himself say that he'd run into a stray halberdier on the road; but that was some time ago.

'Oh,' Gorgas said. 'Well, that's one less to worry about, I suppose.'

There was something in the way he said it, suggesting that if Bardas Loredan met a man on the road, he'd kill him, because that's what he does, of course. Carpenters shape wood, peat-cutters cut peat, charcoal-burners make charcoal, Bardas Loredan kills people. Did any of them get away? Not to worry. It'll give Bardas something to do, now that the evenings are drawing out.

'Isn't that apprentice of yours with you? Damn it, I can't remember his name. He's all right, is he?'

'He's fine,' Bardas replied.

Gorgas nodded. 'I gather he was the boy who gave the alarm at Briora. He did well.'

One step across the floor, slightly to the left to avoid tripping over the footstool; a two-handed feint to the right to draw his guard, in case he has time to draw his sword, then let go with the left hand and swing hard with the right for a point of impact just above the ear. He'd taught that as a basic gambit when he was running his fencing school; simple and fairly obvious, but in all the thousands of years that men have spent killing each other, nobody's yet come up with a sure way to defend against it. Against an unarmed man, of course, it's virtually satisfaction guaranteed, like the easy shot at a sitting rabbit from fifteen yards, where all the difficulty and skill is in the stalk, the actual loosing of the arrow being pretty much a foregone conclusion. Against an unarmed man who happens to be your brother and who's trying to make conversation, no possibility of failure whatsoever.

'What do you want, Gorgas?' Bardas asked.

His brother grinned sheepishly. 'This is going to sound bad,' he said, 'and I won't insult you by trying to make it sound otherwise. Niessa told me to bring you back to Scona Town.'

'I see.'

'Actually,' Gorgas went on, 'she's got a point. The war's escalating, getting out of hand. You're our brother, you live out here alone on the coast, a ship could easily slip in, they could grab you and be away before we could do anything. I'd never forgive myself—'

Bardas opened his mouth to say something, but thought better of it.

'I know you don't want to come to Scona,' Gorgas went on. 'Gods know, I can understand why. Niessa wants you safe, where she knows where you are. It wouldn't be for ever; just till things calm down and this mess with Shastel sorts itself out. After all, this is our mess, it's up to us to solve it without you getting hurt. We think we can see a way to deal with it without it turning into a full-scale war – nobody wants that, it'd be stupid, crazy. Then you could come back here, carry on as you are now—'

'I'm not going to Scona,' Bardas said.

Gorgas took a deep breath and sat down. 'I knew you'd say that,' he said. 'Damn it, you're my brother, I'm not going to bring you in on a rope like a stray calf. All right, here's what we'll do. There's a ship from the Island in port; get on it, go where you like, I don't care where. Just so long as you go somewhere where the Foundation won't find you easily. And your apprentice, of course; and don't worry about money or anything like that, we can sort something out—'

'You're joking,' Bardas said. He felt as if the sky had fallen all around him, and there was nothing between him and the stars. 'She'll kill you,' he said, in a voice that came from somewhere around twenty years ago.

Gorgas shrugged. 'I can handle Niessa when I have to,' he replied. 'The trick lies in not doing it too often. The hell with her, little brother. Is it what you want, or isn't it?'

'You know I never wanted to come here,' Bardas said, the words spilling out like a leak in a wineskin.

Gorgas nodded. 'That was us being selfish,' he said. 'I suppose we both thought that somehow we could make things up to you, put everything right again.' He made a wide gesture with his hands. 'As if. Whatever we do always seems to screw things up even more, so maybe the only thing that might help is to stop trying. I don't know. At least we should stop thinking about what we want.'

Bardas couldn't think of anything to say. He sat down on the edge of the table and looked at Gorgas; with his back to the fire, in control, as if he was in his own house. He let the axe slip out of his hand.

The halberdier yawned. After everything he'd been through – the march up from the sea, the fighting in the villages, being holed up in that awful place with the leaky roof, and then the unexpected attack and the fire and the narrowness of his escape – more than anything else he wanted to go to sleep, if sleep was actually possible in this horrible country.

Just Ramo and himself, the only survivors. There could be no possible reason why they'd made it and nobody else had, it could only be something random, meaningless. Now, as if to make fun of them, everything seemed to be going their way. They'd stumbled on this house, nicely off the beaten track, with nobody home; a few scraps of cold roast rabbit and some flat beer on the table in the main room; a comfortable hayloft to sleep in, where he'd be relatively safe until such time as he and Ramo felt strong enough and brave enough to go and look for someone to surrender to. He thought of his fellow survivor, pacing up and down outside on sentry-duty (Ramo had insisted on setting a watch, just like the real army. Fair enough; if he wanted to play sentry instead of getting some sleep, good luck to him).

He stared with painful, gritty eyes into a patchy red sunrise. Before he'd been accepted into the armed forces of the Foundation he'd been the son of a hectemore, making some sort of a living off sixty or so acres of hill-side and bog in the far west of the Shastel peninsula. The hayloft had always been a good place to hide, on a hot day when there was work to be done, or when his father was in a foul mood. It's a basic rule of life that all haylofts are virtually identical, and this one had the same smells and sounds as the one he'd taken refuge in not so many years ago. So, although he was weary and aggrieved and painfully hungry, for the first time in a long while at least he felt reasonably safe.

Which was a mistake on his part; because, as he leant his halberd against the piled stooks and sat back with his hands behind his head, the noise he'd taken for a mouse scuttling about somewhere above his head suddenly got louder. He almost had time to grab his halberd, but not quite. A big man dropped down from the top of the stacked hay, landed beside him, grabbed his halberd just as his fingertips brushed the shaft, and stuck the spike into his windpipe.

Bardas Loredan twisted the blade to free it and pulled it out. Then he dropped down to a crouch and listened. But there was nothing to hear, and he allowed himself the luxury of a moment's rest. He rolled the body along the stack, out of sight of the doorway, pulled off the dead man's coat and draped it round his shoulders, then sat down where he'd been sitting, in case anybody happened to look that way. His knees ached, as well they might after two hours of crouching in the back of his own hayloft, listening to the sentry's tuneless humming and waiting for first light.

One thing he'd had plenty of was time to think, and he'd decided on what he considered the most sensible course of action. He looked down at the halberd, wondering whether he'd have to fight anybody else before he got clear. He had no idea how many of them there were; presumably they were the survivors of the raiding party, but even that was just supposition on his part. If they'd done the job properly they'd have put a man up by the gate, maybe a patrol round the boundary wall. It'd be extremely bad luck if they'd managed to find the hole in the back hedge, so he could slip out through that and almost immediately be on the road down to Briora. But that would mean crossing the yard and walking straight past the workshop window, which would be asking for trouble. If he simply dropped down from here and followed the line of the barn up as far as the gate, he stood a better than average chance of not being seen until he was right on top of the gate sentry, who ought not to know what hit him. He felt the weight of the halberd, and stacked it against the hay; he'd be better off barehanded than trying to do any good with an overgrown staffhook.

He swung his legs out through the hayloft door, braced his hands on the floorboards and slid himself

forward, landing quite comfortably on the soft grass. As
he'd hoped, there was nobody about, and he walked
fairly slowly and calmly up to the gate. Sure enough
there was a sentry, and sure enough the sentry was leaning on the gate looking down the lane, where it was
reasonable to expect any trouble to come from. He'd
even taken his helmet off, just to make Loredan's life a
little easier. Just before he reached him, Loredan stooped
and picked up the stone he used for propping the gate
open. It was the perfect size and shape for the job; there
was a crunch, like the sound you make when you put
your foot through thick ice, and the sentry slumped
forward over the gate, then slid backwards and sprawled
on the ground. Loredan used his head to give himself a
leg-up over the gate.

Well, that was easy; much easier than getting out of
the City. Maybe it just seems easier after all the practice
I've had. He walked briskly down the lane without looking back and kept going until he reached the main road,
where there was an old mortgage-stone sticking out of
the hedge. He sat down on that and took a deep breath.
He wasn't shaking or shivering. He felt fine.

Quick check; alive and walking, not cut about at all, no
broken ribs or head injuries. Can't complain about that,
now can you? There's a couple of dead men back there
who'd give their right arms to be in your position. He
stood up and started to walk down the road, for all the
world as if he was off to the village to buy fish. And
everything I am is coming with me, he thought. Like the
last time, I suppose, except I've been spared a swim in
cold water, and last time I ended up coming here. Won't
make that mistake again.

As he walked, he considered whether it was a true
analogy. After all, it was absolutely certain that Gorgas
and the Scona army would sooner or later come back, to
starve or slash the survivors out of his house. If they
chose the latter course, then it was fairly certain there'd
be nothing to come back to; they'd set fire to the thatch

and shoot them down as they came scampering out, like rabbits flushed out of a burry. But if they surrendered peacefully, there might not be too much damage done - except that then he'd have to go and be polite to his brother if he wanted his house back, and that was more effort than anything was worth. If he managed to find the boy, he could have the place, although he hadn't seen or heard anything of him since Gorgas' visit; either he'd got himself killed by straggling halberdiers, or he'd taken off to Town and caught a ship to the Island (as I told him to, being a melodramatic idiot. Oh, well.) It'd be bad if he'd got himself killed, after escaping from the City and the annihilation of all his family; for a while there, Bardas had fooled himself into thinking that there was some purpose behind his survival, that all the effort and luck expended on bringing him here must mean something. Truth is, I didn't escape at all the last time, because I came here.

He stopped for a moment and looked back. Leaving home, saying goodbye for the last time, wasn't something the Loredan family had ever done particularly well; their exits tended to be hurried, botched affairs, framed by fire and the sword and the imminent danger of getting caught. He crouched down on his heels, tucked into the hedge to disguise his outline, and tried to think of some way of doing it properly, but he lacked any sort of frame of reference and gave up. For him, of course, leaving home always seemed to carry with it unpleasant associations of his brother Gorgas; that first departure from the Mesoge, the strange and sudden appearances of Gorgas Loredan in the last night in Perimadeia, and now this pantomime in a dripping hedge. There seemed to be no end to the places he could render uninhabitable for himself, but always there Gorgas seemed to be, rolling up like the constable on market day to move him along.

I should have killed him while I had the chance.

Bardas listened to the echo of that sentiment in his mind, and grinned. It was true, he'd come very close, but that wasn't the same thing as actually performing the irrevocable act. Home had been Gorgas' fault, no doubt about that; Gorgas had turned him out of the Mesoge as surely as if he'd been the landlord's bailiff, and as a direct result of that, he'd gone to war on the plainspeople with his Uncle Maxen. But there the chain was broken. He could blame Gorgas for putting him there, but not for what he'd done with his own hands, or for the consequences of those irrevocable actions. Whatever else he might have done, Gorgas hadn't performed the act that burnt down Perimadeia. It'd be wrong, wrong on a Gorgas Loredan level of malfeasance, to punish Gorgas for something he'd done himself.

The chain was broken; but here he was, nevertheless. It was a part of it that he couldn't make fit, as if a piece was missing or a page had dropped out. And yes, here he was.

Well, that was something he could alter. He cleared his mind, as if he was putting away his tools at the end of a long day, and considered where he should go next.

There were, of course, certain practical matters to be considered. Assuming he wanted to get off Scona, he'd need to find a ship and some way of paying for his passage. Since the only place where merchant ships put in was Scona Town, it'd mean having to go there, hang around until he found some way of getting money, or a ship's captain who'd let him work his passage (remote chance, since it'd be obvious to anyone he didn't know the first thing about working a ship), or a merchant who'd give him a job and take him back home with him. The third option seemed the likeliest bet; he knew at least two marketable trades, if only he could convince a trader of that with no examples of his work to show, no references or tools of the trade. It was his likeliest bet, but not very likely. Nevertheless, he welcomed the difficulty. Nothing like a horrendously difficult task and an empty stomach to take one's mind off other things.

It's more than that, though; I feel positively cheerful,

as if it were the first day of a month's leave. It's because this is making me leave Scona, which is what I've been wanting to do ever since I got here. This is just an excuse. Well, at least it's a good excuse.

The sun was well up now, and he decided to leave the main road. There was a chance that the Scona army would be bustling down this way fairly soon, and he had no desire to meet them. He took a track he knew – little more than the bed of a stream, now in spate and slippery under the soles of his badly worn boots – that bypassed Briora and brought him out on the cart-track between Ustel and the Town. It was a steep climb, rather more exertion than he'd have chosen after no sleep in a hayloft; but by the time he'd slipped and scrambled along it for about an hour, he was glad he'd chosen it, because as he pulled himself up a steep rise and skidded down the other side, he nearly trod on the dead body of a man, a Shastel soldier with an arrow in his back. He prised the body out of the mud and turned it over; a straggler from one of the various comings and goings there'd been over the last few days, not an ordinary halberdier but an officer, wearing a fine mailshirt and a belt with a gold buckle. There was a ring on one of the man's fingers with a stone in it, and underneath where the man had fallen, nearly submerged in the mud, Loredan found a good-quality sword with a decorated hilt, worth thirty quarters of anybody's money. He had no less than twenty quarters cash in his purse, and his boots were nearly new and, once padded with a few strips of cloth, a passable fit.

He stripped off the mailshirt and packed it up in the dead man's satchel, which turned out to contain half a loaf of bread, an inch of sausage and an onion. Loredan sat down beside his benefactor and solemnly thanked him, with his mouth full, as he did some mental arithmetic – thirty quarters for the sword, twenty cash, say thirty for the mailshirt since it's damaged, ten more for the ring, another ten for the belt-buckle makes a hundred, and he was home and dry, as good as on board ship, not counting another three for the satchel and one for his old boots, maybe even one for the arrow if the blade's not bent; then he went back over the body in case there was anything he'd missed. The padded jacket under the mailshirt (not military issue) was still perfectly service-able and the shirt was better than his own, despite the blood and the hole in the back, so he had them. He pulled off the trousers and held them up; they were torn at the knee and covered in mud, and a Shastel greatcoat probably wasn't a sensible thing to wear in the streets of Scona Town, but in the coat pockets he found a small folding knife and a book – Pacellus on Ethical Theory. The owner's name was scrawled on the flyleaf – Renvaut Soef, whoever he'd been before he became an exploit-able resource. The book was crumpled and illegible in places where rain and blood had got at it, but there was space for it in the satchel, so he took that too. In fact, he realised as he left the naked body behind him, virtually nothing was wasted except the meat.

Machaera woke up with a scream, and opened her eyes.

The dream started to fade, and she was glad to see the back of it; there had been fighting, and men being tram-pled in the mud; her cousin Remo, thin and dirty, leaning against a gate with a halberd couched in his arms, a burning house with men running out and then dropping to the ground, a sky full of arrows hanging in the air and then falling towards her, a man stripping a corpse and many other unpleasant things she didn't want to think about. She got out of bed quickly, as if she was afraid some of the horrible things might still be lurking under the pillow, and splashed cold water from the jug onto her face. That seemed to help; her mind was clearing, and when she looked out of the window she saw that the sun was already up. She sighed; twice in a row now she'd overslept and missed breakfast.

She scrambled into a gown and one sandal; the other one had vanished, and it took her several minutes to run it to ground behind the book-press. She was just fumbling with the straps when the bell went – definitely no breakfast, and only a minute or so to get down the stairs, across the courtyard, up the stairs of the Old Library and into the small lecture hall. She darted out and slammed the door behind her, realised she'd forgotten her wax tablets, went back for them, remembered to check for the stylus, found it wasn't in the loop on the back of the tablets, hunted frantically for it, found it under the bed and this time made it down the stairs and into the yard, just in time to collide with the junior warden who was staggering along under a heaped armful of books, all of which inevitably ended up on the ground. Without daring to look him in the eye, she knelt down and started scooping them up and shovelling them back into his arms. When she'd gathered up the last errant scroll, she embarked on her apology, but the junior warden (who was eighty-two, as opposed to the senior warden, who was forty-one) scowled at her and said, 'What?' She decided to cut her losses and get out of the way as quickly as she could, before she did any more damage.

There wasn't any point going to the lecture hall now; once the lecture started the door was bolted and nobody was allowed in. Nobody knew why this was done, though the favourite explanation was that, years ago, people who weren't members of the Foundation used to sneak in once the lecture was under way and sit at the back, learning things they weren't allowed to know. Machaera started to walk back to her staircase, her mind preoccupied with shame and guilt, and she nearly walked straight into the young woman who had already coughed and said, 'Excuse me,' at her. Fortunately, she avoided a second collision just in time.

'Excuse me,' the young woman repeated.

Machaera stared at her in awe. Creatures like this were never seen on the premises of the Foundation. She was dressed in a dark-blue buckram coat and matching breeches, with shiny black boots and a broad-brimmed black hat. Round her waist was a silk belt, with a purse and a pouch for a set of tablets, both in fine embroidered silk; and over her shoulder was a dark-blue baldrick from which hung a slim silver-hilted sword in a blue silk scabbard. To an Islander, it was just the runaway-princess-disguised-as-a-man look, practically a uniform in the mercantile community (Vetriz had two such outfits in green, which Venart had forbidden her to wear on this trip), but to Machaera it was the most startlingly exotic thing she'd ever seen and she wasn't quite sure whether she could cope with it.

'Can you help me?' the young woman asked. 'I'm looking for a man called Gannadius.' Her voice was faintly exotic too, although the City accent was familiar; but there was a faint overlay of something else. The Island, possibly? Machaera had never met anybody from there, but she'd heard somewhere that some Island women wore trousers and carried swords, just like the men. Then she remembered that the women who did that were generally pirates, so presumably this strange person was a pirate too. If so, the pirate life hadn't had much effect on her fingernails.

'You mean Doctor Gannadius,' Machaera said, wondering what on earth Doctor Gannadius had to do with pirates. Perhaps they brought him rare manuscripts plundered from Southern argosies, or fragments of ancient inscriptions stolen from abandoned temples in the jungles of the West. 'He might just be in his lodgings, if he isn't lecturing. I'll take you there.'

'Thank you,' said the young woman gravely, and followed as Machaera led the way, looking round nervously from time to time as if checking that the lady pirate was still there and hadn't slipped away to loot the buttery.

'Have you been here before?' Machaera asked.

'No,' the young woman replied. 'Which is unusual for someone in my line of work, I know.'

'Oh?' Machaera replied, and then wished she hadn't. If

the Foundation had intimate links with pirates, she wasn't sure she wanted to know. 'Well,' she recovered, 'I hope you're enjoying your visit.'

The young woman smiled. 'There's certainly a lot to see,' she replied. 'Some of it makes me quite nostalgic.'

'Excuse me?'

'It reminds me a lot of Perimadeia,' the lady pirate translated. 'All these courtyards, one opening into the next. And the fountains, too. There were ever so many fountains in the City.'

Machaera nodded. 'Ah,' she said, as if she'd just understood a great mystery. 'Well, Doctor Gannadius' lodgings are through here, turn left at the top of the staircase, the first door you come to.' She hesitated for a moment, torn between fascination and a general desire to get away before somebody saw her in such bizarre company. 'I can show you if you like,' she said.

'Please, don't bother,' the lady pirate said with a smile. 'I'm sure I'll find the way. Thank you for your help.'

'Oh, that's all right,' Machaera replied, trying to give the impression that she conducted heavily armed girls in trousers round the Cloister grounds every day of her life. 'It was nice meeting you.'

I wonder how she manages not to knock things over with her sword, she mused as she made her way back to her room. It sort of sticks out when she walks. It must be a real nuisance in a crowded street.

The young woman found the first door on the left at the top of the staircase, knocked and waited. A familiar voice called out, 'Come in,' and she pressed down the latch and walked inside.

'Hello, Gannadius,' she said.

He was fatter than he'd been the last time she'd seen him, manhandling a heavy trunk up the gangplank of a twin-castle freighter called the *Squirrel* beside the Strand on the Island. His hair was shorter too, which probably explained why more of it seemed grey than she remembered. The long grey gown was presumably what Doctors wore in these parts; it wasn't so different from the long brown robe he'd worn when they first met, in Perimadeia, a place that now existed only in a few people's memories.

'Athli,' Gannadius replied. 'Good gods, what are you doing here?'

Athli grinned, took off her sword and baldrick, and dropped into a chair. 'It's all right,' she said, 'I haven't come for my money. You look well.'

'Thank you,' Gannadius replied, unstoppering the wine jug. 'I'm ashamed to say this dreadful place suits me. And I'll pay you back the money immediately. I'd have done so earlier, but finding someone reliable who was going that way—'

Athli waved the rest of the speech aside. 'Don't worry about it,' she said. 'Keep it for me, in case I need it some day. How's business?'

Gannadius laughed. 'I'm better at this than at the soft-furnishings trade,' he replied. 'Mind you, that's not saying much. What about you? You look prosperous enough, but usually the more prosperous an Island trader looks, the more likely he is to be up to his eyes in debt. I hope that's not the case.'

Athli shook her head and accepted the cup of wine. 'And when she says, couldn't be better, business is booming, you know she's about to try and borrow money. But seriously, everything's going very well indeed. I've got my own ship now,' she added, 'and it's paid for, too. And I've branched out from soft furnishings; I'm now the Island agent for the Grand Foundation of Poverty and Learning; or I will be once I've sorted out some details, which is why I'm here. Who'd have thought it, Gannadius, a fencer's clerk from Perimadeia, running a bank.'

Gannadius looked at her. 'Congratulations,' he said severely.

'I know what you're thinking,' she said. 'But whatever else they may be, they're also a highly successful international banking corporation, and getting their agency is rather better than finding large sums of money in the street. Besides,' she added with a frown, 'you work for them too, so you can't talk.'

Gannadius shrugged. 'There was a job for me here, and I couldn't go on imposing on your good nature indefinitely. Admit it, I was a fairly incompetent clerk.'

'True.' Athli finished her wine. 'Which isn't to say that your old job isn't still there for you if ever you do decide— It's all right,' she added, with a grin, 'I'm only joking. What's it like here, really?'

'Very much like being back in the City,' Gannadius replied. 'I teach my own special brand of nonsense to innocent young things who still insist on believing that really it's all about magic, and if they do their homework and pay attention in class they'll end up being able to turn their enemies into frogs. I still play at research when I'm in the mood, but more for the sake of appearances than out of any desire to increase the sum of human knowledge. As far as I'm concerned, the less people actually know about that subject, the happier we'll all be.'

Athli nodded a few times. 'I tend to agree with you there,' she said. 'And if you ask me, you'd be better off back at your old desk in the counting-house; well, you know what I think about all that stuff. Still, that's your business and not mine, I'm delighted to say. No, I won't thanks,' she said, as Gannadius offered to refill her cup. 'I've got to go and talk business with hard-nosed businessmen in an hour or so, and it won't create a very good impression if I slur my words and breathe fumes in their faces.'

Gannadius nodded. 'It's all dry bread and pure spring water with that lot,' he said. 'Miserable people, most of them; and this latest crisis hasn't exactly improved their humour - oh, I don't suppose you know,' he added. 'About the military situation, I mean.'

Athli shook her head. 'You mean the Scona business,' she said. 'Why, has there been a flare-up or something?'

'You might say that,' Gannadius replied. 'Without

boring you with details, we've got several hundred
soldiers and a few high-ranking members of the Poor
either dead or trapped on Scona, and everybody's going
around with very grim faces. As far as I can tell, it counts
as a pretty serious setback, and there are all sorts of
gloomy predictions about mass defections among the
hectemores, reprisals, naval blockades, even invasions.
It's fairly fresh news and they're doing their best to keep
it quiet, but obviously it's not going to do confidence
in the Foundation any good at all, so bear that in mind
when you're discussing commission rates and franchise
agreements; you're probably in a much stronger bargaining position than you think.'

Athli raised an eyebrow. 'Assuming I still want the
agency,' she said. 'Is it serious? I mean, really? The last
thing I want is for the Foundation to go under and leave
me holding a fistful of outstanding letters of credit.'

'I wouldn't worry too much about it,' Gannadius
replied. 'In the long run, it must come down to a battle of
resources; and the Foundation's a great big bank and
Scona's a little one. I'm not saying the Foundation could
lose three hundred halberdiers and not feel anything, but
if the worst came to the worst, they've got fifty men for
every one of the Scona people. The main headache has
always been the fact that they've got quite a few ships
and we haven't got any. In fact, thinking about it, perhaps that might have something to do with their wanting
to set up an agency on the Island. Where else would you
go if you wanted to hire a fleet of say fifty warships, cash
in hand and no questions asked?'

Athli smiled. 'The same thought had crossed my
mind,' she said. 'Some considerable time after it crossed
the mind of every ship-owner on the Island. They've
been talking to each other for years, but the long and the
short of it is, it'd cost too much compared with the actual
amount of aggravation the Foundation gets from Scona.
I don't imagine that's really changed all that much, no
matter what your friends in the sackcloth tunics are

saying. But thanks for the advice,' she added, with a smile. 'At the very least, it'll leave them wondering how I ever managed to find out. From what I gather, they're quite paranoid about secrecy and security.'

Gannadius pursed his lips. 'Maybe you're right,' he said. 'But it wouldn't be the first time a mob of ill-mannered upstarts managed to bring down a proud and mighty nation, as we both know. Anyway,' he went on, 'that's enough about affairs of state and high finance. How are Venart and Vetriz? And the Buezon sisters? And did you ever manage to get rid of all that magenta lace I managed to lumber you with?'

Absent friends and old times on the Island filled in Athli's spare hour quite comfortably and pleasantly, and she was feeling happy and relaxed when she got up to go off to her meeting. But as she turned to leave, Gannadius said, 'There's just one other thing,' and the tone of his voice was somehow disturbing.

'Yes?' she said.

Gannadius looked down at his feet, and then at the wall. 'I know what you think about, well, what I do—'

'The expressions "mystical claptrap" and "charlatan" do tend to spring to mind, but please go on.'

'That's fine,' Gannadius said. 'But I have a young student who seems to have a depressingly advanced level of natural ability as far as mystical claptrap and charlatanry are concerned—'

'The key word,' Athli said quietly, 'being "natural". Carry on.'

'Quite. And the other day she had one of her extremely tiresome visions, and as usual came to me with it, and I saw it too. And before you ask, it wasn't something useful like the winners of a horse race. It was more to do with an acquaintance of mine and your former employer.'

'Loredan,' Athli said without expression. Gannadius grimaced.

'That's not a name to go saying too loudly in these

parts,' he said, 'as you well know. But yes, this vision did have something to do with Bardas Loredan, which is why I decided to brave your overdeveloped sense of humour and tell you about it. Do you want to—?'

Athli nodded. 'So what was it?'

Gannadius closed his eyes for a moment. 'The girl has a cousin, Ramo or some such name, who was with the raiding party on Scona. She saw him leaning over a gate, apparently on sentry duty or something like that; it was early in the morning, and he was looking tired and bored. That's all she saw – I get the impression she's seen the same thing more than once, which technically speaking is quite significant. But when she showed the vision to me, I saw something else. I saw this cousin Ramo leaning on his gate, but I also saw Bardas coming up behind this man, hitting him over the head with something, scrambling over the gate and hurrying away down a track. And that's not the end of it,' Gannadius went on. 'She – my student – also saw a man on a hillside taking armour and clothes from the dead body of a Shastel soldier, and when I saw that part of it, the man was Bardas Loredan. And that's about it,' he finished lamely. 'I thought I'd tell you, just in case—'

'Yes, thank you,' Athli said, and Gannadius saw that her face had gone white. 'Is there any way – I mean, can I see this vision too? Or isn't that possible for non-believers or whatever you'd call it?'

Gannadius shook his head. 'I know it was Bardas,' he said. 'He seemed perfectly sound and healthy, but I wouldn't go further than that. He took the dead man's shirt and boots in preference to his own, which suggests at the least that he's down on his luck. There wasn't anything in what I saw that confirmed the place was Scona, but that's where Cousin Ramo is, or was. In my opinion, the visions must be either the recent past or the immediate future, for that reason. You see, I do know for a fact that Bardas is on Scona. In fact, he's been there for some time.'

Athli looked at him with cold fury in her eyes. 'I see,' she said. 'And you didn't think to tell me.'

'It's not like that, I only saw him for the first time quite recently. I know he'd been there a while because he had a house and a workshop, what looked like a fairly well-established business, something to do with woodworking; and that suggests—'

'Yes, I see,' Athli interrupted. 'I'm sorry. So you're saying he's on Scona and probably in some sort of trouble.'

Gannadius nodded. 'That's what I make of it, anyway,' he said. 'And I thought - well, I'd better tell you. I know you were—'

'Yes,' Athli said. 'Look, I must go. But thank you for telling me. I may not be able to stop by before I leave, so - well, keep in touch. How do I find the Secretary's office, by the way?'

The door closed behind her, and not long afterwards Gannadius saw her from his window, walking briskly across the courtyard towards the Provost's lodgings. He noticed that she'd forgotten to take her sword, and wondered whether he ought to send someone after her with it. He drew it from the scabbard, and saw that it wasn't a sword at all, just a hilt and six inches of broken-off blade.

'You did what?' Niessa demanded.

'I let him go,' Gorgas repeated wearily.

'But why? I told you—'

'Because it was the only thing I could do in the circumstances,' Gorgas interrupted with a flash of irritation. 'Think, Niessa. He was standing over me with an axe in his hand; I'll swear he was this close to taking a swing at me.'

'Rubbish.'

'You weren't there.' Gorgas shivered a little. 'Come on, look at the alternatives. If I'd tried to make him come back with me, either he'd have killed me or I'd have killed him. Either way, it wouldn't have achieved the required objective. It wouldn't have made things better. Agreed?'

Niessa frowned. 'You had your escort with you, didn't you? Four against one—'

'Oh, sure.' Gorgas sighed. 'Three squaddies and me against the longest-surviving law-fencer in the history of Perimadeia, in a cramped room where numbers wouldn't have helped anyway. It's certain sure he'd have killed one or two of them. It wasn't a military operation, Niessa, it was a private family matter. Soldiers would only have made things worse.'

'It was Bank business,' Niessa replied coldly. 'The whole object of the exercise was to neutralise a threat to the Bank's security. To that extent, yes, I'd rather you'd killed him. Then at least he wouldn't be wandering about just asking to be grabbed and used against us as a hostage.'

The strain of Gorgas keeping his temper was almost audible. 'I'll pretend I didn't hear that,' he said quietly. 'I know you didn't mean it. Look,' he went on, relaxing a little, 'the object was to get him out of harm's way, right? Well, that's what I've done. This time tomorrow he'll be on a ship, heading off somewhere a long way away, probably somewhere they've never even heard of Scona. Problem solved, no violence and everybody's happy; we may even have started him thinking that maybe we're not so bad after all. You'd never have got that result if you'd had him dragged in here against his will.' Gorgas leant forward. 'And there's one other advantage that I'll bet you haven't even thought of.'

'Really? Do tell.'

'It's simple. My confounded niece. If Bardas has gone away, we can let her go. I mean, she can't very well kill him if he isn't here, can she?'

Niessa's expression confirmed that no, she hadn't even considered that. It was an interesting moment.

'It's what I do best,' Gorgas went on. 'I take a problem and I turn it into an opportunity to solve a couple more problems. Of course, it means you do have to be able to see the bigger picture and think in the longer term. But if my life stands for anything, it proves that there's no problem so bad it can't be sorted out somehow, even if it's later rather than sooner, provided you never ever give in. Like Uncle Maxen used to say: never surrender while you've got one man still on his feet, you never know what may turn up.'

CHAPTER TWELVE

'I hate the sea,' confessed Bardas Loredan, clinging to the rail with both hands as the *Fencer* slid over a small wave. 'Or at least I hate being on it. Comes of being a woodworker, I suppose.'

'Really? And how do you make that out?'

'I know a bit about wood,' Bardas replied. 'With particular reference to its tendency to rot, split, warp, fret, feather and just plain bust. And the thought that the only thing separating me from certain death is one inch of pine, probably the cheapest grade they could lay their hands on—'

'Relax. The ship isn't going to sink. It's a good ship.'

Another small wave hit the good ship and wobbled it a little. Bardas lurched, nearly lost his footing and hauled himself back upright, his fingernails leaving little marks in the rail timber. 'I think we should turn back,' he said. 'While we still can.'

'Don't be silly. If you're going to be like this all the way there—'

'It's all right for you,' Bardas grumbled, his eyes shut. 'Though come to think of it, I can't see why you're acting so superior. I mean, what the hell do you know about boats anyway? You're just a carpet and cushion merchant, and before that you were nothing but a clerk. I can picture you turning up your nose at the sea the first time you saw it because the colour didn't go with the rocks.'

'Right. And you're a farmer turned soldier turned

lawyer turned bowyer. All of them occupations that call for an intimate knowledge of seafaring. Bardas Loredan, the human dolphin.' Athli yawned and stretched her arms wide. 'Though it's true, we did do our fair share of shipping disputes. But you weren't the one who had to read through the pleadings, with all those loathsome, incomprehensible technical terms. Bowsprits and luggers and mizensails and I don't know what else. Why they can't say "the bit of flappy cloth that hangs off the middle stick thing" like everybody else beats me.'

Bardas nodded. 'Talking of which,' he said, 'one thing I could never fathom, though I never mentioned it for fear of showing my ignorance, was why all that interminable paperwork was actually needed. After all, the whole thing was settled by three minutes' violence, so what the hell was the point of all those carefully worded petitions and statements and rejoinders and surrejoinders you spent your time writing? It was all so meaningless, you know?'

Athli looked at him in surprise. 'You're joking,' she said. 'Do you really mean to say you didn't know? All that time, and all those fights?'

'If I knew, I wouldn't be asking,' Bardas replied, nettled. 'So, are you going to tell me?'

Athli giggled. 'Sorry,' she said. 'I just find that – well, anyway. The point is, before a case was permitted to go to trial, the parties had to show the court – that means the judge. You remember the judge? Man in a black dressing gown sat up on a bench at the back of the hall.'

'I may have noticed him once or twice,' Bardas conceded. 'I thought he was some sort of referee, to make sure there was no cheating.'

'He was that as well. But the other part of his job was going over the pleadings to see if there was really a case to answer. Otherwise, the system would have broken down into people using the courts as a place to fight duels to settle private grudges, rather than serious commercial and criminal issues.'

'Right,' Bardas said. 'I see. And in all the years we worked together, did a judge ever throw out a lawsuit for, what was it you said, no case to answer?'

'No,' Athli admitted. 'Which goes to show how well the system worked,' she added gamely.

Bardas laughed. 'And the rest,' he said. 'But honestly, I had no idea. Was it difficult?'

Athli nodded. 'Very,' she replied. 'And complicated, and time-consuming and boring. What do you think I did all day, sat around combing my hair?'

'I never realised,' Bardas said. 'All that work, and all you ever got was five per cent. It doesn't seem right, somehow.'

Athli looked him in the eyes. 'I didn't have people trying to kill me,' she said. 'I never had an argument with the way we split money. But no, I can believe you didn't realise. The truth is, if you're not prepared to kill people and risk getting killed yourself, you have to work damned hard to earn a living in this cruel, hard world.'

'Wouldn't suit me,' Bardas said, shaking his head. 'But it's true, I haven't really done a proper day's work since I left the farm; I mean, soldiering's hard but you can't really call it work, it's a lethal mixture of boredom and adventure but it's not *work* because it doesn't actually produce anything, or do anything. And the fencing – well, that was just the soldiering without the boredom but with *very* unpleasant adventures. And as for the bow-making—'

'Yes? Surely that was a fair day's pay for a fair day's work.'

Bardas shook his head. 'Not really,' he replied. 'My brother was making sure I was handsomely subsidised out of the procurement budget. I only had it explicitly confirmed the other day, but I suppose at the back of my mind I'd known it for some time. I was getting paid well over the odds, far more than the work was worth, which meant I was really only playing at it, like a hobby or something.' He closed his eyes. 'In other words, the whole thing was a waste of time. I might just as well have stayed in Scona Town and spent all day lounging around like an old blind dog, the way they wanted me to.'

Athli didn't say anything, and they stood for a while looking at the distant speck on the seam between the sea and the sky where Scona had been. Then Athli muttered something about some chore she had to attend to, and walked away. Bardas stayed where he was.

I should be glad, he chided himself. *Glad and cheerful. After all, look at it sensibly.* It was a valid point; he'd got what he wanted, or should have wanted, a chance to sweep the pieces from the board and set them up again any way he liked, a chance to break away entirely from his family and everything he'd ever been, nothing left over from the past except the boy and Athli, both of them listed in the short column of credits on the right-hand side of the ledger …

He let his head droop forward. He'd found an old and valued friend he'd been sure he'd lost for ever – after the awkwardness of seeing her again, his surprise, the shock of how well she'd done for herself, the disagreeable fact that she'd started making something of her life the moment she'd got away from him; after all that, it was as if they'd never been apart, that same taken-for-granted easiness between them that had been one of the few good things about the years he'd lived in the City. She was, after all, the only friend he had now, but a good enough friend that he didn't really need any others (like the man who was recommended to read Stazio's *Commentaries* and replied that it was all right, he'd already got a book). She'd proved what sort of friend she was many times; just recently, when the boy had turned up on her doorstep with some wild tale about Bardas Loredan having sent him to her for safekeeping (like a bank deposit; how apt), she'd taken him in without question, as if it was the most natural thing in the world. Somehow, when he'd been with her, he hadn't minded being himself so much. That part of it hadn't come back, not so soon after that meeting with Gorgas. But perhaps it might, at that. Presumably that was what had moved him to go and look for her, his first step as a free man, a refugee, an ex-Loredan . . .

Then why are you doing this stupid thing? demanded the voice in the back of his head. *The whole world to choose from, a ship effectively at your disposal, money in your pocket, and look where you decide to go.* And of course there was no answer to that.

'Can I ask you something?'

He hadn't heard the boy approaching over the noise of the sea and the general racket of a ship being worked. He looked round and saw that the boy was worried about something; not difficult to spot, he always scratched his neck when something was bothering him. 'Go ahead,' Bardas replied.

'This place we're going to,' the boy continued, 'Are we staying there? For good, I mean.'

Permanently, yes. Whether good'll have any part in it I'm not sure yet. 'That's my intention, yes,' he said. 'There's nothing for us on Scona, and it wasn't exactly as if we chose to go there in the first place. A ship fished us out of the water and took us there, if you remember.'

'Oh, I know that,' the boy said. 'I'm not bothered about it, I was just asking, that's all.' He leant on the rail; he could just reach. 'What's it like in the Mesoge? Does it really rain all the time?'

Bardas shook his head. 'Gods, no. Tell the truth, it doesn't rain nearly enough if you're trying to grow things. And when it does, it all comes down at once and turns the roads into sludge.'

The boy nodded, and moved on to the next item on his list. 'So it's hot there, is it?'

Bardas considered before answering. 'Muggy rather than hot,' he replied. 'The City was hot, but it was more of a dry heat. In the Mesoge, the temperature's lower but the heat feels hotter, if you see what I mean, in summer at any rate. In the winter we have snow.'

'I've never seen snow,' the boy replied. 'Is it hilly or flat?'

'Flat near the coast, hilly inland. But they're hills rather than mountains, not as tall as the back hills beyond Perimadeia, and more rounded than Scona.' He smiled. 'Scona always struck me as a tatty sort of a place, because you could see where the rock had worn through the grass, like the elbows of an old man's coat. You don't get those spectacular rocky outcrops in the Mesoge. In fact, you don't get spectacular anything. To look at, it's fairly dull compared with what you've been used to. Good cattle country, good for sheep, and horses down on the flat by the sea. In the low hills, where we're going, it's indifferent poor land for grain, plenty of woodland – it was never worth anybody's while to clear it – better climate than the coast or the top hills. It's not so parcelled up into fields as the coast, but it's not moorland, like the top. Up there's only fit for running sheep and cutting peat.'

'I see,' the boy said. 'Are there a lot of people?'

'Depends on where you are,' Bardas said, looking out to sea again. 'Obviously it's more crowded on the plains and sparser up on the moors. The middle part's a bit more heavily populated than Scona was, but not all that much. It seems more crowded because people live out on their farms, rather than living in villages and going out to work every day. You're rarely out of sight of someone's house, but there's never more than one or two houses together.'

'That sounds strange,' the boy said. 'Sort of cramped and lonely all at the same time.'

Bardas nodded. 'You do tend to see a lot of your immediate neighbours and not much of anybody else,' he said. 'It doesn't actually matter very much, because all the Mesoge people are pretty much the same. I mean, they all do the same work, there's precious few foreigners, they even look the same.'

'Like you?' the boy asked.

'I suppose so, yes,' Bardas answered, after a moment's

thought. 'On average we're taller than they are on Scona or in the City, most of us have dark hair. You won't have much trouble understanding what people are saying, though the accent'll sound fairly dull and flat to you. We, on the other hand, find the sing-song City accent rather irritating. But not nearly as bad as the Scona bleat. It's sort of nothingish, like most things about the Mesoge.'

The boy collated the information. 'It doesn't sound so bad,' he pronounced.

'Oh, it isn't,' Bardas said. 'Not bad, not good, just ordinary. It's a sort of leftover soup of a place – bits of everything, but nothing in particular. It's like that with the people, too. Because we don't live in villages we generally have to do everything for ourselves – no specialist tradesmen, you see. So we can all do a bit of smithying, a bit of weaving and building and carpentry and pottery; all the boys your age can make a passable bow, good enough to shoot rabbits with—'

'There's rabbits in the Mesoge?'

'Any amount of them, unfortunately.'

'Oh.'

'Like I was saying,' Bardas continued, 'we can all do a bit of everything, as much as we need to get by and no more. Nobody's *good* at anything, because that'd be a waste of effort and resources. Far more efficient to be competent at everything, because you don't need a *good* bow, or a good plough or a good bucket, just one that works, and usually the one thing you haven't got is time. You get the job done and move on to the next job, and when you've finished that there's always something else. So, a bit of rope'll do to hold a gate shut instead of a latch, and if a bent nail will do the trick as well as a mortice and tenon joint, you use a bent nail.' He caught sight of the boy's expression, and laughed. 'It's not as bad as all that, really. I mean, it has its advantages too. For one thing, there hasn't been a war fought in the Mesoge for over two hundred years. And people don't bolt their doors at night, either.'

'Don't they? You mean there's no stealing?'

'Not really. What'd be the point, when everybody's got more or less the same as everybody else? And besides, you can't do anything without at least two people seeing you. Everybody knows everybody's else's business, and a stranger – well, a stranger wouldn't be able to spit without everybody knowing about it for five farms in each direction.'

'Right,' the boy said. 'So when we get there, what are we going to do?'

The *Fencer* made landfall at Tornoys, where Athli made a half-hearted attempt at justifying the expedition in commercial terms by buying four dozen bales of reasonable-quality local worsted for only slightly more than she would have paid for it on Scona or Colleon, and two dozen caged songthrushes.

'What do you want them for?' Bardas asked, as the wicker hampers of frantically warbling birds were carried up the ramp.

'There's a craze for them on the Island,' Athli replied. 'Bored wives tweet and gurgle at them and feed them crumbs on the ends of silver tweezers. And I know where I can get all the cute little bronze cages I can use, cheap.'

'Ah,' Bardas replied, nodding. 'In the Mesoge, we eat them.'

Athli bought a wagon and two adequate horses for less than the going rate, and they followed the coast road as far as Lihon, which was the nearest thing the Mesoge had to a city. From there they followed the main carters' road, a semi-connected tracery of cart tracks and cattle-droves that meandered from farmstead to farmstead in no particular order. As luck would have it, they were trying to go up country in the week before Lihon Fair, which meant that they were continually fighting their way upstream against a fierce current of sheep, goats and pigs being driven south, which sometimes threatened to overwhelm them and sweep them back the way they'd just come. At the end of the second day, Bardas pointed out the wooded crest of a range of hills, which he said overlooked the small valley they were heading for. At the end of the third day, they were exactly the same distance from it, but now they were approaching it from the west rather than the south.

'Not meaning to be rude,' Athli said, 'but how much longer is this going to take?'

Bardas shrugged. 'I don't honestly know,' he replied. 'I've only ever come this way once, and then I was going in the opposite direction, from home to the coast. Actually, I think I came a different way, or else the roads have moved. I seem to remember it took about five days last time.'

On the fourth day they finally left the plain and found themselves on a straight, horribly rutted track that led up the first range of hills in the direction they wanted to go. 'This is the old Bailiffs' Drove,' Bardas explained. 'When I was a boy, most of this part was owned by big City families and let to local tenants like my father. The City owners' bailiffs had this road made so they could drive cattle direct from a couple of mustering-stations to the coast; they reckoned that if they took their land up here in hand and could arrange continuity of supply, they'd be able to flood the City with cheap beef and mutton from their own estates. It didn't work, though; they couldn't agree wayleave terms with the farmers on the coastal plain, so the big joint droves they'd planned got this far and then had to pick their way through the lanes just like we've been doing. In the end, they gave it up as too expensive and went back to letting the land, or sold it off to the tenants in possession. That's when we bought out our place.'

Athli nodded. The further they got from the sea, the more Bardas was using words like 'we' and 'us' instead of 'they' and 'them', and although most of what he said about the country was a series of variations on themes of inefficiency, stagnation and an utterly provincial mindset, she couldn't remember ever having seen him so animated. To a certain extent she was pleased; it was the nearest she'd ever seen him to being happy, or at the very least taking an interest. On the other hand, she didn't like the Mesoge, for all the reasons Bardas himself had given. All around her she felt an oppressive indifference to anything except the job in hand, which was subsistence farming. She hadn't seen a painted door since they'd left Lihon, and the men they passed in the fields all wore virtually identical smocks of pale undyed wool and sturdy but oafish-looking wooden-soled boots. Once she thought she saw a garden and pointed it out to Bardas, who explained that the cheerful-looking yellow and purple flowers were local varieties of flax, grown as cattle fodder. It was the first time he could remember, he said, that anybody had ever mentioned the colours of the flowers. Athli thought of the times when he'd made fun of her back in the City for caring about what colour things were – what earthly difference did it make if the shirt was grey or green, what was it about a blue-enamelled inkwell that made you write more legibly than you would with a plain brass one, and so on. Back then she'd taken it for a rather endearing deficiency of taste; here, she could see it was just Mesoge, buried two or three layers down under his skin. It wasn't as if he seemed to like the place any more than she did, but his attitude suggested that he somehow thought it was *right*, the way things should be, and that any difficulty he had in accepting it was a fault in himself rather than a difference of opinion. *Five years here and he'll be a farmer again*, she reflected, wondering as she did so why that thought depressed her so much. *And not a particularly good one, either*, she added, with a touch of malice.

When she'd left him, rather melodramatically, just before the fall of Perimadeia, she'd believed for some time that she was three parts in love with him, and when someone had tapped her on the shoulder on the quay at Scona, and the someone had turned out to be Bardas

Loredan, she'd told herself that yes, now she knew for sure what it was she'd been feeling for him. Here and now, in the Mesoge, she wasn't so sure. The differences in him were subtle and apparently contradictory. For one thing he looked younger; he held his head up straighter, talked more, volunteered information instead of waiting to be asked. There was something almost boyish about the way he was showing off his home to his friends from Away. But at the same time he seemed to have diminished. He still spoke in the same way, with his usual inflections and turns of phrase, but in everything he said about the Mesoge and its people there seemed to be an underlying note of involuntary, almost grudged respect, so that every time he criticised something he was acknowledging that he was wrong to do so, and that his opinions were therefore worthless. *This is how it's done here; it's not how I'd do it; therefore I must be wrong.* Athli found this both unsettling and distasteful, and naturally began to wonder whether in fact she knew him at all, or whether the man she'd assumed she was in love with had never in fact existed. Thinking about it objectively, she realised that when she thought of Bardas, she saw him in her mind's eye as a striking figure standing on the floor of the courthouse in Perimadeia, sideways on and with his sword-arm extended in the guard of the Old fence, or as a lost and angry man slumped on a bench in a tavern, drinking hard after an easy victory. Of course, she'd never really seen him as a soldier, certainly not as a bowyer or a farm boy, only as a fencer, a man alone in the middle. It was quite possible that she'd made a mistake. Maybe they just didn't have love here, like they didn't have curtains or decorated pottery, and so loving a Mesoge man was actually impossible. After all, love wouldn't help you squeeze an extra four measures of barley out of a stony terrace or get a good edge on a badly tempered scythe-blade, so why would they give it house-room?

'Do they really eat thrushes?' she asked.

Bardas nodded. 'We smear the branches of trees and bushes with lime,' he said. 'They perch and their feet stick, and all you have to do is pull them off and put them in a covered basket. Roasted, they're not bad. And,' he added, with a sideways glance at the boy, 'it makes a welcome change from rabbit.'

The boy groaned, and Bardas laughed; a father teasing his son, Athli decided, and she wondered if that was one of the things that had made him decide to come back here; that if he was to be responsible for the boy, then the boy had to be brought up properly, in the Mesoge fashion. In all the years they'd known each other in Perimadeia, he'd mentioned home and his father three, maybe four times. Now she had enough information to draw a full mental picture of Clidas Loredan, who had apparently been everything a Mesoge father should be: wise, short-tempered, exacting, impatient with failure, able to turn his hand to anything, practical, realistic and (Athli added, with a malicious grin) doomed. It didn't help that there were quite a few things about the Mesoge that she personally found highly amusing, though she knew for a fact that Bardas wouldn't see the joke.

Well, if he insists on being doomed, he can jolly well be doomed on his ownsome. I think this is a horrid place, and I want to go home, where people wear nice clothes and don't mind paying for them. I think I'd go mad if I had to live here. They can't all be doomed, can they? I mean, if so, how come there are still so many of them left?

For a time it seemed as if they'd reach the wooded crest and the valley below it before nightfall on the fourth day. But, at the last moment, the Bailiff's Drove suddenly ceased to exist and melted away into an overgrown lane too narrow to get the wagon down. Bardas swore and backed up the horses – there wasn't room to turn round – as far as the last turning off they'd passed, which led them off to the east round the brow of another small hill. When the sun set and they put the canopy over the wagon for the night, the wooded crest appeared to be just as far away as it had been at noon, albeit that they were seeing it from a slightly different angle.

'We'll be there tomorrow,' Bardas said cheerfully as he lit the fire. It was colder than it had been the previous evening, and Athli wished she'd brought more than one blanket. 'I know this place, some cousins of ours used to be the tenants here, though they had to give up and move on. Just over the hill, on the slope, is where the landlord made them plant a vineyard. It didn't come to anything, of course, but the landlord insisted and they wasted a hell of a lot of time over it. Apparently he'd read a book about viticulture and was convinced he could cover the slopes of these hills with vines and make a fortune. Unfortunately, he never actually finished the book, so he missed the bit about dry, well-drained soil. In the end he let us pull them up. The vinewood made pretty good toolhandles, as I recall.'

Athli looked up. 'Is that how these people look at everything,' she asked, 'in terms of what it can be made into?'

Bardas looked at her curiously. 'Doesn't everyone?' he replied. 'The last couple of years I've been walking round Scona and every time I pass a tree I say Yes or No, depending on whether I can make bows out of it or not. It's instinctive, I guess; is this thing likely to be any use to me or not? Can I make something out of it? You do the same; you look at the rolls of cloth in the market and think, how much would they go for on the Island and what can I get them for? It's human nature.'

Athli shook her head. 'In a market, yes,' she said. 'That's what markets are for. But I don't go around weighing up everything I see as a potential source of profit, or pricing everything as I go, like an auctioneer's clerk.'

Bardas shrugged. 'I suppose it depends on what you've trained yourself to notice,' he replied. 'But I think that that's what people do, its the essence of being human. You take pieces of junk - a bit of tree, or some lumps of iron ore - and you make them into something useful and good.'

'Even if they were perfectly good as they were?' Athli queried. 'Like the thrushes?'

Bardas laughed. 'Maybe, but they aren't doing *me* any good just flying around in the air and going tweet-tweet. Surely all of life's about change; how we change things and how things change us. Otherwise we'd eat grass and sleep standing up. That was always the City mentality,' he went on, turning his head away and looking at the hillside. 'Everybody in Perimadeia was involved in making things, one way or another. They sat on a rock surrounded by sea and turned everything they could lay their hands on into something useful or valuable. Useful to them, of course – they tended to regard anything they couldn't use as trash and a nuisance, which is how they came to get on the wrong side of Temrai and his people. Here in the Mesoge we're similar, but we tend not to muck about with people, just things. Hence, no wars.'

Athli decided that she didn't want to continue with the discussion. 'One thing they can't make here,' she said, 'and that's a decent road. But then, if you don't ever go anywhere, what do you need roads for? Pass me the bread-bag, please, I'm starting to feel hungry.'

'And no rabbit,' added the boy. 'Please.'

'Or thrushes,' Athli said. 'Or squirrels or weasels or frogs or any other free delicacies from Mother Nature's larder. Just bread and cheese and some of that apple chutney will do me.'

'Are you sure?' Bardas said, with a concerned look on his face. 'I bet you that if I looked around for a minute or so I could find you something to go with it – a few beetles, maybe, or a handful of woodlice. Though personally I prefer my woodlice marinaded in honey, with just a faint garnish of chives—'

'Oh, shut up,' Athli said.

'You again.'

'That's right,' Gorgas said cheerfully, 'me again. No,' he

added, as the warder started to close the door, 'leave it. She's free to go.'

The warder didn't say anything, but he didn't need to. His face reminded Gorgas of the bas reliefs of allegorical subjects that City architects loved to decorate the top of arches with: all melodrama and action, with every face registering extremes of graphic emotion. Any archtop in Perimadeia would have been pleased to have the warder up there, radiating the very essence of Relief and Deliverance From Tribulation. Gorgas denied himself the smile.

'You're kidding,' said Iseutz. 'She's letting me go?'

'That's right. Normally I'd say get your things together, but I really can't imagine anybody wanting to take anything out of here except to burn it.' Now he smiled. 'Present company excepted, of course.'

'Witty, Uncle Gorgas, witty. It's nice to think that when you're a beggar scratching a living on the street corners of Shastel, you'll have a valuable talent like that to fall back on.'

Gorgas nodded gravely. 'Clearly it runs in the family,' he said. 'Well, what are you waiting for? You can go. Now. Soon as you like.'

She shook her head. 'Not till I know what's involved,' she said. 'You don't expect me to believe that you and my mother have had a sudden change of heart and realised the error of your ways, do you? It's some sort of game, isn't it?'

'Oh, for gods' sakes. Get out of here, will you, before I change my mind.'

Iseutz grinned at him, leant against the wall, slid down it and squatted on her heels. 'The more you want me to do something, Uncle Gorgas, the harder I'll fight not to do it. There now, do you think I'll be the first person in history ever to be thrown *out* of jail?'

Gorgas sighed and settled himself comfortably on the bed, lying on his back with his hands behind his head. 'Actually,' he said, 'there is a certain appeal to this place.

I can see how you could get used to it; it'd be so easy to wallow in that feeling of the worst having already happened. When you've reached that point, of course, there's absolutely nothing left to be afraid of. It must be wonderful not to be afraid of anything any more.' He yawned. 'Shut the door on your way out, there's a good girl.'

Iseutz scrambled up and stood over him, her arms folded. 'Oh, there's plenty to be afraid of in a place like this,' she said. 'Like the thought that you're never going to get out of here. The thought that they might even *bury* you in here – or I suppose they've got a pit or a wellshaft they sling the bodies down. Sometimes I think about that, and I run over to the door and bash on it till my wrists bleed, yelling for them to let me out. I don't like it in here, Uncle, I don't like it one little bit. But I'm not leaving till you tell me why.'

'Please yourself,' Gorgas muttered drowsily. 'It's no big secret. I've been on at Niessa to let you out ever since she put you in here, and now, bless her heart, she's agreed. Simple as that. I expect she got sick and tired of the sound of my voice, the way I'm sick and tired of yours.'

She didn't move, just went on looking down at him. 'So I can go, can I? Go wherever I like?'

'Mhm.'

'All right,' she said. 'And what if I tell you I'm going straight to Briora – that's the name of the village, isn't it? – to find Uncle Bardas and kill him?'

'You're welcome to try.'

'Really?' She frowned. 'And you won't try and stop me?'

'You can give it your very best shot if you like. It won't get you very far, but that's your business. You go right ahead.'

She knelt down beside him, and he noticed how graceful the movement had been. 'Come on, Uncle Gorgas, be a sport, tell me what you're up to. Please.' She folded her arms, rested her cheek on them and smiled.

'For gods' sakes,' Gorgas snapped, 'leave it alone, will

you?' It wasn't right to see her acting girlish, acting her
age. She looked like a monster, with her matted hair,
thin, bony arms, hands unnaturally large; there were
white scars along the blades of her hands, from the base
of the little finger to the projecting bones at her wrists.
'Get away from me, will you? You're disgusting.'

'Thank you,' she replied gravely. 'Tell me what's going
on.'

'For the last time, nothing's going on.'

'Then why are you letting me go, when the first thing
I'll do is ...'

'No, you won't,' Gorgas said angrily, 'because he's not
here. He's gone. Left Scona. And before you ask, I don't
have a clue where, and that's the truth.'

'I see.' She looked steadily at him, her eyes very large
and round and brown; then she spat in his face. Gorgas
shuddered and slapped her across the cheek, striking her
on her hard, fleshless cheekbone so hard that she lost her
balance and fell over backwards.

'I'm sorry,' Gorgas said immediately, 'I didn't mean to
do that, you just ...'

'You were provoked,' she said, as she got up from the
floor. 'My fault. Really, Uncle Gorgas, I don't have any
quarrel with you. But why did you let him go?'

Gorgas shrugged. 'He wanted to go, and I couldn't
stop him. Simple as that.'

'And now me. All the baby chicks flying the coop,
Uncle Gorgas. I expect Mother's livid.'

'She's not best pleased.' He stood up. 'Look, are you all
right? I didn't mean to hit so hard, it's just – well, things
are getting to me and I took it out on you. I shouldn't
have done that.'

'It's all right, really.' Iseutz smiled, and Gorgas noticed
that her eye was already beginning to swell. 'You know,
part of you is a decent human being. That's the strange
thing about you. In spite of the really incredible things
you did, you're not really a monster either. You know, I
used to lie here thinking about that – what sort of person

could do something like that, murder his own father without a moment's hesitation? Well, obviously a monster, I thought, something more and less than human. But I don't see that somehow.'

Gorgas slumped against the wall and rubbed his cheeks with the palms of his hands. 'It was a mistake,' he said. 'I made a mistake. People do, you know. And the stupid part of it is, the whole thing only took - what, three minutes, four at the most. True, there was all that stuff with Niessa and the City boys before, but so what? Pimping for your sister's part of growing up in the Mesoge, it's one of the things you do for a little extra money when you're young, like scaring crows or picking blueberries on the moors. No, when you analyse it rationally, it was a few minutes, less time than it takes to boil a kettle. Everything else bad I've done in my life has been in the normal course of business, the sort of thing you're never really ashamed of, deep down; there was just one thing I did, and that's all, but it's the only thing about me anybody ever sees. I'm Gorgas the patricide, the man who killed his own father. They talk about me as if it was what I did for a living, like I do it every day; like I kiss my wife and children goodbye every morning and go off to spend the day murdering members of my family. And that's not me. That's putting me on a level with some lunatic who kills people for no reason and keeps on doing it till someone stops him, or an assassin who murders people for money.' He stopped short, and shook his head. 'The gods only know why I'm telling you this,' he said. 'Ask anybody who knows me, I don't lie about what happened but I don't wear my heart on my sleeve, either.'

'That's all right,' Iseutz said soothingly. 'You can talk to me about things you can't tell other people because we're so much alike. Well, aren't we?'

Gorgas looked at her. 'No offence, but I don't think so,' he said. 'Beyond the fact that I killed my father and you want to kill your uncle, I'd say we're very different.'

She shook her head. 'You're forgetting,' she said. 'One thing we've definitely got in common. My mother.'

'I beg to differ,' Gorgas yawned. 'You forget, I've known her all my life, and you hardly know her at all. I imagine you've invented this other monster while you've been in here, but I'd be really surprised if you knew the first thing about what Niessa's really like.'

She frowned. 'But you hate her, don't you? Because of the way she uses you, makes you do things you don't want to, the way she's ruined your life—'

'Don't say things like that,' Gorgas interrupted. 'I love my sister. The gods only know what'd have become of me without her. For all these years, she's been the only person I've got in the world. You just look at what she's achieved—'

Iseutz laughed. 'You really mean it, don't you?' she said. 'You really do believe all that stuff. That's bizarre, Uncle Gorgas, truly it is.'

Gorgas leant forward and straightened his back. 'You've lost me, I'm afraid,' he said. 'Surely what I believe about my own feelings has got to be the truth, hasn't it? I think this time you're being just a bit too clever.'

'Perhaps.' She put her hands behind her back and stood on her toes, like a young girl about to be taken on an outing or a treat. 'So what happens now?' she asked. 'Where am I supposed to go now?'

'Wherever you like, we've been into all this—'

'Being practical, I mean. Like, I've got no money, nowhere to go, no way of earning a living. Do I go and live with Mother, or am I going to be shipped off the island and sent somewhere, or what? I was assuming you'd got all that sorted out.'

Gorgas shook his head. 'House arrest, you mean. Are you expected to go and play the good, dutiful daughter in your mother's house, doing chores and being shown off to visitors? I don't think so.'

'Why not?' She grinned crookedly. 'It's what normal daughters do.'

Gorgas thought for a moment. 'All right,' he said, 'here's the deal. If you want, you can come and stay with me. A week or as long as you want to, but I'd want you to think of it as your home. The gods know, having a home to go to's probably the most important thing in the whole world. How about it?'

She stared at him, trying to laugh. 'Gods,' she said, 'you really do believe in all that stuff. Happy family life, the pleasures of having one's nearest and dearest about one. You live in a strange world, Uncle Gorgas. It must be a bit like those brass bowls we used to have in the City, the ones that come from Colleon and got passed off as City-made. Remember how, when you first looked at them, you thought you could see the usual writing on the side, who made it and where and some motto or other? And then, when you looked closely, you saw it wasn't writing at all, just shapes made to look like writing, because the people who make them in Colleon can't read or write. I think that's your life, Uncle Gorgas, made by someone who's never had one but thinks he knows what they're supposed to look like.'

Gorgas sighed. 'Is that a yes or a no?' he asked. 'Come on, this is all highly entertaining but I've got other things I should be doing, like running a war.'

'Why not?' she replied with a shrug. 'It's not as if I'm spoilt for choice, and yes, it's thoughtful of you to make the offer, whatever your reasons may be. Of course,' she added, 'it's not such a big deal for you, since I don't suppose you're actually at home very often, it's your wife and kids who're going to have to put up with the mad woman. Still, I don't suppose that thought even crossed your mind.'

'It didn't,' Gorgas confessed. 'But they'll be all right about it. After all, you're family.'

'I'm a member of the Loredan family,' Iseutz replied with a smile. 'That alone's grounds for any sane person to lock the door on me and set the house on fire. We're an evil bunch, aren't we, Uncle Gorgas?'

'Yes, I suppose we are,' Gorgas answered. 'But we're *our* evil bunch.'

'Not prisoners,' Alexius said gravely. 'Guests. Valued and respected guests.' He shifted uncomfortably on the stone bench. 'If I was sixty years younger,' he added, 'I'd scratch my initials on this bench, like I did on the bench outside the Preceptor's chambers, where I used to sit and wait when I'd got myself in trouble and had been sent for to be judged and found wanting. I spent a great deal of time sitting on that bench, in a room not entirely unlike this one, and the feeling of unspecified but acute dread is also remarkably similar. I'd hoped that at my age I wouldn't have to go through all that again, but it seems I was wrong.'

Vetriz smiled. 'It was a bit like that when we were children,' she said. 'It was always, "Wait till your father gets home," because of course he was away most of the time on business, and when he was actually there we were as good as gold. But when he'd been away for a couple of months and then we heard that his ship had been sighted and was due in later that day – well, it was always an uncomfortable time, because there'd always be this terrible catalogue of crimes and misdemeanours ready to greet him; the poor man only just had time to take his hat off, and Mother would march us forward, and he'd look at her with this *Can't-it-wait* expression ... Of course,' she went on with a grin, 'I always got away with it, because I was a girl and all I had to do was let my little face fall and start snuffling and Father would believe anything I said. So I always put the blame on poor Ven, and, bless him, he never did come to terms with that; he'd always protest his innocence and be really upset when he got punished for naughty things I'd done. He honestly believed that all he had to do was tell the truth and somehow Right would always prevail. You know, deep down in his soul, I think he really still believes that to this day.'

Alexius considered that for a moment. 'That's rather a fine thing, don't you think?' he said. 'Not the most suitable mindset for a trader perhaps, but nevertheless admirable, in a way.' He sighed, and shifted again. 'Have you heard any more about how the war's going?' he asked. 'The man who sold me my breakfast was convinced that Shastel is striking a deal with a great confederacy of pirates; they'll ship the halberdiers over to Scona and in return they'll get to sack Scona Town. On the other hand, he also believes that if they try, Gorgas Loredan will drive them back into the sea, and Niessa Loredan will command her tame wizards to summon up a great storm and sink all their ships, so perhaps his value as a source of information isn't as high as one might think.'

Vetriz shrugged her slim shoulders. 'I think this war's like a fight I once saw,' she said, 'where there were these two young men at a wedding dance, and they'd had too much to drink, the way people do, and there was some sort of a quarrel over a girl or something. Anyway, everybody expected these two to start fighting and I suppose they didn't want to disappoint everyone, so they started prancing round and swishing about with their fists; and, quite by accident, one of them made a wild swing and knocked over one of those big iron lampstands, you know the sort I mean, and the lamp toppled off and fell on the other man's shoulder and gave him a nasty knock. And the other one – the one the lamp hit – sat down in the middle of the floor cursing and swearing and rubbing his shoulder and calling the first man a clumsy idiot, and the first man was apologising and getting into a terrible state because he was convinced he'd broken the other man's collarbone; he was jumping up and down and bawling, "Send for a doctor, send for a doctor," and then someone else tried to shut him up, so he took a swing at this other man and hit him on the nose; and that really finished him off, because the man's nose started bleeding and he was staggering about with a napkin pressed to his face; and of course everybody else in the place was laughing like mad, and then the bride burst into tears because of all this fuss spoiling her wedding dance, so the groom got angry with the man who'd done all the damage and took a swing at him himself, and of course he missed and smacked his fist against the wall and broke a bone in his hand—'

Alexius nodded. 'Most wars start because someone makes a mistake, and most battles are lost by the losing side rather than won by the victors. I'm not sure if that makes things better or worse. I suppose it depends which you disapprove of more, malice or stupidity.' He massaged the calf of his left leg, which had gone to sleep. 'It's possible she's forgotten all about us,' he said. 'I wonder, if we simply got up and walked away, would anybody actually try to stop us?'

'We could try—' Vetriz began to say; at which point the door of the Director's office opened and the clerk scurried out, his arms full of hastily rolled maps. 'She's ready for you now,' he said. 'And I'd watch it if I were you. It's a bad day.'

Alexius stood up, then staggered and grabbed hold of Vetriz's arm to steady himself. 'Pins and needles,' he explained. 'Oh, confound it. Now I'm going to have to stagger in there and look as if I'm drunk.'

There was a new piece of furniture in the Director's office: a small, round three-legged table between the two visitors' chairs, on which someone had put a jug of weak, sweet wine and two beautifully made horn cups, with silver rims and bases and dainty little silver stands to hold them upright. Vetriz recognised them as City manufacture and quite old, and it occurred to her that there were probably casks and chests of such things squirrelled away somewhere in the building – gifts from visiting embassies, foreign heads of state anxious to curry favour, wealthy individuals trying to secure private concessions, bribes, inducements and sweeteners, not to mention spoils of war. It looked hopelessly out of place in the deliberate dourness of the office; *I wonder why she did it*, she asked herself. *Probably just to disconcert us. Third rule of negotiation: confuse and conquer.* She sat down and made a deliberate show of not having noticed.

'My brother Bardas,' said Niessa Loredan, 'has left Scona. I didn't want him to go and I don't know where he's gone. Did you know that already?'

Vetriz looked at Alexius, who shook his head. 'I had no idea,' he said.

'I believe you.' Niessa stood up, went to the little table and poured wine into the two cups. 'Flavoured with honey and cinnamon,' she said to Vetriz. 'Your favourite, I believe.'

Vetriz smiled wanly. 'That's very kind of you,' she said, taking the cup and holding it slightly away from her. 'Please don't take this the wrong way, but if he's gone, do you really need us here? I mean, there doesn't seem to be any point—'

'On the contrary,' Niessa replied. She was pouring water from a pottery jug into a plain wooden cup. 'This is exactly the sort of contingency I needed you for. You aren't going to be difficult, are you?'

'What do you want us to do?' Alexius asked.

Niessa sat down and folded her hands. 'First,' she said, 'find out where he is and what he's doing. Then I want you to bring him back. It's all right, I'll tell you how to go about it when the time comes. It's quite simple, really; like this—'

—And all three of them were standing beside a river, looking at two young men and a girl. The girl was holding a big wicker basket full of clothes, and the men were trying to grab hold of her. She was trying to avoid them and pull away without dropping the basket, until one of the men pulled it away from her and let it fall into the water. The girl swore at him; he laughed and grabbed a handful of her dress where it covered her shoulder.

'I'd forgotten that,' Niessa said.

The fabric tore, and the girl stumbled backwards,

putting down a hand to steady herself. The other man came up behind her and reached out, and she swung at his face; she had picked up a stone, and it cracked loudly against the bridge of his nose.

'Look,' Niessa said, pointing. 'There's Gorgas, over there.'

She was gesturing at a tall young man standing behind a single cypress tree, holding the reins of two horses. He wasn't watching what was going on down in the river; he was looking over his shoulder, with an expression of panic on his face. Vetriz couldn't see what he was staring at because there was a ridge in the way, but she saw him pull a short, heavily recurved bow from a scabbard on the nearest horse's saddle. He pressed the hooked end of the bottom limb against the outside of his right ankle, then lifted his left foot over so as to trap the bow between his legs, bringing his left knee to bear on it just below the handle and applying enough pressure to bend it until he could slip the string over the top nock. It was a graceful manoeuvre, smooth and unhurried, like a dance step practised over and over again until it had become perfect and could be executed without any thought whatsoever.

'I often come here,' Niessa said casually. 'But I still notice something new every time. Did you see? He did that without once looking down.'

He pulled a handful of arrows out of the quiver that hung down beside the horse's neck, ducked under a low branch of the tree and wedged himself in a slot between two boulders. There was the faintest of clicks as he drew an arrow onto the bowstring.

'He was really attached to that bow,' Niessa was saying. 'Bardas made it for him. I was surprised he lent it to the Ferian boy; I never knew him lend it to anybody else, he was that jealous of it. I think it was mostly because it was a present from Bardas.'

Now Vetriz could see what he'd been looking at: three men with mattocks in their hands.

(*At least, I assume those are mattocks*, Alexius said to

himself. *We called what those men are holding rasters where I come from, but I've never heard that word anywhere else. I thought a mattock was more like a hoe. Gorgas said they were mattocks when he told me the story, so maybe I'm just filling in.*)

The girl in the river was screaming now, and the two men were panicking, apologising, shouting at her, trying to shut her up; one was yelling he was sorry, he didn't mean to, it was just in fun; the other slapped her across the face so hard that the running men could hear it. The youngest man stumbled, fell, landed heavily on his side, tried to get up, twitched, went still. The oldest man didn't appear to have noticed, but the third man swung round, almost losing his footing on the stony ground, looked up in the direction the arrow had come from and shouted something. Then he fell over too, flopping backwards as if he'd been pushed. The older man stopped then, and a moment later he fell down too; the arrow hit him just above the heart and went through diagonally, the arrowhead poking out a finger's breadth under his right shoulder-blade.

'Forty yards, I'd say,' Niessa commented, 'and two out of three as clean a pair of kills as you could possibly wish for. In an archery contest, it'd have scored something like two bulls and an inner; thoroughly respectable, good enough for silver. In the field, though, a botched shot's a botched shot.'

Then he stood up, pulled a few more arrows from the quiver and walked over to where the slope overhung the river. The two men had stopped bothering with the girl and were staring at the bodies; the girl was hitting one of them across the back of the shoulders with the sides of her fists and he wasn't even taking any notice. They watched as the archer drew and took a quick aim, sighting down the arrow and making the adjustment for aiming off; then one of the men dropped like a stone into the water, and the archer reached to his belt for an arrow. The other man started to run without looking round; the girl started to say something, and then the arrow hit her. She went down—

'Now there's the bit I wish I could slow down,' Niessa remarked. 'Unfortunately, it all happens so quickly, I can't really make anything out for sure. Does his hand wobble on the loose, or is he deliberately shooting low? Believe it or not, it didn't really hurt all that much.'

'Have we got to watch the rest of this?' Alexius interrupted.

'All right,' Niessa said, with a hint of disappointment in her voice. 'Actually, there's not much more to see. He goes chasing off after the Hedin boy – he had nice eyes, Cleras Hedin, but really bad teeth; the joke is that he and I had been quietly amusing ourselves for days before all this happened – money changed hands, obviously, but it was all quite amiable – so there was really no need for him to be involved, it was young Ferian I drew the line at. But Gorgas doesn't know that.' They were back in the Director's office now, and the wine in Vetriz's hand was still pleasantly warm. 'Anyway, he'll catch young Hedin and bash his brains out, and when he gets back he'll find Clefas and Zonaras scampering up the track, and Bardas and me not dead, and he'll give it up as a bad job and run away. The rest of it's just shouting and screaming and not knowing what to do, and Zonaras being sick at the sight of blood; it's just as well Clefas stayed calm or we'd both be dead. But he's solid brick from the shoulders up, nothing ever seems to get a reaction out of him. Typical farmer.'

There was a moment of complete silence. Then Alexius cleared his throat.

'I'm sorry,' he said. 'I still don't see the point. Why did you want us to see that?'

Niessa smiled charmingly. 'I didn't,' she replied. 'You just helped me answer my question. Now I know where Bardas is – he's gone home. In fact,' she added, refilling Alexius' cup, 'I think I know precisely where he is, right now.'

* * *

'This river,' Bardas was saying, 'used to mark the boundary; our land on that side, from here over to where you can see that little clump of firs. The ford is just round the bend here.'

He stopped and reined in the horses. Two men were approaching on the other side of the river, just emerging from the shade of a tall cypress tree. They were wearing the usual broad-rimmed leather hats and carrying mattocks over their shoulders.

'There now,' Bardas said, and jumped down off the cart. 'If that isn't good timing.' He raised his hands over his head and waved to the two men, who turned and looked at him. 'Now I'm home,' he said.

CHAPTER THIRTEEN

'Bardas,' said the short one.

'Hello, Clefas,' Bardas replied. 'Hello, Zonaras. It's good to see you again.' The two men regarded him steadily, exhibiting no emotion of any kind. *Some sort of Mesoge recognition ritual*, Athli speculated, *wouldn't surprise me in the least.* Doing her best not to be obvious about it, she took a long look at Bardas' two long-lost brothers. There was a family resemblance, to be sure, particularly round the jaw and chin, and Zonaras, the taller of the two, had Bardas' eyes. Even so, it was almost shocking to see Bardas' features mirrored in these two nondescript middle-aged farmers; it was like walking through a bazaar in somewhere like Inagoa or Sizma, some primitive backwater of a place where they used seashells for money, and coming across an obvious piece of loot plundered by pirates from an Island ship, an enamelled silver jug or an ivory-framed mirror among the asymmetrical coil-made pots and scraped-out wooden bowls. Clefas, the short one, was pot-bellied with fat cheeks and an enormously thick neck; he looked about ten years older than Bardas, though she knew for a fact he was the youngest of the brothers. The other one, Zonaras, seemed shorter than he actually was because of a bandy-legged stoop, and the hair on the top of his head was beginning to go. His ears stuck out, and he had a straggly beard that was thin at the point of his chin and absurdly bushy at the sides. Both of them had huge red hands with bitten fingernails.

'This is Athli Zeuxis,' Bardas went on, 'a friend of mine from the Island. She's a trader.'

The brothers looked at her as if she was something on a stick at a puppet show. Neither of them said anything, but there wasn't any need. Their expressions fairly shouted, *So her name's Athli Zeuxis; what d'you expect us to do about it?* She'd certainly never felt less comfortable in her life. A minute or so dragged away, and still neither of them had said a word, except for Clefas' perfunctory greeting. She glanced at Bardas out of the corner of her eye and saw with relief and amusement that he seemed to be feeling just as embarrassed and out of his depth as she was. It occurred to her that Bardas hadn't even tried to introduce the boy, but that at least seemed to be in keeping with what passed for normal behaviour here. Children, it seemed, were like dogs; everybody had one or two huddled round their feet or trotting round in the background looking for a fight while the big people talked to each other (or at least while they stood stock still and practised their glowering) and nobody ever seemed to notice they were even there.

Just when Athli was about to scream, or fall asleep on her feet, Clefas gave a little sigh and said, 'You staying long?'

Bardas blinked once. 'I'm not sure yet,' he said. 'I haven't really got any plans in any direction at the moment.'

'You'd better come up to the house,' murmured Zonaras, in the tone of voice of someone who's just found a badly injured stranger in the road, right at the most inconvenient moment possible. The total lack of expression had subtly changed into a hostile, suspicious stare, the face of a man who fears the worst. *That's odd*, Athli said to herself. *I'm the one who's a complete and utter stranger among these lunatics.*

It wasn't far to the house, which proved to be a long thatched affair with a steeply angled roof and tiny, almost token windows. There was a huge front door,

solid oak studded with the heads of big square nails, and
a doorway at the side with no door whatsoever, just a
board put across to keep the pullets from escaping. The
yard was littered with junk; smashed and mossy barrels
with ferns growing up through the gaps between the
slats, what looked like a perfectly good and serviceable
chain harrow almost completely overgrown with bind-
weed, any number of holed and rusty iron buckets, the
green and decaying skeleton of a cart that had been
gradually robbed of its boards and fittings, like a beached
whale after the local people have cut off the best meat
for salting; a water-butt with a bubbling leak in the side,
and green moss marking the course of the escaping
water; a pile of bones stacked up like logs against an
outhouse wall; the skin and bones of a huge rat nailed to
the planked-in sides of the woodshed half a century ago,
now tanned and cured by the wind and sun to
a brittle crispness; a sheep's skull on a pole, set up as a
slingshot target gods only knew how long ago, chipped
and cracked and still incredibly in one piece; a leaf-thin
rusty scythe blade lodged between loose stones on top of
a crumbling wall. A fat, blind old ewe nibbled lichen off
the stones of the mounting block. *Oh, for gods' sakes*,
Athli muttered to herself as she passed through, *surely it
wouldn't kill them to tidy the place up say once every
seventy-five years?*

'Cosy,' she whispered in Bardas' ear, as Zonaras laboriously shooed away the pullets from the doorway and
lifted away the board.

'Personally, I preferred it when it was just left scruffy,'
Bardas replied. 'Mind you wipe your feet before you go
indoors.'

Because it was so dark inside the house, Athli's first
impression was of the smell, a bizarre mixture of cheese,
smoke and apples. It was strong, rich and delicious, and
not at all what she'd been expecting. It was also pleasantly cool, thanks to the thick stone walls and flagged
floor. When her eyes became accustomed to the light,

she saw a long, bare room with a huge fireplace at one end, almost hidden behind a massive iron spit with an elaborate mechanism for turning it, and beside it a cavernous bread oven; there were sunken alcoves with steps leading down on both sides of the room, and a massive table in the middle that was almost as long as the room, with a low bench on either side. From the crossbeams hung ropes of onions, low enough that Bardas and Zonaras had to duck, and a bewildering collection of tools and implements, some of which looked as if they hadn't been disturbed for a hundred and fifty years.

'Where's Father's chair?' Bardas asked.

'Broke,' Clefas replied. 'We put it up in the hayloft.'

'Pity,' Bardas said. 'I'll see if I can't mend it.' He sat down on the bench and planted his elbows on the table. 'And the pot-hook too,' he added. 'I see nobody's got around to fixing that since I've been away.'

Clefas and Zonaras looked at each other, then sat down opposite him; it reminded Athli of some tense moment in a long, drawn-out business deal, the point when the parties stop pussyfooting around and get down to cases. She perched on the edge of the table at the far end, while the boy pulled up a low three-legged stool and crouched on that.

Clefas drew in a deep breath. 'If it's the money you're after,' he said, 'you're out of luck.'

Bardas frowned. 'I wasn't, actually,' he said. 'I sent it to you for you to use, though I can't say there's much sign of it.'

'It's all gone,' Zonaras said.

That seemed to throw Bardas completely. 'What do you mean, gone?' he said. 'Come on, talk sense.'

Zonaras shrugged. 'It's gone,' he said. 'We haven't got it any more. Simple as that.'

Athli knew what that look meant – Bardas, keeping his temper. 'Don't talk soft,' he said cheerfully. 'I sent you enough money to buy this whole damned valley. Which is what I assume you did with it, right?

Clefas and Zonaras looked at each other. 'We bought the farm,' Clefas said. 'This place.'

'And?' Bardas leant forward across the table. 'Come on, I sent you enough for that in the first year. What did you do with the rest of it?'

So that's it, Athli said to herself. *That's what he did with it all. He sent it home.* All the time she'd known him in the City, when he'd been earning enormous sums of money as a fencer-at-law and never seeming to spend a copper quarter of it, when he'd been living in a bleak, miserable apartment in an 'island' block and eating dry bread and coarse, cheap cheese; he'd sent the rest of it back to his brothers here in the Mesoge. She felt her mouth drop open; she knew more or less exactly how much money was involved, since she'd been his clerk, living very comfortably off her five per cent share. More than enough to buy this dismal valley; the Loredan brothers should have been living in a castle in the middle of an ornamental lake, with long avenues of sycamores lining the road and a model village set back at a discreet distance for the estate workers to live in. Every fight, every burdening of the already obscene odds against him, every drop of blood he'd shed, every morning he'd woken up and looked out through his tiny window at a sun that might not be there that evening; where in the gods' names could all that have gone, and leave the brothers still living in this squalor?

'We bought the mill,' said Zonaras after a while. 'But it burnt down.'

'We built it again,' Clefas added, 'but then Leucas Meuzin built another one over at Ladywood and he charged less than we did, so we gave it up.'

'All right,' Bardas said, 'so you make one mistake. That would have been a drop in the ocean. What about the rest of it?'

And then the long, dreary catalogue began; a ludicrous recital that made Athli want to howl with laughter – if only she could remember it when she got back to the

Island, what a party piece it would make, with the funny accents and the two of them interrupting each other like a pair of professional storytellers. There was the cattle-ship, which was going to make the run to Perimadeia once a month and bring in a king's ransom in easy profit, except that it hit rock on its first run out and sank. There was the weir across the Blackwater, to catch the salmon; but there were problems, and instead of a month to build, it had taken a year and huge quantities of stone shipped in specially from Basleen in a specially modified ship; and it worked so well the first year that now salmon were extinct in the Blackwater, and the weir had clogged up and flooded and they'd had to pay all the neighbours the cost of draining their flooded land. There was the seam of pure tin someone had discovered up on top of the moor, an absolute fortune just waiting to be carted away; the salt pans and oyster beds on the coast; the deposit of fine white sand in the dunes beyond Turnoys that was going to be the foundation for a glassmaking industry to rival anything in the world; the wagon in Lihon; the diamond mine and the carpet-weaving syndi-cate and the cedar plantation, and of course the Bank of the Mesoge—

'But why?' Bardas interrupted. 'For pity's sake, Clefas, why didn't you just buy land like I told you to?'

Clefas scowled at him. 'But we don't want to be farm-ers any more,' he said. 'We want to be like – we wanted to make money and be rich.'

'You wanted to be like Niessa,' Bardas said softly. 'If she could do it, so could you.'

Zonaras slapped the table with his huge palm. 'It didn't seem fair,' he said, 'her running a bank and having money pouring in, when by rights she'd married Gallas and should have been an ordinary person. If she could have all that, we wanted it too. I guess we just weren't as lucky as her. And now the City's fallen,' he added bitterly, 'and there's no more money, and here we bloody well are.'

At that moment, what Athli wanted more than anything else she could think of was for Bardas to pull Zonaras across the table and bash his face in. But he didn't move. After a long time, he pushed his hair back from his forehead and said, 'What have you got left? Anything?'

Clefas nodded. 'There's the farm, like I said. And we bought Palas Rafenin's place when he died, that's another thirty acres. And there's the rap up on the moors where the tin mine was going to be, we let the keep on that to Teufas Tron for nine quarters a year. And there's the rosewood plantation, of course, but that won't be worth anything for fifty years—'

'Nothing,' Bardas said. 'All gone. Wonderful. I've kept every swindler and chancer in the Mesoge for all these years and my own brothers are still chasing sheep and hoeing onions.' He drew his fingertips down his cheeks as far as his chin. 'You bloody fools, I was trying to look after you, all of us. I wanted it to be so that none of us would ever have to worry about anything ever again; and like you said, Zonaras, here we bloody well are, right back where we started.'

'Heris,' Gorgas Loredan called out, 'I'm home.'

'We're in the cloister,' his wife replied. He smiled, dumped the heavy bag he'd been carrying and strolled through the dark shade of the hall out into the courtyard.

An appealing sight, if ever there was one; his wife sitting in her favourite cedarwood chair, sewing. At her feet, his daughter Niessa playing with her little wooden horse on wheels. Behind her, his son Luha lying on his stomach on the grass, propping himself up on his elbows and reading a book; and to his right, perched on a small ebony stool, the latest addition to the family, his niece, who was having her hair combed by the maid. Gratifying how well she'd scrubbed up - oh, for sure she'd never be a beauty or anything more than ordinary with a hint of strange-looking, all bones and eye-sockets. But at least she was clean and respectably dressed in one of Heris' old linen smocks and a good plain pair of sandals. 'Hello,' he said. 'That's what I like to see, a hive of industry. Any messages?'

Heris looked down at a wax tablet balanced on the arm of her chair. 'Vido brought over the excise figures, they're on your desk. A man called Bemond Grus would like to talk to you about five hundred pairs of boots, FOB the *Sea Falcon*, whatever that means. *She* sent someone to see if you were back yet, but there wasn't a message. Oh, and I've done those transfer deeds, all except the long one that needs a coloured plan.'

'You have? That's splendid,' Gorgas replied, trying to remember which deeds she was talking about. It seemed a long time since he'd had nothing more urgent to think about than paperwork. How wonderful it must be, he thought, to be bored.

He grabbed a cushion from the pile, dropped it on the grass and stretched out, like a good dog after a long day herding sheep. 'So what's been going on since I've been away?' he asked. 'Luha, how did you do in your verse-composition test?'

'Nine out of ten, Father,' the boy replied, without looking up from his book.

'That's not bad,' Gorgas said. 'Did anybody get ten?'

'No. Well, yes. Ruan Acher did, but his dad's a poet, so—'

Gorgas frowned. 'Doesn't matter,' he said. 'Nine out of ten's good, don't get me wrong, but ten would have been better. If Ruan Acher can do it, then so can you.'

'Yes, but Father, verse composition,' the boy said. 'When am I ever going to want to do verse composition? It's not like it's any good for anything.'

The frown condensed into a scowl. 'Don't let me hear you talking like that,' Gorgas said. 'And don't go spoiling good work with a bad attitude. After dinner I want to look at your work, and we'll go over it and see if we can spot where you went wrong. Niessa,' he continued, turning his head a precise few degrees towards her, 'have you been practising your flute like you promised?'

'Yes, Daddy,' the little girl answered proudly. 'And Doctor Nearchus says I'm nearly a grade ahead of everyone else in the class. Shall I get my flute and play you my piece, Daddy?'

'That'd be nice,' Gorgas said. 'You're excused.'

Niessa scampered off, and Gorgas lifted up on one elbow. 'What about you, Iseutz?' he said. 'Settling in?'

His niece looked at him, and one corner of her lip twitched. 'Absolutely, Uncle Gorgas,' she said. 'Yesterday we did my teeth, and today we've been doing my hair. And tomorrow we're going to do my fingernails, though I don't suppose there's really a full day's work to be done there. Can I have the afternoon off if we finish early?'

Gorgas breathed out through his nose. 'I take it that means you haven't been to see your mother yet,' he said. 'You know, the sooner you do it, the sooner it'll be done.'

'But Uncle,' she replied, with a nice touch of horror in her voice, 'you can't expect me to go and see Mother until I'm *finished*. It wouldn't be right.'

Gorgas shrugged. 'You do what you like,' he said. 'Just don't expect me to keep the peace between you indefinitely, that's all. You know you're welcome to stay here as long as you like, but—'

'We'll just have to try and get my toenails done ahead of schedule, then,' she said. 'Maybe we should get in a night shift.'

Heris turned her head and looked at Iseutz sharply, but didn't say anything. The girl looked uncomfortable for a moment, then said, 'For what it's worth, I really am doing my best. If I could sew, I'd sew. But I can't. And I don't want to go and see my mother. I can't imagine saying anything to her that wouldn't make things ten times worse.'

'I don't believe that,' Gorgas said.

'And besides,' she went on, ignoring him, 'what on earth makes you think she wants to see me? If she was that keen on the idea, why hasn't she come here? Or at least sent a message or something?'

'She's a busy—' Gorgas started.

'Yes,' the girl interrupted, 'I know. And that's fine. She can be busy, and I can sit here being put back together again, like something the cat's knocked over, and everybody can be happy. Come on, Uncle, what exactly is it that makes you believe we all *want* to love each other?'

There was a moment of complete silence; then Heris quickly gathered up her sewing and wasn't there any more, and Gorgas got slowly to his feet, walked across and sat beside her. She kept the rest of her body still, but couldn't keep her head from flinching away just a little.

'That's all right,' Gorgas said, so quietly that she could hardly hear him. 'That's fine. You go ahead and give up. After all, you proved your point while you were in the prison, and before that in the City. You had this fine life all lined up for you, you were going to get married and live the way people are meant to, and then a man called Bardas Loredan came along and he killed the man you were going to marry, and that life wasn't there any more. So you decided, right there on the spot, you decided: no compromise, no giving an inch, you wanted justice, or revenge, or whatever you want to call it, not that it matters a great deal. And you know what? You failed. Total waste of time and blood, and all for melodrama.' He was right up close to her ear now, like an awkward boy edging nervously along a bench at a wedding towards the girl he's afraid to talk to. 'Look at you. You're a mess. There are bits of you *missing*. But here I am, and here's your mother, and we *never* give up on anything; not because it's impossible, not for armies or storms at sea or plagues or fires or the earth opening up and swallowing whole cities, and certainly not for melodrama. Now I don't care what you want or what you're feeling or even what a complete and utter mess and waste of good food and water you happen to be; *nobody* gives up in this family, because there's a lot of enemies out there, more than Shastel and Temrai put together, and on our side, there's just *us*. Understood?'

'That's it, is it? We've got to love each other because nobody else ever could?'

A wide smile spread gradually over Gorgas' face. 'You've got it,' he said. 'There's me; well, that doesn't need explaining. There's your Uncle Bardas, who killed people for a living and brought the plainspeople down on Perimadeia. There's you. And there's your mother.'

Iseutz nodded slowly. 'All right,' she said. 'Just out of interest, what did she do?'

'Oh, she's the pick of us,' Gorgas said softly. 'I kill in self-defence, Bardas killed for other people, you want to kill for revenge, or whatever it is that's eating those holes in your poor little brain. But your mother killed a whole damn city, and you want to know why? Not for revenge, though the gods know she had cause. Not because she had to. She killed Perimadeia to save money.' He grinned suddenly, as if remembering a marvellous joke. 'Not to *make* money, you understand, to *save* it. She was sick and tired of paying interest on the money she borrowed in Perimadeia to set up this stupid bloody bank – money down the drain, she said, and nothing to show for it – so she sent me to open the gates and kill the whole damned city. Isn't that wonderful? Well, I think so. She may be an evil bitch, but you've got to admire her single-mindedness.'

Iseutz moved her head a little and looked him in the eye. 'It was you who opened the gates,' she said.

'It was me. Your mother's idea, and I did it.'

'I see,' Iseutz nodded. 'And you did it.'

'It happened to coincide with my own interests,' Gorgas said, 'but I'm not the one who takes the initiative. She suggested it, and I agreed.'

Iseutz looked at him for a long time. 'Uncle Gorgas,' she said, 'why do you pretend to love your family when you hate them more than I do?'

Gorgas thought for a moment. 'You're confusing the

issue,' he said. 'You're mixing up hating and recognising evil.' He looked away for a moment, a man at home enjoying his garden. 'Do you really think it's not possible to love someone when you know they've got this bit of evil inside them? You surprise me, I thought you were more grown-up than that. You think my wife doesn't love me, in some part of her mind? You think I don't love Bardas, my brother? Or Niessa, or you? This is strange,' he added, leaning back in his chair, 'being able to talk freely like this; I suppose it's because I've got so much in common with you.'

'You think so?'

'Don't be offended. I like you. You're helping me put into words a lot of stuff that's just been churning round in my mind for years and years. Come on,' he said, sitting up again, 'tell me what you think of me. I don't mind.'

Iseutz considered her reply, thoughtful, like a student in a tutorial. 'What you've just told me,' she said. 'It's not something I can begin to understand. I mean, I can see it's possible; one man can open a gate, it's just a matter of sliding back some bolts, lifting a bar, and because that gate's open, a city can fall and thousands of people can die. It's the idea that someone could do that *deliberately* that I'm having trouble with.' She ran the stumps of her fingers across her lower lip. 'Is it something you enjoyed?' she asked. 'Did you like doing it?'

'Do I need to answer that?' Gorgas replied.

She shook her head. 'No, it was a silly question. It'd be too easy to write it down to some sort of madness, on a par with the crazy people who kill small children in the woods. What's the answer, then? Their rules don't apply to us, is that it?'

Gorgas pursed his lips. 'I think you're getting there,' he said. 'I see our family as being a small group of soldiers, like those Shastel raiders; we're deep in enemy territory, outnumbered, every man's hand against us, can't expect help or relief from outside; so we do whatever we have to do, and we make it all right with ourselves because there's so many of them and so few of us, they're the enemy and we have some sort of right to survive. So the raiding party takes what it needs, does what it has to do, it keeps on going, and when you know they don't take prisoners, you forget all about giving yourself up. I like to think of it as being like a different species of animals. It's all right to kill animals to eat, or to wear, or because they've built a nest in your roof and they sting you whenever you go in or out. No, that's not it, not that we're better than them, just different. There's some people you're allowed to kill, and some you're not. That's why I can forgive Bardas; and why you should, too.'

Iseutz shrugged. 'I'll grant you, he's probably the best of us. But he's also the one who's harmed *me*. So he's the only one I hate. I really don't want to think about the rest of it.'

Gorgas nodded. 'No reason why you should,' he said. 'It may sound like I go around agonising about all this, but I don't really. It's that word *evil*, it's not the right one. Would it be better to say it's a different perspective on the value of human life, in absolute as opposed to subjective terms?' He stood up. 'You know, I'm really glad we've had this talk. It's cleared the air, don't you think?'

Iseutz made a vague gesture. 'You really did that?' she said. 'Opened the gates of the City and let the enemy in?'

Gorgas spread his hands. 'One lot of enemies killed another lot,' he said. 'I didn't start that fight. I didn't kill a single Perimadeian. Like you said, I pulled back a bolt or two and lifted a bar. Uncle Bardas didn't start the war. Temrai didn't start the war. Your Great-Uncle Maxen didn't start the war.'

'Oh, gods,' said Iseutz. 'I'd forgotten him.'

'And I'll tell you another thing,' Gorgas said, stooping to pick up an empty plate. 'Your father didn't rape your mother; it was just good business, at the time. There now,' he said, frowning, 'I don't think I've left anything out, have I? At least I've been straight with you, and that's one thing I do pride myself on, being straight with people. It's like the proverb says, you can choose your friends but you can't choose your family.'

'Doctor Gannadius!'

Now if only I was as old as I feel, I'd be deaf and not be able to hear you. Gannadius quickened his pace a little.

'Doctor Gannadius! Wait!'

No chance, Gannadius thought sadly. He couldn't have failed to hear a voice that loud if he'd been stone deaf, or even dead. He looked round and saw Volco Bovert bearing down on him like a fashionable prophecy. 'Master Bovert,' he said politely.

'You're a hard man to find, Doctor,' Bovert said, catching his breath. There was an awful lot of Volco Bovert, probably more than would ever be necessary except in the direst of emergencies; ironic, in a way, since his official post was Tribune of the Poor. 'I think it's time we talked seriously about the Scona problem.'

'My pleasure,' Gannadius sighed. He'd only spoken to Tribune Volco a handful of times, at this or that faculty reception, but he knew him well enough to anticipate that insufferable habit of his of reducing the world and everything that happened in it to an order of business; thus, everything to do with Scona and the war became 'the Scona problem', just as anything connected with the Foundation's commercial activities was swept into 'the balance of payments issue', while the sum of human knowledge and all attempts to expand or clarify it was lumped together under 'the syllabus debate'. It went without saying that the quality that had earned him such a high position in the Shastel hierarchy (apart from being fifth in line to be head of the Bovert family) was his exceptional clarity of thinking and ability to pare away all the fat and concentrate on the meat. *Where I come from*, Gannadius reflected, *we had a word for people like that. It was five letters long and rhymed with 'midiot'.*

The enormous presence of Tribune Volco backed him into a ledge in the Cloister wall, and he perched on the head of a low-level carved lion while Volco settled comfortably on a wide stone seat. 'Thank you for sparing the time,' Volco said. 'Now then, about Scona. We need you to *do* something.'

For a moment, Gannadius was completely confused. All he could think of was that Volco, for some reason to do with the bizarre complexities of faction politics, wanted him to lead the next raiding party; and he didn't really want to do that. He was still swimming in circles round the idea when Volco went on. 'You see,' he said, in a low whisper that was probably inaudible a mile away, 'we believe that the military option – the *conventional* military option – is not the ideal solution for us at this time. We therefore believe that the time has come to explore *other approaches.*'

Gods, Gannadius realised with a mixture of amusement and horror, the fat fool's talking about magic. He wants me to hex the rebels into oblivion. He actually thinks—

The vision, or whatever you choose to call it. The great armada, with the ruins of Scona in the background. And Bardas Loredan leading the army.

He shook himself, like a dog climbing out of a river. 'With respect,' he said, 'I don't see how an abstract philosopher like myself can really presume to advise a practical man of affairs such as yourself—'

'Other approaches,' Volco repeated. 'Oh, I've heard all about the sterling efforts made by yourself and Patriarch Alexius on behalf of Perimadeia. Now it's true that in the long run, those efforts were conspicuously lacking in success; but we feel that in the context of the Perimadeian war, any such efforts, however well conceived and ably executed, were doomed to failure from the start. Whereas in the matter of the Scona problem—'

Gannadius looked into the Tribune's eyes. No doubt about it, the man sincerely believed in magic – of course he did, because magic was such a perfect solution to the problems besetting his faction and the Bovert family, in which case it *had* to work. It would work, if only because Volco Bovert needed it to.

So what are you going to do? Refuse? Not advisable, since your position here is based on a whole series of misleading hints designed to give the impression that magic really does work, and that you know how to do it. Serves you right for trying to make a living selling snake-oil.

'I see what you mean,' Gannadius interrupted; and then inspiration struck. 'And of course, I've been actively investigating the possibilities for quite some time. But I'm sorry to say I've run up against a difficulty.'

'A difficulty,' Volco said, as if referring to some abstruse type of mythical or heraldic beast. 'I see. What kind of difficulty?'

'It's very simple,' Gannadius said. 'You have me, but Scona has the Patriarch Alexius. I'm afraid we cancel each other out. Which means,' he persevered, doggy-paddling frantically in a sea of self-contempt, 'that I'm fending off his curses, and he's fending off mine. The end result is that neither of us can actually achieve anything, other than making sure that magic can't be used as a weapon by either side.'

Volco's nostrils twitched as Gannadius spoke the fatal word *magic*, a word he wouldn't have used if he wasn't more or less at the end of his rope with the enormous Tribune and therefore tending to be dangerously sloppy in his choice of vocabulary. But as soon as the word was out, Volco's whole demeanour changed; suddenly he was like a pig that's heard the sty gate creaking on its hinges.

'Fascinating,' he said. 'But really, we mustn't despair of the, um, metaphysical approach so lightly. If it's simply a matter of resources—'

Ah yes, here we go. Build more ships. Enlist more soldiers. Buy bigger and stronger magic. 'Resources, yes,' Gannadius said, 'but sadly, not resources that are readily available. To put it in its simplest terms, to beat their magic we need more and better magicians, and I'm afraid that as far as our resources of magicians go, you're looking at them.'

Volco blinked, as if a horse had just galloped through a puddle at his feet, spraying him with muddy water. 'I understand,' he said. 'And what about the rebels? Do they have further and better magicians?'

'Not as far as I'm aware,' Gannadius replied cautiously. 'Though to be honest with you, I've really got no foolproof way of knowing. I'm afraid that's the nature of the beast, Tribune, we won't know what they've got till they hit us with it.'

Volco thought for a moment; he looked like a volcano trying to remember the words of a song. 'This Alexius,' he said. 'Would you be able to neutralise him, render him harmless to us?' Unfortunate tone of voice. 'In which case, surely, you would then be able to—'

'Tribune,' Gannadius broke in with what he hoped was a disarming smile, 'I would if I could but I can't. I'm sorry to have to say this, but really, there's nothing doing. I'd hate for you to waste your energies on a dead end.'

Volco stood up. 'Thank you for your opinion, Doctor,' he said. 'No doubt you'll let me know as soon as the situation changes.'

Wonderful, Gannadius reflected, as he watched the Tribune barrelling off down the Cloister, now I've made an enemy of the sort of man who never forgives his hammer if he knocks a nail in crooked. He got up, thought for a moment, and headed back up the Cloister in the direction of the Clerk of Works' office.

The post of Clerk of Works, like every job on Shastel that could be done with manicured nails, was purely formal; that is, the Clerk was a busy man with an important and responsible position, but not the one his title implied. The responsibility for making sure the buildings didn't fall down resided with the Refurbishments Steward, who was nominally in charge of supplying fresh flowers for the war memorials.

What the Clerk did was infinitely more important.

Because, once upon a time, the Clerk had been in charge of allocating meeting rooms to the various groups who wanted to hold regular discussions, the post had gradually mutated into that of semi-official referee of all faction activity. In formal debates in Chapter, the Clerk made sure that all appropriate protocols were observed, and outside Chapter he was the only man who could be seen to act as a mediator in faction disputes. Since the post had to be held by a man of unimpeachable neutrality, all the factions fought like tigers to secure it for one of their leading partisans, and for the time being the Separatists held the prize, in the shape of Jaufrez Mogre.

'Hello, Doctor,' Mogre said, looking up from whatever it was he'd been reading. 'This is a rare treat. Come to get your feet dirty in the political sewers?'

That, Gannadius reflected, was what he liked about Jaufrez Mogre. Alone of all the Shastel factioneers he'd met, Mogre freely admitted that his life's work was a game, and a dangerous and silly one at that. *Useless, yes, and potentially disastrous, almost as bad as abstract philosophy*, he'd cheerfully admitted, when after a long and lugubrious evening over a jar of genuine Colleon applejack Gannadius had actually voiced his opinion of Shastel politics. *The difference is, we don't pretend we can turn each other into frogs. Good applejack, this, have another.*

'Jaufrez, I want to tell you something,' Gannadius replied, sitting down and looking meaningfully at the jug on a nearby table. 'You may remember, a while back, we were talking about various things and I admitted that I couldn't do magic?'

'Yes, I remember.'

'Well,' Gannadius said, with a sheepish grin, 'I was lying.'

Carefully, not allowing his attention to wander, Jaufrez poured two cups of Mavoeson perry in such a way as to make sure the bitter sediment stayed in the jug. 'Is that right?' he said. 'That's interesting.'

'It's true, Jaufrez. Not the sort of magic you're thinking

of, in fact it's not *really* magic, but it's not, well, normal either. I suppose you could say it's halfway between the two.'

'I believe you,' Mogre replied, putting one cup down in front of Gannadius. 'Don't think you're telling me something I don't know, because you're not. That's why I've always regarded you as a dangerous bugger; you can sometimes do this stuff, but you don't know how or why, and usually you can't make it do what you want.' He smiled over the rim of his cup. 'I do read the intelligence reports, you know. I was reading about all this while you still thought the plainspeople would never take Perimadeia.'

'Oh,' Gannadius said. 'I wish you'd told me.'

Jaufrez shrugged. 'I thought you knew. Oh, right then, I'd better tell you some other stuff you might not know. Niessa Loredan,' he went on, wiping his mouth on his sleeve. 'She's a witch.'

'Niessa Loredan?'

Jaufrez nodded. 'Straight up. She knows more about the Principle than you ever will. And if you want proof,' he added with a wry grin, 'you used to live in it.'

Gannadius frowned. 'I don't know what you mean,' he said.

'Think,' Jaufrez replied sternly. 'The original curse, right? And before you ask, this is straight from the bitch's mouth, via one of our most valuable snitches on Scona, so you keep this to yourself and don't even think about it without telling me. The original curse was placed on Bardas Loredan by Alexius at the instigation of Iseutz Hedin, Niessa's daughter. Alexius – and you, of course – then do everything you possibly can to lift the wretched thing, by which time it's got hopelessly tangled up in the affairs of Perimadeia itself, because Bardas Loredan has become Colonel Loredan and is in charge of the City defences. Bardas doesn't get killed by Iseutz, and the City falls. Now that's history. The connection you don't seem to have made is that the City falls *because* Bardas doesn't get killed. Or had you grasped that already?'

Gannadius sat still and quiet for a moment. 'Why?' he said.

'Because Niessa Loredan's a witch,' Jaufrez replied. 'Easy. She brought together two unwitting agents: her daughter, and a man with an innate ability to manipulate the Principle – natural, I think you call them – Patriarch Alexius.'

'What?' Gannadius lurched forward in his seat, spilling his drink. 'Alexius?'

'Ah, you didn't know that either. Interesting.' Jaufrez nodded. 'It's got something to do with the really rather bizarre history of the Loredan family – you do know about that, don't you? Oh, good. Niessa wanted the City to fall, and she wanted Bardas back, and she wanted her daughter back as well. Now I won't even attempt to go into the theoretical stuff, which is all equations and funny notation and long words, but basically, because of all the history of Bardas and Maxen and the systematic destruction of the plainspeople's society, the fall of Perimadeia was Bardas' *fault*. Niessa recognised that, she knew that in consequence the City would be destroyed by them, sooner or later, and it was just a matter of leaning on the right supernatural levers and tweaking the right pulleys to make it happen. But to save Bardas, not to mention Iseutz – remember, she's caught up in this ghastly Loredan family thing, her mother was Maxen's niece just as much as Bardas was Maxen's nephew – she needed to find some way to protect them that wouldn't jeopardise the fall of the City, which she very much wanted to happen. The purpose of the curse was to make Alexius avert it; to keep those two safe from each other, and therefore safe generally, by churning up the Principle all round them with shields and defences and all manner of such things; the result being that while all this was going on, Bardas Loredan could have jumped in the sea with lead boots on and still not have drowned – charmed life, completely safe from anything you care to name.'

Gannadius pulled himself together; not easy to do. 'But that doesn't explain what you said about the City falling because Bardas wasn't killed,' he said. 'Does it?'

'Again, my friend, think it through. Bardas is carrying the blame for what Maxen did to the plainspeople. The necessary outcome should be that the City is punished, *and Bardas dies*. Again, don't ask me to show you the maths, but Niessa worked out that the direction the Principle was tending towards was that Bardas should die defending the City, and the City survive. Not the desired result. But,' he added, 'with a little shuffling, a pair of silly old fools meddling with dangerous stuff they don't understand – no disrespect intended, of course – and everything turns out the way Niessa wanted. Apparently she had a slice of unexpected luck when it turned out there was another natural in there rooting for Bardas, but otherwise it was all according to plan. And that's why I worry about magic, and Niessa Loredan being a witch. And,' he went on, staring hard into Gannadius' eyes, 'why I made damn sure we got you before she could. My big mistake was thinking Alexius was too old and frail to make the journey, or be any use to her if he did. *Bad* mistake, that. I should have realised that it was the Principle that nearly killed him back during the siege, not his own bad health. But,' he added with a sigh, 'when you've got a thousand and one things to take care of, you get lazy and jump to unwarranted conclusions. Sorry, I've been rabbiting on. You came here to tell me something?'

Gannadius was silent for a long time. 'I think I owe you an apology,' he said. 'I thought you were just another of the faction buffoons, and in fact you run the place.'

Jaufrez looked scandalised. 'Me?' he said. 'Not in the least. Shastel is run by the Foundation in Chapter, in accordance with the spirit of the precepts laid down by our founders, and if you think I think otherwise, you really are insulting me.' He relaxed and smiled. 'Gannadius, my dear old friend, what do you think we've all been doing these years? The Grand Order of Poverty and Learning is the greatest repository of knowledge and wisdom the world has ever known. We'd got the hang of the Principle back when your Patriarchs were still learning to do long division. Our problem is, rather like Niessa, we understand it but we aren't much good at making it do useful work. Unnaturally low per capita level of naturals, probably as a result of our intensive study of the subject – don't know why, but it seems that the more interested you are in the subject as a community, the less likely you are to throw up these lethal freaks of nature. Which is why we're so excited about you and young Machaera. That and the link you've presumably still got to Alexius—' his grin broadened. 'Oh, come on,' he said. 'Otherwise why in the gods' names would we hire an old fraud like you to be a Doctor of Philosophy in the greatest academic institution in the world? The boy who cleans your boots knows more philosophy than you do; but of course,' he added, yawning, 'he can't change people into frogs.'

It took Gannadius nearly a minute to get his voice back. 'Volco Bovert,' he said.

'My old tutor in Paranormal Dynamics, and the author of one of the standard commentaries,' Jaufrez replied. 'What about him?'

Gannadius licked his lips to free them. 'And does he know I'm a fraud?' he said.

'But you're not,' Jaufrez said patiently. 'Oh, you may think you are, but you're not. You're that exceptionally rare occurrence, the man who isn't a natural to begin with, but who messes about with naturals for so long that the ability rubs off on him. Which is why, now that the war's starting to go a bit yellow on us, we need you.'

Gannadius let go a deep breath, which he hadn't realised he'd been holding. 'So that's it,' he said. 'You're really a city of wizards.'

Jaufrez shook his head. 'Only in our spare time,' he said.

CHAPTER FOURTEEN

The next morning, Bardas Loredan left the house shortly before sunrise. He took with him a felling axe, three wedges in a leather bag and a quart barrel of cider.

He walked for about twenty minutes, found what he was looking for and set to work. He hadn't been at it long when he saw Athli coming towards him, struggling gamely through the long, wet grass in her fashionable boots.

'There you are,' she said. 'I followed the sound of the axe.'

'Good thinking.' Bardas leant on the axe-handle for a moment. 'I'm out of condition,' he said irritably, 'getting soft and fat in my old age. Did you want something?'

Athli shook her head. 'I felt like a breath of air,' she said.

'Right.' Bardas lifted the axe and pointed with it at the tree he was felling. He'd cut deeply into the trunk on two sides; the cuts looked neat and symmetrical. 'My great-grandfather planted that tree,' he said, 'when he was a boy. It was a tradition in our family – you planted a tree for your eldest son to cut down and make into the roof-tree of his house. Somehow my grandfather never got around to using this one, and it became a sort of family mascot.' He looked up into the branches. 'From up there, you can see right across to Joyous Beacon, assuming it isn't raining.'

'And you're cutting it down,' Athli said.

'That's right.'

'I see.'

Bardas took a step or two to the side, changed his grip on the axe and swung. 'The idea,' he said, punctuating his words with precisely aimed blows, 'is to cut away on three sides, the fourth side being the opposite direction from the one you want the tree to fall in.' He worked briskly and without apparent effort, raising the axe-head and letting it fall under little more than its own weight, making sure that each cut carried on from its predecessor in a planned logical sequence. 'Now, I want this tree to fall that way – right where you're standing, in fact – so the trunk will be supported by that little hump in the ground when I come to start splitting. Important to take the support away from each side equally – that way, when it's ready it'll go, just like that.'

Athli watched for a while, trying to think of something to say. 'What kind of tree is it?' she asked.

'Osage,' Bardas replied. 'Very few of them left in these parts now. People will insist on cutting them down, you see.'

'I see. And why's that?'

Loredan moved across a little. 'It's the best timber of all for bow-making,' he said, his eyes fixed on the cut. 'Better than yew or hickory or ash or elm, if you can find the right stuff. About one tree in twenty's fit for the job; the rest's firewood. Of course, you can't tell if it's any good until you've felled it. Evil stuff to work with, of course. If you violate the growth rings, you're finished.'

Athli watched for a while, as he took out the third side and moved round for the final assault. 'What's a growth ring?' she asked.

'Look at a trunk that's been sawn through, and you'll see lots of concentric rings, right? They're growth rings. If the tree was a family, each ring would be a generation, and the present generation would be the bark. That's the only bit that's actually still alive.'

'I think I follow.' She looked up at the tree. 'Where should I stand?' she asked.

'I'd come behind me, if I were you.'

He was making rapid progress; now, with each blow of his axe, the branches shivered. 'Is this what you're planning to do, then?' she asked. 'Start up a bow-making business here in the Mesoge? I thought you told me the people in these parts were mostly self-sufficient.'

'They are.' His pace was slowing now, and he paused after each cut to make sure he was on line. 'This one's for me. Hence the choice of timber.'

A few more cuts, and the tree made a sharp cracking noise and seemed to nod, as if in agreement with something he'd said. 'Nearly there,' he panted. Two cuts later, the tree groaned again and slowly toppled forward, directly onto the little hump he'd indicated earlier. 'Now we'll see if it's any good,' he said.

He walked up and down the fallen trunk a few times, lopping off small branches and studying the bark. Then he shook the wedges out of his bag, picked a spot and knelt down, holding the axe just below the head. 'Now, if I'm lucky,' he said, 'it'll come apart along this line like a book opening.' He tapped the wedge in just enough to start it, using the back of the axe-head as a hammer; then he stood up and swung. The axe-head rang on the wedge with a sharp, brittle sound that made Athli wince. After a few heavy blows, he took the next wedge and tapped it in a little further down the line, repeating the procedure until all four wedges were started. Then he walked up and down the trunk, hammering each wedge in turn, until one long continuous split appeared quite suddenly in the bark. 'Amazing,' he said, 'how something this big and solid can be taken apart with five bits of metal and a stick. Remind you of anything?'

'Not really,' Athli said, shivering a little in the cold. 'Any luck?'

'Too early to say,' Bardas replied. He carefully knocked out the wedges, hitting them sideways, first one direction and then the other, until they came free. 'Now for the boring bit,' he commented, and he set to work cutting the trunk off at the top, just below where the main spread of branches started. This part of the job seemed to take longer than the actual felling.

'Why didn't you do that first?' Athli demanded.

'If it hadn't split the way it did, I'd have known the whole thing was useless and I wouldn't have bothered cutting it off. That's an important part of felling timber, knowing what's good and what's just waste, and not persevering with something you know you can't salvage. Now I've got to roll it over to get the next line of wedges in.' He knelt down and heaved, just managing to roll the trunk a third of a turn. 'What I'm looking for,' he said, 'are flaws that run through all the way from top to bottom, right down through all the growth rings.'

'From generation to generation, like a family curse. How melodramatic.'

'Oh, it's primal stuff, chopping down trees. A tree's the oldest thing most men ever get to kill. Like I said a while ago, a tree's more like a family than a single thing on its own.' He tapped in the first wedge; it seemed to go in far more freely than the ones on the other side had done. He repeated the procedure, and when he'd driven the four wedges in almost as far as they'd go, there was another crisp crack and a section, like a slice out of an enormously thick cheese, came loose enough for him to lever it out. He laid down the axe and examined the section.

'This bit here's a possibility,' he said. 'The grain's not perfect, but it's straight enough, and I can get these kinks here out by steaming and bending.' He moved back to the remainder of the trunk, heaved again and repeated the wedging process, until he was left with two more cheese-slices. 'Well,' he said, 'this bit's completely useless, the grain's waving up and down like the course of a river. This chunk's all right, though; look, there's a lovely straight bit here, see?'

'Oh, yes,' Athli said, giving it a cursory glance.

'Wrong. There's a knot here, look, it wrecks the whole thing. Sometimes you can work round them, but this one's too big.'

'Pity,' Athli said.

'Waste. Well, what we can't use we can always burn.' He looked up and grinned at her; she looked away. 'It'd be a laugh if I can't get one stave out of the whole of this great big tree, don't you think? All those years, all that waste, and nothing at all to show for it.'

'Quite.'

He drove in the wedges a third time, lugged the three sections around until they lay side by side, and examined them carefully for about a quarter of an hour. 'Useless,' he finally pronounced. 'Not even if I cut the two limbs separately and spliced them in the handle. Isn't that just perfect?' He sat down on the grass and put his face in his hands.

'Bardas.' He didn't answer. Athli studied him as dispassionately as she could, trying to remember what it had been like in the old days. She'd seen him in a mess often enough, but she couldn't now call to mind the exact form the mess used to take. He hadn't touched the cider; now that was different, because back in the City the first thing he did on a bad day was take it out on a bottle. She wished she could remember more of the pathology of his downswings, but it was starting to seem long ago and far away, as if she was the one who'd moved away and he'd stayed where he was, more or less. In a way, this was the right place for him, beside the stump of this particular wasted tree. He looked like he'd been there all his life.

'I think I'll go back to the coast in the morning,' she said. 'I want to have a closer look at the market in Tornoys. There may be things I can buy there.'

He nodded, without looking round. 'Textiles, some of the local ceramics and brassware,' he said. 'The quality's not up to much, but it's cheap. They've been trying to set up factories, trying to find a good use for all the people we have hereabouts.' Now he looked up, but not at her. 'Pity you can't just take an axe to people the way you can with trees,' he said, 'split 'em down the grain and have a look at the way they lie. You'd waste a good few, but you wouldn't make nearly so many mistakes. And there's plenty more where they came from. A man can be ready to fell in twenty years, but a good tree takes generations, and you still can't tell . . .'

Somehow, seeing him like this made it easier, not harder, than she'd imagined. But like this, he was just waste, like the ruins of the tree. Lots of waste here in the Mesoge.

'I expect I'll be back this way from time to time,' she said, glad that he wasn't looking at her when she said that. 'You take care of yourself, you hear?'

'Thanks for the lift,' he replied. 'It was good to see you again. Oh, Athli.'

That tone of voice – would you mind passing me my hat, my sword-case, the bottle? 'Yes?' she said.

'Would you do me a favour and take the boy with you? Between you and me, I don't think he's cut out for peasant farming.'

Athli thought for a moment. 'I don't think I'm taking people on at the moment,' she said.

'I'd consider it a great favour if you did.' Bardas sighed, picked up a chip of wood and looked at it, tossed it away. 'No real future for a kid in these parts, and he's City, after all. This isn't the right place for young kids from the City.'

'I'm not sure I can help you,' she replied. 'I feel sorry for him, but he's no concern of mine.'

He closed his eyes. 'I'll ask you again. Please take him with you. This is a dreadful place. You can't even get a tree to grow straight here.'

Athli sighed. 'I'll tell you what I'll do,' she said. 'I'll take him to the Island and I'll try and find a place for him. And I'll do my best to keep an eye on him, at least till he's settled. And that's it, Bardas. No more souvenirs. These days, I can only carry cargo that pays its way.'

'Thanks,' Bardas said. 'Tell him to take the valuable
stuff – he won't want to, he doesn't like the way we came
by it.' He smiled. 'Robbing the dead, he called it; stupid
kid doesn't realise, that's what they're *for*. Oh, and he'd
better take that old sword of mine, it's worth a lot of
money.'

'The Guelan?'

Bardas nodded. 'Not many of them left,' he said.

'I know,' Athli replied. 'People will insist on breaking
them, you see.'

'Quite.' Bardas moved his head and looked at her, as if
she was a tree he'd split and found to be not suitable for
his purpose. 'Dreadful waste, but that's how things are.'

'The point,' said Avid Soef, for the time being chief
spokesman of the Separatists, 'is quite simple, and all
we're doing is trying to complicate it. That's silly. Let's
recognise that it's simple, and try and deal with it. The
point is, we have two choices before us in this war,
double or quit. There is no third choice. So, which is it to
be?'

Chapter was unusually quiet; and Gannadius, feeling
cold and more than a little out of place, had to try hard
to keep still. It was like those times he'd insisted on staying up when there were visitors, and then the grown-ups
had started talking about things he didn't understand,
strange and frightening, and he hadn't been able to slip
away and go to bed like he wanted to. Beside him,
Jaufrez Bovert was concentrating on the debate, apparently unaware that Gannadius existed.

'On the one hand,' said Avid Soef, 'we can quit. There's
a lot to be said for that argument, and you know as well
as I do that the Separatist movement has been advo-
cating it for some time. In fact, we were opposed to these
reckless military adventures from the start, and we never
hesitated to say so, here on Chapter floor, where everybody can hear what we're saying. But there's a world of
difference between *we should never have started this* and

let's end it now. The difference is, if we back off and make it look like the defeats we've suffered – I'm calling them defeats because that's what they are, nasty, messy defeats that have cost us the lives of good friends and colleagues – then we're lying to the world, and to ourselves. We're saying, in a big loud voice, that Shastel is finished; a few smacks round the head from Gorgas and Niessa is enough to chase us away, and nobody need concern themselves with us again. I don't like telling lies, gentlemen, it doesn't sit well with me and I'd rather not do it. Which only leaves the other option, to double.' He looked around; everybody was paying attention. He paused for a moment. 'And that's all I've got to say, really,' he said, and sat down.

'Mistake,' Jaufrez whispered in Gannadius' ear. 'That's a pity.'

Before Gannadius could reply, another man stood up on the other side of the chapter house. 'Sten Mogre,' Jaufrez muttered. 'Redemptionist. I think we're about to have something sharp inserted right up us.'

Sten Mogre cleared his throat. He was a short, bald, stout man with a little fringe of white beard, and his voice was very deep. 'One thing I enjoy more than most,' he said, 'is agreeing with a Separatist. Now, like all true pleasures, it's very rare, very rare indeed, and when I do get the chance, I like to share it with as many friends as I can. So, friends, enjoy.'

Gannadius heard Jaufrez groan softly beside him. Mogre looked round, then carried on.

'I agree,' he said, 'that we shouldn't abandon this war just because we've had a couple of setbacks. I agree, because the reasons we started the war are as valid now as they ever were, and I agree that patching up some kind of treaty with the Bitch would be dishonest and dishonourable. So it follows that I agree with what my friend Avid has just proposed, that we double. And there we are, basically, all in agreement with one another, the way good friends ought to be. All that's left to discuss, I think, are the details of how we should go about it.'

There was a slight shiver of tension in the chapter house, the sort of ripple of anticipation that used to mark the first drop of blood in the lawcourts of the City. Jaufrez leant back in his seat, folded his hands in his lap and closed his eyes.

'And the first thing I want to say on that score,' Sten Mogre said, 'is that now we're all friends, let's act like friends, put our differences to one side, and pull together. Where the war's concerned, we in the Redemptionist movement have always wanted to co-operate with all the other shades of opinion in this assembly – well, it's only sensible, isn't it, for pity's sake? – but somehow or other it's never quite seemed to work out that way. Don't know why, it's a mystery; fortunately, it's not a mystery we have to bother with any more, so let's put all that rubbish to one side and concentrate on getting it right. Agreed? Well, of course. I mean, who couldn't agree on something as basic as that? Like my good friend Avid just said, it's so very simple.'

'Bastard,' Jaufrez muttered. 'So why not just get on with it?'

Sten Mogre put his hands behind his back and lifted his chin just a little, adjusting his stance and posture as precisely and carefully as an archer squaring up to his shot in a tie-break. 'So here's the deal,' he said. 'We Redemptionists are prepared to admit it: first time round, we didn't do so well. In fact, we made a mess of things. Now, fortunately it wasn't a big mess and the loss is really neither here nor there, but as my good friend over there just implied, for a Foundation as powerful and influential as ours, any loss is a disaster until it's made good. So; I propose that we give up the conduct of this war and hand it over to someone who can be relied on to do a better job. And, after that quite inspiring speech he made just now, who can doubt that the best man for the job is my very good friend, Avid Soef?'

It was clear enough that everybody else in the

building had seen it coming, like a thunderstorm you can watch drifting in from the distant hills. Gannadius, however, was taken by surprise, and had to fight quite hard to stop himself laughing.

'I'll go further,' Sten Mogre said. 'I think we should give Avid Soef all the resources he needs to do this job properly. I propose he be given command of two thousand men and a budget of forty thousand gold City quarters.' He paused and smeared a broad smile on his wide face. 'With resources like that,' he added, 'surely the result has to be a foregone conclusion.'

As he sat down, the Chapter seemed to bubble, like fermenting liquor. Jaufrez was scowling horribly. He nudged the man sitting on his other side and said, 'Do something.' The man nodded and stood up.

'That's easy for you to say, Sten,' he said. 'But I'm not sure I agree with you on one point. Sure, we ought to be able to make a better fist of it than you did, given adequate resources. And I agree that if – given adequate resources – we fail to do the job, then we ought to be ashamed of ourselves. Where I'm taking issue with you is on the definition of "adequate". Two thousand men and forty thousand quarters, Sten? That's a bit cheapskate, surely. Could it be that you haven't really thought this through?'

Jaufrez stirred uncomfortably and hissed, 'Careful, you idiot.' The man nodded imperceptibly and went on. 'Here's what I think,' he said. 'I don't think we can undertake a full-scale attack on Scona with fewer than four thousand men and a hundred thousand quarters. I know it's a lot to ask,' he said, holding up his hand as the hall started to buzz. 'But I'm being practical; no fancy speeches about our wonderful fighting men, or how the enemy's bound to cut and run just as soon as someone stands up to them. As I see it, we go in with overwhelming force or we don't go in at all. And I think we need a vote on this before the debate goes any further.'

Gannadius found himself nodding, though he wasn't

sure why he should be taking sides on this or any other faction issue. Perhaps it was just the grace and skill of the recovery; to ask for a vote on a proposal that was so outrageous as to be inconceivable (half the army and a huge slice of the contingency fund) was inspired thinking, because a vote against the proposal would be a vote against the project, and the Separatists would have escaped the noose Sten Mogre had effectively draped round their necks, of potentially being responsible for a full-scale major defeat at the hands of Gorgas Loredan and his archers.

But it wasn't over yet. 'I'm having a wonderful day,' said Sten Mogre, 'I'm agreeing with two Separatists in one morning. I fully accept what my dear friend Hain Jaun's just said. Two thousand men and forty thousand quarters was downright cheapskate. In fact, four thousand men and a hundred thousand quarters isn't that much better. I say we send six thousand men and put the budget at a hundred and thirty thousand gold City quarters, and I say we vote on it now.'

Brilliant, Gannadius reflected with a shudder. *If they win, they'll get no credit, because with that much power they couldn't lose; in fact, they'll have to win magnificently to avoid accusations of time-wasting and squandering resources. And if they lose – well, I wouldn't give ear-wax for the lives of the whole lot of them. Wonderful. These people are all quite mad. And I have the feeling it isn't even over yet.*

He was right. Before the stewards had a chance to mobilise the assembly for voting, Avid Soef was on his feet again. The expression on his face was odd; it was the sort of look you might expect to see on the face of a man who's falling to his death off a cliff, who manages at the very last moment to grab the ankle of his deadliest enemy and pull him down too.

'Isn't it wonderful,' he said, 'what we can achieve once we put all our squabbles behind us and start acting like grown-ups? Gentlemen, I'm not ashamed to say this, I never thought I'd live to see the day when the various movements in our community would suddenly and simultaneously decide to forget all the garbage and work together. Well, here it is, and isn't it wonderful? I tell you, however the war pans out – even if we lose and lose badly, though thanks to the extremely sensible and statesmanlike proposals you're about to vote on, I can't see that happening, not in a million years – whatever happens in this war we're going to come out the winners, because the best thing we could possibly hope to gain from it has already happened, here, before your very eyes.' He looked round the chapter house, so that everybody could see how wide and ingenuous his smile was. 'And as a token of good faith, not to mention in the interests of the general good, I've got one last amendment to the proposal. Now, my good friend Sten's been kind enough to propose me as the leader of this expedition; I don't know why, because I'm no soldier, the gods know, but a man like me doesn't turn down an opportunity like this for getting into the history books. Still, I've got to say here and now, I'm not going to accept this assignment unless you vote for my really excellent friend and colleague Sten Mogre to accompany me as joint commanding officer. After all, two heads are so much better than one, and if one of those heads is Sten Mogre's, then surely a result's as good as in the bag.'

Jaufrez, who'd been slumped forward with his head in his hands, looked up sharply, as did pretty well everybody in the chapter house – except, of course, for Sten Mogre, who looked like a man who's suddenly forgotten how to breathe. For a moment, Gannadius honestly believed the poor man was about to have some kind of seizure; then he stopped quivering and sat still, his expression beyond description.

The result of the vote was predictable enough: an enormous majority in favour of the proposal to send Avid Soef and Sten Mogre with an army of six thousand halberdiers and a budget of a hundred and thirty thousand gold quarters to attack Scona and end the war. Gannadius, who wasn't eligible to vote, waited for Jaufrez outside the voting lobby.

'Well,' Jaufrez said, 'it's enough to make you believe in pixies. I really thought we were for it that time, and yet here we are, right back where we started, with no advantage whatsoever to either side. Still, I should have known Avid'd pull something out of the hat. Bless the man, he left it right till the end but he got us there.'

Gannadius waited till he'd finished. 'Aren't you forgetting one thing?' he said. 'Your precious Foundation's now committed to an all-out war with Scona, and if you lose—'

Jaufrez shrugged. 'If we lose, that's the end of the Grand Order of Poverty and Learning. Very true. But at least we'll all go down together, and that's all that matters in the final analysis. Besides,' he added cheerfully, 'we aren't going to lose, it's impossible.'

Gannadius shook his head doubtfully. 'I'm not so sure about that,' he said, 'really I'm not. Big armies have been humiliated by small ones before now; in fact, there's a school of opinion that says in wars like this, over a certain level a big army's a positive disadvantage. So—'

Jaufrez nodded, as if he'd just been told that fire can sometimes be hot. 'Of course,' he said. 'You're talking to a Doctor of Military Theory, for gods' sakes. But we're not going to lose because we've got a secret weapon, one that's so powerful and effective that we'd win without putting a single soldier in the field.' He grinned, and clapped a chunky hand on Gannadius' shoulder. 'We've got you.'

An hour or so after the debate, a senior member of the Foundation stopped at a fishmonger's stall in Shastel market and, after a few minutes' negotiation, bought a halibut for two copper quarters. When he'd taken his fish and walked on, the fishmonger's teenage son left the stall and walked briskly across the market square to a livery

stable, where he collected a rather fine chestnut mare
and rode at a sharp canter out of Shastel City down the
coast road to the sea. There he happened to stop and
pass the time of day with an old family friend, a fisherman whom his father and uncles had been doing business with for some thirty years. When he'd ridden on
his way, the fisherman whistled to his own three sons,
who were mending nets on the quayside. They put the
nets down and came over to where he was sitting. Not
long afterwards, the two eldest boys took out the family's
smaller, faster boat and set sail, although it was several
hours too early for the evening run.

They sailed right round Scona and, just as it was
beginning to get dark, they came across an oyster-boat
making its way home from its daily trip to the oyster-
beds of Blutile Shoal. The two Shastel boys hailed the
oysterman and asked if he had anything for them; the
oysterman replied that he had, and he hove to. They
talked for a while as they transferred the oysters to the
boys' boat; then they parted and went their separate
ways, the boys back to Shastel, running in slowly and
cautiously through the dark, the oysterman hurrying it
up so as to reach Scona before the light failed. As soon as
he made it to shore, he tied up on Strangers' Quay and
trotted up the hill with his money to the Bank, where he
barged past the guards (who knew him well enough to
let him through) and straight as a weasel in a warren
through the corridors to the Director's office.

When Niessa Loredan had heard what he had to say,
she thanked him, paid him and shut the door after him.
Then she called a clerk and sent him off with a string of
messages. He went up the corridor and down a flight of
steps to the messengers' room, where five or six boys,
ranging in age between twelve and sixteen, were playing
knucklebones. He gave them their assignments and they
scampered off down the back stairs out into the city. One
of them ran down the hill, weaving in and out of the
evening promenaders with remarkable skill and judge-

ment, and arrived, out of breath and sweating, at the door of Gorgas Loredan's house in Three Lions Street. He banged on the door until the porter came, in bare feet and shirt sleeves, and shot back the bolts. As soon as the porter saw who it was, he left the boy standing there and dashed through the portico and hallway to the dining room, where Gorgas and his family were just about to start dinner.

'Eudo?' Gorgas said, looking up. The conversation died away.

'There's a message at the door,' the porter replied, and the way he said it made any further questions unnecessary. Gorgas stood up, put his napkin on his chair and left the room. 'In my study,' he said. The porter nodded and scuttled back to the porch, where the boy was sitting on the step, getting his breath back.

'Thanks,' the boy said, 'I know the way.'

Another messenger ran up the hill, past the rainwater tanks and the cattle pen and into the tangled mess of streets known, for fairly obvious reasons, as the Drinking Quarter. He was taking a short cut; someone who didn't know the city as well as he did would have gone the long way round, following Drovers' Street around three sides of a square until he reached a cheap but tidy inn called the White Victory. It took him longer than he'd have liked to find the landlord, but as soon as he'd pulled his messenger's badge out of his pocket and waved it under the man's nose, things started to happen a bit more quickly. The landlord yelled for his eldest son, who appeared at the kitchen door with a tray of loaves ready to go in the oven for the morning's bread.

'Leave that,' the landlord said, 'and find the Islander girl and the old foreign git. Message for them from the Bank.'

The landlord's boy stared at the messenger for a second or so, then shoved the tray into his father's hands and set off like a runner in a relay race. He tried the foreigners' rooms, but they weren't there so he doubled back and looked in the common room, and then the side parlour.

'There you are,' he said. 'You've got to come now. There's a message for you from the Director's office.'

Vetriz and Alexius were playing chess; Alexius had the white queen in his hand, holding it in mid-air above the table.

'What do you think she wants?' Vetriz said.

'You're asking the wrong person,' Alexius replied. He put the chess piece back where it had come from. 'We'll call it a draw, shall we?'

'We most certainly won't,' Vetriz answered sharply. 'Make sure nobody touches the board,' she told the landlord's son. 'Very important game. Issues of national security at stake. Have you got that?'

The boy looked at her as if she was mad, very much as he looked at all foreigners, then led the way down the stairs and across the courtyard to the long kitchen, where the messenger was drinking a cup of hot chicken soup he'd managed to blackmail out of the landlord's wife.

'You're to go and see the Director immediately,' he recited, putting the cup down and wiping his mouth. 'I'll show you the way.'

'That's all right,' Vetriz replied. 'We've been there before.'

'I'll show it you anyway,' the boy said firmly.

Vetriz shook her head. 'No, you won't,' she said. 'You'll go away and commandeer, or whatever the right word is, a nice clean, comfortable wagon and a couple of well-behaved horses, and,' she added firmly, 'some cushions. You can show them your badge or something, I expect you know what to do. *Then* you can escort us to the Director's office. Understood?'

'But ...'

Vetriz looked extremely stern. 'Unless,' she said, 'you want to explain to the Director why Patriarch Alexius of Perimadeia died of heart failure trying to keep up with a fifteen-year-old boy running through the Town streets in the dark. I'm sure she'll understand once she's heard your side of the story.'

The boy was back in seventeen minutes, with a small cart and a bewildered-looking drover, who was wearing a horse-blanket over his shirt and stockings. 'Now can we go?' the boy asked pitifully. Vetriz nodded.

'Now we can go,' she replied.

'Thank you,' Alexius said, as the cart bumped and rattled down Drovers' Street. 'I really couldn't have faced a forced march this evening.'

Vetriz nodded. 'Bad headache?' she said.

'That's right.'

'Me too.'

They looked at each other.

'So what did you see?' Vetriz asked.

Alexius frowned. 'It's hard to explain, really,' he said. 'I was sitting in a large building, like a meeting-hall or a chapter house, and it was empty except for my old friend Gannadius – I've mentioned him before, haven't I? Oh, you know him of course, I forgot. Anyway, he was sitting directly in front of me watching something I couldn't see, and I kept tapping him on the shoulder, but I couldn't make him look round. It only lasted a few seconds, and I can't make head or tail of it.'

Vetriz shrugged. 'Beats me too,' she said. 'And mine was – well, if I didn't know better I'd say it was more like a daydream – you know, like *normal* people have? Except for the headache, of course, and that might just be falling asleep with my head at a funny angle. But I don't think so.'

'What was yours about, then?'

Vetriz' nose twitched. 'Well, it sounds silly, really. A bit – personal, let's say. It had Bardas Loredan in it, and whoever I was in it, I certainly wasn't me, if you see what I mean. Pity, really,' she added.

Alexius looked grave. 'It sounds to me,' he said, 'as if you've been using this wonderful gift that's been vouchsafed to you for frivolous and unworthy ends. You must tell me how you do that when you've got a moment.'

Vetriz shrugged. 'It wasn't worth this headache,' she replied. 'Dear gods, I hope I don't have to give a blow-by-blow account to Her. I wouldn't know where to look.'

'I expect the general outline will suffice,' Alexius said. 'Maybe that explains the secret midnight summons, and the urgency. She demands to know whether your intentions towards her brother are honourable.'

Vetriz sniffed. 'Next time,' she said, 'you can jolly well walk.'

There was also a messenger who ran from the Bank down to Strangers' Quay and the customs house, where the Deputy Chief of Excise and the duty watch were mulling a gallon of confiscated Colleon mead over the fire and toasting cheese. When the Deputy had heard what the messenger had to say, he pulled on his coat and his boots and stomped off along the quay, muttering under his breath, until he reached the Hope and Determination, a very plain and functional tavern whose idea of overnight accommodation was letting the customers sleep it off where they dropped. There he found the man he wanted, one Patras Icenego, a Perimadeian refugee and master of the *Charity*, a small, ugly cutter that was always tied up at the far end of the quay, fully rigged and provisioned, but never seemed to go anywhere. The curious thing about Patras Icenego was that, although he spent most of his life in the Hope and Determination, he never paid for anything and was always sober. As soon as he saw the Deputy walk in, he was on his feet. The two men talked together for a minute or so; then the Deputy went away, while Patras Icenego got up and left the tavern, walking quickly up the slope to the centre of town. He called at a variety of inns and taverns, and in a remarkably short space of time had assembled enough men, awake and sober, to crew the *Charity*. An hour later, the small ship was under way, its running lights fading into the sea-fret that hung around Scona like some form of protection.

'I'm getting sick and tired of this bench,' Vetriz said. 'I'll swear there's grooves in it.'

Alexius nodded. 'I'm tired of our cosy chats with the Lady Director,' he replied. 'Nothing ever seems to happen, I always end up with a headache, and I can never seem to remember what we've been talking about. I wonder if cows feel the same way after they've been milked.'

Vetriz looked at him. 'We usually seem to be having two conversations at once; you know, one here and one over there, wherever there is. The trouble is, when we're there it's no earthly use trying to tell lies or pretend; they just don't work. But we never seem to talk about anything significant. In fact, now you come to mention it, I haven't a clue what we do talk about. I wonder if you're right, about cows being milked.' She shuddered. 'Though I'd put it more in terms of flies and a spider.'

Alexius sighed. 'I think the worst part of it's the humiliation. Well, it would be,' he added, 'for me. After all, I was supposed to *know* about these things; Daisy the cow, Emeritus Professor of Dairy Studies.'

The door opened ('Not so bad,' Vetriz whispered. 'Under an hour this time.') and the usual bored-looking clerk collected them and ushered them in. There was a man standing behind the Director's chair. He looked older and thinner than the last time Vetriz had seen him; but also taller and stronger, as if he'd grown. That was odd.

'Hello,' Gorgas said.

Vetriz nodded in reply, then looked at Niessa. She looked awful; her face had somehow collapsed, and even her hair seemed flat and thin. *Perhaps she's ill.*

'No,' Niessa said, 'just worry. Sit down, for pity's sake. Now listen. At Chapter today, the Foundation voted to send six thousand halberdiers to attack Scona. It's inconceivable that we can withstand an assault on that scale – be quiet, Gorgas – and even if we could, the effort would ruin us. Do you understand what I'm saying?'

Alexius nodded. 'I take it you're looking for somewhere else to fight this war,' he said.

'Of course. Obviously, the only sensible course of action is to change their mind.' She paused and closed her eyes for a moment. 'Unfortunately,' she went on, 'I seem to have underestimated quite how big their mind is.'

Gorgas took a step forward and sat down on the edge of the desk. 'What she's saying is,' he said, 'we'd probably have a better chance trying to fight them.'

'I thought I told you to be quiet,' Niessa said. 'In fact, though, what my brother's just said isn't so far from the truth. Trying to fend them off in the Principle is going to be much harder than I'd ever imagined. It's possible, of course, but it's made much harder by the fact that they know what I'm going to do. I simply hadn't anticipated that,' she added. 'I thought I had the world monopoly on magic, and I was wrong. I think that's hurt me more than the prospect of losing the Bank, knowing that I've made such a stupid mistake.'

'Excuse me,' Alexius interrupted. 'Are you saying that the Foundation can – excuse me, they can do magic?'

Niessa shook her head impatiently. 'I'm not in the mood for an academic discussion about terminology,' she said. 'When I heard the news from Chapter, I used the – damn it, terminology again; call it a link or a conduit, whatever you like, the *thing* I've been building between you and your friend Gannadius. I tried to go through you to him, to make him change their minds. But I couldn't get in. You remember, you saw him sitting in front of you, but you couldn't get his attention, or see what he was looking at?'

Alexius stared at her and said nothing.

'It amazes me that they've been able to keep it from me,' Niessa went on. 'But they've closed it all up. If I can't even get in, how the hell can I expect to be able to do useful work there? And now,' she went on, 'as if that's not bad enough, they're attacking *me*.' She turned her head and glared at Vetriz. 'Attacking *us*, through Bardas.'

Vetriz felt herself go suddenly cold, the way you feel sometimes when you cut yourself deeply. 'Oh,' was all she said. Niessa looked at her unpleasantly, and Vetriz remembered Alexius' joke about honourable intentions.

'Of course,' she went on, 'I've taken such steps as I can. Bardas will be back here in a day or so, where he belongs.' Here she gave Gorgas a filthy look; he turned his head away. 'And now it seems that you've suddenly become terribly important to us all, which I must admit surprises me a great deal; another mistake on my part which no doubt I'll live to regret. Really,' she added, 'I only kept you here for tidiness' sake. Thank the gods I've had the sense to keep a few peasant virtues.'

Gorgas smiled at that. She ignored him. 'So there we are,' she sighed. 'The defence of the realm depends on the three of you. Gorgas can go through the motions of trying to fend off six thousand halberdiers. Alexius – well, we'll have to see what we can do. I have an unpleasant feeling that you're going to be needed for defence more than anything more productive, now that they've got control of your wretched friend. And you,' she went on, giving Vetriz her nastiest look yet; it made Vetriz want to giggle but fortunately she managed not to. 'You're going to have to look after our gods-damned liability of a brother, and I wish you the very best of luck. It's something we've been trying to do these past twenty years, and you can judge for yourself what sort of a fist we've made of it.'

CHAPTER FIFTEEN

'Sleep,' said Gorgas Loredan, 'is wrong. I don't hold with it. If a tax-collector showed up on your doorstep and demanded a third of everything you own, you'd cut his throat and start a riot. But along comes sleep, demanding a third of your life, and you snuggle your face into the pillow and let him rob you. Well, maybe you do. Not me.' He yawned, and covered his mouth with his fist. 'When I was a kid, I made the decision not to let the bastard grind me down; I started cutting back, slowly and gradually, half an hour per year, and now I can get by easily on four hours a night, and go without sleep entirely for three or four days in a row if I have to. Net result is, by the time I'm your age I'll have lived eight whole years longer than you have – that's four more hours a day for forty-eight years, you can get out your counters and check the arithmetic if you don't believe me. Think of it, eight more years of life. It's like what market traders do with the coinage; you know, the way they clip a tiny bit of silver off the edge of each coin that passes through their hands, and after a while they've got a jar full of silver they can take down to the Mint and exchange for new coin.'

The sergeant smiled. 'Right,' he said. 'You Loredans cheat everybody else, so why not Death as well? Sounds only fair to me.'

Gorgas shook his head. 'Not all us Loredans, just me. Niessa's got the staying power of a cheap tallow candle.

About the time I'm settling down to make a start on a useful night's work, she's dead on her feet and sleep-walking back to her bed. Bardas was a bit better than that, but still no night-owl.' He sighed, and put his hand over the side of the boat, letting his fingers trail in the water. 'I'm telling you,' he said, 'if I were to invent some medicine you could buy in a bottle that guaranteed you an extra eight years of life, guaranteed to work, money back if not, I'd be so rich I could buy Shastel instead of fighting it. But you try and convince people to do with-out a few hours' sleep, they look at you as if you were murdering their children. Crazy.'

The sergeant grunted. 'You'd get on well with my youngest boy,' he said sorrowfully. 'Four years old and he never goes to bed before his mother. If you make him go to bed, he only waits till we're all asleep and then gets up again. I caught him trying to light the lamp the other night – well after midnight, and he nearly burnt the house down. Four years old,' he repeated, shaking his head. 'By your reckoning, if he keeps at it he'll be older than me by the time he's thirty.'

Gorgas laughed. 'You send him to me when he's twelve and I'll put him to work as my night clerk,' he said. 'No point in all that extra time going to waste.'

'I'll hold you to that,' the sergeant replied.

The narrow quay of the factory island was already busier than usual. One of the first orders Gorgas had given when the news broke was for the stockpiles of arms and materials in the factories to be shifted up to the Town and every available ship and barge was being loaded up with bales and barrels, sacks, crates, jars and boxes. 'Not a bad start,' Gorgas commented, as they disembarked. 'But we're going to need to set up another shift, maybe two, and that'll mean we'll need more labour, not to men-tion materials. Then there's transport, and storage too, of course. Fat lot of good it'll do us having a cellarful of barrels of arrows here if we can't find the barges to ship them a few hundred yards over the water to the city.'

'Build more barges, then,' the sergeant said. 'Or you could requisition some of the cattle-boats.'

Gorgas shook his head. 'Not likely,' he said. 'They'll be too busy hauling timber and pig-iron from Colleon and the South. And as for building barges, I can't spare the shipyard capacity. I've got ten commerce raiders to build and a couple of months to do it in, so the hell with building barges.'

The sergeant raised an eyebrow. 'Commerce raiders?'

Gorgas nodded. 'It's about the only way I can think of to take the war to the enemy. That said, though, they may just find they've got themselves into something they can't handle. Have you ever stopped to think what proportion of its population Shastel can feed from its own farmland? Twenty thousand people living on a rock are likely to get hungry if the grain-ships can't get through.'

'Good point,' the sergeant said.

Gorgas stopped to let a cart laden with oxhides pass. 'And their timing isn't exactly wonderful, either,' he went on, 'declaring war when the early barley's just coming up to being ready to cut. Catches fire easily at this time of year; believe me, I'm a farm boy, I know these things. We aren't through yet, my friend, not by a long way. And those bastards up there in their castle might just learn a few things about what wars really mean that aren't anywhere in their textbooks.'

The first visit on the itinerary was to the sawmill. It was fortuitous, to say the least, that Gorgas had insisted that Scona have its own top-class sawmill, and had cajoled his sister into parting with the money to build it. He'd based it on the sea-mills of Perimadeia, but the Scona version was bigger and rather more efficient. The tide surging up the narrow straits between the factory island and Scona trapped water in a system of weirs, which powered five enormous water wheels, in turn connected by a fabulously complicated array of gears and drives to the flywheels that dominated the sawmill itself. Ten huge circular blades, each one as tall as a man, ran

day and night in the sawpits, while another feed powered
the rollers that drew the logs into the blades. Three shifts
of a hundred men, women and children loaded the rollers,
took off and stacked the cut planks, cleaned out the mountains of sawdust and made sure the mill kept going.
There were even two orderlies on duty at all times, to
patch up cuts and pull out splinters for workers who weren't
careful or quick enough around the spinning blades.

'I could stand here all day just watching,' Gorgas
shouted over the deafening noise. 'When I think of how
long it used to take us when I was a kid, fooling around
with hammer and wedges, it makes me realise I've
achieved something in my life.'

The mill foreman made a great show of being proud
and honoured, which Gorgas completely ignored; instead,
he immediately started talking about extra shifts, which
stripped away the foreman's jovial obsequiousness like
raw vinegar stripping a pearl.

'We simply haven't got the capacity,' he kept repeating. 'All ten saws are fully occupied as it is, except when
we stand down for an hour at night for sharpening and
general maintenance. And we've got to do that, or they'd
be scrap within a week.'

Gorgas shook his head. 'That's your department,' he
said. 'I want output up by a tenth in three weeks. How
you do it is up to you. Still,' he went on, 'if you want a
suggestion, I couldn't help noticing that you stop the blades
for ten minutes or so after every cut length. Why's that?'

'To grease them,' the foreman replied. 'It stops them
jamming and means we can go longer without having to
sharpen them up.'

'Fair enough,' Gorgas conceded. 'But can't you keep
them running while you're at it? It only takes a few
seconds to swab on the grease; the rest of the wasted
time is stopping and starting the train.'

'It's a safety measure,' the foreman replied. 'I wouldn't
fancy smearing grease on those things while they're
running, would you?'

Gorgas nodded. 'I can see you'd rather be here in the office, where it's safe and quiet. And if you want to stay in here, I suggest you get me my extra ten per cent. Otherwise you'll be out there with a pot of grease and a rag on a stick. Understood?'

Next they went to the burnishing shop, where a feed from the water wheel drove two massive circular mops, on which weapons and armour were given their final polish. Ten women and sixteen children were employed there, coating the items to be polished with grit in a base of runny wet clay and holding them on the wheels. The air was full of grit and dust, and Gorgas was glad to get out again after a perfunctory inspection, his eyes painful and watering. Nobody lasted very long in the burnishing shop.

'We could close the whole thing down,' the sergeant pointed out. 'It's only to make the stuff look pretty.'

Gorgas shook his head. 'Shame on you,' he said, 'and you a sergeant. How can you bawl a man out for not being able to see his face in his helmet if the helmet's not shiny to start with? You could undermine the whole basis of military discipline.'

After that they visited the tannery, another of Gorgas' improvements on a Perimadeian original. The four main vats were as big as cottages, with scaffolding towers to support the cranes that lowered and raised the bales of hides. If anything, the atmosphere was worse than in the burnishing shop, and everybody who worked there had their faces muffled up in any piece of cloth they could lay their hands on. It was generally held that you could spot a tannery worker from the other side of the Square, because his arms were permanently black to the elbows; assuming, of course, the unlikely event of a tannery worker ever finding himself in Scona Square, among the cheerful stalls and strolling promenaders.

'Our main problem is getting the materials,' the foreman said. 'You find me another ten tons of oak-bark a month and I'll up production by a quarter. And using anything else is a false economy.'

Gorgas scratched his head. 'That's a lot of bald trees,' he admitted. 'Still, that's my problem, not yours. What I need you to do for me is start producing stuff I can use for covering the hulls of boats; barges, mostly, and landing-craft for putting marines ashore on shallow beaches. You'll need to talk to the shipyard masters about what's needed. Pretty soon that's going to be your top priority, so be ready.'

Gorgas toured the brass foundry, the armoury and fletching shops, the bowyers' shop (where he joked with the foreman about having a brother who could use a place, if there was one going) and the ropewalk, and then it was time to head back to the city for a meeting with the treasury clerks. They were just as sullen and difficult as he'd anticipated; they had their orders from Niessa to make sure he didn't spend a copper quarter more than was necessary, and they'd learnt by his own example that attack was the best form of defence. Before he could even begin setting out his requirements for building the commerce raiders they were querying his last set of accounts and telling him there wouldn't be any money for new projects until he'd sorted out the waste in his present budget. He dealt with this obstacle by punching the chief clerk in the face, knocking him to the ground and breaking his nose, then he helped him up, gave him a bit of rag to staunch the bleeding and carried on the discussion where he'd left it. The clerks' attitude improved substantially after that.

'It's not the things that are the problem, you see,' Gorgas explained, as he and the sergeant crossed the city on their way to the barracks. 'It's the people. Sort out the people, and the people will sort out the things. And that's all there is to it.'

As he'd expected, the mood in the barracks was ambivalent, the usual mixture of enthusiasm and terror that mobilisation brings to a standing army. There was scarcely any room at the butts; five or six men were shooting on each target instead of the usual two, and the red and gold rings were so clogged that there wasn't room to squeeze another arrow in. Gorgas stopped to watch, and the chief instructor gave orders for a target to be cleared for him.

'I'll have to borrow a bow,' he admitted. 'I'm ashamed to say I haven't got a decent one of my own any more, not since my old favourite broke.'

After that, of course, he was spoilt for choice; but he made a point of choosing the plainest standard-issue ash bow he could find, and a dozen issue bodkinheads straight from the barrel. The crowd gathered around him was so thick that he was amazed any of them could breathe.

'Three up for sighters and then straight in,' he announced, as he flexed the bow against his calf to string it. 'That sound fair to you lads?'

A chorus of shouts assured him that it was. He picked up the first arrow, drew smoothly to the corner of his mouth, sighted low and to the right and loosed; the arrow struck a palm's width high and on line, not bad for a first shot with a strange bow. He cleared his mind and concentrated, well aware that he had a fearsome reputation as an archer to defend, checking his stance and the length of his draw and calculating the allowance. The next arrow only just brushed the bottom left edge of the target-boss, however, and he changed his ideas; after all, he'd shot on impulse all his life, letting his eyes and hands think for him ever since he was a boy in the Mesoge. For his third sighter he simply drew, looked at the target and loosed without thinking, and the arrow landed plumb in the top left of the gold. He put nine more beside it as quickly as he could draw and nock, then unstrung the bow and handed it back to the instructor without a word, while the soldiers cheered themselves hoarse.

'There you go,' he said, 'nothing to it. Now, if there's anybody here who wants to tell me the issue bow's a cross-eyed bastard, step right up. No takers? Just as well.' He grinned, as if at some private joke. 'I'm here to tell you, we make good bows on Scona.'

* * *

'The first issue we have to address,' said Avid Soef, 'is ships. Agreed?'

At the far end of the enormous table, someone yawned. Over on the right, a very bald man whose name generally got left out of the minutes was eating a chicken leg, noisily.

'No,' replied Sten Mogre. 'Absolutely not. Our first priority is an overall strategy, a game plan. Once we've got that, *then* we can start worrying about details such as ships.'

Soef glowered at him. 'Ships are just a detail,' he said. 'I see. I suppose you're planning to walk to Scona?'

Mogre smiled indulgently and folded his hands over his smooth, round belly. 'Save it for Chapter,' he sighed. 'This is neither the time nor the place for the celebrated Soef wit. Thanks to you, we're both in this mess up to our necks; if you want to have any chance of getting out of it in one piece, I suggest you lay off the cheap point-scoring and try to be positive. Obviously ships are an important detail; so are lines of supply, and communications, and battlefield tactics. In a war, everything's important. What I'm saying is, begin at the beginning. Let's start again, shall we?'

Avid Soef hesitated for a moment, then nodded. 'All right,' he said. 'My suggestion's fairly self-evident, I reckon. Let's hear what you've got to say.'

'Thank you.' Mogre leant across the table and drew the big chart towards him. 'All right,' he went on, 'here's the map of Scona.' He jabbed at a corner with a sausagelike finger. 'Here's Scona Town. Point to bear in mind: it's the only sheltered anchorage capable of receiving more than a handful of ships, so from that angle it'd be a good place to land. Against that, of course, it'll be the most heavily defended place on the island. Looked at another way, if we're going to win this war then sooner or later we've got to take Scona Town, either by assault or siege, and siege is out of the question unless we can maintain an effective blockade.'

Rehamon Faim, a tall, broad-shouldered man in his early forties, nodded vigorously. 'Exactly,' he said. 'Sooner or later we've got to take them on at their strongest point, so why not sooner? The key phrase for this whole war, it seems to me, has got to be *overwhelming force*. There's a point in any battle where, if you outnumber the enemy by a sufficient proportion, you can hit so hard and so overwhelmingly that there's absolutely nothing they can do about it – smother the bastards, in other words – and that way you keep your losses to a minimum. Well,' he added, 'that's how I see it, anyway.'

Avid Soef shook his head. 'I've read the same books as you, Rehamon,' he said, 'and you haven't quite got that right. In a land battle, on the flat and in the open, then yes, I'd have to agree with you. But an opposed landing on a defended position like Strangers' Quay – that's asking for trouble. Now, if you'd ever *finished* the book, you'd have read the bit where it's explained how, in a bottleneck or defended-causeway scenario, too many is actually worse than too few; and I say that's basically what a seaborne attack on Scona would be.'

Sten Mogre, who'd been pouring himself a drink, rapped the table for attention. 'You're both of you getting too far ahead,' he said. 'Scona Town's obviously the key to this war, but it's not the only potential beach-head, not by a long way. If you'd care to look at the map, you'll see the other choices ringed in red.'

With a general scraping of chairs and hunching of shoulders, the committee studied the map. 'You're being a bit optimistic, aren't you?' said Mihel Bovert, the acting treasurer. 'Some of these you've marked are just little coves, places you'd be hard put to it to land more than a fishing boat.'

'I'm coming to that,' Mogre replied patiently. 'Here's my point. Now, before I start, this isn't a suggestion or a proposal, so there's no call to go jumping down my throat. It's a straightforward question. Which is going to be better, a single landing in force, or a number of simultaneous landings all round the island?'

Soef shrugged his shoulders. 'You've obviously been mugging up on this, Sten,' he said. 'You tell us what you think.'

'All right.' Mogre resumed his comfortable sprawl. 'Let's just think for a moment about how the rebels fight. Quick word-association game: someone says Shastel, you say "halberdiers". Someone says Scona, immediately you think "archers". Right? So, we agree on that, now what we've got to do, the way I see it, is to organise this war so that halberdiers will be at an advantage over archers. And where are archers at their best? I'll tell you what the books say – not me, the books, the people who know about these things. And they'll tell you, archers are most effective when deployed defensively from a position of strength against a massed advance of the enemy across open ground.'

'We know all this,' interrupted Mihel Bovert. 'Make your point.'

'All right.' Sten Mogre nodded pleasantly. 'A massed advance of the enemy across open ground, gentlemen: that's what we've got to avoid. And here's where Avid's point about numbers sometimes being a handicap is important. When you're marching down the throat of a line of archers, the more of you there are, the better their chance of hitting something; simple as that. Better to have smaller, more mobile assault units converging on the enemy from different directions; you make them divide their forces – and with archers, as everybody knows, there's a magic ratio, somewhere between thirteen and ten to one, depending on distance between the armies and quality of troops. Once you go below the magic number, archers simply can't stop a determined advance of heavy infantry. So, our aim's got to be, split them up enough to take the individual units below that threshold. And we do that by dividing our own forces and making them do the same.' He paused and looked round. 'How are we doing so far? All agreed?'

Avid Soef did his best to look bored. 'Like you keep saying, Sten,' he said, 'we've all read the books. All you're really saying is, let's use a basic encircling strategy. Common sense.'

Mogre smiled at him. 'It looks that way, doesn't it, until you look at the map. Look at the map, Avid. You see these brown bits, all round the edges? They're mountains. Scona is basically one big mountain, with pockets of straight and level stuff scattered here and there. And when I was doing the first year of the course, they made me write out a hundred times, where there's mountains, there's problems. You know the sort of thing – ambushes, supply, communications, the right hand not knowing where in hell the left hand's got to, basic stuff really. If we turn six thousand men loose in parties of a few hundred in the Scona hills, sprinkled all over the shop like handfuls of seedcorn, we'll deserve what we'll undoubtedly get. Are you following all this, or shall I go back?'

Avid Soef scowled impatiently. 'Now what are you trying to say?' he sighed. 'First it's *Let's divide our forces*, now its *We've got to stick together*. Would you please make up your mind?'

'Calm down, Avid,' Mogre replied, 'nobody's getting at you. All I'm doing is trying to point out what I think is a pretty obvious fact about this war, which is that there's no simple answer; we can't just copy out a few relevant passages from the set books and follow them to the letter, we've got to use our heads. We've thought about the enemy, sorted out their strengths and given a little preliminary thought about how to avoid them; now let's do the same for the terrain.'

Pier Epaiz, the youngest member of the committee, raised his hand. 'As it happens,' he said, 'I've been doing a bit of work on this very point. I teach a class in property law, and I had my second years go through the Cartulary records and pull out all the old copy mortgages and leases from way back, anything to do with land transactions on Scona. We're correlating them now, and once we've married up our findings with the old tithe maps and census returns, we should be able to put together a far more detailed geographical survey than anything we've got in the main archive. Which means,' he went on, grinning nervously, 'that if we do a proper job, we ought to be able to produce reliable maps that actually show our people where things are.'

'Now *that's* the most intelligent thing—' Avid Soef started to say; but Mogre interrupted him.

'Point of interest,' he said. 'Any idea how long this exercise is likely to take?'

Pier Epaiz thought for a moment. 'Six months at the very most,' he said, 'and there's every chance we can do it in four, if I can get some more people assigned from other classes. In fact—'

'Four months,' Mogre repeated. 'You're suggesting we hold up the war for four months while your students read their way through old property deeds.' He shook his head. 'Tell me you can let me have something that's an improvement on what we've already got in four *weeks*, and yes, that'll be a useful contribution. Otherwise I guess we're just going to have to make do with the tithe maps, from which,' he added, 'if I remember my law classes, all the plans and diagrams you get in title deeds were originally copied anyway.'

'Yes, but there's usually further details in the text—' Epaiz tried to say, but the rest of the tables was looking at him, so he sat down again and pushed his chair back. 'All right,' Mogre went on, 'there is actually a valid point here. Geography - know the terrain. Maps - where we've got two or more units working towards a common objective, make sure they're all using copies of the same map, drawn to the same scale. Don't laugh,' he added, 'it's been known. One commander runs a pair of calipers over the map, calculates it's two days to the city. His colleague on the other side of the city's got a different scale map so he gets a different time estimate - result, one of them gets there before the other one does, ends up facing the enemy on his own and gets a hammering. What I'd like you to do,' he went on, looking across at Pier Epaiz, 'is get this mapping school of yours turning out precisely identical campaign charts copied from the tithe map, beginning with twenty copies just for starters and then keep 'em coming till I say When. All right?'

Epaiz nodded silently.

'This is wonderful,' said Sten Mogre, 'we're actually starting to make some progress. Let's see if we can make some more. Now then, we've got Pier on map-making, what else needs to be done before we can make a proper start? Ernan, would you like to put together some figures for me on, first, what we're likely to need in the way of supplies and materials – right across the board, from halberds to boot-buckles to bacon – and then second, what we've actually got, and finally third, what we need to get, where's our best chance of getting it, how long and how much. Are you happy with that?' Ernan Mines, small and painfully nervous sub-dean of the faculty of Mathematics, nodded several times. 'That's fine, then,' Mogre went on, turning to the tall grey-haired man sitting to his immediate left. 'Hiors, why don't you get your History students cracking on the best profile we can put together of the rebel forces – number, training, equipment, everything you can get? Grab hold of as many traders, fishermen, spies, whatever as you can lay hands on, anybody who's likely to know anything useful – recent shipments of military supplies, best guess at manpower reserves, all the demographic stuff, accounts of previous engagements in the dispatches archives; see if you can scrape together a few samples of rebel kit so we can see what we'll be up against.'

He paused to draw breath, then leant forward a little and looked straight at Avid Soef. 'And what I'd like from you, Avid,' he continued, taking no notice at all of the expression on his colleague's face, 'since you raised the issue, is a rundown on what kind of ships we'll need, how many of them, where we can hire them from and how much it's likely to cost. Keep in touch with Hiors, he'll be able to tell you what the rebels have got in the way of fighting ships so you'll be able to make provision for keeping them off our backs while we're trying to land troops. Now then, anybody, have I forgotten anything?' He waited for two seconds, then went on, 'Nobody? Well, if anything occurs to anybody after the meeting, let me know. Meanwhile, I'd like to suggest that we meet up in two days' time and see where we've reached. Agreed? Splendid.' He stood up. 'I think we've actually managed to get some valuable work done here today, so thank you, all of you. If we keep on at this rate, who knows, we might just all still be alive this time next year.'

The committee filed out, except for Avid Soef and Mihel Bovert.

'I know,' Bovert said, before Soef could speak, 'it's a disaster.'

'You reckon?' Soef smiled cheerfully. 'I don't think so. In fact, I think it's all going wonderfully well.'

Bovert stared at him. 'Really?' he said. 'That Redemptionist pig hijacks the meeting, hijacks the whole damn war, makes us look like idiot children—'

'Relax.' Avid Soef perched on the edge of the table and pulled a discarded map towards him. 'Use your brains. So Sten's taken charge; if you remember, we aren't exactly here by choice. Now, if it all goes wrong, we can turn round and say, Nothing to do with us, you want to talk to Sten Mogre.'

Bovert conceded the point with a brisk nod. 'And if all goes well?'

'In that case, we share the credit and nobody's any worse off. And besides, there's still a long way to go. But my guess is, since Sten would insist on taking everything on himself, he's going to be so busy running the damn war that he won't have time to remember why we're fighting the wretched thing in the first place.'

* * *

'Don't take this the wrong way,' Zonaras said over breakfast, 'but just how long are you planning on staying?'

Breakfast consisted of the remains of the previous
day's loaf, a slab of cheese aged to translucence and a jug
of cider in urgent need of using up. Nobody seemed particularly hungry.

'I don't know,' Bardas replied. 'To be honest, I hadn't
given it any thought. Why? Do you want to get rid of me?'

Zonaras and Clefas looked at each other. 'This is your
home too, you know that,' Clefas said. 'But we've got to
be realistic.'

Bardas raised an eyebrow. 'Realistic,' he repeated.

'That's right,' Zonaras said. 'Face facts, Bardas. We
produce enough to keep the two of us, just about. Three
would make it tight.'

Bardas stirred in his seat. 'That depends,' he said.
'Three useless losers like you, perhaps. Shut up, Clefas,
when I want to hear from you I'll let you know. This is a
good farm, or it was in Father's day. All right, we were
never rich; but it provided for all of us and paid the rent
as well, and nobody ever went hungry or barefoot that I
can remember.'

Zonaras was bright red in the face. 'We work damned
hard, Bardas,' he said. 'We were up and seeing to the herd
while you were still asleep in your pit. Don't you come
here telling us how to do our job.'

'Someone's got to,' Bardas replied calmly. 'Oh, I'm not
saying you're idle,' he went on. 'Nobody could accuse you
of that. You're just useless. Stupid. Everything you touch
goes hopelessly wrong. If there's ninety-nine right ways
of doing a thing and one wrong way, you'll choose the
wrong way every time. And you know why?'

Clefas got to his feet, hesitated, then sat down again. 'I
suppose you're going to tell us,' he said.

'You bet. It's because you're losers, simple as that. It's
not your fault,' he went on. 'You're younger sons, you
weren't brought up to think. In the ordinary way of
things, you'd have spent all your lives having someone to

tell you what to do, how and when to do it; Father, then Gorgas or me, then Gorgas' sons or my sons. You'd have been looked after, working hard would have been enough, all that anyone'd ever have expected of you. As it is, you've had to shift for yourselves, and you just aren't up to it. Well? You aren't going to try and tell me I'm wrong, are you?'

There was a long, heavy silence.

'All right,' Zonaras said. 'But whose fault is that? Who went prancing off because he just couldn't stick it round here any more? Now, if you'd stuck around, if you'd had the guts to stay here where you belonged instead of running off and leaving us—'

'For gods' sakes, I did my best for you,' Bardas replied angrily. 'All those years I spent risking my life, living in places you wouldn't stall a pig, just so you'd be looked after—'

Clefas jumped up again. 'Oh, yes, that was fine,' he shouted. 'All you had to do was send us money and that was supposed to make everything all right, like we were cripples or wrong in the head or something. All we wanted was one lucky break, so we could turn round and tell you where to stuff your damned money. Well, if you think you can come poncing back after all these years and start in being head of the family like nothing's happened, you're stupider than you look.'

Bardas gave him a cold stare. 'Sit down, you idiot,' he said. 'And stop bobbing up and down, the both of you, you're giving me a headache. The fact remains, I can take over the running of this farm and within a year we'll all be comfortable and have more than enough for the three of us. You carry on the way you're doing and you'll still be breaking your backs to scrape a living when you're old men. And for why? Stupid pride. You're like sulking kids, the two of you.'

'Really?' Zonaras said. 'All right, big brother, you go ahead and tell us how you're going to make such a hell of a difference.'

Bardas shrugged. 'Where do I start?' he said. 'All right, here's ten things you're doing wrong, taken completely at random. One to five inclusive: you take a look out of the window there, you'll see ten rows of vines, all leaf and no bloody grapes. You want to know why? Because you've overpruned, overwatered, overfed, overtrellised and over-thinned. Next to that you've got ten rows of beans you've burnt alive by smothering them in manure. Moving on from the withered beans, we come to the dead plum trees, which you managed to kill by girdling 'em right down to the quick, and just beyond that, your pride and joy, the new olive stands. Must have taken weeks of backbreaking work to lay them out like that, all neat and tidy; but they're all going to die, because slap bang in the middle there's two great big oak trees, and any fool knows that oak roots poison olives. Now then, your onions—'

'All right,' Zonaras growled, 'you made your point. Everybody makes mistakes.'

'Yes,' Bardas sighed, 'but not in every single bloody thing they do. It takes real talent to spoil *everything*. And you know the really sad thing about it?' He closed his eyes, rubbed them, and opened them again. 'Most of these disasters are because you're trying too hard. Really, if you'd just done the bare minimum and spent the rest of the day sitting on your backsides under a tree chewing blades of grass, you'd have ended up far better off. And that's ridiculous.'

'All *right*.' Zonaras was beside himself with anger now; Bardas could recognise the symptoms of the man who's going to come out swinging at any moment, and braced himself. 'So we're no good at it,' Zonaras continued. 'So what? Nobody ever told us. Father never told us how to do things - oh, he told you and Gorgas all right, made sure you knew all there was to know about every bloody thing. If we stopped and asked, we got a clip round the ear and told to get on with our work. It was always, you don't need to know that, Bardas knows. You do as you're told and leave the thinking to your elders and betters. So all right, we did as we were told, and where did it get us? All we ever learnt was hard work, not what the hell you're supposed to use it for. And all that time, where in the gods' names were you? You were up in that bloody City, killing people.'

Bardas could feel his breath shortening; anger, bad temper, not problems he usually had to cope with. A man who fights and kills for money almost never has occasion to get angry. 'I'd leave off that line of argument if I were you,' he said. His brothers stared at him contemptuously.

'That's a threat, isn't it?' Clefas said. 'I knew that's how it'd be, sooner or later. Bardas the big fighting man, Bardas the mighty fencer, do as I say or I'll bash your face in. Well then, is that what you're going to do? Going to bash my face in if I say what you don't like?' He relaxed, and grinned viciously. 'I tell you, Bardas, I always reckoned you and Gorgas were out of the same pod.'

'That's—' Bardas said, and got no further. Instead, he made himself calm down. 'That's not a very nice thing to say, Clefas. All right, I've done a lot of things I'm not proud of, but comparing me to *him*—'

Clefas looked at him curiously. 'Everyone else round here does,' he said. 'Why shouldn't we?'

Bardas stared at him. 'What do you mean, everyone else?'

'We're ashamed of you, brother,' Zonaras interrupted. 'Both of you. Like when you used to send the money; decent people wouldn't have anything to do with it, not even when we were offering to pay over the odds. We all know where that's come from, they'd say. All three of 'em, they're as bad as each other – that's what they said, but what they meant was, the whole damn family, as if we were like you two and her. And what did we ever do except stay home and try and make a living?' He laughed. 'Well, we tried that and we weren't any good at that either, and now we're just here and we aren't rightly bothered any more. So understand this, will you, Bardas?

We don't want you coming back here, not if you were to double and triple all the yields and gods know what else, because we're through with you, all three of you. Why don't you just push off and leave us alone?'

'Zonaras?' Bardas looked up at his other brother.

'Like Clefas just said,' he replied, 'we don't want you here. This isn't your home any more. Go back wherever the hell it is you belong and don't come bothering us any more.'

Bardas nodded. 'All right,' he said. 'I certainly can't see any point in staying here. So where do you suggest I go?'

Neither of his brothers said anything. He waited, then went on, 'I can't go back to the City because some bastard burnt it down. I'm too old to go fooling about soldiering any more, even if anybody'd have me. Come on, you tell me, where am I supposed to go?'

Clefas shrugged. 'None of our business,' he said. 'Why not back where you just came from? You've been there two years, it can't have been that bad. Besides,' he added, 'if you want to be all cosy and homely, why don't you make up with Gorgas and Niessa? You're all made for each other, if you ask me.'

Bardas looked at him for a long time. 'You say that like you mean it,' he said quietly. 'In which case, you're right. I don't belong here any more. And that's a shame.'

Zonaras shook his head. 'You may be a big fighting man, Bardas,' he said, 'but you don't know spit about your own family. You face it, brother, we're the Loredan boys, no good to anybody, no good for anything. Everybody round here says so.'

'Do they?' Bardas smiled. 'Well, if everybody says it, I guess it must be so.' He stood up and walked to the door. 'If you had any idea how I used to dream about this place, back when I was in the cavalry, and then afterwards, when I was fencing. I used to think, all right, my life's never going to be worth anything, but at least I'm making good for my family, looking after them, doing my bit as the eldest. For gods' sakes, that's all I've ever cared about. That's why I stayed away, because I was never going to be any good for you here, only if I was away, making money to send home. It was all just for family.'

Clefas looked him in the eyes. 'I reckon you were wasting your time, then,' he said.

Bardas nodded, and walked out. It was warm in the yard, the sun just beginning to mull the air, and the previous night's rain smelt sweet. On an impulse, Bardas stooped, picked up a small stone and let fly at the old sheep's skull; the stone hit it squarely in the middle with a crack that echoed off the back wall of the house, but it didn't budge. He shrugged his shoulders and lounged slowly towards the gate that led into the back orchard. He was untying the scrap of cord that made do in place of the long-since-rusted-up latch when he heard the sound of boots behind him and turned back.

Standing between him and the house were four men, four Scona archers; a sergeant and three troopers. 'Bardas Loredan?' the sergeant said.

Bardas nodded. 'That's me.'

The sergeant hesitated for just a split second, then took a single step forward. 'You've got to come with us,' he said. There was real fear in his eyes, and Bardas could see it was a stranger there.

'All right,' he said.

'Now,' the sergeant went on. 'That's my orders.'

'All right,' Bardas repeated. 'I haven't got anything to bring. We might as well go.'

The soldiers stepped back as he walked between them – *they're terrified of me*, he realised, with a flicker of amusement, *is that because they're afraid I'll hurt them or afraid they'll have to hurt me? Come to think of it, they'd have had cause if they'd shown up an hour earlier. I'd have killed all four of them then, if I'd had to.*

He wondered if he ought to mention it to them, just so that they'd know how well they stood with fortune, but decided against it. Instead he reached over and pulled the bow out of the hand of the man nearest to him, a quick snatch the man could do nothing about.

'It's all right,' he said, before his wretched escort had time to react, 'it's just professional interest. Is this the sort of kit they're issuing you lads with now, then?'

The archer nodded and reached out for his bow. Loredan held it out of his reach and studied it. Then he slid his thumbnail under a tiny split in the wood of the back, where a splinter was just starting to pull away. 'Just as well you haven't tried drawing this piece of shit recently,' he said, 'or first thing you know, you'd have got the top limb in your face and the bottom limb between your legs, and your mates'd have had to take you home on a door. Garbage,' he added, sticking one end in the soft ground, putting his weight against the splintered limb and leaning till it snapped – a long, messy, diagonal fracture, full of splinters and needles. The soldier watched him in silent agony. *Oh, gods, I suppose he'll have it stopped out of his pay, I didn't think. Oh, but wouldn't that be Niessa all over?* 'So I've just done you a favour, son, haven't I?'

The archer looked at him. 'Yes, sir,' he said.

'And you don't have to sir me, I'm just a civilian.'

'No, sir.'

'Whatever.' He handed the two bits back to the archer; it felt like he was a general giving out medals. 'I used to make them, you see,' he went on. 'Bows. For a living. Fortunately, that wasn't one of mine.'

'No, sir.'

'Not that mine didn't break sometimes,' he went on, just so he could listen to his own voice, 'but not like that. That's where some clown shaved down through the growth rings; do that and the whole thing pulls to pieces, past all saving.' He started to turn his head for a last look, but didn't. 'One little slip with something sharp, you see, and you'd be amazed the number of things you can comprehensively ruin without even trying.'

CHAPTER SIXTEEN

The war was born prematurely and, as is often the case with infants who come into the world before their time, to begin with it was touch and go whether it would survive.

The first blow was struck on the deck of a Colleon freighter riding at anchor in Leucas Bay, two hundred miles from Scona, and none of the men involved in the fighting were from either Scona or Shastel. The freighter's master, whose name is not recorded, was on his way to Shastel in the hope of hiring his ship to the Foundation as a troop-carrier. So as not to make the journey with an empty hold, he'd taken on a cargo of one hundred and six barrels of prime Colleon raisins, always a profitable commodity in the market at Shastel. The captain of a Leucas coaster happened to overhear him talking in a dockside inn about what he had on board and resolved to help himself to it. In order to justify this action, he decided to take advantage of Leucas' famous neutrality decree, which stated that the Senate and people absolutely declined to intervene in any military action fought on their land or in their home waters, by declaring himself to be a Scona privateer and running up the ensign of the Loredan Bank, which he had taken the precaution of buying from the Bank's agent a few hours earlier. In order to make absolutely sure that the coastguard wouldn't intervene, he also gave formal notice of his intentions to the nearest available state officer, who happened to be the customs inspector; who, having been given a generous token of respect by the master of the Colleon freighter in return for a fairly cursory inspection of his ship's hold (declared as empty in the landing manifest), decided it would only be fair and reasonable to send a customs clerk after the freighter to warn them what to expect. In consequence, when the coaster pulled alongside and declared the raisins legally seized in furtherance of legitimate harassment of enemy shipping, it found the sides fenced in with loosely gathered tarpaulins to foil grappling-hooks, and the crew lined up on deck with such weapons as they possessed, ready for a fight.

These were not the sort of terms on which level-headed Leucas merchant venturers chose to do business, and so the captain of the coaster broke off the engagement and fell back. For some unaccountable reason, however, the freighter decided to give chase. Among its crew were four Santeans, all of them enthusiastic cross-bowmen, and they were amusing themselves by taking long-distance shots at the departing coaster. One shot happened to hit the coaster's first officer in the leg, making him slip and fall overboard. The coaster came to a full stop in order to rescue him, allowing the freighter to come alongside and show signs of preparing to board the coaster. In order to do this, its master ordered the tarpaulins to be lowered, and the coaster captain, who on balance preferred the thought of fighting on someone else's ship, immediately sent across a boarding party of his own to prevent this. As a result, a Leucanian sailor by the name of Sepren Orcas, being the first man aboard the freighter, inaugurated the Scona-Shastel war by striking the freighter's sergeant-at-arms a glancing blow across the back of his shoulders with a cutlass.

As it happened, the battle was relatively short. The Leucanians were better armed and more experienced fighters, but the freighter's crew outnumbered them three to one, making a successful opposed capture of the freighter virtually impossible. Having done enough damage to make sure the freighter's men had other things on their minds beside boarding the coaster, they pulled out, struck the Loredan ensign and resumed their course back to the harbour. No one on either side was killed, and the only serious injury was accidental – one of the freighter's crew was in such a hurry to scramble up into the rigging to avoid the boarding party that he lost his footing, fell to the deck and gave himself severe concussion, eventually leading to the loss of one eye. In the reliable accounts of the engagement his name is variously given as Horg Pilomb of Colleon, Mias Conodin of Perimadeia and Huil Laphin from the Island.

It was, in short, the sort of battle that gives proper, serious-minded warfare a bad name: confused, inconclusive and largely pointless. When news reached the Foundation on Shastel, they immediately issued a proclamation that no ships were to be described as in the service of the Foundation without prior consultation with and agreement from the Shastel Faculty of Navigation and Commerce, with the intention of safeguarding commerce by discouraging any repetition of the Leucas affair, not to mention their own reputation – after all, the battle would be remembered as the first in their war, and they didn't really want that sort of foolish behaviour attributed to graduates of the Cloister.

The bench was uncomfortable and Bardas Loredan, who hated aimless sitting around under any circumstances, was tired and bored and wanted very much to get out of his wet clothes and warm up in front of a fire. He felt a strong urge to stand and walk away, but he couldn't quite muster the energy and besides, he had nowhere to go and no money.

Eventually a clerk found him, his head lolled forward onto his chest like a man who's died in his sleep, and woke him up.

'She'll see you now,' he said.

'Right,' Bardas replied hazily. 'All right, yes.' He stood

up and followed the clerk into Niessa's office. She was alone.

'Hello, Bardas,' she said.

'Hello, Niessa. Can I sit down?'

'Of course you can, you don't have to ask. Would you like some hot soup?'

It crossed his mind that he'd been kept waiting outside while his sister made the soup; but he was hungry, and said, 'Yes, please.' Niessa filled a wooden bowl from a ladle and handed it to him; he tilted the bowl back and swallowed a mouthful. It was a thick, spicy fish soup and quite palatable.

'That's good,' he said.

'Shastel recipe,' she replied. 'They have people who study *everything* over there.'

He nodded and drank some more. 'How about some cider?' she asked.

'Fine,' he replied, 'though I'd just as soon have table beer, if you've got any. I've a headache from sleeping awkwardly.'

Niessa smiled and poured him a cup of weak beer. 'Sweet dreams?' she asked.

'I don't know,' Bardas replied, 'I can't remember them. And the headache's just from sleeping at an awkward angle, I'm sure.'

'It's your headache. So,' she went on, sitting down behind her desk and steepling her fingers, 'just what are we going to do with you this time, Bardas?'

He looked at her. 'Don't ask me,' he said. 'Nothing strenuous, if it's all the same to you. That boat you sent was awful.' He sneezed.

'You'll have to stay here in Town,' Niessa went on. 'After what nearly happened last time, I'm not having you wandering about on your own where some roaming band of halberdiers can grab you and drag you back to Shastel to be a hostage.'

Bardas nodded slowly and drank the rest of his soup. 'That's the explanation, is it?' he said. 'Well, I suppose it makes sense.'

'It's just as well I thought of it before they did,' Niessa replied. 'After all, if I could find you so easily, so could they. Home was an obvious place to look.'

Bardas sighed. 'So tell me about this precious war of yours,' he said. 'You seem to be taking it very seriously, to go by what the men in the boat were saying. I take it it's a bit more than just an escalation of the stuff I got caught up in.'

'Six thousand halberdiers,' Niessa replied. 'Gorgas keeps insisting we can fight them; I have to keep reminding him that's not the point. You remember the old story Father used to tell, about the old man and the barrel of pears?'

Bardas thought for a moment. 'Actually,' he said, 'no.'

'Oh.' Niessa looked surprised. 'Perhaps it wasn't Father then. Anyway, it's a good story. There was an old man who had a fine pear tree, and one year he grew the best pears he'd ever seen. "I'm not going to waste these on the market in our village," he said to himself, "I'll take these to the City, where they pay top dollar for quality merchandise." So he put the pears in a barrel, loaded it onto his handcart and set off. But he'd never been to the City and underestimated how long it would take him to get there, so he only took with him enough food for three days. Five days later, when it ran out and still he was less than halfway, he was starving and there was no sign of anybody living in the desert he was crossing; so he opened the barrel, chose the smallest and meanest pears he could find, and ate them. To cut a long story short, he reached the town all right, but along the way he'd eaten all the pears. Good story?'

'It was all right,' Bardas replied. 'Not one of Father's, though.'

'Maybe you're right,' Niessa replied. 'Anyway, I don't want Gorgas spending all our money and resources just to win a war; that'd be like the old man eating the pears. And business has been all right lately, but not wonderful. No point fighting a war unless you know what the objective is.'

'Now I do recognise that,' Bardas said. 'That's what Uncle Maxen used to say.'

Niessa shook her head. 'He used to say it, but I made it up, when I was just a little girl. He came to visit once, do you remember? Well, of course you do; that was when you told Father you were going to leave home and join Uncle Maxen and the cavalry.'

'I didn't, though,' Bardas replied, 'not till Father died.' He pulled up short, waited, then went on. 'Anyway, he got that from you. Whatever. It's still a good saying.'

'Thank you.' Niessa studied him for a moment, her head slightly on one side, as if he was a puzzle she was just about to solve. 'Either you've mellowed or you've lost interest,' she said. 'I'd like to think it's the former, but I can't see it. I take it Home wasn't what you expected it to be.'

Bardas shrugged. 'In case you were wondering,' he said, 'Clefas and Zonaras are just fine. Clefas and Zonaras. Your brothers.'

Niessa frowned. 'Thank you,' she said, 'but I knew that already. I pay through the nose for a monthly report on exactly how they're doing and what they're up to. If you'd only asked, I could have told you and saved you a trip.'

Bardas looked up. 'That's interesting,' he said. 'Who's your spy?'

'It's not spying, it's looking after the family. And since you ask, it's Mihas Seudan – you remember, he goes round with a cart mending pots and selling bits and pieces.'

'Dear gods, is he still alive? He must be a hundred years old.'

'Seventy-seven,' Niessa replied. 'Every month he calls in at the True Discovery at Tornoys, and he gives the report to the landlord, who passes it on to my courier when he comes back that way from Silain. I've been keeping an eye on them for years, just to make sure they don't come to any harm.'

'I see.' Bardas thought for a moment. 'So you knew all about the money I was sending them.'

Niessa nodded. 'You never were terribly good with money, Bardas,' she said. 'Always inclined to throw good after bad. Like Mother used to say, you'd try and mend a leaking kettle by sealing it with water.'

Bardas shook his head. 'Serves me right, I suppose,' he said, 'for assuming they could be trusted to do a simple thing like receiving money.' He smiled ruefully. 'Do you remember the Witch, who used to live over at Joyous Beacon in that fallen-down old shed? Her son had been sending her money home for years, and she'd carefully buried it all under the floorboards, while she was living on turnips and gleanings and wearing old sacks. She reckoned she was putting it aside just in case she ever fell on hard times; and when she died and they dug it up, there was the best part of three hundred gold quarters there, enough to buy a whole valley. I don't know. Is that better or worse than squandering it all?'

Niessa clicked her tongue. 'A peasant with money's like a monkey with a crossbow - he'll do no good with it, and probably a great deal of harm. Talking of family, by the way, you haven't asked about Gorgas.'

'No,' Bardas replied, 'I haven't.'

'Well, he's been away for a day or so buying timber - masts for the commerce raiders he's having built, and why I'm indulging him in that, gods only know; we can't afford them, and I fail to see what good they'll do when they're done - but he ought to be back tomorrow for the next day. I want you here when he comes home. I'm not having any more of this daggers-drawn business between you two; I've got quite enough to cope with right now. I'm not saying you've got to love him; just don't make any trouble, that's all.'

Bardas smiled. 'Me?' he said. 'Like you said a moment ago, I think I've lost interest. I tell you what; you make sure he stays out of my way, and I'll stay out of his, and that way nobody'll get hurt, fair enough?'

'No, it isn't.' Niessa looked at him as if he was refusing to eat up his dinner. 'I can't afford to have him all upset and brooding, he's got a war to fight. But we'll deal with that later. One other thing, while I think of it. My daughter; she's living with Gorgas now. We're doing our best to make sure she doesn't find out you're here, but sooner or later she will, and then there'll be more trouble. Oh, Gorgas says he can control her now, she's much better than she was; but I'm her mother, I understand her, and she's long past the stage where anything can be done with her. I don't want to have to put her back in custody, but I can't really see any other way. I'll say this for her, she's remarkably single-minded.'

Bardas rubbed his chin. 'You're going to lock her up,' he said. 'That's interesting. How long for? Forever?'

Niessa looked at him impatiently. 'For the time being,' she said. 'I'm just facing facts, she isn't fit to be let loose. I shall have to organise something suitable this time. I admit I made a mistake putting her in prison; that was just feeding cream to a cat. No, I think she needs a nice quiet place with people to look after her, make sure she's taken care of and eats properly, at least for now, so long as we're here. As and when we move on, we'll sort out something more appropriate. Anyway, provided you keep out of her way you shouldn't have anything to worry about.'

Bardas nodded. 'Everything's under control,' he said. 'That's all right, then. Can I go now, please?'

'I suppose so,' Niessa replied. 'I want you here in the main building for now – the clerk'll show you the way, it'll take you a while to find your way around. I don't know what you're going to do with yourself, that's up to you. You're old enough to keep yourself entertained, I'm sure. But I don't want you leaving the building without telling me, and you're not to go sneaking out without a guard. Is that understood? It's not too much to ask,' she added. 'You can see as well as I can that it's for your own good as well as ours.'

Bardas sighed. 'Whatever,' he said. 'But if it's no trouble, I'd like to have somewhere I can work, and some tools and materials and such. Just enough to give me the illusion of doing something useful, you know.'

'No problem,' Niessa replied. 'I'm sure Gorgas'll say all contributions to the war effort will be gratefully received. He seems to think quite highly of your work, though I dare say he's a little bit biased.'

'I know,' Bardas said. 'He always was too soft-hearted for his own good.'

It was typical of the Islanders that they should build the grandest and most ornate council chamber in the known world, and refer to the assemblies they held in it as Town Meetings.

The Meeting House had been built seventy years previously, and it was the Islanders' proud boast that every copper quarter of its cost had been raised by voluntary contribution. Quite how voluntary the contributions were in a society where failing to keep up with the neighbours was the greatest conceivable disgrace is another matter entirely; the fact remains that once the project was under way and there was no realistic chance of stopping it, the people of the Island dealt with it as they dealt with all their enduring problems: they enjoyed it.

More than anything else, it was this capacity for turning duty and obligation into pleasure that made them unique, and uniquely successful. Mostly it was a continuation of their obsessive need to compete; once one of them had given twenty gold quarters to the Meeting House fund, it was inevitable that the next contributor should give twenty-five, and the next thirty. It became a point of honour for every trader to bring back something for the project from every journey he made; a barrel of coloured mosaic chips, a bolt of red velvet, a silver candlestick, a load of beautifully figured yew planks, ten thousand Colleon steel nails, a Perimadeian stonemason. When eventually the Meeting House was declared complete, there were howls of rage and anguish from merchants who hadn't yet had a chance to top their closest rivals' latest offerings, and there were old rumours of cellars beneath the building crammed with unopened books of gold leaf, mildewed bales of samite, barrels of gesso set rock hard and crated frescos chipped off walls the length and breadth of the trade routes. Once it was done and the fun was over, interest shifted elsewhere and the flow of offerings slowed down and dried up, and these days nobody bothered to look at the dazzling mosaics or give the breathtaking span of the roof a second thought; the Meeting House had become an accepted part of daily life, as if it had always been there, and people thought of it simply as the place where meetings were held – an improvement on holding them in the open air, and that was all there was to say on the matter.

Venart Auzeil arrived an hour early for the Town Meeting, but in the event he was very lucky to get a seat at all. The news that Shastel was looking to hire seventy ships and crews for their war against Scona had gone round the Island like a rumour of free beer, starting as an approximation of the truth and ending up as an open invitation to anybody in possession of a vessel bigger than a large soup bowl to come along and take a shovel to the contents of the Foundation's treasury. In the end he managed to find a gap on a bench in the middle of the seventh row between a very fat lamp wholesaler he'd spoken to once at a fair and a group of sour-faced old men he suspected of being a herring syndicate.

After a very long time (time spent in the immediate vicinity of herring traders passes very slowly) the sponsors of the meeting got up on the dais at the front, introduced themselves and stated the purpose of the meeting; yes, Shastel was looking to hire ships, mostly bulk transports that could act as troop carriers, although they were also interested in a few fast cutters to serve as escorts. As accredited representatives of the Foundation on the Island, the sponsors were empowered to accept tenders for the contract from individuals, syndicates or companies; tenders were to be in writing, delivered to the Foundation's main office in the Little Market Yard, and the results would be posted in the Square in three days' time. Were there any questions?

Venart took a deep breath and pushed himself up out of his seat. 'I'd like to say something,' he roared, having underestimated the quality of the House's legendary acoustics. Everybody in the building stared at him.

'I'd like to say something, please,' he repeated, in a quieter voice. 'Now, for those of you who don't know me, my name's Venart Auzeil; you may well have known my father, Hui Auzeil. The point is, I have a sister, and she's being held against her will by the Loredan family on Scona. Why, I don't know; the bitch who runs the Loredan Bank sent for us both when we were over there a short while ago, and the upshot was that she arrested my sister and gave me two days to get off Scona. Well, I'm not going to stand here pointing out to you the implications of this for each and every one of us; it's enough to say that our whole livelihood depends on our being able to go anywhere in the world, knowing that people aren't going to push us around, because we're Islanders and nobody messes with us. Obviously I'm biased; it's my sister, and I'm going out of my mind with worry - well, you can imagine. But before you say, "That's tough, but what's it got to do with me?" I want you to consider this. If we let this matter ride, we'll be sending a message to every thief and bully in the world that we can't look after our own, and if that's your idea of how to conduct business, I have to tell you it isn't mine. Anyway,' he added, 'that's enough from me. All I'm trying to say is that there's other reasons apart from money why we should help Shastel against Scona; and while we're at it, I think we should insist that Shastel makes the release of my sister one of their bottom-line peace-treaty demands.'

Venart sat down, and there was a brief silence, apparently made up of equal parts of pity and embarrassment.

Eventually, someone got up in the middle of the eleventh row. Venart didn't recognise him.

'Actually,' he said, 'the last speaker – I'm afraid I didn't catch his name – does have a valid point, or at least he's raised one; I'm not sure it's the point he intended to make. In fact, I'm quite sure it isn't, but it's a good one nevertheless. Anyway, it's this. We're traders, businessmen, that's what we do. And one of the reasons why we do it so exceptionally well is that we all live here together on this island in the middle of the sea, with nobody from the outside daring to bother us because we've got more and better ships than anyone else, and nobody here on the Island trying to tell us what to do because we've proved over the last two hundred years or so that a society like ours neither wants nor needs a government of any sort. And it's wonderful,' the speaker went on cheerfully. 'If we all had the whole world to live in and we could do whatever the hell we wanted to, we'd still all want to be traders living here on the Island, because nothing and nowhere even comes close. Think about that, neighbours. Think carefully.'

He paused for a moment. There was no sound of any kind.

'Now then,' he went on, 'our friends here who hold the Shastel Bank franchise have come along today and offered us large sums of money for the hire of our ships. That sounds wonderful, doesn't it? I tell you, when I heard the rumour I was up here like a squirrel up a tree; I've got two ships, a damn great timber freighter that'll make a wonderful insurance claim one day when I can find a big enough rock to sail it onto but otherwise isn't good for anything much, and a sweet little cutter that skips along like skimming a flat stone on a rock-pool and carries about as much cargo as I could comfortably fit in my pockets; and these kind people here are prepared to pay me more for a month's work than I usually make in a season. But then I got to thinking, and this is what I want to share with you. The point is, Shastel wants to hire my ships for a *war*.

'Now don't get me wrong, if Shastel and Scona want to beat up on each other, they're more than welcome to do so, and if while they're at it they need to buy any stuff, such as food or timber or iron ore or any damn thing, I'll be more than happy to sell it to either of them, or both, for choice. Taking a slightly longer-term view, I'd be delighted to see Scona getting a bloody good hiding, simply because it's a stated policy of the Loredan Bank to diversify and expand – I'll translate that for you, friends, it means barging in on our business, making stuff cheaper than we can buy it, supplying only their own trading syndicate and generally cutting us wherever we go. I really don't like the sound of that, a government getting involved in business; it's like a fox going in for chicken farming. So, if they come to a bad end, you can expect to see me walking around with a sprig of heather in my cap and a big grin on my face.'

There was a ripple of laughter from the crowd. The speaker let it die down before continuing.

'But,' he said, making his voice a little harder and sterner, 'here's the problem as I see it. Suppose we get involved in this war, and Shastel loses. Good for business? I don't think so. I can't see any of us being welcome on Scona ever again. All right, you say, not much chance of that happening, so what's your worry? Fair enough; but suppose we get involved in this war and Shastel wins? Is that going to be any better? Come on, everyone, think about it. How's it going to look everywhere else we go? It's going to look like we, the people of the Island, formed an alliance with Shastel to make war on Scona. Put it another way: up till now we've always been individuals wherever we go, and as a result nobody bothers us. We're good people to trade with, we deal fairly and by and large our prices are the best; there's no advantage in turning us over, because all that means is that they'll lose our repeat business, which is pretty much like putting money in a sack and chucking it in the sea. Now imagine what it's going to be like if we start acting like a nation, a government. The Island joins Shastel against Scona. The Island demands the return of the hostage. I'm not going to spell it out for you, neighbours, I imagine you can see what I'm getting at perfectly well without me having to hammer the point into the ground.

'All right, you say; what are you suggesting we should do? Boycott the offer? Turn down this highly lucrative new business on account of some vague fears about how the rest of the world's going to feel about us? Doesn't sound like a desperately smart move, does it? And suppose you're a good boy and don't take up the offer; how're you going to feel when the man next door decides he can't be doing with all this political bull getting in the way of business, and signs up with Shastel for the duration?

'Here's the deal. A big thank you to Athli what's-her-name – Zeuxis, that's right; Athli Zeuxis – and the rest of the Shastel Bank consortium, and anybody who wants to sign up with them should go right ahead and do so. That's fine. But I'd like this meeting to send back a big fat raspberry to the Foundation, with the message, we don't take sides, we don't give or ask for either help or treaties with the outside world, because we aren't a nation; we're just a lot of people who happen to live in the same place, and most of us do the same kind of work. And whatever we do, we don't mention this man's sister at all; not one word. Especially we don't interfere by making demands on the governments of other countries. Sorry, neighbour, and you really do have my sincerest sympathies, but that's the way I see it. No foreign adventures, no taking sides, no moral support, nothing. None of our business.'

Venart left the meeting feeling angry and confused. At the start of the proceedings, it looked like everybody was in favour of the Shastel deal except for the small number of traders who did substantial business with Scona (later he found out that the speaker was one of this group, thereby learning as fact something that every other man in the Meeting House had guessed immediately after

he'd started talking). The upshot had been that the
Shastel agents had been given a rather insulting little
homily to pass on to Head Office, along with a large
number of signed contracts for the hire of ships. As the
speaker had urged, there was no reference whatsoever in
the homily or the contracts to a girl by the name of
Vetriz Auzeil.

Venart went home, slammed the door behind him and
went through into the counting house, where his clerks
were copying letters and doing chequer-board calculations. He was in a foul mood by this stage; he swore at
one clerk for lighting a lamp when there was still the last
knockings of daylight left, and at another for taking a
new pen from the pot when a bit of careful sharpening
would have got another hour or so out of the old one,
and the room was extremely quiet and tense when the
doorkeeper came in and announced that Athli Zeuxis
had called and was waiting to see the boss.

'Rest assured,' she said, as Venart poured her a drink
of warm wine and honey with mint and grated cinnamon, 'I'll be doing whatever I can. Have you any idea
what Niessa Loredan's up to?'

Venart shook his head. 'Well,' he amended, 'I've got a
vague notion it's all to do with that magic stuff we got
mixed up in that time in the City, with old Alexius and
Bardas Loredan. Which means,' he added with a long
sigh, 'that even if someone told me what was going on, I
wouldn't understand a word of it.'

Athli nodded. 'I know what you mean,' she said. 'I'm
not sure I believe in it, even. Well, be certain that I'll be
doing whatever I can to get Vetriz out of there. It shouldn't
be beyond me to spin Head Office a report dropping
great big heavy hints about things they can do that
would go a long way towards getting the Island firmly on
their side. I wouldn't be at all surprised if they took the
bait; they simply can't get their heads around the idea of
the Island not having a government of any kind; they
much prefer inventing some extremely secretive and

well-hidden ruling class manipulating everything from behind the scenes and being incredibly devious about it all. The idea of a secret agenda of freeing hostages concealed behind a public declaration of neutrality is just the sort of twisted scheme they'd really go for. But,' Athli went on, 'even if they do go for it, I'm not making any promises about getting anywhere. The plain fact is, as far as I can tell, they want this to be an all-out war to the death; the idea behind it is to get rid of Scona for good and all, and nobody's going to be all that interested in peace negotiations or making deals; not unless Gorgas Loredan manages to give them a couple of damn good hidings. Sorry to sound negative about it, but it'd be cruel to get your hopes up.'

'Please do what you can,' Venart replied, pouring himself another long drink. 'I really can't think of anything else I can do, short of tripping over some vital piece of military intelligence about Shastel war plans that I could trade for her with Niessa Loredan. And the chances of finding out something she doesn't know already are pretty slim, to say the least. That's one tough woman, Athli. I don't think there's much she wouldn't do if it suited her.'

'I promise I'll do my best,' Athli replied, refusing a refill. 'At the very least, I ought to be able to find some way of getting a message through to Vetriz, if that's any use to you.'

Venart smiled, for the first time in a while. 'Thanks,' he said. 'I'll write something tonight and send it over to you first thing tomorrow. At least I can let her know she hasn't been entirely forgotten. Anyway,' he said with an effort, 'that's enough about that. What do you make of this war, then? Is it a foregone conclusion like everybody says?'

Athli made a vague gesture with her hands. 'If you do the arithmetic, it's got to be,' she said. 'Six thousand halberdiers against – what, seven hundred regular archers and whatever conscripts Gorgas can chase up. You don't need to be a treasury clerk to figure that one out. On the other hand,' she continued, looking out of the window, 'take a look at the run-up to this situation and maybe the numbers aren't so important after all. We were getting close to the stage where Gorgas was running out of floors to wipe with Shastel raiding parties; not that he's some kind of military genius, it's just that the raiders made such bad mistakes.' She smiled thinly. 'We had a saying back in Perimadeia – it was attributed to General Maxen, Bardas' uncle – that ninety-nine out of a hundred decisive battles are lost by the losers rather than won by the victors, and the art of strategy was little more than giving the other side rope to hang themselves with while trying not to make too many stupid mistakes of your own. Basically, that's what Gorgas has been doing so far, and it's worked pretty well; unless you count winning so often you provoke a full-scale war as a mistake, which is an arguable case. No, I could see Gorgas winning one or two very impressive victories and killing an awful lot of halberdiers; and my guess is that all he'd achieve that way would be an even bigger number of halberdiers assigned to catching him.' She shook her head. 'It'll be interesting to watch,' she said. 'I'd say his only hope would be a big victory resulting in a major blow-up in Shastel faction politics; but it could just as easily be his own death warrant.'

The ink was full of dust again, and the pen was worn out and spluttering; the scraps of parchment had been scraped down so many times there were holes in them, and the ink just soaked away in places, making the letters look like trees grown shaggy and shapeless with moss and ivy; and the lamp needed a new wick. But Machaera kept on writing, because calligraphy was seventy marks (seventy marks just for the writing, regardless of what she wrote) and a good score would go a long way towards offsetting the inevitable disaster of Applied Geometry, and she *had* to do well in

Moderations if she wanted to get into the top stream of Third Year ...

There was a nick in the shaft of the pen, and it had worn a raw patch on her middle finger between the top knuckle and the side of her fingernail, and it *hurt* ... There had to be some way to harden her skin up before the exam, something she could put on it to stop it rubbing away. Hadn't she read somewhere that raw grain spirit did the trick? Not that that would be a lot of help, since she didn't happen to have any raw grain spirit; although she had an idea they used the stuff in the Natural Philosophy workshops, and wasn't that moon-faced boy who kept oh-so-accidentally bumping into her in the Buttery (Name? Can't remember) a Nat. Phil. second-year?

She narrowed her eyes and squinted at the page she was copying from. The main text was clear enough; it was the bold, cursive script of about a hundred and twenty years ago, written in Perimadeia in a commercial copying shop by someone who understood how to lay out a legible page of text. Her problem was with the commentary, scrawled between the lines and crammed into the margins, running right to left as often as left to right, contorted with scholarly space-saving abbreviations and written with a pen shaved down to the thickness of a hair. *Mcrb thnks th Passg prob corrupt, cf Euseb On Philos chp 23 ll.34 to 60 but cf opp Comm on Silen Gen Summary chp 9 ll.17ff wh var readings pref;* all squashed into the gap above one line, with the last few words bulging out into the margin and marching upside down along the underside of the end of the line, like a column of ants on the stem of a flower. It could, of course, have been worse; there could be three or four generations of commentary squeezed in there, rendering the main text as illegible as the subsidiaries and making reading the thing as slow and painful as a child picking its way through its first horn-book.

Macrobius thinks this passage is corrupt, she wrote

carefully, *compare Eusebius,* On Philosophy, *chapter 23 lines 34 to 60; but note the opposite view in the commentary on Silentius,* General Summary, *chapter 9 lines 17 and following, where variant readings are preferred.* Quite, she thought. And does it really matter, given that the text all this attention has been lavished on is nothing more than the trivial bickering of two scholars, both of them dead for over four hundred years, over a fine point of dogma in a theory long since discarded as quaintly primitive? Apparently it did, or else why was she crouched here copying it out on slivers of vellum scrounged from the bellows-mender's shop in the vague hope that writing it out would somehow help fix it in her memory? It mattered because the men who set the exam thought it mattered, probably because they'd had to sit in this same library staring at this same copy of this book when they were her age, and that was the only criterion that counted for anything. Still, it would be interesting to know when this book was last read by someone who *wasn't* studying for the second-year Mods; two hundred years ago? Three?

She looked at the page in front of her and considered the next line in the main text. *But that same foolish and opinionated clerk, in averring that the same essence could be at one and the same time corporeal and non-corporeal, commits a grave error; indeed, his ignorance and folly are such that no scholar would pay any heed to them. In consequence—*

Machaera yawned and lifted her head until she could see out of the window. Outside it was a clear, crisp day, and the menacing silhouette of Scona Island was painfully sharp against the hard blue sky. Over there, apparently, lurked the Enemy, the latest incarnation of the dark and malevolent force that waited eternally for the weak, the helpless, and bad girls who didn't eat up their dinners. She found it extremely unsettling to think that the Enemy was so close, only the width of a narrow channel away; if she wasn't careful, she could easily spend hours staring at the water, imagining shadowy coracles flitting over the dark water, spear-points and helmet-ridges gleaming in the thin light of a watchful star – and then she'd never get any work done, and she'd fail Mods completely and have to go home. Oh, *damn* Scona, for being at war and distracting her from her revision!

She didn't look up, because she knew that the man standing beside her wasn't real, and that she was in another of those involuntary and unfortunately extra-curricular visions (if only they counted towards the year-end continuous assessment grades – but they didn't, and a headache right now would be *so inconvenient* …)

'Machaera,' Alexius said. 'I'm sorry, am I disturbing you?'

'A bit,' she replied, trying not to let her resentment show; after all, Patriarch Alexius was one of the greatest scholars ever, she should be proud—

'You work too hard, you know,' he said. 'You aren't getting enough sleep. Fine thing it'd be if you're so exhausted you fall asleep in the exam. Don't laugh; it happened to a friend of mine. He'd spent a whole year cramming for that one subject, got as far as writing his name, and the next thing he knew was the invigilator shaking him by the shoulder and taking his paper. He gave up philosophy after that and went into the wine trade, where he made a great deal of money and would have done very well for himself if he hadn't been killed when the City fell. At least, I assume that's what happened to him; it's a fairly safe assumption. What's that you're reading?'

'Veutses, *On Obscurity*,' Machaera replied. 'Doctor Gannadius says it's the key to understanding the whole of neo-Tractarianism.'

'He's right,' Alexius said, 'surprisingly enough, since I happen to know for a fact he's never read it. Oh, he's read the *Epitome* and the *Digest*, which contain everything you need to know; but as for sitting down and actually ploughing through the wretched thing, he told me himself, life's too short. I did read it, once – a long time ago now, of course – and frankly I couldn't make head or tail of it. So I went back and read the *Digest* entry and for the life of me I couldn't remember any of the important points listed in the *Digest* article being in the original text. So I went back and read Veutses again, from beginning to end, and blow me down if I wasn't right. All the important ground-breaking stuff was made up by whichever poor little clerk it was who did the *Digest* entry, not Veutses at all.'

'Oh,' said Machaera, visibly shaken. 'But it says in the *Commentary*—'

'Ah.' Alexius smiled. 'The purpose of the *Commentary*, which was written two hundred years later, was to take the conclusions reached in the *Digest* and then go back into the original text and find obscure and badly written bits which could be interpreted to seem as if they were the bits the writer of the *Digest* got his ideas from. It's a wonderfully imaginative and inventive piece of academic writing, and just shows what you can achieve if you really set your mind to something.'

'Oh.'

'But for pity's sake don't go pointing that out in the exam,' Alexius went on, 'or they'll fail you on the spot.'

'Oh ...'

'As is quite right and proper,' Alexius continued. 'Because what you've been taught is that Veutses discovered Veutses' Law of Obscurity, and the exam's to test what you've learnt, not some theory or other you may have dreamt up for yourself. After all,' he went on, 'the conclusions drawn by the *Digest* writer are still just as valid and important, so why does it matter who wrote them?'

'I suppose not,' Machaera replied, frowning. 'But it still doesn't seem fair, really.'

'Doesn't it?' Alexius shrugged his shoulders. 'I don't think it was ever supposed to be. If I were you, though,

I'd skip the rest of the book and just read the *Digest*. After all, you can't go far wrong if you emulate someone as distinguished as Doctor Gannadius.'

Machaera looked at him, then nodded obediently. 'If you say so,' she said. 'But I still think—'

'Give it thirty years and it'll wear off,' Alexius interrupted. 'Thinking, I mean. It's something you grow out of, like greasy skin and spots. And, all due respect, I didn't come here to discuss Veutses and intellectual dishonesty. Do you mind if I sit down, by the way? I know this isn't my real body, but even notional cramp in imaginary legs can be quite painful.'

'Oh. I mean, sorry. Yes, please sit down.'

Alexius perched on the edge of the desk. 'That's better,' he said. 'Now then, let's get to the point. You and I are deadly enemies.'

Machaera looked shocked. 'But we can't be,' she said. 'Really, I would never—'

Alexius raised a hand, palm towards her. 'I know, I know,' he said. 'But it isn't up to us. It's because of the war, you see. And it seems that you and I are like – oh, I don't know - we're two siege engines mounted high on towers, facing each other across the straits, ready to bombard each other and turn each other's cities into rubble. Believe me, it's true. I was brought here - to Scona, I mean - and you've been carefully encouraged when under normal circumstances you'd either have been scared into never using your latent abilities or strangled or something, just so we can be part of the war.'

Machaera looked at him gravely. 'I'm not sure I want that,' she said. 'But you can't be right about me,' she went on. 'Why me, when we've got people like Doctor Gannadius?'

Alexius chuckled. 'Gannadius is a nice enough man, and quite bright too, in his own way, but he's got about as much ability to use the Principle as I have wings to fly through the air. Anything he can do in the Principle he has to do through a natural. It's the same with Niessa Loredan, and she's the one using me.'

'Oh.'

'So I thought,' Alexius went on, 'why don't you and I come to an agreement? Call it a private peace treaty all of our own. Because one of these days, quite soon, you'll find yourself in one of these visions, and you'll be at some critical point in the future of the war, and you'll be standing there looking at a single moment in time where either of two things can happen. I haven't the faintest idea what it'll be; it could be a soldier standing in a doorway, or an engineer aiming a trebuchet, or a general putting his head up above a slit-trench to see what's happening, whatever. That's when you'll find yourself making a decision about what should happen next – let's say you decide that the soldier in the doorway sees the enemy approaching and runs away, instead of holding his ground and keeping them back until reinforcements arrive, or the engineer decides to add an extra two degrees to allow for windage, or the general thinks better of it and isn't shot down by a sniper. When that happens, I'd like you to make a conscious effort not to make a decision. Switch off your mind, say out loud, "I don't know what's going to happen next." And if we both do that—'

'Excuse me,' Machaera said.

'Sorry?'

'Excuse me,' she repeated, 'and please don't take this the wrong way; but if we're really on opposite sides, and I don't make the decision, how will I know that you won't make the decision either? I know this sounds awful,' she went on wretchedly, 'but if I do as you're saying, won't I be hurting my side and helping yours? And besides, I *do* want Shastel to win the war. It can't be wrong to want that, can it? I mean, shouldn't people do everything they can to help their side win, if there's a war?'

Alexius narrowed his eyes. 'But they're using you,' he said. 'Just like Niessa's using me. Surely you can see that's not right.'

'It's all right if I don't mind,' Machaera replied. 'And yes, the war's a dreadful thing, and I wish ever so much there didn't have to be one, because lots of my friends will have to go and fight and some of them may get killed or badly hurt, which is probably worse in a way, because then they'll have to live their lives without an arm or an eye or something. But if I don't do something to help, that won't mean there won't be a war, it just means we're less likely to win; and what if I keep my side and you don't? Then I'd really be hurting my side—'

Alexius scowled at her for a moment, and stood up; he raised his hand, drew it back and slapped her hard across the side of her head, at which point he wasn't Alexius any more but a short, stout middle-aged woman she'd never seen before but somehow knew as Niessa Loredan. Machaera tried to scramble out of the way, but Niessa was coming after her; now she had a knife in her hand, and behind her shoulder Machaera could see Patriarch Alexius, looking horrified but not moving. She got as far as the doorway when Niessa managed to reach out and grab her by the hair. Machaera screamed, and as Niessa slashed at her with the knife she tried to fend the blade off with her hands. She could feel the knife cutting her fingers and palms, slicing through the knuckles of her right hand just below the first joint; but the sensation wasn't pain, it was more like a kind of fear she could feel with her body as well as her mind. She screamed again, and then Niessa got past her flailing hands and stuck the knife into her, just below her ribs, in the place her father used to stick in the knife when he was skinning rabbits he'd snared up in the mountains orchard. She could feel the knife inside her, an intrusion, something that shouldn't be there—

And she was sitting looking out of the window at a distant prospect of Scona, with her hands clasped in front of her, as if she was trying to keep her intestines from falling out. She'd scattered her bits of parchment and knocked over the inkwell.

'What the hell do you think you're playing at?' someone said behind her; and the librarian stepped smartly forward and rescued the copy of Veutses' *On Obscurity* just before the spreading pool of ink reached it. 'For gods' sakes, be careful, this book's irreplaceable.' He scowled down at her, just as someone had done a moment or so ago (but she couldn't remember who, and she had a headache) and then sighed. 'You fell asleep,' he said, not quite so ferociously, 'and knocked over the ink. Second year, I take it?'

Machaera nodded.

'Swotting for Mods and not getting enough sleep,' the librarian went on. 'Well, you wouldn't be the first. Go on, get out of my sight while I clear this up. Go to bed. You aren't safe to be around innocent books.'

Alexius woke up with a start and opened his eyes.

'You nodded off,' said Niessa Loredan, smiling indulgently like a fond daughter. 'In the middle of a sentence. You were just about to explain to me about Parazygus' theory of simultaneous displacement, and suddenly you went out like a snuffed candle.'

'Did I?' Alexius put a hand to the side of his head, where something was banging away like a trip-hammer in a foundry. 'How terribly rude of me,' he said, 'I do apologise. It must be old age.'

'That's all right,' Niessa said. 'And it's rather warm in here, and you did eat four slices of cinnamon cake.' She stood and picked up the knife. 'Let me cut you another,' she said.

CHAPTER SEVENTEEN

It could have been any village in the mountains of Scona; the same red sandstone houses, the same grey mossy thatch, rutted muddy street, open doors, ubiquitous chickens and children. But this village was barely twelve miles from Shastel, and its people were downtrodden serfs of the Foundation rather than satisfied clients of the Loredan Bank. And although they weren't showing a tremendous amount of enthusiasm for the idea, they were on the point of throwing off their chains and joining the great war for freedom. Assuming, of course, that they knew what was good for them.

The harbinger of liberty in this instance was Sergeant Mohan Bar, a thirty-year man who'd served in a wide variety of armies, official and unofficial, before drifting into the Scona archers as a sergeant instructor. Organising successful revolutions was largely uncharted territory as far as he was concerned, and he wasn't sure he was temperamentally suited to it. There was far too much diplomacy involved, and not enough giving and obeying orders; in fact, he had the uneasy feeling that what these downtrodden serfs on the verge of throwing off their chains wanted him to do was go away. That, however, wasn't an option.

The villagers were holding yet another meeting, which Sergeant Bar was watching from the comfort of a bench outside the village's anonymous and extremely scruffy inn. The mug of cider in his hand had been on the house (or at least he'd assumed so; as far as he could recall, the issue of payment hadn't been addressed in his short conversation with the innkeeper), it was a pleasantly warm day for the time of year and there was nothing else he was supposed to be doing; a soldier on active service learns to recognise such quiet interludes and make the most of them while they last.

'It's very simple,' one of the village worthies was saying. 'They're here, for sure the Foundation knows they're here, whether we like it or not we'll already have been convicted of treason just because they're here; so what the hell, why don't we do as he says? We haven't got anything to lose by it. More to the point, we don't exactly have a choice.'

The rest of the meeting grumbled, the way people do when facing an unpopular truth.

'We can still explain,' someone at the back replied. 'Grab hold of these jokers, tie them up, send a message to the Foundation telling them what's happened and asking for an escort to take them on as soon as possible. If we do that, then how can they possibly say we've acted treasonably?'

The first speaker shook his head. 'Don't you believe it,' he said. 'It's like it's some sort of contagious disease; if you come in contact with the enemy, you're assumed to be infected. As far as the Foundation's concerned, we're dead men. So, we fight or we go quietly and end up in a labour gang or dangling from a tree beside the road somewhere. Oh, yes, and just one thing you may have missed: you're talking ever so bravely about arresting these men and tying them up. If you try it, I'll be interested to see how far you get. In case you hadn't noticed, they're heavily armed soldiers, not a few kids you've caught scrumping apples.'

'This is wonderful,' someone else said. 'Whatever we do, we're going to get killed. Why don't we all just get out of here up into the hills till all these lunatics have wiped each other out? Then we can come back down and steal their boots.'

Sergeant Bar smiled, finished his cider and went for a walk to stretch his legs. He couldn't help thinking that he wasn't getting the most out of what should have been a thoroughly desirable assignment – out of the camp, left to his own devices, no officers and no fighting, in a village where they had booze and (presumably, though he hadn't seen any) women. Somehow, unfortunately, he couldn't see it in that light.

He walked to the top of the hill that overlooked the village and stared out in the direction of Shastel. There was a taller hill between him and the Citadel, which was probably just as well for his peace of mind, but he had a good view of the only road in these parts, along which any intercepting force would have to come if it didn't want to scramble through bogs and rocky outcrops. From sheer force of habit he planned a defence; his twelve archers, six on either side of the road in among those trees directly below where he was standing, the local levy (big joke!) blocking the road behind a barricade of carts and barrels, with a reserve force halfway up the slope behind those rocks, where they'd be out of sight and nicely placed for a quick uninterrupted sprint down onto the enemy's rear to conclude the engagement. If he'd been fabricating a battlefield on the barrack-room floor, with rolled-up blankets for the hills, water bottles for the trees and a stretched-out sword-belt for the road, he couldn't have designed anything much more favourable for a defence against superior numbers.

He frowned, and shuddered; bad luck, wishing a fight on himself and his men. If he had the sense he was born with, he'd be more concerned with his lines of retreat, the fastest way back to the inlet where their ship was waiting. Fortunately, that was pretty straightforward, too. Provided they had enough advance notice, they could double back round the edge of the far hill and down the path they'd come up in the first place long before the enemy even reached the village. Sergeant Bar shook his head. It'd be as well to post a sentry up here, and place another man in the village to watch for a signal. If he did that, there was nothing to worry about. Safe as houses.

Archers Venin and Bool weren't overjoyed at their assignment; but once Bar had explained that he'd chosen them for the job because he didn't like them very much and didn't see why they should lay around villages relaxing when they could be sitting on hillsides, they saw the logic behind it and took their lookout positions. Bar went back to his bench outside the inn and checked on the progress of the meeting, which was still going round in the same dreary, reassuring circle. Bar yawned. He didn't really know what he was supposed to do at this point; his mission was to organise the resistance in Shantein, issue the warlike partisans with twenty slightly sub-standard ash flatbows and a less than generous allocation of arrows, teach them the arts of archery and war, inspire them with courage and the will to win, and then come home. At a guess, he was somewhere in phase one and (he suspected) running a little behind schedule.

The morning drifted into noon and the combination of warm sun and tolerable cider lapped him gradually into sleep. He was snuggling his cheek into the crook of his elbow and dreaming comfortably when he heard his name and looked up.

'Bool?' he mumbled. 'I thought I told you—'

'They're coming,' Bool interrupted. 'Forty men, just come into sight on the road.'

It took Bar a second or so to work out what Bool was talking about. 'Right,' he said. 'That's all right. Signal Venin to get back here. I'll get the men fell in and we'll be on our way.'

Venin arrived, out of breath and dusty, and Bar jerked his head towards the far hill and gave the order to move out; at which point he noticed that the meeting had fallen silent and everybody was looking at him.

'They're coming, aren't they?' someone said.

Bar felt a little uncomfortable. 'That's right,' he said.

'And you're leaving.'

Bar frowned. 'Yes,' he said. 'We're leaving.'

The man who'd been talking the closest approximation to sense jumped up and came over, blocking his way. He looked angry and scared. 'You can't just go,' he said. 'They'll kill us all. We won't stand a chance.'

Bar thought for a moment. 'Sorry,' he said. 'But it's too late now. You should've done what I asked four hours ago, instead of sitting around gabbing.'

Four or five other villagers had joined the first speaker. 'You can't just walk out on us,' one of them protested. 'Now you've got us into this mess, you damn well get us out again.'

'Forget it,' another one replied. 'Just suppose he did stick around, and just suppose he managed to give 'em a good hiding, though I can't say I see it myself. Then he goes home, and tomorrow another lot comes down the road and we still get killed. I say we head up into the mountains while there's time.'

'What about their ship?' someone else put in. 'Why don't we go to Scona? Hey, you, how many of us can get on your ship?'

Bar raised his hand for silence but didn't get any; so he slapped the face of the man nearest to him, making him overbalance and topple over backwards. That worked just fine.

'Listen to me,' he said. 'Nobody's going on any ship. Doesn't matter to me what you do, fight, give in or run away. We're leaving, so you'd better do what you think is right. Best of luck,' he added, remembering the diplomatic aspect of his mission.

There was a moment's silence; then the first speaker folded his arms. 'We'll fight,' he said. 'Tell us what you want us to do.'

'Get out of my way,' Bar replied. 'I won't ask you again.'

For some reason, that had the reverse effect to the one he'd intended; there was a ring of villagers round them now, all angry, scowling, shouting, waving their arms. *Well now*, said a small, wicked voice at the back of his mind, *that's phase one. What was phase two again?* 'All right,' he heard himself say. 'All right, we're staying, now back off before my men get nervous and hurt somebody.' The ring of angry people loosened up a little; they were looking at him, hanging on his every word. Even so, forty halberdiers against a dozen archers and these fools. It didn't bear thinking about.

'All right,' he said again. 'First things first, weapons. How many of you have got any?' He waited. Nobody moved. 'Right. Well, get anything sharp or heavy or pointed. Hurry, you've got two minutes. Go.'

At least that dispersed them. Bar turned to his platoon. 'Now listen to me,' he said. 'This lot's worse than useless, so mostly it'll be up to us. The odds are crap, but we've got surprise and a good position. Venin, you remember where you were just now? All right, take five men with you, wait for my signal before you start shooting. Bool, follow on behind but take the trees on this side of the road. You'll get three, maybe four shots each, and that'll be it, your only chance to end this and get out in one piece, so for gods' sakes concentrate, we've got to take down at least half of them in those first three volleys. You can do it easy, it's well within your capabilities. Right. Go.'

They moved out without a word, leaving him standing on his own in the middle of the village. *Wonderful*, he said angrily to himself, *now we're in a war. Should've been more careful what you wished for. Still, you'll never get a better position, so why the hell not?*

He reviewed his remaining forces. There were twenty-six of them, comprising seven felling axes, one genuine Shastel military halberd, twelve hayforks – there had been no more formidable weapon in the world when he was thirteen years old and running away from one with a dozen freshly stolen onions down the front of his shirt – six mattocks and a spade. *Put 'em together and what d'you get? A massacre, most likely. But we'll see.* 'The axes, the halberd and you, the big man with the fork. You know where I had my sentry? A hundred yards beyond that and further down the slope there's a pile of rocks. Can you get yourselves there quick without being seen from the road?'

One of the axes nodded. 'No problem,' he said.

Bar nodded. 'Fine,' he said. 'In that case, you're in charge. Now, when I give the signal and *only* then, you get yourselves down the slope quick as you can and take the enemy in the rear. The signal will be three short blasts on this horn,' he went on, patting the small copper bugle at his belt. 'Stay awake and remember, don't move a hair till you hear the signal and we ought to be all right.'

The assault party (*my picked men. Oh, gods*) set off briskly, leaving Bar with the eighteen remaining peasants. There were three boys no more than seventeen and four old men with grey hair or no hair at all (but he had the idea they were probably the pick of the bunch). The rest of them were that indeterminate age that only peasants ever attain, the stage in their life-cycle where childhood and courtship are over and there's nothing left to do but work and die. They were tough, strong, determined men, and no match in a million years for trained armoured halberdiers. Oh, well. They were only there for decoration, bait to draw the halberdiers into enfilading fire from a dozen Scona archers shooting at between seventy-five yards and point-blank. With any luck, a canteen of hot soup taken off the fire just before the start of this action should still be palatably warm by the time his victorious forces came back again.

There wasn't time to build a road-block or a barricade; a nuisance, that, because it meant his centre guard would be out in the open where the enemy could count them, maybe notice the absence of archers if they were bright enough. As he formed his line, pushing and shoving the plainly terrified farmers into some semblance of formation, he tried to figure out an escape route, but nothing obvious met the eye; just headlong down the road back to the village, or up the sides of the combe and hope nobody follows. Damn the cheapskates, they should have assigned an officer for this mission, not just sent out a sergeant.

In due course the halberdiers came into view; at first just a coloured smudge on the margin of the sky, then discernible human shapes, then identifiable people. Beside him, his makeshift platoon were standing still and quiet, staring at the oncoming enemy as if they were strange monsters walking up out of the sea onto the beach, something unnatural and inhuman. But to Bar they were just soldiers; after a while, all soldiers look the same, act the same. At this distance, you could be forgiven for mistaking them for people, but that would be foolish. When a man puts on a second skin of steel, hardened leather or padded cotton, he becomes something more and less than human, and the usual rules don't apply. Slickly and competently, Bar braced his bow, checked the lie of the string between the nocks, drew an arrow from the quiver at his belt and fitted it carefully over the served point opposite the arrow-shelf. He took up a few pounds of pressure, checked the position of his feet, and scanned for a target. In the dead centre of the front rank there was a tall man, a whole head taller than the men on either side, an obvious choice for the first shot of the day. Bar squinted a little, trying to assess range, something he'd never found easy. The only way he'd ever made any sense of it was by practising at roving marks – walk through woods and fields, choose a mark, measure off fifty or a hundred paces, remember what a head or body-sized target looks like at that range, then experiment with elevation and windage (allowing for paradox) until you can hit the mark three shots out of four. If in doubt, shoot high, so that if you miss your target you stand some chance of hitting another further back in the column. All standard elementary stuff, the sort of thing he made his living teaching to other people. Shouldn't be a problem.

When the tall man was about ninety yards distant, Bar raised the bow to an angle of forty-five degrees, pushed with his left hand, pulled with his right until the tip of his index finger brushed the corner of his lip while lowering the bow to what he estimated was just below the right elevation and looking down the arrow over the bodkinhead, directly at the target, then up with the aim an inch while pushing his left hand forward just a touch more until he could feel his shoulder blades pinch the skin over his spine, at which point his fingers knew to relax of their own accord, letting the arrow fly and the string come smartly forward to slap against the bracer on his left wrist. He held the loose position for half a second of follow-through, then reached for the next arrow as he looked to see what he'd done.

The tall man was still there, but there was a disturbance in the row behind as the column shifted a little to step round a fallen body; good enough for government work, as the engineers said. He had time for one more shot before giving the signal to the archers in the wood—

And down from the hillside in a flurry of mud and loosened stones came his assault squad, his sting in the tail, far too early. They slithered the last few yards, trying to slow down but only making things worse for themselves; the halberdiers saw them in plenty of time, halted and formed to receive them in flank and rear. Sheer impetus carried them into the line and sent them spilling out round the back of the column, so that they masked both sides of it, making it impossible for the archers in the wood to shoot without hitting them. Bar felt his mouth drop open - honest to gods, he simply hadn't imagined such a thing could happen, not when he'd been at such pains to tell them to wait - and for a long time (in context) he couldn't think of anything he could do. But it wasn't long before the halberdiers had the better of it; the peasants fought for themselves, the way people do, but the halberdiers fought like soldiers, engaging the enemy facing the next man down the line on the right so as to get the best advantage from the design of their weapons, assuming as an article of faith that the next man in the line would do the same for them. Nothing is more disconcerting for the amateur fighter than being ignored by the man you think you're fighting while being attacked by the man you thought was fighting your neighbour; and in a battle, few men live long enough to be disconcerted twice.

That cup of soup's still warm, Bar said to himself. *This would be a good time to go.* It would be the logical thing to do, draw the attack onto his platoon of peasants, and the enemy would never even realise there were a dozen men in the wood. They could stay still and quiet and then discreetly withdraw, go back to the ship and away home in safety. Instead, he nocked, drew and loosed another arrow, this time reducing the elevation by a quarter of an inch. Second time lucky. He pulled the bugle round on its strap and blew once, the signal to the archers in the wood.

It turned out to have been a lucky mistake. The mistimed attack had had the effect of halting the column seventy-five yards or so from the archers, a comfortable range for three aimed shots. The first volley took the halberdiers completely by surprise, and by a lucky chance the officer was one of the eight men who went down. The rest of the company were just about to break up and run for cover when the second volley hit them – seven down this time, making a total of seventeen out of forty, leaving twenty-three standing. Quite possibly, the Shastel Faculty of Military Mathematics has a formula for the critical percentage, the point at which the survivors give it up and run. In Bar's experience, it was somewhere around the one-third mark, which meant this lot ought to break now. But they didn't. Instead they came on at the run.

Hell, Bar thought. There wasn't a third volley – they'd

have been shooting towards the standing line, with the risk of overshots hitting their own side, and they weren't to know that as far as Bar was concerned it would have been a justifiable risk. He had time for a snatched shot (clean miss; pulled left) before the halberdiers were on top of his line, which broke and melted away, leaving him standing. But not for long.

After the halberdiers had burnt the village and rounded up the male survivors, they fished Bar's body out of the mud – he was seven-eighths dead, with two puncture wounds in his stomach and a cracked skull – cut off his head and stuck it on a pole, and dropped the trunk down the well. Their bad grace was understandable; twenty-one dead out of forty, and only one dead Scona archer to show for it. The rest of Bar's command had reached their ship and were well away before the halberdiers even came looking for them.

Apart from being the first real engagement of the war, the battle of Shantein was important as the first major victory of the Redemptionists over the opposing factions. It had long been a plank in the Redemptionist platform that the Scona archers were not invincible and that traditional halberdier tactics would always prevail if properly and faithfully applied. The timing was impeccable, since it coincided with elections to five crucial faculty appointments, all of which went to Redemptionists. This in turn altered the balance of power in three sub-committees, causing a snowball effect that brought the faction an extra seat on the Appropriations and Establishments Committee, seriously shifting the voting patterns in Chapter. By clever manipulation of the agenda, the faction leaders were able to reschedule a delicately poised research funding vote they were expected to lose so that it came after a Redemptionist motion to bring back the Scona archer's head from Shantein and mount it on the main watchtower of the Citadel. The faction won both votes by a surprisingly comfortable margin, and the head of Sergeant Mohan

Bar was duly and ceremoniously put in its appointed place, its empty eyes looking out over the straits towards home, where it stayed for some time until it was removed as an eyesore following complaints from the Dean of the Faculty of Military Geography, whose window looked out over the tower platform.

As for the surviving villagers, they were kept in an open-air stockade for a fortnight, during which time four men died of wounds or fever, then they were marched back home and turned loose, with a substantial figure for damages and indemnities being added to their total mortgage debt. No further rebellions among the hectemores of Shastel are recorded.

On Scona, where they used a somewhat different basis for their accounting, the Shantein incident was regarded as a qualified success. The mathematics, it was held, spoke for themselves – twenty-odd halberdiers killed for the loss of one archer, a respectable return on capital. Factor in the confusion caused by the botched attack and the desertion of the peasant line, and the net result was a substantial victory of bow over halberd, giving grounds for genuine optimism.

'The fact remains,' Gorgas argued in committee, 'we were let down by lack of support for the archers, and that's a problem that isn't going to go away. They're bound to learn something from their mistake, we can't expect them to go on charging down the archers' throats like that.'

'So what do you suggest?' someone asked. Gorgas took a sip of water and dried his lips with a linen handkerchief.

'Mercenaries,' he said. 'A minimum one hundred heavy infantry. Professional soldiers, the type who know that when things go wrong, their best chance of survival is standing firm and staying cool, not running away. Half a dozen pikemen at Shantein would have turned the battle for us; the centre would have held, the hectemores wouldn't have run, the halberdiers would have ended up withdrawing under fire, we'd have half of Shastel territory up in arms for us by now. Carry that through to a major battle here on Scona, and you can work out the implications for yourselves.'

There was a brief silence, as the committee waited for Niessa to speak.

'I can see your point,' she said, looking up from the tablets she was keeping notes on. 'Now let's work it through. Last point first: substantial hectemore uprisings. Well, the fact of the matter is, we simply couldn't have afforded to arm and supply more than a token number of rebels, which is precisely why that mission was specified the way it was. I didn't want a mass defection; I wanted a few pockets of rebellion, enough to be a nuisance and a worry, no more. Anything bigger than that would have looked like a mortal threat to the very survival of the Foundation, and any chance of a settlement would have gone out the window for ever. And that's aside from the question of the cost and the drain on our resources that a big rebellion would've been, and that'd have done us more harm than a major defeat in the field. So,' she continued acidly, 'we came close to a disaster there, but luckily we just fell clear. We've learnt our lesson, no more troublemaking in Shastel territory. You've got to stop thinking like a soldier, Gorgas. We aren't soldiers, we're bankers; what we understand is profit and loss and return on investments. On that basis, we're well out of it.'

There was a rumble of approval from round the table. Gorgas looked as if he wanted to say something, but didn't.

'Next point,' Niessa went on briskly. 'I'm afraid this mercenaries business is pure fantasy. Now, I'm not even going to discuss the practicalities – recruiting men we could actually trust, getting them here and so on – because none of it's relevant. We can't hire mercenaries for the simple reason that we can't afford to; which brings me neatly on to the main point we've got to cover today, which is budgets. The plain fact of the matter is that unless we stop spending like farmers at a fair and cut a third off these projections, we'll be bankrupt in a matter of months. And that,' she added, 'isn't up for discussion, it's plain truth, and we've got to deal with it.'

'Go on,' said a man at the end of the table.

'I've cancelled the following projects,' Niessa said. 'Forca, I'm sorry but your grain depots are going to have to wait. Gorgas, the commerce raiders. Lehin, the curtain walls across Novice point. Thanis, we'll have to postpone repayment on the unsecured loan stock; let's just cross our fingers and pray it doesn't start a run on the rest of our securities. If we cut those, and if we all make sure we've trimmed all waste right back to the bone in our respective departments, we've at least got a chance of seeing it through to the end of the quarter without bleeding ourselves dry. Obviously there's not going to be a dividend for the foreseeable future, which means a lot of our securities are going to be sold off cheap on the foreign exchanges; I've got no option but to buy in at least a major percentage, just to keep confidence in the markets from caving in. With deferred payment options and using nominees I can put off settlement to next quarter, but it means we'll be looking for a further ten per cent cutback then, so you'd better start planning ahead for that.'

'Easy,' Gorgas muttered. 'To begin with, there's the wages of all the men who're going to get killed because of this quarter's cuts. All it'd take is one massacre and we could be back in the black.' He leant forward across the table, his weight braced on the palms of his hands. 'Niessa, don't you understand anything about this war? Or are you just ignoring it, hoping it'll go away? I invite you to think of it in these terms. Each major defeat makes us weaker. The weaker we get, the harder it'll be for us to keep trading; which means reduced revenues, further cuts, further weakness. We can't run this war according to best counting-house practice, Niessa; those rules don't work here.'

'Nonsense,' Niessa replied. 'Everything we do is war in some form or another. We're at war with every major bank in the world. It so happens that this war is in three dimensions rather than the usual two.'

Ironically, the first ship to reach Shastel from the Island was the privateer *Reprisal*. A few days later, she was joined by five others, the *Butterfly, True Virtue, Meriz's Chance, Return* and *Equal Measure*. The crews were the usual mix of Islander underclass and foreign miscellany, and the first thing they did was take their melodramatic privateer thirst to the usually quiet and sombre inns of Shastel Quay.

One exception was the midshipman of the *Return*. He walked up the hill from the Quay as far as the middle gate, turned left, climbed the hundred and fifteen steps of the Cloister Stairs and stopped to ask the way to the Faculty of Applied Philosophy. The research fellow who pointed him in the right direction was puzzled by the unlikely combination of scruffy third-hand cuir-bouilli armour, neat short white hair and cultured Perimadeian accent, but really didn't want to get involved, and so made no comment. The stranger, who had somehow made it up the steepest stairway on Shastel without getting out of breath, thanked her politely and walked briskly away, leaving the research fellow to her speculations.

At the faculty gate, the Perimadeian stopped again and asked the porter where he might find Doctor Gannadius.

'Depends,' the porter replied. Like most Shastel porters he was a retired sergeant-at-arms, fully capable of recognising a pirate when he saw one; and the halberd leaning against the corner of the front office of the lodge was definitely not just a war souvenir. 'You tell me what you want with him first. Then we'll see.'

The Perimadeian smiled. 'Certainly,' he said. 'I'm his cousin. And of course,' he went on, before the porter had a chance to speak, 'you can't just take my word for that; so I suggest that I stay here where you can keep an eye on me while you send your boy to ask the good Doctor if he can spare a minute or so for Olybras Morosin.'

The boy was duly despatched. He came back a few minutes later, trying to keep up with Doctor Gannadius, who was exhibiting a turn of speed that was quite possibly unique in the Faculty's history.

'Olybras?' he panted, leaning on the pillar of the lodge gateway. 'Is that you under all that leather?'

'Hello, Theudas,' the stranger replied. 'You've put on weight, haven't you? Mind you, it's been thirty years.'

'I—' Gannadius stopped, took a deep breath. 'You're alive, then?' he said.

'Apparently. And so, it seems, are you. I always said that if we lived long enough, eventually we'd find something we had in common. For pity's sake, Theudas,' he went on, scowling, 'either invite me inside or tell me to go away, before your porter stares me to death.'

'I – Oh, come in. Follow me.' Gannadius nodded to the porter, who nodded back and retreated into the lodge like a watchdog who's been forbidden to bite a dinner guest. 'This way. Olybras, it's – well, it's good to see you.'

'Really?' Olybras shrugged. 'There'd no accounting for tastes, I suppose. I don't remember us ever liking each other terribly much in the past.'

A flicker of annoyance moved the corner of Gannadius' mouth. 'All right,' he said. 'But this morning I really believed that I had no family at all left in the whole world, and now, right out the blue, I've got one again.'

'Quite so,' Olybras replied. 'A pity it has to be you, but on balance it's a good thing. By the way, how come the funny name? Last time I saw you, you were still just plain old Theudas Morosin. Presumably it's some sort of magic thing.'

'It's not magic,' Gannadius started petulantly; then he

took another deep breath and moderated his tone of voice. 'It's – it *was* traditional in my Order that when you reached a certain status, you assumed one of the traditional names. Gannadius was the second Patriarch of the City, and since I'd always admired—'

'I get you,' Olybras interrupted. 'Swank, in other words. Putting on airs. Well, jolly good luck. I know that sort of thing always meant a great deal to you. It's nice to know you nearly made it to the top of the greasy pole before the whole thing ceased to have any vestige of meaning.'

Gannadius stopped and glowered at him, to no apparent effect. 'And what about you, Olybras?' he asked sweetly. 'Doing all right for yourself, I see?'

Olybras laughed and shook his head. 'Obviously not,' he said. 'The best I can say for myself is that I gracefully reclined on hard times rather than falling on them. This time last year I still had my own ship, even if it was just a floating coal scuttle. But it simply fell apart one day, died of old age and malice, and now here I am, chief beetle-crusher on an Island privateer, at my age. My only consolation is, I never had any talents to fritter or promise to unfulfil.'

Gannadius pushed open the door to his lodgings and led the way in. 'Well,' he said, 'the life seems to agree with you. You look revoltingly fit and healthy.'

'Oh, I am,' Olybras said. 'It's one of the few benefits of having to work for a living. Plenty of exercise, only just enough food, and lots and lots and lots of bracing sea air.' He looked around, chose the most comfortable chair and sat in it. 'Have you got anything to drink?'

'Wine or cider,' Gannadius said.

'Oh, wine, with a bit of honey and cinnamon if there's any going. We acquired a barrel of that fortified Jairec stuff last month, and we're still only halfway through it. It makes your teeth hurt for days afterwards.'

Gannadius sighed and grated his last half-inch of cinnamon. 'So that's what you do, is it? Acquire things?'

'Go on,' Olybras said, 'you can use it if you like. The P word. I don't mind.'

'I suppose piracy is an honourable profession, in its way. It all depends on who you rob.'

Olybras shook his head. 'Anybody who can't get out of the way quick enough,' he replied sadly. 'Remember when we used to play pirates, Theudas? I seem to remember you always insisted on being the pirate captain, and I was the hapless merchant. Of course, you were bigger than me then. You had a mean left hook in those days.'

Gannadius winced a little. 'True,' he said. 'But you never showed any early aptitude for speculative philosophy, so the irony isn't quite symmetrical. Still, you were always the bookish one back then. Poetry, wasn't it, and metrical romances?'

Olybras smiled. 'Tales of adventure and heroism on the high seas,' he said. 'Anything not directly concerned with the tanning industry. Just my horrible luck to end up wearing the foul stuff. Father would be proud to see me today, I guess.' He slouched back into the chair and sipped his wine. 'By the way,' he said, 'whatever became of the yard? I lost touch.'

'Cousin Pallas took it over from your father,' Gannadius said, rather severely. 'And when he died—'

'Pallas died?' Olybras frowned. 'Well, of course he did. But I'd assumed he died when the City fell. Somehow that doesn't hurt so much. When did he die?'

'Oh, twelve years ago now,' Gannadius said. 'One of the chemicals disagreed with him, and in the end it poisoned him.'

Olybras shook his head. 'He was like me,' he said, 'he never wanted anything to do with the business. He should have cleared out, like I did. Like we did,' he added. 'Let's not forget that, Theudas. All right, you didn't run away to sea, you ran away and turned respectable instead. None of us stuck around though, except poor old Pallas. Sorry, you were saying.'

'After he died,' Gannadius continued, 'his daughter took it over. You never knew Pallas had a daughter, did you?'

Olybras put down his cup. 'Actually, I did,' he said. 'Asbeli, I seem to remember. But I never met her. Presumably she—'

'As far as I know,' Gannadius said. 'Like I said, until today I thought I was the last one left. I somehow assumed you'd come to a bad end somewhere along the line, after we hadn't heard anything for such a long time.'

'There was no reason for me to stay in touch,' Olybras muttered. 'For a while, in fact, I had something which could have passed for a life of my own. Things looked as if they were starting to go well. I had a wife. In fact,' he added, 'I had two, but the second one was purely a matter of convenience, for when I made the Moa run. Everybody has a second wife in Moa, it's how their society's organised. And anyway, she died a few years ago. But I had a real wife in Perimadeia. And a son.'

Gannadius looked up. 'You've got a son?' he said. 'Congratulations.'

'Ah.' Olybras looked at him. 'That's a moot point. In fact, that's what I came here to ask you.'

'Ask me?' Gannadius raised his eyebrows. 'What do you mean?'

'I mean, you might be able to tell me if I've still got a son,' he said, standing up and helping himself to more wine. 'No more cinnamon? Oh, well, never mind. I'll bring you some up from the ship a bit later on, we've got five cases of the stuff. No, I had a son all right, though I wasn't any sort of father to him. I left him and his mother to get on with it when I lost the *White Rose* — that was my fourth ship, or was it my fifth? Anyway, when she went down I somehow never got around to going home, and I heard a bit later that Methli'd found someone else, which was her good luck. And Theudas — did I happen to mention I named my son Theudas, Theudas? — he would only have been, what, four years old at the time. They were better off. Anyway, I naturally assumed they'd shared in the common misfortune when the City was destroyed, and I made myself deal with it accordingly.'

Olybras stopped talking for a moment and sat still, rocking the wine round in the bottom of his cup. Gannadius waited until he was ready to continue.

'And then,' Olybras went on, 'this job came up; this business between Shastel and Scona. I'd gone to the meeting about it, and afterwards I heard a lot of City voices coming from a wine shop and went in to investigate. I don't know if there's enough of us here, but we've got a fair number of people from Home on the Island and we like to make a bit of a show of sticking together, that sort of thing – anyway, the point is, when you hear City voices, you go over and introduce yourself, just in case they've got any news about anyone you want to know about. I got talking with a man who knew some people who'd known some people I knew, and after we'd been chatting aimlessly for half an hour or so I suddenly realised from what he was saying that the Doctor Gannadius of Shastel he'd mentioned a few times as an example of one of us who'd fallen on his feet was really my cousin Theudas Morosin hiding behind a silly name. Obviously I found that nugget of information mildly intriguing, and I started paying a bit more attention; just as well, because that was when it started to get interesting. You see, talking about you led on to talking about the people you worked for briefly when you first came to the Island, and there was another City name: Athli Zeuxis. That led us on to the Loredans; and then this man let fly with the thunderbolt. "What did you say your name was again?" he said, so I told him; and he thought about it and said, "And you reckon you had a cousin, Theudas Morosin?" and I said yes, that's right. "Well," he said, "that's odd, because I heard that name recently, Theudas Morosin; but it wasn't a man our age, it was a kid, maybe around twelve, thirteen years old." Well, I stayed calm and tried not to let myself go all to pieces.

"What about Methli Morosin?" I asked, but he hadn't heard of anyone by that name, just a boy. Well, to cut a long story short, I asked for details and he said this boy lived on Scona and was apprenticed to one of the Loredan brothers; the crazy one, he said, the one who lives out in the wilderness and makes furniture or something of the sort. It was common knowledge up that end of Scona, he said; what with him being a stranger and the Boss's brother.'

'You mean Bardas Loredan,' Gannadius said in a small, apprehensive voice.

'That's it,' Olybras replied. 'And then I heard some story about Bardas Loredan having taken the boy with him when he got out of the City at the end; I tried to follow it, but I didn't have much luck, I was too busy stopping myself from falling off the settle.'

'Bardas Loredan's apprentice is your *son*?' Gannadius interrupted.

'That's right. And presumably your cousin, once removed. Or should that be second cousin? Gods know. Anyway, once I'd got as much out of this fool as I could, I went round the docks asking after a berth on anything that was going to Scona. And that's when the horrible irony of it hit me: because of the war and this big charter deal with Shastel being talked about all over the place, of course nobody was going anywhere near Scona under any circumstances. I nearly burst into tears, I'm telling you; it was unbelievable. But I pulled myself together and kept ferreting away, until I heard a rumour that the colonel and his apprentice had been sent away by the family and weren't even on Scona any more.'

Gannadius nodded. 'That rumour's almost certainly true,' he said. 'In case you're wondering why I sound so sure, Bardas Loredan's a friend of a friend – Patriarch Alexius, as a matter of fact. Apparently they met up during the war.'

'That's what I heard,' Olybras said. 'But beyond that, nobody knew anything; like where he went or whether there was a boy with him. And, like I just told you, there was no chance of getting through to Scona, so I made up my mind to try the next best thing and came here. And now I'm asking you: do you know anything about where Bardas Loredan's gone? And if you don't, what about this magic of yours, is it any good for doing useful work, like finding people? I've heard stories that suggest it just might be.' He put his cup down on the table and leant forward. 'And before you say it, yes, I know there's no such thing as magic, just applied philosophy. Which is why I want you to apply your philosophy and find my son. Your cousin. Or is that too much to ask, for family, when you're already doing as much for strangers?'

'How did you–?' Gannadius started to say; then he leant back in his chair, feeling ill. 'Damn you, cousin,' he said, 'you're not another one, are you?'

Olybras laughed. 'I suppose it must run in the family.' He shook his head. 'I have a slight ability, nothing more; I used to think it was just occasional bursts of good luck, except that didn't fit in with the general pattern of my life. After all, it didn't make sense; most of the time my luck is reliably lousy. I can predict with a fair degree of certainty that when I come to a crossroads in my life where things could go either way, good or bad, they'll go bad. Except that just occasionally, I could see the cross-roads, or turning-point, whatever you care to call it, I could actually *see* it coming, like a dream, and then if I was quick and extremely careful, I could get hold of my luck and bend it, the way you can bend steel when it's red hot. If I got it wrong, of course, it'd snap instead. I'd try and bend it my way, but something would go wrong and I'd have made everything worse. But this dream-vision thing only happens once in a blue moon, and there doesn't seem to be any proportion to it; it can be something really important, like a bad storm or a pirate attack, or something really trivial, like losing an anchor. I really didn't give it much thought until I got talking one day with my ship's cook on the *White Rose*. He was a City man - fascinating life he'd led, I'll tell you about it one day when we've got time - and he'd been a student at the Academy for a couple of years, till he got into trouble and dropped out. He explained the basics of the Principle to me and I found out the rest for myself. But he was the one who taught me how to eavesdrop on the voices I hear in my sleep sometimes.'

Gannadius blinked. 'You hear voices in your sleep?'

'Oh, yes,' Olybras replied casually. 'It's like you're in a house with thin walls, and you can hear there's a conversation going on in the next room, but unless you really concentrate you can't make out the words. As far as I can gather, what I'm hearing is the people who can really do magic, eavesdropping if you like, except that I can't do it on purpose, it just happens sometimes. And that's how I know you're being used by the Shastel wizards to play some kind of war with the Scona wizards; Niessa, Alexius and the Auzeil girl—'

'What the hell are you talking about?' Gannadius demanded. 'I don't—'

'Oh, of course.' Olybras chuckled. 'Most of it you wouldn't know anything about. I imagine you catch yourself nodding off in the middle of a conversation and waking up a minute or so later with a bit of a headache. Well, for your information there's a really first-rate war going on inside your head; even the snippets I see and hear are little short of spectacular sometimes. Actual fighting; men with bows and halberds, ships, siege engines - cavalry too, sometimes, which I find a bit odd since neither side's got any. Maybe it's all a whatsisname, a metaphor.'

'Oh, for pity's sake,' Gannadius said, disgustedly. 'Am I really the only person around here who can't see what's going on inside my head?'

—And he fell forwards into mud; nasty, thick mud under a thin layer of leaf-mould. He felt his legs sink in, right up to the knees, and he knew he wouldn't be able to free them but he tried anyway. All he succeeded in doing was to pull his foot out of his boot. The feel of the mud on his bare foot was disgusting.

'Hang on,' someone said behind him (he was too firmly stuck to be able to look round and see who it was). 'Don't thrash about, you'll just make it worse.'

Someone grabbed him under the arms and lifted; someone very strong, much stronger than he was. He angled his other foot so as not to lose that boot as well.

'There you are,' said the voice. He could turn his head now; he was looking at a young man, no more than eighteen, but enormously tall and broad across the shoulders, with a broad, stupid-looking face, wispy white-blond hair already beginning to recede, a small, flat nose, pale blue eyes. 'You really should look where you're going,' he said. 'Come on, it's time we weren't here.'

Gannadius opened his mouth to demand an explanation, but his voice didn't work. The giant had started lumbering off through the undergrowth - he hadn't noticed it before, but they were in a dense forest overgrown with brambles and squelching wet underfoot - and he had to hurry to keep up. By following the giant exactly and walking where he'd trampled a path, he was able to pick his way through the tangle.

'I don't like the look of this,' the giant said; and a moment later, men appeared out of the mess of briars and bracken, stumbling and struggling, wallowing in the mud and ripping their coats and trousers on the thorns. It would've been hilariously funny to watch, but for the fact that in spite of their difficulties they were clearly set on killing him and the giant, and unlike the two of them, they were in armour and carried weapons.

'Damn,' the giant said, ducking under a wildly swishing halberd. He straightened up, took the halberd away from the man who'd been using it and smashed him in the face with the butt end of the shaft. Another attacker was struggling towards him, his boots so loaded with mud that he could only just waddle. He was holding a big pole-axe, but as he swung it, he caught the head in a clump of briars, and before he could get it free the giant stabbed him in the stomach with his newly acquired halberd; he wobbled, let go of the pole-axe and waved his arms frantically for balance, then collapsed backwards, his feet now firmly stuck, just as Gannadius' had been, and lay helplessly on his back in the slimy mud, dying. 'Come *on*,' the giant said, leaning back and grabbing Gannadius' wrist while fending off a blow from a billhook with the halberd, gripped one-handed near the socket. 'Gods damn it, if you weren't my—'

—And sat up in his chair, suddenly awake, with a murderous pounding in his temples.

'Well,' Olybras said, 'that was fascinating. Not to mention pleasing too, of course; he's obviously a brave, good-hearted lad and he can look after himself, though of course I'd much rather he stayed out of situations like that altogether. But do you think possibly that next time you could try for something a little bit earlier? Say by about six years?'

Gannadius looked at him. The light from the window behind him hurt terribly, but he ignored it. 'You knew who that was?' he said.

'Oh, yes,' Olybras replied. 'I don't know how, mind, but I recognised him at once. That was my son.'

CHAPTER EIGHTEEN

'I'll be careful, I promise,' he'd said as he waved goodbye; but now he came to think of it, he couldn't remember any of them saying, *Now you will be careful, won't you? Or Look after yourself, Uncle,* or *Please come home soon, Daddy.* Little Niessa had waved, or at least she'd waggled her hand up and down; but Luha hadn't, he'd just stood there as if he was watching some dreary ceremony in the Square, Heris had simply smiled wanly and his niece – had she even been there to see him off? He wasn't sure she had been. That wasn't right. It grieved him.

'That's the place, there,' the sergeant said, and pointed. 'Of course, that's where they were six hours ago. Where they are now's another matter entirely.'

Bardas hadn't been there, either, but he hadn't really expected him to be. It was infuriating that Bardas was here, living quietly in the Bank headquarters, making no fuss, being peaceful; but every time he'd suggested to Niessa that he should pay his brother a visit, she'd just looked at him and changed the subject. And now here he was, at the head of the nation's army about to engage an enemy force that outnumbered him six to one in what might well prove to be the decisive battle of the war, and none of them seemed to care that they might very well never see him again; it was almost as if Heris had said, 'Have a nice day at the office,' without looking up from her mending, while the children got ready for the day's lessons. Gorgas could imagine no more noble or desirable way to die than defending one's home and family, but apathy on such a scale did tend to undercut the whole concept.

'We'll find them,' he replied calmly, 'don't you worry about that. Though on balance I think I'd prefer it if they didn't find us. Does that make any sense?'

The sergeant shrugged. 'Not really,' he said. 'I don't see how we can fight them without letting them know we're here.'

'Ah,' Gorgas said with a smile. 'Now there's an idea.'

Bol Affem, Junior Dean of the Faculty of Military Logistics and second-in-command of the vanguard of the faculty regiment, knew the meaning of fear, but only because he'd once had occasion to look it up in a dictionary. His father, Luha Affem, had died fighting corsairs in the Fleve delta when he was six. His grandfather had been the first man to be killed in the attack on the Jaun hill-fort, seventy years ago. Death in battle was so much a part of the traditions of the Affem family that Bol could conceive of no other way of dying; if he was afraid of anything, it was of ending his life in a bed, surrounded by doctors, in the middle of a perfectly good war.

Nevertheless, the landscape in front of him inspired a certain degree of unease. Not fear, which he knew to be a negative, worthless thing, but apprehension, a sharpening of the instincts and a quickening of the wits when faced with a potential challenge, a healthy and quite useful reaction to a subconscious recognition of danger.

He called a halt and, as the men grounded their halberds and began to climb out of their packs, he walked ahead to the edge of the bluff. There was no obvious way to proceed. If he led his column along the brow of the ridge, he'd be advertising his position for all to see, sacrificing any element of surprise he might still have, and so far he'd seen no sign of scouts or advance parties to suggest that the enemy knew he was here. But if he followed the road through this rocky combe, he could easily walk into a copybook ambush and allow himself to be bottled up, pinned down by the rebel archers. On balance, he decided a little self-advertisement wouldn't do any harm; let the rebels know he was coming—he had the advantage of overwhelming force, which in turn would breed terror and despair. Let them see just how strong his army was.

He slipped off his own pack and sat down on it, unbuckling the front flap and pulling out his water bottle. It was a third empty already; not a problem, but a timely reminder that water might be a problem later on if he didn't monitor the situation. He felt in his pocket for the map and studied it; a wavy blue line across the shoulders of the combe marked the course of some sort of water-way, but it could be anything from a brook to a full-sized river. He put the map away and glanced up at the sky, which was still cloudless and blue. Hot weather for marching at top speed, but even that wasn't necessarily a bad thing. *Let your army march a day before it fights,* his great-grandfather had written in his *Standard Commentary* (still required reading in first-year Tactics); *marching exercises the unfit body and regulates the ill-disciplined mind.* A forced march was as good as a week's training for men just out of the comfort of barracks.

He called to his sergeant; a good man, twenty years with the colours. 'We'll follow the ridge,' he said, 'then drop down into the valley and pick up the road on the flat. We'll be crossing a river or stream of some sort, so take the opportunity to fill water bottles.'

The sergeant acknowledged the order in the appropriate manner and withdrew to a respectful distance. Affem allowed the men five more minutes, then gave the order to proceed.

It was about an hour later, while Bol Affem was drawing up contingency plans in his mind in case it proved impossible to take up water at the river, that the enemy appeared. It was a disconcerting sight; they simply appeared on the ridge, walking up from the steep northern side of the combe and shuffling into a rather slovenly double line directly in front of him. There were no more than fifty of them, all archers, with no more than a dozen helmets and mailshirts between them. They looked more like a gang of unruly children in a village street waiting to pick on an enemy than a military unit. Bol Affem called a halt, and waited. This was so obviously the bait for some attempt at a trap that he wondered whether they really believed that a professional soldier would fall for it. Where was the rest of the trap, though? Waiting down on the slope, to take him in flank as he charged the road-block? Surely not, they'd have to charge up a steep rise, which would be suicide. There wasn't anywhere else they could come from. If this was the rebels' idea of an ambush, he'd be only too delighted to oblige them.

Then, while he stood and tried to puzzle it out, the archers took their bows off their shoulders, nocked arrows in an insultingly leisurely fashion, aimed carefully and started shooting. Seven men went down in the front rank, and another two in the second. The archers each nocked another arrow, took another deliberate aim and loosed; Affem could see them congratulating each other for good shots, commiserating on near misses.

There are no circumstances in all the vicissitudes of war, the elder Affem had written in a passage every boy on Shastel was required to know by heart, *that can ever justify a trained soldier losing his temper.* Bol Affem rubbed his face with the palm of his hand, admitting to himself that, for the first time he could remember since he was a little boy, he didn't know what to do. It had to be a trap, but for the life of him he couldn't see what the trap could possibly consist of. There could be no trap. It was . . .

An arrow hit the man standing one step back to his left, passing through the man's right arm between the bicep and the bone. Affem watched him wince without crying out or moving; he knew better than to leave formation in the face of the enemy, as a good soldier should. Affem felt proud, but also ridiculous; what possible excuse was there for standing still, like the straw target-bosses at a fair, while the rebel archers praised and jeered at their neighbours' technique, made helpful comments about footwork and follow-through. It was ludicrous . . .

'Sergeant,' he said, 'take the front three ranks and get rid of those hooligans.'

The men charged well. They kept exactly in step, so that the points of their levelled halberds made a precise straight line of steel. After a desultory shot or two (though two men went down and stayed down; inevitable at this range), the rebel line simply melted away, the archers scattering down both sides of the ridge, running as fast as they could go. Naturally, the sergeant didn't pursue; he called a halt, turned about and brought the detachment back to rejoin the main column.

'Well done, sergeant,' Affem said. 'Get the wounded seen to as quickly as possible, we're wasting time here.'

Half an hour later, the same thing happened.

This time, the rebels only had time for one shot before the charge dispersed them; but four more halberdiers went down, three killed outright, one shot in the knee and unable to move. Bol Affem swore under his breath and pictured what he'd like to do to the cowards, as and when he had an opportunity.

Half an hour later, again. And again, forty minutes after that. And again; this time, as soon as the pursuit party broke off and turned, a dozen or so archers popped back over the ridge and shot at them, hitting two men in the back. The rest of the party turned and charged again; as the sergeant called them back from the pursuit, an archer materialised only a few yards away from him and shot him through the groin; he bled to death before the next attack, which was a mere fifteen minutes later. This time the archers didn't even drop back down the slopes.

They danced out of the way, daring the halberdiers to put distance between themselves and the main column; and, while the advance party were dithering about whether or not to pursue further, another party of archers jumped up quite unnoticed at the rear of the column, killed six men and faded away.

Proportion, Bol Affem thundered to himself. *These losses are visible and insulting, but trivial in proportion to the size of the army. If we march faster, we'll reach the village quicker, and either they'll fight us properly there and we'll tear them apart, or they can stand by and watch while we kill every living thing in the village. They'll be sorry they started this by the time I've finished it.*

Around the middle of the afternoon they did manage to catch one archer, who slipped and fell and didn't get up again quickly enough; five minutes later, there was hardly enough flesh left on his bones to feed a couple of dogs. But Affem couldn't help noticing that the number of rebels in the harrying parties was increasing, and where there'd been fifty-odd to begin with, there were now over seventy-five. Trying to increase the pace of the march turned out to be impractical; if he ordered quick march, the rebels stepped up the rate of their attacks to slow him down again. He'd confidently anticipated being off the ridge by nightfall, but it didn't turn out that way, so he kept going in the dark – a miserable business on the crown of a steep-sided ridge, but he had no choice; the archers couldn't see to shoot in the darkness, and besides, unless they reached the river by dawn, lack of water would be a serious problem. He ordered the men not to drink except at designated rests, and kept going.

Dawn broke, and still the end of the ridge wasn't in sight. But as soon as there was light to shoot by, the archers were back; still slouching and unsoldierly, loosing their arrows like men shooting for a goose at a wedding, running like terrified children as soon as he sent his men forward; at the last count he'd lost eighty-two killed and twenty-six too badly injured to walk, including thirty-one sergeants. The army was becoming unmanageable, with no one to order the lines or relay the words of command.

Just before midday, having covered no more than two miles since dawn, he caught sight of a rocky outcrop just under the ridge and led the army down to it. There was just enough cover, providing everyone crouched low and kept perfectly still. It was a hot day, but nobody was prepared to shed helmets or breastplates. The last of the water ran out in the middle of the afternoon. The archers killed another sixteen men and wounded twenty-one more, mostly shot through arms and legs that wouldn't quite fit behind the rocks. It was heartbreaking to see men huddled up with an arm or a leg exposed, while a half-dozen archers honed their skills and wagered on who would be the first to hit the small, difficult target. Two halberdiers finally lost control and ran out, brandishing their halberds and yelling bloody murder. The second one managed to get ten yards.

That night the archers brought up lanterns, but the light wasn't good enough; they gave up and went away, allowing the army to continue. Just after midnight the ground began to slope sharply downhill, and just before dawn they reached the flat and the river. At first light they were still filling water bottles; the archers had been waiting for them behind rocks and trees, and shot down twenty-one before they could be chased off.

Somehow Bol Affem had assumed that, once he reached the flat, his problems would be over. Of course, this wasn't the case. The only difference was that instead of jumping up unexpectedly, the archers trailed the army in full view, like wild, mad dogs that follow you down a village street. They came no closer than ninety yards, but there were nearly two hundred of them now, and by noon they'd picked off another twenty men and slowed the march to a crawl. By this point, the army were exhausted, having marched two nights and crouched half a day in the hot sun. Thanks to strict rationing there was enough water; but Affem had banked on reaching the

village a whole day earlier, and food was running low.
Just before evening, he was shot in the calf of his left leg.
The arrow passed through cleanly and without cutting a
vein, and he was able to hobble, using his halberd as a
crutch, but by midnight he had to lean on a man's shoulder. Nevertheless, he made himself continue, because he
knew that at dawn they would reach the village.

And so they did. It was easy enough to find; for the
last hour of darkness, they had a bright orange glow to
guide them. The fire was pretty much burnt out by dawn,
when the archers attacked again. When Affem finally
limped down what had been the village street, swinging
between two men with his wounded leg dragging behind
him, there was nothing but ash and charred timbers. The
well was blocked with the bodies of dead halberdiers,
men killed on the first day. There was no food, and no
cover. Nothing for it, therefore, but to press on to the
next village, which was only four miles away.

'I don't know about you,' Gorgas said, his mouth full of
cheese, 'But I'm exhausted. This not fighting certainly
takes it out of you.'

Behind him in the distance, a pillar of smoke rose in
the still air. He made a point of not looking at it; that was
the village of Lambye, burning, and he'd given the order
to burn it. The thought that he'd set his men to burn
down one of his own villages made him angry, for all that
he knew it was the way to win the war. Nevertheless, the
act disgusted him. And what Niessa was going to say
when she found out, he shuddered to think.

'How much further is it to the river?' the sergeant
asked. Gorgas glanced down at the map spread across
his knees and brushed away a few crumbs that had fallen
in the folds.

'At the rate they're going, four hours,' he replied, 'give
or take an hour. I'll say this for them, they've got a hell of
a lot more staying power than I'd have given them credit
for.'

'Training,' the sergeant said. 'Discipline. It's what sets your professional soldiers aside from your bandits and hooligans.'

'I think you're right,' Gorgas said, cutting himself another slice of cheese. 'For a start, it gets them killed.'

They saw the smoke rising from the second village almost as soon as they left the first.

'That's it, then,' said the colour-sergeant, stopping and shading his eyes. 'It's going to be like this all the way. No food and no cover. We don't stand a chance.'

'Then why don't we charge them?' growled the young soldier to his left. 'Go out there and get the bastards? Got nothing to lose by it, have we? If we all charged, the whole lot of us—'

Nobody was listening, and he gave it up. For the last eighteen hours, he'd found it progressively harder not to think about water. Up till then, the other desperate issues of the march had been enough to distract his attention – hunger, exhaustion, the incessant nibbling inroads of the archers. Now he could hardly spare them a thought. *Which is good,* he tried to re-assure himself. *Nothing like being thirsty for taking your mind off your troubles.* He wriggled his shoulders against the hard straps of his pack, which were crushing the rings of his mailshirt through the buckskin jerkin underneath and into his skin. He had a blister on each heel where the backs of his boots nipped against the tendon. He tried not to think about water.

'There's one thing he haven't tried,' somebody muttered in the row behind.

'Uh? What's that?'

'We could always surrender.'

Several men took it as a joke and laughed. 'He's got a point there,' the young soldier said. 'Why don't we do that?'

'Ah, go to hell,' someone jeered. 'We can do without that kind of talk.'

The young soldier frowned. 'What's your problem?' he said. 'Face it. Either we give in or we're going to die.'

'Make him shut up, Sarge,' someone sighed. 'Put him on a charge or something.'

The colour-sergeant shook his head. 'We won't surrender,' he said. 'Not while we still outnumber them five to one, or whatever it is now. It's still overwhelming odds. We can't surrender, we can't get near enough to fight, we're getting slower all the time and in a few hours we're going to start keeling over without the bastards having to raise a finger. Craziest thing you ever heard of, but they've done us. It'll be the biggest, most spectacular victory in history; they'll be teaching it in their damned faculties for the next thousand years. Pity we got to be on the wrong side, really.'

Bol Affem was thinking along broadly similar lines, as he stumbled and dragged along between his two supporters. *Amazing innovation,* he thought, *just when you thought every possible tactic had been tried and there couldn't be anything new. After this, they'll have to rewrite every textbook and treatise in the library – unless we win the war, of course, in which case we can forget this ever happened and go back to the proper ways of making war, the ones in the syllabus.* He could feel his eyes closing all the time now; such an effort to keep them open, to stay awake, to be bothered. Now that he was being dragged along rather than having to make the effort of walking, he was beginning to feel removed, outside, not involved; it was like being a child again, carried on his father's shoulders, too small to be any use or any trouble. He didn't really feel hungry or thirsty; the pain in his leg was still there but even pain didn't seem to work properly any more. Most of all, he could no longer make the effort to be afraid of Death. Foolish, pointless. It was like the fear he'd felt when he was a little boy, just before he went to a children's party. *It'll be all right,* his mother used to say, *you'll enjoy it once you get there.*

'Here they come again,' someone nearby observed in

a matter-of-fact voice. Nobody seemed very interested. Affem lifted his head and saw in the middle distance the line of archers walking towards them, not hurrying, moving up like a party of merchants on a long journey. He saw his soldiers wearily closing ranks, like very old monks performing a ritual they've long since lost all belief in. He let his head droop.

There had been a point, presumably, where they'd stopped believing in survival, but he couldn't remember it coming and going. It had been gradual, gentle, the death of hope; the slow realisation and acceptance, made easier by the fact that none of them really cared any more. Water, shade, shelter, food – give them any of those and they'd stop and stay stopped. A future after water or shade or shelter or food wasn't a realistic aspiration, and besides, where would be the point in it? It had become obvious that this march would never end, that somehow this rocky scrub and moorland stretched away into infinity. Given time, a man might eventually climb the stairs to the moon; but no one could ever reach the edge of this country.

We could surrender.

Bol Affem laughed. Yes, why not? In another life, perhaps, the next time round, the next army to be caught like this, in a siege without a city, a prison without walls, surrender might be an option. But not while there are still a thousand of us to a couple of hundred of them; because any minute now, we'll reach the water or the shade or the shelter or the food, and there'll be fighting, and when there's fighting we'll win. Or we could surrender, right now, we could refuse to go on. In theory.

Something was happening.

Affem looked up again, and saw that the men at the head of the column were quickening their pace, walking instead of slouching, breaking into a run. He tried to see what all the fuss was about; not the enemy, surely, they'd given up trying to engage them hours ago. Besides, he could see the archers on either side coming in close, shooting, taking men down in dozens and being ignored.

'What's the matter?' he asked.

'Don't know,' said one of the soldiers. 'Here,' he called out, 'what's the rush?'

'Water', someone shouted back. 'There's a bloody river.'

To begin with, Gorgas had worried. It would be just like life, he reckoned, if at the very last moment, when all the hard work had been done and everything had worked out so perfectly, one little mistake cost them everything and turned this victory into a ghastly defeat. It would only take a little carelessness, allowing the enemy to get close enough to engage, getting between them and the water, with the odds still so desperately uneven, his army could be wiped out in a few minutes.

Then he stopped worrying, as soon as he saw the enemy scrambling and tumbling down the steep sides of the combe, dumping their packs and their weapons, hurling themselves into the water. Instead, he joined the line of archers steadily, methodically shooting them down as they drank and splashed.

They aren't taking any notice. They don't seem to know we're here.

He nocked an arrow, drew, aimed, pushed with his left hand and let the load on the string pull it clear of his fingers, then watched the arrow lift and drop into the mark; a good one, seven hits on the trot now. There was another arrow on the string before he even knew it. He'd always done well, shooting from a distance.

Up till then, it had just been the front end of the column; now the main body had caught up and was pouring down the slope like a landslide, like a stampede, like sheep being driven down a narrow lane, like water splashing messily out of an over-filled bucket and slopping onto the floor. They were tripping over each other, shoving, falling and making others fall with them, sliding down the dry slope on their backsides like children tobogganing on rush mats; but all they were aware of was the presence of water. Gorgas shot a man and watched him still gulping down water as he died.

'Extraordinary,' said the sergeant, disgusted. 'Never seen anything like it in all my life.'

'You'll be feeling sorry for them next,' someone commented. The sergeant shook his head.

'I wouldn't go that far,' he said, as he drew his bow. 'Nobody could feel sorry for *them*.'

It was true, Gorgas reflected. The sight was so obscene, that scrambling, crawling, inhuman mass - it was like watching ants or wasps, or a nest of woodlice revealed by the lifting of a rock. The only emotion he felt was revulsion, the urge to stamp on them and make them stop moving, put a stop to the indecent spectacle. *That's a point*, he reflected. *How long's it going to take us? And are we going to have enough arrows? I really don't want to have to come back tomorrow to finish off.*

There was a raft of bodies on the surface of the water now, like the clogged mess that collects in a stream after a rainstorm, when hedge-clippings and dead leaves get washed into the watercourse and drift up against a rock or a tree root, forming an impromptu dam. 'How many do you reckon we've done so far?' someone speculated. 'Three hundred?'

'Not so many as that,' someone else replied. 'Say two hundred.'

'Two-fifty, surely. At least two-fifty.'

'Cease fire,' Gorgas said.

They did as they were told; but they were staring at him as if he'd gone crazy. He took no notice. This had gone far enough. Any more would just be a waste.

'You two,' he said, 'go and tell them to throw down their weapons and put their hands on their heads and they won't be harmed. Find me their commanding officer.'

Had they noticed that the shooting had stopped? He could see no sign of it. Most of the men who'd made it into the water looked like they were dead, but that couldn't be right, they couldn't have shot that many. He looked again and saw that there were men just lying in the river, floating, full to bursting with water and waiting for something to happen, or just floating. The rest, the ones still scrabbling for a way in, seemed totally pre-occupied with getting to the water. Calling for them to throw away their weapons was a waste of time: they'd all done that already. 'All right, the rest of you,' Gorgas said. 'Make sure your quivers are full, we may not be done shooting yet. Where's those carts with the arrows? Come on, just because we're winning there's no call for every-thing to grind to a halt.'

Some time later the two men came back. With them were three of the enemy; two men carrying a third, all three of them soaked to the skin, their clothes, arms and legs dipped a sort of rosy pink. Down there in the river they were drinking the stuff. Gorgas felt sick.

'This is Master Bol Affem,' said one of the two hal-berdiers. 'He's in charge, but I don't know if he can hear you.'

'Unlikely,' Gorgas replied. 'He's dead.'

'Oh.' The halberdiers let go, and the dead body flopped to the ground like a sack of flour. 'So now what?'

Gorgas put his toe against Affem's jaw and flipped it over so that he could see the man's face. He smiled bleakly. 'Consider yourselves promoted to the rank of acting generals. Surrender or I'll kill the lot of you.'

'We surrender,' one of the halberdiers replied prompt-ly. 'Now what?'

It was a very good question. There was no force on earth short of death that was going to persuade the halberdiers to stop and get out of the water before they'd finished guzzling it. All he could think of was to make it look like there had been a proper official surrender, and trust that they'd all accept that that was what had hap-pened. His knowledge of human nature suggested that they would. 'Down the slope,' he ordered. 'Form a ring around them, forty yards out, and slowly close it up till they're all herded together into a mass; then we'll start pulling them out in groups of thirty and marching them out. And we're going to need food for the buggers, and somebody'd better go ahead and make a start on a stockade; and you three, start assigning men to prisoner-guarding squads. The gods know, I never expected anything like this, so I haven't a clue how you'll go about it.'

'Hang on,' said a sergeant, 'isn't there an old slate-pit a mile or so up the road? We could put 'em in that for the time being.'

Gorgas shrugged. 'If you say so,' he said. 'If it'll work, let's do it. This is *embarrassing*.' Suddenly he grinned.

'What's the joke?' the sergeant asked.

'Oh, nothing,' Gorgas replied, smiling. 'I'm just imagining what my sister's going to say when I tell her I've brought some people home for dinner.'

'We don't need to wait for Affem's column,' said Sten Mogre. 'Gorgas and the army simply aren't here. We can press on and be in Scona Town by the end of the week.'

Avid Soef glowered at him over the wine jug. 'Fine,' he said. 'Then what was the point of sending him?'

'The point,' Mogre replied smugly, 'was a half-hearted attempt to lure Gorgas away on a wild goose chase while we made a dash for the Town. I never for one moment imagined he'd be stupid enough to fall for it, but I thought what the hell, we don't need Affem's army anyway, the extra numbers'd just get under our feet and complicate logistics, and it'd be nice to have a third army loose behind their backs while we're bashing them up in front of Scona. The fact that he went for the bait surprises me, but I'm damned if I'm going to let the opportunity slip.'

Soef thought for a moment. If there was a hidden agenda behind the manoeuvre he couldn't see it. 'Fair enough,' he said. 'But we should still divide our forces, come at the Town from two sides. I don't like the thought of four thousand men all marching up the same road.'

'That's a good point,' said someone from the far end of the table. 'It's the same principle you referred to a moment ago. Too many men in the army's often worse than too few.'

Sten Mogre frowned, and tilted the jug over his cup. It was empty, and he licked his fingers. 'Obviously I've considered that,' he said. 'But the fact is, there's only one realistic approach to the Town by land: along the heights and down the north road. Which direction do you suggest our other army should come from? In from the west, threading their way through all those rocks and rubbish? Or do you envisage them squelching their way through the south marshes?'

Avid Soef hadn't thought of that. 'You're being a bit glib, aren't you?' he said to buy himself time to think. 'Just how much do we know about the southern approach?'

Mogre smiled. 'I've been there,' he said. 'I won't say I know it like the back of my hand, but I remember having to pay a couple of peasants to pull my chaise out of the bog. Unless you know your way in that stuff, you're asking for trouble.'

Soef nodded. 'Exactly,' he said. 'And I'll bet you money they'll think so too, and they won't bother setting up proper defences. Which is why we should send a force that way – picking up a few locals as guides, of course. Surely you haven't forgotten your Guerenz?'

'Remind me,' Mogre said patiently.

'Guerenz, chapter seven, section four or five, can't remember which offhand. *Avoid the enemy's weaknesses, which he will fortify into strengths, and address instead his strengths, which complacency will render weak.* Always been a favourite of mine, that.'

Mogre sighed. 'Far be it from me to argue with Guerenz,' he said. 'But do we actually need to bother? What's that other passage in Guerenz? *To strike unexpectedly with overwhelming force is the only strategy;*

everything else is compromise forced by circumstance. And that's not scripture,' he went on, leaning back and clasping his hands behind his head, *'that's just ordinary common sense.'*

'Not so fast,' someone else said. 'I've been with you every step of the way up till now, but I think Avid's making sense on this one. Suppose Gorgas comes back and engages us in front of the Town, somewhere in the high passes where a handful of men can easily hold up an army. Unless we're prepared to bash through and take heavy losses, we could be held up for days, and remember, we're on a knife-edge with logistics as it is, this far from home. I hear they're already burning villages between here and Polmies. But if we had a second attack going home, we could afford to waste time playing games with Gorgas, because while we're doing that, our second army'll be in Scona Town ending the war. And if Gorgas just falls back on Scona and shuts the door, it won't make any odds.'

One of the big candles in the middle of the table guttered and went out. A batman quickly replaced it with a fresh one. 'All right, I'll go along with that,' said Sten Mogre. 'Actually, it's a good idea, though nobody's mentioned the real reason; which is, the purpose of this exercise isn't just burning Scona Town, it's wiping out the rebel army and capturing or killing the Loredans. I like the idea of our second army coming up *from* Scona once we've taken it and catching Gorgas in the rear while he's defending this notional pass we're all assuming he'll lay us up in. Now that's neat.'

Avid Soef went to bed in a foul mood. True, he'd won the day and got his army, but once again that damned fat man had nipped out all the credit right from under his nose. There was also the slight possibility that taking an army across these marshes might not be the simple walk-through he'd assumed it was when he came up with the idea; and that Mogre was well aware of it when he so graciously conceded. On reflection, what he should have done was insist that Mogre lead the southern army – yes, but then Mogre would be the one to take Scona and catch Gorgas, while he was stuck fast in a mountain bottleneck fussing over water rationing and acceptable loss ratios.

Confound it; why did war have to be so *difficult*?

'Uncle Gorgas will be just fine,' Iseutz said confidently. 'His sort never come to harm. The bad luck just sort of glances off them and hits the person standing next to them.'

Heris Loredan bit her tongue and made no reply. It was only to be expected that the child would be the next best thing to impossible given the life she'd led, and since Gorgas seemed to dote on her it would be imprudent to pick a fight. 'I hope so,' she mumbled. 'I suppose he can look after himself.' She put the stopper in her ink bottle, picked up the document she'd been copying and sprinkled it with sand to dry it off. 'Aren't you cold, sitting there without even a shawl?' she asked.

Iseutz shook her head. 'I don't feel the cold any more,' she said, 'or at least not the way you people do. You forget, it was *really* cold in the prison.'

Heris didn't think she could take much more of her husband's niece without doing something she'd later regret, so she took the original document and the copy and went back into the house. Irritating, to be chased out of her favourite seat in the cloister by this horrible, sad creature; but being married to Gorgas Loredan had taught her the value of strategic retreats and the avoidance of conflict. She retreated into the office and busied herself with the filing backlog.

When she'd gone, Iseutz picked up her book and read for a while. It was a Perimadeian technical treatise on applied metallurgy, dealing with such topics as the extraction of mercury and the refining of precious metals; for some bizarre reason, the subject interested her. Behind her, Luha (solid, dull, insignificant, tree-like

Luha) was dutifully doing his homework. Thankfully, little Niessa had gone off to be a pest somewhere else. Iseutz had finally managed to control Niessa by convincing her that she was a witch who ate cats and rats and turned little girls into insects; Niessa avoided her whenever possible now, and peered anxiously at her from behind furniture when it was required that they share a part of the house for any length of time. Heris she could banish from her presence just by being aggravating, and Luha was the easiest of them all; she only needed to wave her mutilated hand under his squeamish little nose and he was off and away like a flushed partridge. As for Uncle Gorgas – well, she didn't mind him. But while he was away, it was imperative that she should be able to exercise some degree of control over her environment.

'Excuse me, miss.' Iseutz looked up; it was that damned obsequious porter. 'Is the mistress in the house, do you know?'

'Yes,' Iseutz replied. 'Why?'

The porter looked at her. 'Well, miss, there's a man at the door. He says he's the master's brother, miss. Bardas Loredan.'

Iseutz kept perfectly still. 'That's all right,' she said. 'Show him in here, I'll deal with him.'

As soon as the porter had gone she jumped up and looked round frantically, but there was nothing to be seen. Hardly surprising; civilised men like Gorgas Loredan don't leave deadly weapons lying around in their houses. There was always a heavy blunt object, like a chair leg; or she could hide in the doorway and strangle him with her dressing-gown cord. Both ideas seemed faintly comic. She stayed where she was.

'Hello, Uncle Bardas,' she said.

It was amusing to see his reaction. To do him credit, he didn't shrink away or yelp, but he was visibly startled.

'Hello,' he replied.

Iseutz smiled and waved him to a chair. 'What are you

doing here?' she said. 'Last place on earth I'd expect you to turn up of your own free will.'

Bardas nodded and sat down, never taking his eyes off her. 'Ordinarily yes,' he said. 'But since I know for a fact that Gorgas isn't here—'

'And you either didn't know I was, or you'd forgotten. Bad staff work on either count, Colonel. Would you like some of this wine? It's not bad, and I didn't have a chance to poison it.'

He shook his head. 'Not thirsty,' he said. 'And these days I don't drink much, anyway.'

'That's a change,' Iseutz said. 'When you were teaching me to fence there was always booze on your breath.'

'I'm a reformed character,' Bardas replied.

'I'm sure. So what are you doing here?'

Bardas grinned feebly. 'To tell you the truth, I'm here to meet my nephew. Is that him, there in the corner?'

'That's him,' Iseutz replied. 'Luha, come and meet your Uncle Bardas. Your Uncle Bardas is a great man, Luha; he's a soldier and a fencer and a craftsman and the gods only know what else besides.'

The boy looked at Bardas warily; a wise reaction, Bardas thought, on meeting a new Loredan. Wiser still would have been to run away.

'Hello, Luha,' he said. 'What are you doing?'

'Geometry,' Luha replied. 'I'm not very good at it.'

Bardas smiled. 'You and me both. I had to learn it in the army, calculating angles for aiming catapults. I could never get the hang of it, though.'

Luha looked at him blankly and said nothing. 'Don't worry,' Iseutz said cheerfully, 'it's nothing personal, he's always like this, aren't you, Luha? The quiet sort.'

'Yes,' Luha said. 'Can I get on with my homework now?'

Bardas nodded. 'Would you like me to try and help you?' he said.

Luha frowned. 'I thought you said you weren't any good at it.'

'I'm not,' Bardas replied. 'But that doesn't necessarily mean I'm not better at it than you.'

Luha thought for a moment; he was one of those boys you can watch thinking. 'If you like,' he said, 'but I'm not bothered. I always do my homework on my own. Father says I should.'

'You carry on, then,' Bardas said. 'I'll sit here and talk to my niece.'

Luha nodded and went back to his corner. Bardas sat back in his chair and let his hands trail on the grass.

'This is cozy,' Iseutz said. 'If you like, I'll send him to fetch Heris and little Niessa.'

'Don't trouble him on my account,' Bardas replied. 'But thank you for being so civil,' he added. 'I must admit, I expected a scene when we next met.'

Iseutz shrugged. 'You'll keep,' she said. 'But I still can't get over seeing you here. You must be really demoralised.'

Bardas nodded. 'That's a fair assessment,' he said. 'Mostly, though, it's only morbid curiosity. Try as I might, I just couldn't imagine Gorgas with a home and a family. It'd be like going round to Death's house for dinner. But apparently I was wrong.'

Iseutz smiled. 'Don't be fooled,' she said. 'It's like those toy houses they sell for little girls' dolls; it's all perfect, absolutely true to life, all the doors and windows actually open, and it was all ordered sight unseen from a catalogue. Except me, of course, and I'm in the process of being slowly digested. In a few years' time I'll probably be quite housebroken. Hey, if I'm really good maybe my fingers'll grow back.'

'I think you came with the set,' Bardas replied. 'I think you're the token skeleton in the cupboard, utterly lifelike but made of wax and only three inches tall. Now you're upset,' he added, grinning. 'Didn't I teach you always to keep your guard up?'

She nodded. 'All right,' she said. 'You know what I'm going to do now? I was just going to bide my time, be patient and kill you when I had the chance. But that'd be too good for you. So I'm going to hurt you.'

Bardas raised an eyebrow. 'Really?' he said. 'And how do you propose doing that?'

Iseutz smiled. Under other circumstances, she might have had a nice smile. 'I'll tell you something I know and you don't, something Uncle Gorgas told me. I'm guessing it'll burn you up.' She shrugged her bony shoulders. 'And if it doesn't, I'll just have to find something that does. But this ought to do the trick.'

Bardas made a show of yawning. 'I'm listening,' he said. 'What's this tremendous secret that you know and I don't?'

Iseutz turned her head away, flipped her fringe out of her eyes, and then looked back, like a young girl flirting. 'It's about who opened the gates of Perimadeia,' she said.

Later that evening, Bardas Loredan went back to the Bank. He was allowed to come and go freely now, so long as he told his sister where he was going. A little clerk from the back office followed him everywhere and told Niessa where he'd really gone and what he'd really been doing. He knew this. It didn't matter.

He had two rooms, one to sleep in and the other for amusing himself. The second room was large and airy, with one big window about seven feet off the ground, looking out over a back alley, and a midden. It was empty except for a chair, a stool, and a long table robust enough to be used as a workbench. There were also two caskets full of the tools he'd asked for, though so far he hadn't had the energy to unpack them.

He unpacked them now, carefully arranging them in a logical order on or under the bench, wiping the preservative grease off the blades with handfuls of the hay they'd been packed in. Three saws; two drawknives, one straight, one curved; five assorted planes, ranging from the long, bulky boxwood trying plane to the neat little brass-bodied block plane; four spokeshaves, straight and curved; any number of files, rasps, chisels and gouges; three short-bladed knives for whittling and scraping; abrasive reeds and pots of sand and grit and resin for bonding them to blocks, wood, brass and iron clamps, in a great variety of shapes and sizes; pots and jars of glues and gessos, and a pestle and mortar; beeswax and the makings of lacquers and polishes; a glue kettle; steel and brass hammers, bastard, ball-pein, planishing and tack; drifts and punches; copper, hide, lead and lignum vitae mallets; whetstones, oilstones, slipstones; a bow-drill, a breast-drill, a screw-drill, all with boxed sets of various collets and a rosewood tray of fine steel drill-bits; three ebony rules and two squares, one boxwood and one brass; charcoal and chalk; calipers and dividers and contour gauges; an awl and a fretsaw and a couple of handy-looking little objects even Bardas didn't immediately recognise; all new and clean and of the finest quality, their edges fresh from their first grinding, their faces true and unbattered, enough tools to build the world.

When he'd finished unpacking he took a stick of charcoal and started drawing sketches on the benchtop.

CHAPTER NINETEEN

Gorgas had seriously underestimated the skill of his archers; there were just over three hundred and fifty bodies clogging up the river, bobbing gently up and down like a raft of logs on its way from the forest to the sawmill.

The good news was that they'd pulled off one of the most remarkable feats of arms in recorded military history; the total defeat of a hugely superior force, with negligible losses to themselves, in a remarkably short period of time. The bad news was that they now had nearly five hundred prisoners, dying of starvation and exhaustion, in desperate need of food and a secure billet. The disused stone quarry was almost large enough and the sides were far too steep to climb, except for one easily guarded track, but they were open to the violence of the sun, and of course there was no water. At a bare minimum of a pint and a half of water and half an Ordnance loaf per man per day, that came to nearly a hundred gallon jugs to be filled at the river, carried four miles along difficult roads, lugged down the steep track and up again; sixty trays of Ordnance loaves to be got from somewhere (Where, for pity's sake? Keeping his own men fed was a serious strain on his ingenuity); two shifts of forty guards, making up a third of his mobile army. As if that wasn't bad enough, he had a major river blocked with dead bodies, and deputations from the four villages downstream whose drinking water was red and stinking. He was going to have to order his battle-weary soldiers to wade chest-high in that disgusting water to drag out all the swollen, sodden corpses, heap them up in stacks like bricks of newly cut peat, and dig three broad, deep pits in stony ground before they could even think of resting, patching up their worn and damaged kit, dressing their own minor wounds - assuming, of course, that they weren't facing an overnight forced march to take on one of the other two armies he knew were still on the loose somewhere on the island. *Only one thing worse than a defeat*, somebody once said, *and that's a victory.* Trite, Gorgas reflected, but true.

His rapid inspection tour of the holding camp in the quarry only depressed him further. He didn't have enough medical orderlies for his own men, let alone any to spare for the enemy; but there were men dying of comparatively minor injuries, and that was a waste. He didn't have to be a doctor or a scientist to know that unless the prisoners were moved on soon, a great many of them would die in the quarry from poisoned wounds, dysentery, malnutrition, any number of combinations of injuries and afflictions exacerbated by heat and squalor. Under any other circumstances he wouldn't let such a dreadful thing happen, but as it was there was very little he could do. If any of them did survive and make it back to Shastel, the tales they'd have to tell of their treatment at his hands would be enough to harden the enemy's resolve to fight to the last man if needs be, to make sure Scona was erased from the earth and rubbed out of human memory. It was what he'd want to see happen if he was in their place.

One final, painful look at the prisoners, bodies and clothes caked in dried bloody mud, squashed up tight together like children hitching a ride on top of a hay-cart; but he had a war to run, the deplorable consequences of victory to cope with, and he'd already done all that was humanly possible. He wiped the picture from his mind and went away.

Back at the burnt-out village he was using as his operational base – more shambles, more mess – he was just in time to hear the depressing news from his commissariat; yes, there were plenty of arrows, bows, shoes, food, everything he desperately needed, but there were only seven roadworthy wagons available to transport them, and the journey would take them a day and a half. Which did he want first? Arrows, without which his men couldn't fight? Shoes, without which they couldn't march, unless he ordered his victorious army to hobble and squelch their way across Scona in the footwear they'd been wading through mud and water in? Food? His choice. Oh, and by the way, Sten Mogre is marching on Scona Town; if you're really quick, you might just catch up with him before he burns it to the ground.

Having obtained the raw materials, Bardas started to build the bow.

First, he put the fresh sinew up on the window ledge to dry in the sun. Then he mixed the sizing glue (fortunately he had plenty of sawdust to thicken it with) and pinned the rawhide up on boards to cure. Even in this heat, these three ingredients needed to be left alone for a few days before he could go any further. Fortunately, there was plenty more to be getting on with.

He made the wooden core, to which the back and belly would be glued. Among the billets of suitable wood he'd been supplied with (sent straight from the Bank's own bow-factory, hand-selected by the superintendent; nothing too good for a Loredan) was a fine, straight-grained mulberry blank, taken from an old, fat tree, which he worked down with the drawknife and the plane into an even half-inch-thick square section some fifty-five inches long. When he was happy with it, he made the bending-jig, a complicated assembly of planks, blocks and clamps to hold the bow in the shape he wanted while he steamed it to make the wood take the drastic permanent curves the design called for. The contour was the traditional kissing mouth, like a full-mouthed woman's upper lip. After he'd bathed the wood evenly in steam for a full hour, it lost its will to resist and sagged into the clamps like a fat man sitting down.

While the wood was cooling down and taking its set, he cleaned the last few ribbons of meat off the bones that would make up the belly, flicking the scraps into the sizing glue pot to give the mixture a touch more texture.

('What do you want with all this junk?' Niessa had demanded suspiciously.

'I want to make a bow for Gorgas,' he'd replied.

That had taken her by surprise. 'I thought you couldn't stand him,' she'd said.

'I've reformed,' he'd replied. 'Forgive and forget, that's me from now on. After all, family's family, and we're all in this together whether we like it or not.'

She hadn't known what to say to that. 'You're going to booby-trap it, aren't you?' she'd said. 'Or put poison on the handle, or saw through it so it breaks in the middle of a battle.'

He'd scowled at her for that. 'Give me some credit,' he'd said. 'I may not be much, but I take a pride in my craft. If I build Gorgas a bow, you can be sure it'll be the best bow the world's ever seen. Besides, when all is said and done, I owe him. He gave me a Guelan sword to defend myself with when Perimadeia fell. I want him to have a really fine bow,' he'd gone on, 'for when the Foundation sacks Scona.')

Once he'd pared the rib-bones down to firm material, he cut the splices to join the sections together, using his finest fretsaw blade and a narrow scraper ground out of a razor. Cutting the double fishtail splice in each section was a long, difficult, nerve-racking job, one which had to be done right. It took him the best part of the day on which Gorgas fought the battle in the river bed.

Sergeant Cerl Baiss had been a sergeant for precisely three weeks. Before that, he'd been the superintendent of the second-largest flour mill on Scona, managing a staff of sixty men, doing a job he liked and doing it exceptionally well. Gorgas Loredan had decided he had leadership and administrative abilities that were badly needed for the war effort, and had drafted him into the reserves a fortnight ago. He'd just had time to master the basic elements of archery, such as how to string the bow and fit an arrow on the string so that it didn't fall off again as soon as he took his hand away, when the reserves became the Town garrison, making Cerl Baiss the man responsible for the defence of Scona Town in Gorgas' absence.

The news that Sten Mogre was fifteen miles from the Town gate with two thousand halberdiers hit Sergeant Baiss like a falling wall.

'If Gorgas got our message,' the young, brash ensign was saying, 'he'll most likely take this road here.' He pointed to a squiggle on the map that Baiss had been assuming was a river, or a village boundary. 'If he really gets a move on, he could be here –' (another prod with the finger) '– by midday tomorrow, by which time Sten will be here, right on our doorstep, where he'd dearly love to be. Which really only leaves us with one course of action.'

One vice Baiss had never indulged in was false pride. 'You'd better explain,' he said. 'I don't want to get this wrong.'

The young ensign nodded. 'These mountains here—'

'Oh. Those are mountains. Right. Sorry.'

'These mountains here,' the ensign repeated, 'are our only chance. Sten'll have to come through them here,' (prod) 'or here,' (prod) 'and my guess is he'll take this fork here, even though it's three miles out of his way, because he knows we could really string him up on the other pass. So we intercept him – he'll be expecting it, mind, but that doesn't alter the fact that we can make life pretty bloody for him – and just hope and pray Gorgas catches up in time to give him a boot up the bum. If everything holds together – if Gorgas comes – we might do ourselves a bit of good. If not, well.'

Sergeant Baiss stared at the map – he'd never understood maps – and tried to think like a soldier, something which came as naturally to him as swimming under the surface in mercury. Why was it, he wondered, that everybody in the army referred to the enemy generals by their first names, as if they were old friends?'

'I think we should defend the other pass,' he said.

The young ensign looked at him. 'But that'd be asking for trouble,' he said. 'Sten's too bright for that.'

Baiss shook his head. 'Forgive me,' he said, 'this is probably all first-grade stuff to professional soldiers, but if the obvious thing to do is go this way, wouldn't he be better off going that way and missing us altogether? Especially as that's the shorter way.'

The ensign shrugged. 'You could go mad playing that game. I could say, "He'll expect us to expect him to do that, so he'll do the unexpected." No way of knowing how many double-crosses to allow for, is there?'

Baiss felt his patience getting thin. 'All right,' he said, 'we'll toss a coin for it.'

'Might just as well,' the ensign said with a grin. 'You're the boss, it's your decision, thank the gods.'

That wasn't what Baiss wanted to hear, but if he'd been a soldier rather than a naturally gifted mill superintendent, he'd have chosen the shorter road. 'We'll defend this one,' he said. 'How soon do you think we can get there?'

The young ensign walked his fingers across the map. 'Four hours,' he said. 'If you're right, my guess is that Sten'll be there in eight.'

In the event, it took Baiss and his three hundred archers two and a half hours to reach the pass, which was just as well since they'd been two hours behind schedule setting off. As a token gesture, he'd sent fifty men to the other pass, trusting the young ensign's assurance that any more than two hundred and fifty men would be a hindrance rather than a help in the sort of battle he was anticipating. Fifty men wouldn't be enough to do more than make Sten Mogre angry if he chose the other way, but that was really beside the point.

An hour later, the enemy arrived; a great surge of armoured men squeezed so tight into the narrow gallery between two sheer sandstone walls that Baiss could hear shields and armguards scraping against rock. That was good, but not as good as he'd hoped. He'd been relying on being able to deploy his archers so that they'd all get a shot, but with the best will in the world he couldn't accommodate a firing line more than sixty strong, and the pass curved about so much that the longest distance the enemy would have to cross in full view of the defending force was less than a hundred yards.

'Five volleys if we're lucky,' the ensign said gloomily, 'and then they'll be on us like a dog on a rat. Of course, hand-to-hand in this sort of terrain will suit them down to the ground.'

Baiss frowned, trying to concentrate. Six fives are thirty, so three hundred; but of course, not every shot will count, so reduce that by, what, half? He had no idea. Say by a third. A hundred of the enemy shot down before they made contact. Was that enough to break an army's morale? Or would it just make them so mad they'd fight like demons?

(*An idiotic war; a bank, led by a baker, is fighting a university in a place where of necessity both sides will cut each other to ribbons.*)

'Here they come, anyhow,' the young ensign said, and his voice was weak with fear. To his surprise, Baiss realised that the terror he'd been trying to cope with ever since Mogre's army had been traced had somehow slipped away. Rationalising, he came to the conclusion that it was because there was nothing he could do now, no options remaining except to stick by what he'd decided and see it through. The prospect of his own death didn't worry him, and the men under his command were proper soldiers, they'd know how to deal with the matter in hand.

'Does everybody know what to do?' he asked. The young ensign nodded. *Except me, of course.* Not for the first time, he wondered what in the gods' names had possessed Gorgas Loredan to drop a civilian into a position in the chain of command where he might just possibly be called upon to lead an army into a major battle. When he'd asked Gorgas that question, though not in so many words, he'd been told that there were only ten regular sergeants in the army and four of those weren't fit to lead a goat on a short string. 'It's all right,' Gorgas had told him with a wide smile, '*none* of us have done anything like this before. I know I haven't. You've got what it takes, you'll manage.'

'On my mark,' the young ensign shouted, his voice high and shrill but clear nevertheless. 'Draw. Aim. Loose.'

Baiss had never seen anything like it in all his life. The nearest he could come to it was a clump of tall thistles, the sort that grow head-high in overgrown pasture, toppling and falling together as one scythe-stroke slices through them. The front rank of the halberdiers had simply gone down, and the men behind had walked right over them; not because they were callous or exceptionally well disciplined, but because there wasn't time to slow down or swerve to avoid them. Someone in the advancing mass shouted an order, and the formation changed from a brisk walk to a trot, the pace at which a middle-aged clerk runs after a hat blown off in a wind. The second volley took down two full ranks and made a mess of the third; this time there was stumbling and falling over, jogging men trying to jump clear over the fallen and either barely succeeding or spectacularly failing; the ranks behind running into the scrambling men in front and shoving them forward, so that more still went down and joined the jerking, twitching tangle; men wading through a sprawl of arms and legs like foresters picking a way over ten years' growth of brambles in an abandoned ride; the young ensign, his eyes tight shut, calling *Loose* a third time.

They're still coming, Baiss thought in astonishment; but of course, it was the safe thing to do, much safer to go forward than try and fall back through that unspeakable hedge of dead bodies and trampled men. They were running now; no more formation trotting, these were men running for their lives away from the shambles, ducking under the inslanting arrows, following the line of least danger. The third volley hit them at no more than thirty yards; it was like watching water flung hard from a bucket splashing against a wall as they went down in a flop, gone from all movement to dead still in a bare moment. Maybe five men, all told, were still on their feet; the line parted to let them through (standard drill manoeuvre, so he'd learnt a whole eight days ago) and as soon as they skidded to a halt they were grabbed by the reserve lines like fighting drunks scooped up by their friends and made harmless. That was all that was left of that charge; the detachment behind stayed where they were, for some reason, and didn't join in.

Victory, Baiss thought. *Well, bugger me.*

'Stand to,' the ensign yelled – Baiss still hadn't a clue what that actually meant, and he remained none the wiser since nobody in his army appeared to react to it at all. 'Casualties, report.'

'All present and correct,' someone shouted back, and a few enthusiastic souls cheered.

Baiss tried hard not to look at the bodies of the enemy who were still alive out in the heaps and drifts of corpses. It was another hot day; if he was lucky enough to live through it, he'd have the privilege of watching them slowly dying.

Nothing happened for a long time after that. Where was Gorgas Loredan? Shouldn't he be here now, with his *professional* army, to take over and make this slaughter worthwhile? Baiss had done his bit, he'd won his victory. Surely he ought to be allowed to go home now?

'The scouts just got back.' It was the young ensign again, looking slightly crazy and grinning like a skull. 'Guess what.'

'You'll have to tell me,' Baiss said.

'There's not two thousand men out there,' he said. 'More like four hundred. The rest of Sten's army must have gone the other way. We've been had.'

'I think they came this way,' someone said.

Gorgas walked to the head of the column and examined the scene. A few halberdier bodies were scattered among the rocks, like hastily discarded clothes on a bedroom floor. A little further on he found a mat of dead archers. They'd been backed into a dead end and cut to pieces. In this confined space, with bodies tightly packed together, there hadn't been room to use the six-inch spike of the issue Shastel halberd; it had been an awkward affair of carving and slicing with the long curved blade, held overhead and brought down on throats, faces and shoulders. Afterwards, the halberdiers had tracked bloody footprints over the rocks.

'These things happen,' Gorgas said, stooping down and dipping a finger in a sticky brown pool. 'This wasn't long ago,' he added. 'We'll catch up with them.'

'What happened to the rest of the army?' someone asked. 'There's only about, what, fifty of ours here?'

'They ran, I suppose,' someone else said.

Gorgas shook his head. 'No, I don't think so,' he said. 'My guess is this lot was a token force just to show willing; the main army must be guarding the other pass. In which case,' he went on with a sigh, 'we'll have to deal with Sten Mogre on our own. Let's go.'

For men who hadn't eaten or rested properly since the night before the battle in the river bed, they kept up a respectable pace in their disintegrating shoes. They seemed to have mastered the quick trudge, the characteristic tempo of men who won't have time to be exhausted until the job's done. In many respects, they reminded Gorgas of what he'd heard about his Uncle Maxen's legendary army, which had reputedly lived like this from battle to battle for something like seven years. The thought of that made him wince.

Even so, it was nearly dark by the time they came down out of the mountains onto the more gentle downlands that lay between them and Scona Town. From this point the road ran straight, with nothing to hold Mogre up except a shallow river and a small wood. Gorgas sent out a few scouts, but he was fairly sure he could guess what the enemy were doing. If he was Sten Mogre, he'd hide his army in Lox Wood for the night and make his attack on Scona first thing in the morning, planning to arrive there just after first light. In which case, he had two choices: to try and get to Scona before Mogre did, shut the gates and stand him off in a formal siege – not a bad plan, on the assumption that Scona still controlled the sea, but effectively giving up on the rest of the island – or to make a stand between Lox and Scona and take his chances in a pitched battle in the open. In either case, it meant marching all night, again. It would be asking a lot of his men to expect them to be able to stand up straight in the morning, let alone fight. There was also the small matter of arrows, shortage of.

Two valid points against risking a pitched battle; and Scona, as far as his sister was concerned, meant the Town, or to be exact, the Bank. The rest of the island was just the view from an office window. No doubt at all about what Niessa would want him to do. She'd been resigned to a siege since this escalation of the war began; he'd virtually had to plead with her for permission to engage the enemy in the field. And that, in Gorgas' opinion, was wrong. The islanders were their people, they owed them a defence; he'd seen the mess the halberdiers had made at Briora. The thought of that sort of thing happening in every village on Scona was more than he could live with. If he retreated back into the Town now, he'd feel like a father shutting his door on his own children. No; the Loredan name stood for something in these parts, it had led these people to stand up against the Foundation and try for something better than the life of serfs and slaves. It was a matter of obligation.

The scouts confirmed his guess: Sten Mogre was making camp just inside the wood. There was a substantial clearing where a generation of straight-growing pines had been felled recently, and the army was there. Mogre wasn't taking any chances. He'd placed pickets on the edges of the wood and a ring of sentries fifty yards or so out from the perimeter of the clearing, so there was precious little chance of sneaking up in the night to attack the camp. A battle inside the wood would suit Mogre well, since the archers would have no substantial advantage of distance in the thick undergrowth; at best, it would be another confused mess. His original idea of looping round the wood and barring Mogre's way on the downs was still his best option, in spite of the disastrous odds. He gave the necessary orders, which were accepted with resignation, as if sleep and rest were politicians' promises, often mentioned and never realised.

Sten Mogre was usually the sort of man who could sleep anywhere, but for once he found he couldn't quite let go. After a couple of hours of lying in the dark in his tent with his eyes wide open, he gave up the struggle, lit the lamp and called a council of war. There wasn't really anything left to discuss, but if he was going to be awake all night, he might as well have company.

'We haven't seen anything of Hain Eir's relief party,' someone reported. 'Looks like we're going to have to do without them.'

Mogre shrugged. If Eir had lost all four hundred of his men, it was worth it to keep the rebel home army occupied while he made his assault; besides, Eir was a Separatist, not to mention Avid Soef's brother-in-law, which was why he'd been chosen for the job in the first place. Sixteen hundred men were more than enough for the task in hand. His only real worry was that Gorgas might not get there in time. It would be galling to have to kick his heels outside Scona Town waiting for him to catch up.

'That's enough shop for one night,' he said. 'Let's talk about something else, for pity's sake. I know – has anyone here read that thing Elard Doce wrote last month?'

Someone laughed; two or three others murmured. 'Actually,' someone said, 'I liked it. Especially that bit about the forked roots of consequence. The man should have been a poet, not a philosopher.'

Mogre smiled. 'I remember that bit,' he said. 'And to give him credit, there's just a trace of a valid point in there somewhere, tucked away in a dark corner.'

Various people made sceptical noises. 'You reckon?' someone said. 'I thought it was just the old Obscurist line in a new hat.'

'Oh, it was, no question,' Mogre replied. 'But the Obscurists had a point – no, don't laugh, they were all as mad as a barrel of rats, but that doesn't alter the fact they'd come up with the Law of Conservation of Alternatives when Dormand was still learning two-and-two-is-four.'

'From entirely false premises,' someone else pointed out. 'And arse-about-face and back-to-front. If Dormand hadn't taken it and turned it on its head, nobody would ever have given it a second thought.'

'Actually,' a thin man sitting near the tent-flap interrupted. 'I heard that City man, Gannadius, say something interesting about that not so long ago. He was basically agreeing with Dormand—'

'Big of him,' someone broke in.

'But he made the point that Dormand didn't take it to its logical conclusion. Think about it,' the thin man went on. 'Let's say you've got a number of alternatives contingent on one moment of choice; all right, for the sake of argument, let's say you're Gorgas, right now, sitting in your tent trying to figure out what to do. You can scuttle into Town and lock the gates, you can take your chances in the field, you can slink off into the hills. Three alternatives. Now, Dormand says that the consequences resultant on those choices are not truly infinite. For a start, he says, all three options could result in Scona falling.'

'The word *could*,' someone interrupted, 'in this context . . .'

'Quiet, Marin,' Mogre said. 'This is interesting.'

'Likewise,' the thin man went on, 'the pitched battle and siege options share a large number of possible outcomes; in other words, the lines of possibility diverge at the point of choice, but then try and join up again as if the choice had never existed. The Obscurists - all right, we know about them, but let's give them their say - the Obscurists would have us believe in the Obscure Design that overrides the choice; Destiny, all that crap. Dormand says there's no destiny, just a natural law that keeps the number of real alternatives to a minimum. What Gannadius was saying, and coming from him it's worth considering, is that there's also a human element - human interference with the natural development of alternatives through the medium of interference with the Principle.'

'In other words,' someone said, 'magic. Sure thing. And then Doctor Gannadius pulls a toad out of his ear and vanishes up his own pointy hat. Somehow I'm not convinced.'

'It's a leap of faith, I agree,' Mogre intervened, 'but not an insurmountable one.'

'A hop of faith, you mean.'

'Yes, I like that, a hop of faith. Let's just suppose for argument's sake that there is this thing called magic, and the likes of Gannadius and his toad-abusing cronies can sometimes bend the Principle at will. Dormand would say it's still random, it's just individuals making choices, only carrying them out through a different medium - doesn't matter whether I exercise the choice by walking through the door myself or influencing you to walk through it, the door still gets walked through, the choice happens.'

'Ah,' said the thin man, 'but Gannadius would say that the sort of event that attracts magical interference follows a pattern. Battles, the fate of cities, blood curses and family feuds, that's when magic gets used; and that in itself creates a trend, which in turn corrupts the purely random development of choice. In other words, there is an obscure design. It may not be Destiny, Obscurist-style; it's purely artificial. But it's a trend nonetheless, and unlike Dormand's law, it's not natural. Then consider the knock-on effect, and you can see where it's leading.'

'Obscurist crap,' someone replied. 'All this talk about something being corrupted implies there's something to corrupt, an Obscure Design. If there's a trend, it's just part of the ordinary trend of human nature, just like Sten said a moment ago.'

'Ah, yes,' someone else objected, 'but a *supervening* trend, a trend that's bigger and stronger than just ordinary motivation, because it pushes people around, makes them do what they otherwise wouldn't have done.'

'In other words,' Mogre said, 'further economising on the number of possible alternatives. Pure Dormand. The State rests.'

'Talking of which,' said one of the council, standing up and stifling a yawn, 'what's good enough for the State's good enough for me. You lot may be able to stay up all night and fight a battle next day, but I need my eight hours. Oh, and a word of advice: make sure Sten wins the argument, unless you want to find yourself posted in the front rank tomorrow.'

'Funny you should mention that,' Mogre said.

The departing councillor stared at him; there was a little twinkle of pure fear in his eyes. 'You're joking, aren't you?' said he. 'Sten, that's not funny.'

There was a long moment of silence; then Mogre smiled and said, 'Of course I'm joking, Hain. This time, at any rate. See you in the morning.' The circle around the small brass brazier had gone rather quiet, but Mogre didn't appear to have noticed any change in mood. 'Right,' he said, 'where he'd got to? Ah, yes—'

Revision. Ack.

Machaera looked up at the guttering candle, then back at the page in front of her. Sometimes a momentary break in eye contact with the book helped jolt her out of drowsiness. This time it didn't look like it had worked. She'd read the same twenty lines at least five times now, and still it didn't mean anything to her.

She tried again.

Although, in refuting the foolish and frivolous claims of Maddianus and his fellow adherents to the so-called Doctrine of the Obscure Design, I have in part sought to disallow the notion that the number of such possible alternatives is restricted through the agency and at the whim of an unknown and imperceptible supervening external agency—

Machaera's head nodded forward onto her chest. She snored—

—And was sitting in darkness, looking down into a circle of light. To be more precise, she was balanced on a rickety folding stool that wobbled as she shifted her weight slightly. The canvas top sagged at one corner, and as she tried to get away from the sag she felt the material tear a little more. She sat perfectly still, and tried to make out her surroundings.

There seemed to be two circles; an inner circle of men sitting round a glowing brazier, whose light and heat scarcely leaked past them; and an outer circle, dim silhouettes of heads and shoulders at the back of the tent (*I'm in a tent*, she realised. *I haven't been in a tent since I was seven, and it wasn't this kind of tent*), of whom she was apparently one. Directly opposite her in the inner circle, just visible between the heads of two other men with their backs to her, was a face she recognised. Everybody who'd been to see the army off would recognise that face. General Mogre. Presumably she was eavesdropping on a council of war. Fascinated, she craned her neck as far forward as she could without further provoking her derelict stool, and tried to catch what the great man was saying.

'It's all in Dormand,' said General Mogre. 'Everything you ever need to know about anything; you look in Dormand long enough, you'll find the answer.'

(*Rubbish*, Machaera said; but here, the words only sounded inside her own head. *And I should know; I'm reading the horrid thing, right now.*)

'Let's hope Gorgas hasn't got a copy,' said one of the men with his back to her. 'Assuming he can read, that is.'

'I'll bet you Niessa's read it,' someone she couldn't quite see chimed in. 'Though I see her more as a disciple of the sainted Maddianus. The complete witch, in fact.'

Sten Mogre grinned. 'Maybe that's why she had Patriarch Alexius kidnapped,' he said. 'To explain the long words to her.'

'It's a nice picture,' someone else said. 'You can just see her, flicking through trying to find the recipes for love potions and raising-storms-at-sea-made-simple.'

'Probably reckons it's written in code,' said another. 'You know the sort of thing, pick out every sixth word and it'll spell out the true message.'

(*I must try that*, Machaera said.

It's been tried, replied the person next to her. *Doesn't work. At least, it makes as much sense as reading the whole thing, but that's not saying much.*

Who are you? Machaera asked.

Alexius. You're that star pupil of Gannadius', aren't you?

I – Machaera couldn't think what to say. *It's an honour to meet you*, she mumbled.

You think so? Good gods. By the way, Gannadius is over there somewhere. Hello, Gannadius.

Hello yourself. And hello, Machaera. Shouldn't you be revising Dormand? Though I suppose this almost counts.

Alexius, what in the gods' names are we doing here? I don't understand. This can't be a crucial turning point, they're just talking horse manure about abstract philosophy.)

'To get back to what we were talking about,' said a thin man. 'You should read what this fellow Gannadius wrote. It really does make a lot of sense.'

(*Horse manure?* Alexius said.

Oh, be quiet. Actually, it was. Pure drivel, from start to finish. You wouldn't want me to tell these lunatics the truth, would you?

Hush, someone said.)

'The heart of the problem as I see it,' one of the inner circle said, 'is identifying your crucial moment. Well, how *do* you recognise the things? All right, let's suppose that Huic over there stays here another half hour, then goes back to his tent. On his way he trips over a guy-rope and pulls a muscle. In the battle tomorrow, that pulled muscle slows him up just a fraction at a crucial moment, his unit just fails to make its ground in time, and in consequence we lose a battle we'd have won if he'd gone to his tent five minutes earlier or five minutes later. Suppose one of us says something about the operation of the Principle that burrows its way into the back of Sten's mind and influences him in some minor way when he's making a decision tomorrow. Suppose if I leave here in two minutes' time for a piss, I'll be outside at precisely the moment Gorgas and his army try to sneak past us, and I'll just catch the faint echo of someone coughing, or see the moonlight on a belt buckle. All right so far? Very good. Now, suppose I'm a wizard or a witch, trying to find the crucial moment so I can prise it open and make things happen differently. How'm I going to know that was the crucial moment? Chances are I'll be snooping round Gorgas while he's trying to figure out what he should do, or else I'll be at the battle itself. And of course, I'll find heaps and heaps of crucial moments there, because *every damn moment's* a crucial moment, or it could be. At this precise moment, maybe there's a crucial moment going on wherever Gorgas is, and there's a whole mob of wizards and witches crowding round him playing tug-o'-war. Now they can't be there *and* here; but if they change his critical moment, who's to say my crucial moment's still going to be crucial? Like, if they make Gorgas go a different way round the wood, then when I leave this tent he won't be there for me to see.'

Sten Mogre nodded. 'What you're saying is,' he said, 'either magic can't work, because there's no real economy of alternatives and Dormand is a pack of nonsense, or every moment is crucial, in which case it doesn't matter where your witches and wizards stop and peel off the skin, they'll always find a point where they can change everything. Avert, you should have been a lawyer, not a soldier.'

'I wasn't saying either of those,' the man called Avert replied. 'I was just pointing out something you've got to address if you want to believe in magic.'

'Which you don't, presumably.'

'I try and keep an open mind, actually.'

(*If he calls me a witch one more time*, someone said, *I'll smack his head, even if I'm not really here.*

Niessa Loredan, Alexius whispered. Machaera shuddered a little. *It's all right*, Alexius went on, *for some reason we're all very polite here, nobody tries to stab anybody else or bully them into betraying secrets. It's quite the nicest, friendliest war you ever heard of. Isn't that right, Gannadius? For instance, Gannadius and I are on opposite sides.*

Oh, Machaera said. *Isn't that awkward? I thought you were friends.*

We are, Gannadius said. *But we aren't really here, so it doesn't matter.*

Speak for yourself, interrupted the voice that had said, 'Hush!' a while back. *I'm Vetriz Auzeil, by the way. And I'm definitely here.*

Excuse me, Machaera said. *But does any of you know, if we're here, why we're here?*)

Sten Mogre suddenly yawned and stretched. 'That's

enough of that for tonight,' he said. 'We'll finish this discussion tomorrow, in Scona Town. Everybody clear about what they're doing?'

'Actually—' someone replied.

(*I think we just decided the result of the war*, Gannadius said. *Any idea who won?*)

—And found himself sitting upright in bed, with a pain in his temples that made him cry out loud. For some reason he felt cold and frightened, as if he'd just seen some horrible accident in the street. 'Machaera?' he said aloud, not really knowing why.

He climbed slowly out of bed and looked out of the window; still pitch dark outside, and the night-light was only just over half gone. He flopped down into his chair and reached for the wine jug.

Magic, he thought, *someone's been making me do magic*. For some reason, he felt sick. He swallowed three mouthfuls of wine, stood up again and washed his face and hands thoroughly in the big stone bowl by his bed. He felt an urgent need for light; he had three candles and an oil-lamp in the room as well as the night-light, and he lit them all. It helped a little.

There was a knock at the door. He opened it.

'Machaera?' he said. 'What's the matter?'

She looked up at him with those terribly young, rather gormless eyes. 'I'm sorry,' she said. 'I had a dream—'

Gannadius stepped out into the passage and looked both ways. Middle-aged teachers weren't encouraged to receive young female students in their quarters in the small hours of the morning. 'I know,' he said, drawing her inside and closing the door. 'Can you remember what it was?'

She nodded. 'I think so,' she added, picking at the edges of her fingernails. 'I'm not sure.'

'Oh, sit down, for pity's sake.' Gannadius found his slippers and eased his feet into them, then slouched down opposite her and poured himself another drink. He didn't offer her one. 'All I can remember is waking up hearing you asking a question,' he said. 'By the way, does your head hurt?'

She nodded. 'A bit,' she said.

'A bit. Fine. Tell me what you remember about your dream.'

She told him. When she'd finished, she saw that he had his eyes shut, his face turned away. 'Is something the matter?' she said.

'I think so,' he replied. 'I think we've just sent hundreds of men to their deaths, and I don't even know who.'

There was still an hour to go before the first cracks of light would appear in the sky. Gorgas Loredan, who'd always had exceptional night vision, couldn't see his hand in front of his face. He'd estimated the distance once they'd passed the wood by counting his own footsteps. There was every chance he'd got it wrong. He knew where he wanted to be, but he hadn't the faintest idea where he actually was.

One hell of a way to choose the site for the most important battle of the war, he reflected. It would be a sad thing if Scona fell because he'd underestimated the length of his own stride.

'All right,' he said, hoping someone was close enough to hear him, 'fan out and dress your ranks. And let's all hope we're facing in the right direction.'

My decision, he kept telling himself, mine and mine alone. Niessa doesn't want me here. I assume the people I'm doing this for are relying on me, but I don't know that; for all I really know, they're welcoming the halberdiers as liberators. The only thing I've relied on in making my decision is my sense of what's right. *My* sense, for gods' sakes. That's comedy.

He closed his eyes. For Bardas; for Niessa; for Luha and little Niessa; for Iseutz and Heris; for them, whether they wanted his help or not. For us and what's ours, right or wrong. Never, not once, have I ever regretted anything

I've done, I stand by it all, and I suppose this is where it all gets put to the test. Victory will be vindication of what I once did and all I've done since. Well. We shall see.

And then the sun rose on Sten Mogre's army.

CHAPTER TWENTY

At first light, Bardas Loredan embarked
on the next stage of the project.

All through the night before, he'd drawn down the
sun-dried tendons and pounded them on an oak board
with a hide mallet until the sinew began to disintegrate
into its component fibres; these he'd slowly and pain-
stakingly drawn off with a purpose-made ivory comb,
sorting the coarse, translucent yellow fibres into bundles
of roughly matching length and laying them out on the
bench in order of size so that they'd be handy when he
came to use them. Now all that remained by way of
preparation was to clean the ribs and make up the glue.

The bone was slippery with its own grease, so he
scoured each section with lye and boiling water, paying
particular attention to the insides of the splices, and set
them aside to cool down while he made the different
sorts of glue that would be needed for what was to
follow.

He made the sizing glue by mixing congealed blood
with sawdust, and the main fixing glue by boiling scrapings of rawhide and the waste sinew in water vigorously
for an hour, skimming off the chaff as it rose to the
surface and stirring from time to time. He separated off
the first pouring, which would make the strongest join,
and put the residue back to simmer for the rest of the
day. The smell was disgusting, but he scarcely noticed it.

With the blood glue he carefully sized both the bone and the wood to seal them, and put them to one side, delicately balanced on wooden blocks where the sunlight poured in through the window. While the size hardened, he pounded more sinew into fibre and made a wooden jig for winding gut into a bowstring. Finally he stretched pieces of soaked rawhide to make the outside wrapping.

('Of course I'd like to help,' young Luha had said, 'if it's for the war. What do you want me to do?'

'Oh, fairly basic things, nothing difficult. I wouldn't bother you, only I've got so used to having an apprentice, and I don't know anybody else who'd be able to help.'

Luha had smiled. 'I've always wanted to learn a trade,' he'd said. 'Something with my hands, that is, not just bookwork or fighting. Making things. I've always wanted to make things.'

'It must run in the family,' he'd replied encouragingly. 'Well, you and I, we'll make the best bow ever seen outside the Mesoge, you can bet your life on it.'

Luha's smile had widened; like so many apparently sullen and withdrawn children, he had a nice smile. 'Father will be so pleased,' he'd said.

'Let's hope so,' he'd replied.)

At roughly the same time as the battle of Lox Wood reached its climax, he finished the preparation of materials and was ready to start building the bow itself.

'Subtlety,' said Sten Mogre, 'is for losers. On the other hand, we really don't want to mess up this battle, so let's take it nice and steady.'

It was a blindingly hot, bright morning, with no trace of a breeze. The sun blazed and sparkled off the sea to the east so fiercely that it was painful to look at, and flashed on the copper-washed roof of the Bank as if it was already on fire. Between Lox Wood, to his rear, and Scona Town itself there was nothing but the open downs, gently sweeping towards the cliffs that flanked the bay. Perfect country for an infantry charge; enough of a gradient to add worthwhile impetus, but not steep enough to make the going treacherous. Below him, he could see Gorgas' little army lying across the line of the road, like a thin billet of steel on an anvil ready to be beaten into shape. 'Thirty gold quarters for Gorgas' head,' Mogre called out, 'twenty more if he's still attached to it and capable of breathing. Apart from him, we don't need any of them for anything, so feel free to indulge yourselves. Keep in line and don't dawdle, and it ought to be easy as treading on beetles.'

He'd put three hundred men in two ranks in the centre, and thrown out the rest in equal numbers on the wings; six hundred and fifty men to each wing, in two long lines. The plan was to advance the wings wide, giving Gorgas the impression that they were sweeping round him to avoid him altogether and attack the Town. If he took the bait, he'd either divide his forces in an attempt to stop them and be encircled before he knew it, or else he'd lose his nerve and try and fall back on the Town, in which case the centre would charge and catch him in rear while the flanks joined ahead of him and formed a noose to cut him off. In any event, so long as he kept his men spread out and moving, he'd rob the archers of any chance of snatching a fluke victory; there simply wouldn't be enough halberdiers in any one place at any time to give them anything worthwhile to shoot at. Fond though he'd become of Gorgas since the war started – hard not to become attached to someone you've studied so intensely – he couldn't for the life of him see any way that two hundred and fifty archers stood a chance against sixteen hundred halberdiers in this terrain. Briefly he toyed with the idea of offering terms, but decided against it without much internal debate. Technically this was putting down a rebellion, not a legitimate war; accordingly, rebellion protocols applied.

'All right,' he said calmly. 'Let's go. Advance the wings, steady the centre. Let's make this one neat and tidy.'

* * *

Gorgas watched the halberdiers coming towards him on either side, and realised that he hadn't the faintest idea what he was going to do.

Stupid, stupid. For some reason he'd got it into his head that they'd form a strong, packed centre and charge from there – an absurd notion, since that was the only scenario in which he'd have a chance of winning. Now it looked like they were ignoring him altogether, stepping round him as if he was a drunk slumped in the street.

'Well?' someone asked. 'What do we do now?'

Gorgas shrugged. 'Engage the enemy, I suppose. I think that's what we're here for.'

'Which ones?'

Gorgas thought for a moment. 'Them,' he said, pointing at the centre of the line, 'the buggers standing still. They'll be easier to hit. All right, form two ranks, loose and advance in turn.'

The first volley lifted and soared like a flock of rooks scared off newly cut stubble. The range was just over two hundred yards – clout-shooting distance, and wasn't it just as well he'd had them all training at the clout for the past six months? Just over halfway towards the enemy, the arrows faltered, stopped climbing, hung in the air for a fraction of a second –

(one tiny fragment of time; the beam of the scale balanced on a razor-thin fulcrum.)

– and dropped, gathering speed and force as their trajectory decayed. They always fall short of where you think they're going to fall; you think they're almost directly overhead at the high point of their ascent, but the trajectory decays, they rise gradually and fall steeply, and their momentum is greater going down than going up. The volley pitched square on the first and second ranks of the centre; and by the time it pitched, the second volley was in the air, fired by Gorgas' second rank after it had passed through the first, advanced five paces and shot. Now the first rank came on another five paces, drew and loosed; as the volley went up, the second rank advanced, drew, loosed. The first rank held their ground, since there was nothing left for them to shoot at.

(*I never thought he'd do that*, Sten Mogre said to himself as he died.)

Now the wings were coming in fast, wondering what in hell was going on. Gorgas took a deep breath and gave the order to form a tight square. *If they've got the sense they were born with, they'll make for the Town*, he reflected, reaching for another arrow. *If they come for us, it'll all depend on whether the arrows hold out. In the end, it comes down to supplies, economics.*

They were coming on, the lines on either side extending so as to join and complete the encirclement. That didn't bother him in the slightest. He'd made his square as small as he could; if they wanted to fight him, they'd have to squeeze in close, turning their extended widely spaced line into a thick, jostling mob just right for shooting arrows into, like the mess he'd seen in the river bed. 'Hold your fire,' he called out in a loud, clear voice. 'At eighty-five, no further. Front rank, draw.'

The first volley thinned them a little, but the gaps soon filled, so that was all right. The staggered ranks of the square worked just as he'd hoped; as one rank loosed, the other drew, so that there was never a moment when there wasn't a cloud of arrows in the air. The enemy were stumbling now, as if they'd been tripped by a rope across their path. Forty yards out from the square they became so tangled that they couldn't move forward fast enough to live long enough to get past the banked-up dead and wounded and go in closer. The bank grew; it was like watching the sand forming high drifts in the bottom of an hourglass, or the moment when the incoming wave dissipates on the sand just before it's pulled back into the sea. At forty yards out, the crucial moment was tangible, although as a problem in applied philosophy it was hardly worthy of attention. It would be decided by nothing more obscure or profound than elementary arithmetic – which was going to run out first, Gorgas' supply of arrows, or the enemy's supply of men? It would be very close, close enough for a recount. It might yet come down to the last arrow or the last man, the accuracy of one archer's aim, the care with which one halberdier put on his breastplate, the true tiller of one bow, the straightness of one arrow, the turning of a head to left or right at one particular moment, to decide whether the attack broke off and fell back or surged over the bank and pressed home.

Gorgas reached down without looking and felt the fletchings of another arrow, one more than he thought he had left. The skin between the first and second joints of his draw fingers was rubbed away into a mush of raw flesh, and the muscles of his back screamed as he took up the weight of the draw, pushing against the handle of the bow with his left hand, drawing back the string with his right. As he drove his left arm forward, straightening the elbow, he heard a sharp crack and felt the top limb of his broken bow smash into his mouth, as hard as a punch from a skilful boxer, while the lower limb welted across the side of his knee. He stood for a moment with the ruins of his bow hanging comically around him – damn the thing, the useless, cheapskate heap of crap, lousy unbacked ash that couldn't take the racking stretch across the back and crushing in the belly, it had left him defenceless in the very moment when everything was to be decided; suddenly there was nothing more he could do except drop two pieces of firewood, stand still and wait.

'The hell with this,' someone shouted (Huic Bovert, who'd tripped over a guy-rope on his way back from the council of war last night, the pain from his twisted ankle was draining his strength like a hole in a bucket). 'Pull back; dress your ranks and for gods' sakes pull back.' Slowly at first, simply because there was so much mess on the ground to pick their way through, the halberdiers edged back; the arrows carried on hitting them, of course, and they continued to fall in roughly the same numbers as before. At seventy-five yards they checked and rallied, and saw for the first time how few of them there were. 'The hell with this,' Huic Bovert repeated, and they withdrew, walking reluctantly away, guiltily, like a man walking away from a woman he no longer loves. Limping slowly behind the main body, his broad back a distinct target, Huic Bovert was the last man to fall, although it was hours before he died.

'I don't believe it,' Gorgas said.

'Don't knock it,' someone beside him replied. 'Close, yes, but it beats losing.'

Someone else had assumed command of the remnants of the army; they had fallen in and formed a column, they were marching away. 'No more than seven hundred,' someone said. 'If that. Probably closer to six.'

Gorgas snapped himself out of it. 'What about us?' he said. 'Casualties?'

'They never got that close,' someone else replied. 'Another three arrows fewer each and they'd have made soup with us, but we got away with it. All present and correct, it looks like.'

'We're getting good at this,' Gorgas said.

Late in the afternoon, while Gorgas was organising men from the Town into parties to collect arrows, parties to strip the dead, parties to bury them, a messenger came in from Sergeant Baiss' detachment; he was pleased to be able to report that Baiss had ambushed the retreating column as they climbed up into the mountains. Out of an estimated seven hundred halberdiers, he was confident that no more than ninety had escaped and were still at large. Was he to pursue the fugitives or return to Scona Town?

Gorgas felt sick. He told the messenger to bring Baiss back and leave the poor devils alone; then he set off up the hill to see his sister.

The Bank was nearly deserted; no clerks scuttling down corridors or peering up at him from their desks. Nobody waiting on the stone bench outside Niessa's office. He pushed the door open and went in. Nobody home.

Eventually he caught up with a clerk in the exchequer; the man was scooping up the silver counters from the counting boards and putting them into a large, clinking sack.

'You,' he said, 'where's the Director?'

The clerk stared at him as if he had two heads. Gorgas glanced down at his bloodstained clothes and shredded hands. 'It's all right,' he said, 'we won. Have you seen my sister?'

The clerk looked as if he didn't know whether to giggle or run. 'Don't you know?' he said. 'She's cleared out. Left Scona. Taken all the ready money and the best ship and gone.'

Avid Soef? thought Avid Soef. *Yeah, I remember him, wasn't he the clown who showed up in Scona Town three days after the other two armies, soaked to the skin and covered from head to foot in mud and pine needles? What a joke!*

According to the locals, the bog-carpeted forest that covered the southern tip of Scona was far drier than usual; the recent heavy rains had all run away into the sea, and the scouring heat of the past few days was drying out patches of marsh and bog that had been submerged for as long as anybody could remember. Mires that usually swallowed you up to the waist now only engulfed you as far as the knee.

Wretched, dismal, every step laboured and difficult; tracks that might just have been passable for five men and a mule becoming lime-traps with two thousand men squelching through them; mud-encrusted boots, almost too heavy to lift, so saturated that their wearers would almost have been drier walking barefoot; tussocks of couch grass, tripping men up and turning over ankles; all under a dark, nasty-smelling canopy of spindly firs and wind-twisted beeches, through waist-high clumps of briar and bramble, in and out of the branches and roots of fallen trees that blocked the way. How utterly superfluous, in all this natural torment, was any trace of the enemy.

The enemy wouldn't come in here. More sense.

Nevertheless, Soef knew, if he *didn't* send out scouts and advance parties, then undoubtedly there *would* be ambushes, roadblocks, landslides, pickets, snipers. The whole army could be cut down in their tracks, all because of carelessness, a general thinking he knew better than Regulations. At any moment he expected to bump into the remnants of the rebel army in flight from the sack of the Town – presumably it had fallen by now, it was hard to imagine anything that could stop an army of four thousand men. When he met them, would they keep running or turn and fight? A battle in this mud and filth among these dark and gloomy trees would be unspeakably awful, for both sides. Surely they'd have more sense. (Ah, but if they had any sense they'd have stayed out of the marshes.)

'They reckon there's a clearing up ahead,' said the colour-sergeant.

'Let's hope they're right this time,' Soef answered. 'For a while back there I thought they were deliberately misleading us – reasonable enough, since we're the enemy. But I don't think so now. I think they're as lost as we are. After all, why in hell should anybody ever come here?'

The colour-sergeant nodded. 'Apparently some of them do,' he said. 'Hunters – there's supposed to be deer and wild pigs in here somewhere, I guess we must be making too much noise. And a few old men bring their yard-pigs to look for truffles.'

'Never could understand what people see in those things. With honey, I suppose, or diced in a— Good gods, they were right. There *is* a clearing.'

'That's not all. Look.'

In the clearing there were men putting up tents, men trying vainly to make fires with wet timber and sodden kindling, men stacking bows in stands, hanging clothes from branches to dry. In the five or so seconds it took for

Soef to realise what he was looking at, a few of them made an effort to get to their weapons. Most of them simply stood and stared, as if they were sitting at home and mythical beasts had just battered their way in through the wall.

'Front three ranks,' Soef shouted, but he was too late; the army was already surging forward all around him, not waiting for orders in their eagerness to take out their feelings after a week in the forest on someone else. The action didn't last long. Half of the two hundred and fifty rebels made it into the forest, unarmed, some barefoot and in their undershirts. The rest were chopped down as if they were the brambles, briars, bracken, saplings and undergrowth of the forest that had caused the army so much suffering and aggravation. It was a swift, efficient, slashing clearance, a lopping of exposed limbs, all blade-work, very little stabbing. Soef didn't try to intervene; he might as well have asked his men to consider the feelings of the couch grass and the bog-cotton and besides, he didn't want to. A week in the forest had got to him too.

By the time the army lost interest, there were about fifty of them left. Most of them had at least a cut or a slice, some were missing fingers or a hand or an ear; it had been like watching spiteful children aimlessly bashing at the trunks of trees, smashing off branches, crushing and scarring the bark till the sap flows. Scarcely any of them had tried to fight.

'That'll do,' Soef called out. 'We're just wasting energy now. Secure the prisoners, we'll move on in an hour. Somebody see if there's any clean water nearby, and find out if there's anything fit to eat in the rebel tents. No point letting good stuff go to waste, when we don't know when we'll next have a chance to stock up.'

Quite. We might just as well eat what we kill.

The prisoners' story cheered him up. They'd got lost as well, trying to find the halberdiers and ambush them. After three days of crashing through bush and sliding in mud, they'd resolved to give it up, pull back to the edge of the forest and either pick the Shastel men off as they came out or harass them all the way back to Scona, the way Gorgas had done with the first army –

'What do you mean?' Soef interrupted.

The prisoner looked worried. 'You don't know?' he said. 'We heard just before we left: General Loredan defeated your first army. He's got hundreds of prisoners.'

Soef frowned. 'General Mogre's army?' he queried. 'Or General Affem's?'

'No idea,' the prisoner said. 'Gorgas hadn't reached Scona, all we heard was dispatches and the order to guard the forest. We only heard about you when we ran into the foresters.'

'You're seriously telling me Gorgas defeated one of the other two armies?' Soef said. The prisoner dipped his head nervously. 'And then he was going to fall back on Scona Town, presumably.'

'I suppose so.' The prisoner wiped blood from a slash across his scalp out of his eyes; blood was running down his hair, dripping off his sheepdog fringe, like rainwater running off leaves. 'The message we got didn't say; all we were told was we'd won a big victory, and we'd been ordered to keep this end tidy.'

'And you're sure you don't know which army it was? If you're lying I'll have you strung up.'

'I'm sure,' the prisoner said wearily. 'I don't even know where the battle was, or where Gorgas was when he sent the message, come to that. I suppose the sergeant might know, if he's still alive.'

Avid Soef looked up at the colour-sergeant, who shook his head. 'All right,' he said. 'Sergeant, fall the prisoners in, we'll have to take them with us. There's a thought; they can show us the way they came. *They* don't look like they've been wading up to their chins in mud.'

The prisoner shook his head. 'It's really very dry the other side of the clearing, where the side of this combe slopes upward. But I can't show you exactly which way we came; we were lost, remember. I'm sure we spent about half a day just drifting round in circles.'

The thought that it might be Sten Mogre's army that had been beaten and captured or put to flight troubled Avid Soef more than he'd imagined such news ever could. He thoroughly disliked the man and knew Mogre felt the same about him, with contempt added in on top. But ever since they'd landed Mogre had been running the show, and Soef hadn't really given much thought himself to any overall strategy, only various small ways to embarrass Mogre and his constituents back in Shastel Chapter. If Mogre had truly suffered a serious defeat, it could be days, even a whole week, before he'd be able to rally his men and play any further useful part in the war. That meant Soef would effectively be in charge of the whole expedition. Whatever happened next could be his fault.

Bloody war, he thought bitterly. *Even when things go right, it's a hiding to nothing.*

'What do you mean, gone?' Gorgas said.

'Gone,' the clerk repeated helplessly. 'And she's resigned as Director. She took all the silver plate and most of the valuable furniture and stuff. But she's left all the books and the accounts.'

Gorgas took a deep breath and let it out slowly. 'All right,' he said. 'Did her daughter go with her?'

The clerk looked puzzled. 'Sorry?' he said.

'Her daughter. The Lady Iseutz.'

'Oh. No, I don't think so. I don't think she took anyone with her, just some bodyguards and the crew of the ship.'

Gorgas leant against the wall and rubbed his cheeks with his fingertips. 'All right,' he said again. 'There just isn't time for this now. Who are the headquarters staff reporting to?'

The clerk shrugged. 'I don't think anybody's bothering with any of that,' he said. 'I think most of the clerks are, well, getting ready to leave too.'

Gorgas scowled and snatched the sack of counters out of the clerk's hand, spilling them all over the floor. 'I bet,' he said. 'Well, that'd better stop. Anybody caught trying to leave his post will have to explain himself to me; you make sure that reaches all your colleagues, or I'll hold you responsible. What did you say your name was?'

The clerk sighed. 'Riert Varil,' he said. 'Chief deputy, copying pool.'

'Right. Pass the message round, then get back to your desk. No, forget that. Find out if there's been any messages, and where in hell the southern guard units have got to. I need to know if there's any more of the enemy left.'

'Oh, I shouldn't have thought so,' the clerk replied. 'I thought you said you'd just wiped them out.'

'Find me as soon as you know. I'll be in the Director's office.'

It was true, Gorgas said to himself, lifting his feet and planting them in the middle of her desk, she must have gone, or where's that little applewood cup of hers, the one Bardas made for her out of the stump of the kitchen tree? It isn't here, so she must have gone. And so, he observed, has everything else, except for the few bits and pieces that weren't worth anything or were too firmly fastened to the walls to be easily removed. He'd known she was gone when he'd put his feet up on her desk without being worried in case she suddenly came in through the door. He couldn't feel her in any part of the building. She'd gone because she couldn't trust him to defend her against her enemies. Again.

The clerk reappeared, looking distinctly nervous. 'No messages, Director,' he said. 'And I've spoken to the heads of department—'

'Director,' Gorgas repeated. 'All right, carry on.'

'I've spoken to the heads of department, and the staff are being put back to work. Sergeant Graiz and the southern guard left for the marshes as you ordered, but nothing's been heard of any enemy units.' The clerk hesitated. 'The war would appear to be over for now,' he said. 'Will there be anything else?'

Gorgas looked at him for a moment. 'Does anybody know why she left?' he asked. 'Did she say anything?'

The clerk nodded. 'I gather she decided the war had become too expensive to pursue any further,' he said.

'Too expensive.'

'So I gather. She formed the view that it was time to cut her losses by closing down her operation here and concentrate on her other business interests.'

Gorgas stared. 'What other business interests?' he demanded.

'You mean you don't know?'

'Oh, for gods' sakes,' said Gorgas angrily. 'No, I don't. What other business interests?'

So the clerk told him: the half-share in a Colleon merchant venturers' company, the tannery on Gasail; the lumber mill at Visuntha; the vineyards at Byshest; the stake in the Dakas copper-mining syndicate; the ropewalk on the Island—

'Go away,' Gorgas said.

Bardas picked up the bow.

Ideally, he would have liked to have left the glue to cure for at least a week, preferably longer than that; but time was a luxury and besides, the glue he'd made from this batch of exotic, expensive rawhide dried remarkably quickly in the fierce sunlight. He picked up the string and dropped one loop over the bottom nock, then hesitated. There was every chance that, when he flexed the bow for the first time to string it, the thing would snap in two and all his work and hard-to-come-by materials would be wasted.

The first stage had been shaping and fitting the butt-spliced sections of bone to the belly of the wooden core; a slow, frustrating business for a man aware that he was working to a tight deadline. But it had to be right; unless the sections fitted together exactly, the belly would be weak, the terrifying forces of compression would find the vulnerable points where the sections met and tear the work to pieces. So he had filed and scraped and polished, smearing soot onto one face of each join with the tip of his finger, assembling them, taking them apart, until the soot marked both faces evenly and they came together so tightly that he couldn't pull a hair into the fissure of the joint. Having located, sized and numbered each section, he smeared on the glue, pressed each one into place against the core and wrapped it round tightly with stout cord, one turn every eighth of an inch. To make sure, he added clamps packed with slivers shaved from the spare bone to distribute the force of the clamps evenly. To help pass the time while the glue set, he carded and sorted the sinew for the backing once again, and wove and served the string.

As soon as the glue was hard and he'd slipped off the clamps and unwound the cord, he'd mixed up another batch and begun the tedious, messy work of putting on the sinew backing. First, he'd sized the back of the core once again, this time with the residue of the last batch of hide glue. Next, he set it up on blocks at the front of the workbench, on which lay forty neatly sorted bundles of sinew fibres at convenient intervals. The glue was right – still warm and the consistency of new thin honey. He picked up the sliver of bone he'd chosen to use as a smoother and put it in a small clay cup full of water.

He selected the first bundle of sinew, the longest he had, and dipped it in the glue until it was saturated and limp. He squeezed out the excess, starting at the top and working the runout down to the bottom, flattening the bundle in the process, then carefully laid it down the middle of the core's back above the handle, spreading it from the centre outwards with the piece of dampened bone until it was just over half an inch wide. The next bundle he butt-ended onto the first, pushing firmly with the smoother to stretch the fibres slightly, and repeated the process until he'd covered a strip up the centre of the back from nock to nock. When that was done he paused briefly to wash some of the surplus glue off his hands.

As he laid in the next row, to the left of the first, he made sure that the butt-seams didn't line up to create a weak spot, two seams side by side; instead he staggered them like rows of bricks in a wall, then worked each bundle over with the smoother until it was indistinguishable from the material above, below and beside it. He continued until the whole of the back and sides of the core were covered in a homogenous mat of glue-sodden sinew, a long, flat artificial muscle that, once dry, would be next best thing to impossible to break no matter how hard it was stretched. As soon as he'd done one layer he laid on the second, working fast while the glue was still tacky and malleable so that each bundle of fibres would be fused with its neighbour and no weak spots could form. Finally he used up the last of the sinew in wrapping the joints in the bone on the belly, and smoothed all the leftover glue over the back; every last fibre of sinew and smear of glue used up, without waste or spoilage.

Because time was so short, he'd made up a drying oven out of slabs of firebrick; he heated the bricks in the fire until they were just too hot to hold and stacked them round the blocks on which the bow was mounted, where the sunlight through the window would catch them and keep the bricks warm once the heat of the fire had dissipated. He'd never used this technique before, and was afraid that the intensity of the heat would warp or spoil the bow, or that the glue would dry brittle, or that the sinew would dry too fast and pull away from the back as it shrank (and those were only the disasters he could easily anticipate; the unforeseen problems would doubtless be even worse).

Now all that was done, and he held the bow in his hands, to be strung and tillered, trimmed, smoothed and polished, the final layer of parchment-thin rawhide to be wrapped round.

In his hands now, it was as ugly and messy as a new-born baby; a man-made limb, put together out of bone, tendon, blood and skin, with all the body parts refined, corrected, pulled out and put back together again in a better, more efficient way. On the back, the tendons to be stretched, in the belly the bone to be crushed and compressed, the two held apart by an intrusive wafer of timber, held together by blood, skin and bone-dust; an arm stronger than any man's arm when stretched and crushed to the very point of destruction, made by violence for violence out of body parts, heat, desiccation and skill. Wonderful beyond words, if the dead muscle still remembered its function, if the dead bone withstood the unbearable force of compression, if dead limbs could take lives, if nothing but a smear of blood and the scrapings of skin could bind the bits of dead body together as they strove with all their stored-up might to tear apart from each other—

(*Like the Loredan family,* Bardas thought with a smile; *some of us bend and stretch, some of us crush and are crushed, but a little blood and sawdust and a shared skin keep us glued helplessly together, and when we bend and stretch and crush together, at the moment before breaking, we have infinite capacity for doing damage. I have been at the back of this family for many years, and now I'm in the belly of the bow, in the place where compression turns to expansion, where the stored force is converted into violence. And I have made this bow for my brother Gorgas.*)

He lifted his left leg and stepped over the handle, trapping the lower limb over the instep of his right foot and drawing the belly-side of the handle up into the hollow of his left knee, then pulled as hard as he could with his left hand on the upper limb, bending it back until he could slip the top loop of the string over the nock. It was amazingly stiff to bend; he could feel the bone trying its utmost to break – but there was nowhere for it to break to, it was trapped against an equally unbearable tension in the sinew of the back, each tension preventing the other from giving way; trapped like the members of a family at war with each other, held by bonds they can never escape but which create the very tension that stresses them to their limit. Just when he thought he would never be able to string the bow, he managed to edge the loop of twisted gut over the sinew-wrapped nock. The bowstring took the strain, the loops and serving held, and Bardas let the bow lie across the palm of his hand, finding its balance around its centre of gravity. Against all his expectations, the tiller was perfect: two beautifully balanced convexes on either side of the concave handle, utterly symmetrical, the recurves bent back on themselves to create yet another tension. He held his breath and lifted the bow – how light it was – set his fingers to the served middle of the string, pushed with his left hand and pulled with his right (*again the power of forces in opposition, working against each other to produce force, violence*), straining the tendons and bones of his arm, back and shoulders; carefully testing, an inch further with each flex, until the base of his thumb touched his chin, and then it would go no further.

He rested for a moment, flexing his tortured muscles, thinking, *So, the wretched thing draws short and stacks like crazy; that's a hundred-pound bow with a twenty-five-inch draw. It'll never be much for accuracy, but the power's there. Well, it wouldn't suit me. But Gorgas was always the strong one in our family, he can draw a hundred without breaking into a sweat, and a short draw suits fast, instinctive shooting. And Gorgas has always shot on instinct, ever since he was a boy.* He picked an arrow out of the quiver that leant against the doorframe, fitted its nock to the string, aimed at a flat oak board three inches thick on the other side of the room, drew and loosed, letting the force of the draw pull the string off his fingers. The arrow struck high and its shaft disintegrated, leaving the bodkinhead driven clean through the board. The power was terrifying, and Bardas stood and stared for a while before unstringing the bow and laying it carefully down on the bench.

Later he tidied it up with scrapers and abrasive reeds and grits, wrapped the handle with more fine rawhide, waxed it thoroughly to keep out the damp and finished it with two thick coats of pure, horrendously expensive Colleon lacquer, which dries fast and is completely waterproof. It looked a bit smarter now, all milk-white except for the dark line of the wooden core, and shining.

He took the last scrap of the fine hide, which was every bit as good for writing on as the best parchment, and wrote *To Gorgas, from Bardas, with love.* Then he opened the door and yelled. Quite soon a clerk came hurrying up.

'Is Gorgas Loredan still in the Bank?' Bardas asked.

'I think so,' the clerk replied. 'But he won't be here much longer. Word's come in that Avid Soef and the third army have just turned up, away to the south. He's getting ready to leave.'

Bardas smiled. 'Wonderful timing,' he said. 'Take him this bow, quick as you like, it's very important.'

The clerk nodded. 'Straight away,' he said.

'Good man. It's just what he always wanted, so he ought to be pleased.'

When the clerk has gone, Bardas shut the door, sat down on the floor, put his head in his hands and tried not to think about what he'd just done.

Gorgas took the handle in his left hand and rested the raw, scabbed pads of his draw fingers on the centre of the string. The bow was perfect, as if it was part of him, his own arm, but made infinitely more strong. He felt as if he'd owned it for years, knew it and was familiar with it, the easy familiarity of flesh and blood.

'It's beautiful,' he said. 'And Bardas made it for me.'

The sergeant was tapping his foot. 'That's really nice,' he said. 'But we do have a war to fight, so when you're quite finished playing with it—'

Gorgas didn't look up. 'I've got to go and say thank you,' he said. 'You don't realise. I've lost my sister, but I've found my brother. We're a family again.'

The sergeant breathed out through his nose. 'Gorgas, we've got to go,' he said. 'If we don't get down the mountain before dark, we won't be able to see to get in position. We could lose the battle—'

'You're right,' Gorgas said. 'Bardas didn't make me a bow so I could lose the war with it. I guess it'll just have to wait till I get back.' Reluctantly, he slid the bow into his bow-case, letting his fingers glide over the lacquered back. 'It's funny,' he said. 'The last bow he made me I did some pretty bad things with. I have the feeling that this time it's all going to be different; like a whole new start.'

'Really,' the sergeant said. 'You mean, with this one, you might miss?'

CHAPTER TWENTY-ONE

'Sten Mogre is dead,' Gannadius said.

The people he was talking to looked at him as if he'd just taken off his clothes. 'I beg your pardon?' one of them said.

'Sten Mogre,' Gannadius repeated. 'He's dead. His army's been wiped out too. In fact, we've lost something in the order of four thousand men, and nothing to show for it. Avid Soef's still alive, of course.'

Mihel Bovert's wife came in with a tray of doves marinaded in bacon fat. 'Eat them while they're hot, everybody,' she announced. 'Oh dear, what long faces. Is everything all right?'

There was an embarrassed silence, broken by one Bimond Faim saying, 'According to our mystical friend here, the army's been cut to ribbons.'

'Oh,' said Mihel Bovert's wife. 'Which army? You mean the great big one that's dealing with those horrid rebels?'

'That's right,' grunted Mihel Bovert, 'the one our son's serving with. Doctor Gannadius, would you say you're mad, divinely inspired or just very, very tactless?'

'I'm sorry,' Gannadius said. 'I – Something came over me, I suppose.'

'Quite,' replied Bimond Faim, lifting a dove off the tray with his fingers. 'The spirit moved you, or whatever. Apart from what your inner voice tells you, have you any proof of this rather disturbing claim?'

'No,' Gannadius said. 'Please, I'm so sorry, forget I said anything. Really—'

One of the dinner guests, a big grey-bearded man, shook his head. 'Easier said than done, I'm afraid,' he said. 'The plain fact is, you don't import a genuine Perimadeian wizard and then ignore his occult sayings. Be straight with us, Doctor: should we pay attention to what you're saying or not? Presumably this sort of thing's happened to you before.'

Gannadius nodded. 'I'm afraid so,' he said. 'Well, similar things.'

'And on these previous occasions, has the little angel voice been right or wrong? Or is it hit and miss?'

'It's hard to say,' Gannadius replied defensively. Mihel Bovert's wife went out, and came back a moment later with a silver sauce-boat. 'You see, I'm only telling you what someone else is telling me.'

'Someone on Scona, though,' said a small, stout woman at the opposite end of the table. 'Your spirit guide, or whatever the technical term is.'

Gannadius didn't correct her choice of terminology; his head was starting to hurt, making it hard for him to concentrate. 'Someone on Scona, yes. Patriarch Alexius, as it happens. And he wouldn't lie to me, so I do know for a fact that Alexius believes that Sten Mogre is dead and his army has been defeated. That's all I can be certain about, though.'

A bald, heavily built middle-aged man opposite him frowned. 'But you can't be *certain*,' he said. 'Let's be scientific, shall we? After all, we're supposed to be men of science. On previous occasions, when you've had these—' He hesitated.

'Funny turns?' suggested Bimond Faim.

'These experiences,' the bald man said. 'On your word of honour as a philosopher, can you honestly tell me you've proved to your own satisfaction that these insights are genuine? That you've somehow communicated with someone far away?'

Gannadius nodded. 'I've spoken to the other person involved – face to face, I mean, in the usual way – and they've confirmed that they had the same, or roughly the same, experience, and that they said the words I heard. Particularly Alexius; I've communicated with him quite a few times, it's as if we have some sort of link. I'm not saying there aren't alternative explanations,' he added. 'For a start, it's perfectly possible that two people of very similar backgrounds who know each other well, thinking about the same problem, might come up with the same idea at roughly the same time, in a way that makes it look like they're in contact with each other.'

'Highly likely, I'd say,' Bimond Faim said, through a mouthful of rye bread.

'I think so too,' Gannadius replied. 'In fact, I have an idea that's something to do with how this link works; literally, a meeting of like-thinking minds. But that's just theory. I *know* Alexius thinks what I just told you is true.'

The silence that followed was distinctly uncomfortable.

'All right,' said Mihel Bovert, his thick brows furrowed. 'As scientists and philosophers, we'll take your word for it that you've verified your findings in an acceptable manner, at least for now. Obviously, the next question is what we do about it.'

Faim looked up from his plate. 'Oh, for pity's sake, Mihel. You aren't seriously suggesting we should base *policy* on this magical nonsense?'

Bovert shook his head. 'That's not up to us,' he said, 'it's up to Chapter. If you're asking me whether we should pass this information on to Chapter, then I think I have to say yes, we should.'

'Leave me out of it, please,' someone else said hastily. 'I really don't like the mental image I'm getting of what our esteemed Separatist colleagues are going to say when we tell them we want to rethink the war because some - excuse me, Doctor - some foreign self-proclaimed wizard has been hearing distant voices in his head.'

'There'll be bite-sized bits of our credibility scattered between here and Tornoys,' growled Bimond Faim. 'We'll be lucky if any of us gets so much as a junior fellowship ever again.'

Bovert smiled. 'There's ways and ways,' he said. 'Jaufre,' he continued, turning to the young man on his right, 'you play chess with Anaut Mogre's son, don't you?'

'Occasionally.'

'Splendid. Go round there now, spin him some yarn about having fallen out dreadfully with your uncle or me, and by way of a terrible revenge on us, tell young Mogre we've got vital information about the war but we're keeping it hushed up for faction reasons. You don't know what the information is, of course, you just know it's terribly important, and we've all been locked in a secret meeting for the last couple of hours. If you're quick, we'll get the summons to Chapter in about an hour and a half, just time to finish dinner and digest.'

Bovert's prediction was reasonably accurate; two hours later he was getting to his feet in a packed, bad-tempered Chapter.

'Essentially,' he said, 'what Anaut's just said is true. I have received what could be important news about the war, and I haven't told anybody. The reason is, I don't believe a word of it.'

On the Separatist benches, Anaut Mogre didn't seem to be aware of his closeness to the mouth of the trap. 'Perhaps this assembly ought to be the judge of that,' he said. 'Be so kind as to share your news with us.'

Mihel Bovert was only too happy to oblige. 'So you see,' he concluded after making his report, 'I really didn't feel justified in troubling this assembly with a cock-and-bull story based on magic and mysticism, when even the magician himself isn't sure the message is actually true.' Redemptionist laughter; awkward silence on the Separatist side. They knew they were now going to have to believe officially in Doctor Gannadius' inspiration – it was that or agree with the Redemptionists, and admit they'd wasted everybody's time calling the Chapter – and demand that action be taken based on it. If the crisis turned out to be a false alarm, they'd be ridiculed for believing in magic. If the crisis proved to be real, the Redemptionists wouldn't find it hard to snatch the credit for sending the reinforcements, since it was their man, at their dinner-party, who'd obtained the vital information. It was time for quick thinking.

'I'm a scientist,' said Anaut Mogre. 'And one of the most important things in science is being able to admit you don't know. I admit, I don't know whether to believe in this magic story or not. For all I know, it could be meaningless babble, or a true vision, maybe something in between. Personally, I've always preferred to keep an open mind about this whole applied-philosophy issue, as anybody who heard my keynote address at Convocation last year will confirm. But what I'd like you all to consider is this. If there's no crisis and we send another army, what's the worst outcome? We look idiots - I look an idiot, as do my colleagues on this side of the chamber - the army comes home again, no harm done. Now, suppose we ignore this message and there really has been a disaster on Scona? Worst outcome: we lose the war. Colleagues, in this case I'd far rather be humiliated than justified, because I'd really like this all to be a hoax or a mistake, I really want to find out that my cousin Sten and his army are safely in one piece and getting on with the job in hand. But if there's the slightest chance otherwise, I say send an army, and I don't care who hears me.'

The general consensus in the courtyard after Chapter was that being sent to Scona with a further three thousand men was a fitting punishment for Anaut Mogre for not seeing that one coming a mile off; if he was truly the best the Separatists had, then pretty soon the balance of power was going to undergo a significant shift. But as far as the war went, regardless of Anaut Mogre's ineptitude, sending another army was no bad thing; after all, another three thousand men couldn't do any harm, and there was an outside chance that, purely by coincidence, they might do a power of good.

When Bovert and his party returned home, they were much more polite to Gannadius and kept pouring him drinks he didn't want; on the strict understanding, they added, that his vision was really a gigantic hoax, and he'd been talking through his rear end. Prophets, they gave him to understand, were fine by them, just so long as their prophecies were guaranteed to be false.

In the heat of the battle, Gorgas couldn't help smiling. When asked by his sergeants what was so very amusing about being attacked on three sides by a greatly superior force on unfavourable ground, he simply shook his head and said it was a personal thing.

They'd had the misfortune to come upon Avid Soef just as he was emerging from the Baudel marshes; his men were exhausted and in bad order, scattered and confused and caked with mud that made their boots almost too heavy to lift, and in consequence he stood still and resolutely refused to attack. As far as Gorgas was concerned, this was a serious problem. Even with Sergeant Baiss's company added to his own, he still had no more than four hundred men, as against Soef's two thousand, so he was in no position to launch an attack. On the other hand, he really didn't want to wait around in open country, with the Baudel marshes in front of him and the Baudel river behind him, not knowing whether yet another army of two thousand-odd halberdiers might suddenly appear behind him and cut off his retreat. All he could think of was to try the harassment tactics that had worked so well in the mountains, and see if he could lure Soef after him into the equally treacherous wetlands to the west or the north. The trouble was that if he did that, he'd have to go there too, and in the mud and ooze of the bogs he'd lose the mobility that gave him his killing advantage. At least here on the level Baudel plain his men could outrun the halberdiers as far as the river. He set about trying to provoke an attack.

Soef, however, didn't want to know. As the first sparse

line of archers strolled up the field towards him, he ordered general retreat and fell back on Sheepridge, a rocky hog's back that provided a natural rampart behind which his men could take cover. If Gorgas wanted to get a shot, he'd have to come within twenty yards; too close for comfort even for light-footed archers against dog-tired halberdiers.

Baffled, Gorgas withdrew to his previous position and ordered his men to dig trenches, cut and hammer in stakes. It was, he reckoned, a matter of nerve and patience. The bottom line was that Soef was the invader, the one whose mission it was to seek out and destroy the enemy; eventually he was going to have to mount an attack whether he liked it or not. For one thing, sooner or later the halberdiers would run out of food; it would turn into a siege without walls. As for his fear of another Shastel army, he had no reason to suppose there was such a thing loose on the island. The fact that he hadn't known about Soef didn't necessarily mean that the enemy had an infinite supply of soldiers wandering around the place. He would sit tight and wait; and, since by retreating to the ridge Soef had obligingly added another hundred and ten yards to the distance his men would eventually have to cross in the face of Gorgas' archers, he didn't mind.

Whether he'd overestimated or underestimated his enemy, he could never be sure. Whether the force that suddenly materialised forty yards from his right flank in the middle of the night was a daring sneak attack or a foraging party that had got hopelessly lost and blundered into his pickets thinking they were halberdiers didn't really matter; the important thing was that they burst into Gorgas' camp with only a few shouts and screams for warning, and it was too dark to shoot. Gorgas woke up from a dream he couldn't remember, with a crick in his neck and a headache, already aware that something was wrong. He stuffed his feet into his boots (either his feet had grown or his boots had shrunk, but he'd never before had so much difficulty doing such a simple thing), grabbed his coat, his quiver and the new, the wonderful bow, and thrashed his way through his tent-flap.

He bumped head-on into a halberdier. Luckily, he was pressed right up close against Gorgas so that his halberd was jammed across his chest. With a great effort the halberdier shoved him away, which gave Gorgas a chance to jerk an arrow out of his quiver and hold it out in front of him, just handy for the halberdier to impale himself on as he rushed forward. The amazed look in the man's eyes as he flopped to the ground said *I didn't expect that* more eloquently than words ever could.

The camp fires were little islands of light; beyond them there was nothing but noise and invisible movement. Gorgas nocked another arrow on his string and stepped nervously out of the light, trying to think what the hell to do. All around him were confused single combats, men shoving and kicking and slashing at sounds, shapes, partial evidence of movement. Someone ran past him, about five yards away; before he knew it, he'd swung the bow up, reached forward with his left hand and let the string pull off his loosing fingers. He had no idea if the shot had gone home, or who he'd been shooting at; reflex, his old, reliable, get-out-of-trouble-quick reflex, faster than thought, which had shaped his entire life. Before he could nock another arrow, someone else collided with him from behind, treading on the back of his knees and sending him sprawling. He managed to avoid landing on the bow but lost his grip on it; he rolled sideways and jumped to his feet. The man, whoever he was, didn't recover so quickly. Gorgas reckoned he could make out the shape of a man on his hands and knees, and kicked hard at where the head should be. His toes jarred on heavy plate, painful in spite of the thick toe-caps, and whoever it was grabbed his ankle and threw him. He landed on his left shoulder, and his floundering left leg cracked into something half soft, which could have been a man's face. The grip on his ankle relaxed; he slid his hands along the ground to help push himself up, and felt something under his left hand, either a bow-handle or a halberd shaft. The shape was rearing up, so he flipped onto his back and kicked up at it with both heels. That seemed to have some effect and the shape collapsed backwards, giving him time to scramble up with the halberd (*which means he's the enemy, what a relief*) and lunge with it towards the other man's last known position. Nothing there but empty air.

He stood still for a moment, and realised that he was waiting to see what happened – bad idea, bad idea. It also dawned on him that the nebulous, undecided duel he'd just fought had left him more frightened than he'd ever been in his life before. No good, he thought, unless he did something quickly it was going to turn into a disaster, a massacre.

Do something. Quickly. Do what?

There were lights coming; in the distance – was that Sheepridge over there? He'd completely lost his sense of direction – in rows, like an army marching with torches or lanterns. The likeliest explanation was Avid Soef and the rest of the two thousand, coming to finish the job, in which case the only sensible thing he could do was run away and hope nobody killed him, deliberately or by mistake, while he was at it. One thing for sure; those lights couldn't mean anything good. Better to run away on general principles, while he still had arms and legs and eyes, the full working capital he'd managed to bring with him from the Mesoge. As usual, Niessa had been right; he had nothing to stay here for.

Trumpets were blowing. *Do we use trumpets for signalling? I can't remember. No, we don't. Avid Soef is giving an order.*

There was movement all round him, but there was a pattern to it; men were leaving the camp, steaming away towards the lights and the noise. *Avid Soef is recalling his men.* 'Hold your ground!' he heard himself yell – to his own side, presumably, not the enemy; hell, they wouldn't obey him anyway. Why would Avid Soef be pulling out when he was winning the battle, the war? Maybe he doesn't know he's winning. Maybe he thinks his men are getting slaughtered, and this advance with lights and trumpet-calls is a desperate attempt to rescue them. The thought was so amusing that he laughed out loud.

'Make for the centre of camp,' he shouted. 'Form ranks, and don't move!' It was worth a try, he supposed. He had no way of knowing how much of an army he had left, four hundred men or twenty - gods damn it, but what a difference the absence of light makes, it changes everything, turns us from demigods into buffoons, makes it possible for two opposing nations each to lose a war in the course of half an hour.

Mercifully, someone got a fire going in the middle of the camp, enough light to see a few yards by. He had the sergeants call the roll; thirty men unaccounted for, presumed dead, and another sixteen cut up to a greater or lesser extent. The lights in the distance weren't going back the way they'd come. Avid Soef was doing something, moving men about. He could hear trumpets and shouts, orders (but he couldn't make out what they were). Patterns of light shuffled about all round the camp, while Gorgas sat on the ground holding his captured halberd and saying nothing, almost unable to think.

It was a long night to sit through. In the first dimpsy half light, he sent men out to collect bows, arrows, weapons, helmets, whatever. The sergeants did most of the organising; for once, he didn't want to be in charge. He had a theory - no more than that - about what Soef had been doing in the pitch dark; he'd been setting up an encirclement, moving his troops into position, setting up a trap that was almost as deadly and likely to result in victory as the unholy mess he'd pulled them out of the night before. Gorgas gave the order to form a square. Then someone brought him his bow.

He recognised it while the man was still quite a few

yards away; its white limbs seemed to shine in the thick coagulated light. The relief he felt as soon as he had it in his hands again was foolish, utterly illogical; it was like having a brother or a father or a son come and stand beside him, a cheerful grin and a hand on the shoulder, saying, *It's all right, I'm here now.* He realised with alarm that the poor thing had been lying strung all night, and in the dew as well. He checked it over with the utmost care; no harm done, as far as he could see. So that was all right.

Avid Soef attacked about half an hour after sunrise. His men walked up briskly, men going to work in the morning after sleep and breakfast. Gorgas' army weren't like that; they were still in the nightmare they'd dreamt last night, bewildered and scared, tense as a half-drawn bow.

Tactically speaking, the position wasn't good. Somehow or other, Soef had left the eastern side of the camp uncovered, but his men were advancing evenly on the other three sides, which meant that each division of his two thousand, less the ten or so who'd been killed in the night, were facing just under a hundred archers, forming two ranks of fifty, with the eastern side of the square standing idle. Quickly, Gorgas did the mental arithmetic; to wipe out two thousand men, each archer would have to make seven successful shots before the enemy reached them. To halt the advance and turn it back, maybe four successful shots, more likely five. At between a hundred yards and fifteen yards, against an advancing target, the acceptable ratio for archery training in the butts was three hits out of five. Gorgas scowled, trying to do the maths – call it eight, nine volleys. In theory, there was time. Assuming, of course, that the enemy were content to lumber placidly forward into the arrow-storm.

Can't be bothered to think. Draw the bow. You wouldn't have the bow if you weren't going to win.

He heard it creak as he drew the first arrow; but that wasn't unusual with a new composite bow, just the sinew and the belly material getting used to taking up the strain. His arrows were all too long for it, given the way it stacked immovably at twenty-five inches, and the spine wasn't right, because the first arrow fishtailed away to the left as well as overshooting; it was chance and the overcrowding in Avid Soef's line of march that made the arrow pick out a man in the very back row of the column. Gorgas couldn't see where he'd hit him, he only saw a break in the pattern, something slumping, a gap just discernible in the hedge of shouldered halberds. With a desperate effort, ignoring the pain in his fingers, he managed to draw the next arrow an extra inch, and allowed for paradox; at eighty yards he hit exactly what he'd been aiming at, a man on the end of a line. He could see the man drop to his knees, the man behind hopelessly trying to jump over him from a standing start, tripping on his shoulder and sprawling down, just avoided by the man behind him. He drew again, making the full twenty-five inches, dropping half an inch, aiming into the brown of the middle of the column. Before he was ready, the string scraped across his raw fingers and slipped away, sending the arrow up into the air and down like an osprey dipping for fish into some place in the army. Men were falling down in that part of the column, but he couldn't be sure that any one of them was his, particularly. Only after the fourth shot did he steal a moment to look at the shape of the advance. They were still coming, but very slowly, picking their way through the dead and fallen like men in a bramble patch who have to keep stopping to unhook the thorns from their clothes and skin, rather than pressing onwards and feeling cloth and skin rip. By now they should have been running; but it'd have been like running in thick mud, to wade through the killed and the twitching. They were near enough to charge, to charge home and win the war, but their dead were like great dollops of mud clinging to their boots, slowing them up and draining their strength.

Some bow. Seven shots, six confirmed hits, one possible.
At that moment, Gorgas noticed Avid Soef.

That man, he thought. *That man looks like Gorgas Loredan.*

There was an old story in the Soef family, about one Mihan Soef who'd won a famous victory for the Foundation by charging the enemy at a crucial turning point, a fulcrum or pivot of the war, and killing the enemy general with his own hands. Up till then, so said Soef family history, it had been a hiding to nothing – the Foundation army was being led by some nullity from an opposing faction, so it was inevitable that they should be losing. According to the story, Mihan Soef saved the day and went on to become Dean of Military Geometry, the first of the family to head a sub-faculty. That part of the story was a lie – look at the great inscribed stone in Shastel Hall, see the dozen or so Soefs listed there above Mihan, up among the dust-clogged cobwebs – but nobody cared, because it was the Soef family version of history, relevant only to themselves, and they had every right to do what they liked in it.

Ridiculous notion, of course; and anybody who tried anything of the sort under his command would answer for it at a court martial, whether it won the battle or not.

I wish I knew how we were doing, Avid Soef said to himself as he stepped over a dead man. *It's only a few yards more, but we're hardly moving. It feels like everything's stopped, as if we're waiting to see what's going to happen.*

The arrow hit him on the right side of his body, two inches or so below the nipple. He knew it would be all right, because his breastplate would have turned the arrow, or at least stopped it penetrating. He took one hand off the shaft of his halberd and tried to tug the thing loose, but it wouldn't come; also, there was suddenly a great deal of pain, which made him stop concentrating on where he was going. His foot caught in something and suddenly he was watching grass coming straight at him; his forehead hit the ground hard, painfully, and the arrow jarred agonisingly inside him. Someone trod on his back, squeezing all the air out of his chest. He heard it whistle out, and knew then that the arrow had punctured his lung. Quite soon, but not all that soon, the lung would flood with blood (Military Medicine, foundation course, year two of Tripos) and that would be the end of him. Another boot clouted against the side of his head and a great weight landed on his back; there were feet in front of his eyes, but his eyes were growing dark, like the sun setting very quickly. *Just a moment*, he thought.

Shot, Gorgas thought, and chose another target.

He had six arrows left; he'd be lucky to have time to loose two of them. He felt like a boy in an exam who's left the easy question till last and suddenly finds he won't have time to answer it. Four wasted arrows, four opportunities gone by; the twisted-gut string rasped the bloody flesh of his fingers, burning and tearing them as the bone kicked back the desperate load of compression, as the sinew jerked in contraction like an arm punching. He didn't watch the arrow on its way (at thirty yards, no point; foregone conclusion. This close, he could see their faces, their eyes – they were hardly moving now, they were standing waiting to see what would happen) and instead concentrated on a clean nock for the next arrow, a good fast draw, bustling the bow open to exert that terrible force on bone and sinew – his wrenched muscles and jarred bones, still drawing the monstrous, over-powered hundred-pound composite recurve that was wrecking his body, flaying his fingers.

He reached down to his quiver. It was empty.

Slowly, Gorgas lowered the bow, relaxed sinew and bone, stood and waited to see what would happen.

They broke and ran at fifteen yards' distance from the line of archers. Between seventeen and fifteen yards' distance, two hundred and seventy-four of them were killed, in just over three seconds.

'I think we won,' muttered the sergeant. 'Again.'

Gorgas opened his eyes. 'Good,' he said.

Nobody was moving. They were watching a little wisp of a line, a hundred or so men, walking gingerly backwards and away from them. 'Bugger me,' someone said, 'there's more of us than there are of them. We outnumber the bastards.'

'Makes a pleasant change,' someone else replied. 'Can we go home now?'

Someone laughed. 'You'll be lucky. First Gorgas'll make us bury the buggers.'

'The hell with that. Let some other poor sod do it. I'm sick of burying bloody halberdiers.'

Apart from the conversation, it was very quiet. There wasn't much noise coming from the thick wedge of bodies – a few moans, some sobbing, but less than they'd come to expect. 'Shame there's no use we can put them to,' someone observed. 'If anybody could think of something we could make out of dead soldiers, we'd all be rich.'

Someone else laughed nervously. 'You know,' he said, 'it still doesn't feel like we've fought a battle. I mean, you can't call this proper fighting, can you?'

Gorgas realised that he was on his knees and stood up. It wasn't easy to do; his back was tensed up into a knot of wrenched, twisted muscle, and he could hardly breathe for the pain. Thirty shots rapid with a hundred-pound bow makes a mess of the human body.

The fact that he felt pain strongly suggested that he was still alive. Pain is as reliable a test for the presence of life as any.

'All right,' he said. 'Break camp, form burial details. Once we've tidied up, we're going home.'

He thought about what he had done.

He had committed violent acts against members of

his own family; wounding and killing. He had shed blood of his own blood to save his own life, to resolve a difficulty. There had been a time when he'd loved his family; he had come to evil through love. He had used his own kin, flesh and blood, for an evil purpose. He hadn't wanted to do evil.

As a soldier he had killed – what, hundreds? As a commander of soldiers, he'd arranged the deaths of thousands. He had caused a war that brought an insatiable enemy down on his people, and he'd fought in that war, responsible for the deaths of thousands. He had committed an act of betrayal for his own personal ends, regardless of the consequences for a whole nation.

Mostly, he'd done what he thought was right.

Mostly, he thought of himself as a good man, a decent human being. Apart from the violence against his family (and he claimed mitigation even in that) he'd done violence doing his duty, meaning to help and protect his people.

He had devoted most of his life to trying to help the flesh of his flesh, and in the end all his effort had been wasted, thrown away. He had tried to be a good man, and somehow through good he always came to evil.

Always, at the crucial moment, the fulcrum, the turning point, the moment of loose, the result had been evil, or something that led to evil. It was, to use familiar imagery, like the bending of a bow. Force was applied; on the outside he stretched, seeking to accommodate, while on the inside he was crushed, compressed, compacted in on himself. The old proverb says that a full-drawn bow is nine-tenths broken; a bow is made so that it does best what it does best just before the point is reached at which it must destroy itself and collapse.

He had believed in his family. He had left his home and gone to another country, accepted responsibility for a whole nation. He had come to believe in that nation. Through belief, he had come to evil.

Hitherto, he hadn't regretted what he'd done. Mostly,

he'd done what he thought was right.

He was the belly of the bow.

It had been a long day, and he hurt all over. He wanted to go home, see his wife and children, see his long-lost niece; but first there was something that had to be done. He had to say thank you.

He hadn't seen Bardas alone since that night at the cottage, and he felt nervous, like a young man hesitating before knocking at his beloved's door. But Bardas had made him the bow, which implied, if not forgiveness, then at least a willingness to establish diplomatic relations. He would visit his brother, thank him for the bow, say a few words and then leave. He would tell Bardas that Niessa had gone, that Bardas was free to go if he wanted, that anything he could give him or do for him was his for the asking, that he wanted nothing in return. And then he would go home.

'Come in,' Bardas said.

The smell inside the room was nauseating. Bardas, noticing Gorgas' involuntary reaction, grinned and said, 'That's the glue. Making bows can be a pretty disgusting business. But we get used to it.'

'Right,' Gorgas said. 'Listen, I just came to thank you. I—'

'That's all right,' Bardas replied. 'It was the least I could do, considering what you've done for me.'

Gorgas didn't know what to say. 'Sit down, make yourself at home,' Bardas was saying. 'You don't have to rush off straight away, do you?'

'No,' Gorgas said. 'By the way, we won. The battle. Probably the war.'

'That's good,' Bardas said. 'I won a war once, against the plainspeople. In fact, I won it so thoroughly and well, they came back and burnt my city to the ground. With help, of course.'

Gorgas waited for him to add something, but he didn't seem inclined to. 'It's a wonderful bow,' he said. 'I don't think I've ever seen one like it. What's it made of?'

'I'll tell you in a moment,' Bardas replied. 'I'm glad you found it useful. I was worried for a while that it might be a bit stiff.'

Gorgas grinned ruefully. 'Stiff's putting it mildly,' he replied. 'As witness my back, hands and arms. At the time, though, it didn't seem to worry me.'

Bardas nodded. 'Plenty of power?' he said. 'Penetration?'

'No question about that. Looked to me that it sent arrows through armour like it wasn't there.'

'That's good,' Bardas said. 'Well, it was only a small contribution to the war effort – I made it, but you were the one who shot it. You always shot well with the bows I made you.'

'Very true.'

Bardas shrugged. 'And I always made 'em better than I could shoot 'em. Ironic, really. Take the bow you shot Dad with, for instance.' Gorgas tensed up, the muscles in his belly tightening, but Bardas went on as before. 'Originally I made that one for myself, but try as I might I could never hit a barn door with it; and the new one – well, I can only just draw the horrid thing.'

'It's a knack,' Gorgas replied quietly.

'Ironic, though; if I'd had that old bow that day, I'd never have hit all those long-range moving targets, if I'd been in your shoes.'

'You weren't.'

'But I could have been. Damn it, we were both young, we hadn't started being the people we are now. I can imagine a set of circumstances that'd have put me where you were, that day. I could have been the one who did what you did. Only,' he added with a smile, 'I'd have missed.'

Gorgas was silent for a moment. 'Well,' he said, 'you turned out to be better with the sword than I ever was with the bow.'

'It's kind of you to say so,' Bardas replied gravely.

'Coming from you, that's an accolade. Can I ask you something?'

Gorgas didn't like the sound of his voice, but he said, 'Sure, ask away.'

Bardas nodded and relaxed a little more into his chair. 'When you opened the gates of Perimadeia,' he said, 'what was the *real* reason? Iseutz said it was because Niessa told you to, but I have my doubts.'

'I was there because Niessa sent me,' he said. 'And her reasons benefited me too, remember.'

Bardas acknowledged that with a gesture of his hand. 'But I bet I know the real reason,' he said. 'Well, the two real reasons. First, you'd always hated Perimadeia, because that's where young Hedin and the other boy came from; if they hadn't come to visit, the landlords' sons with their money and position, being better than us, you'd never have done it. In that respect, Perimadeia ruined your life, just like it ruined Temrai's. That's the first reason. What do you think?'

'There's truth in what you say, Bardas.'

'Thought so. But the other reason,' he went on, 'that was something of your own. Now I'm not saying you'd ever have done it of your own hook just for this reason; Niessa gave you the order, and you thought of this and it was this that made you agree, so it's not all your responsibility. But I think you engineered the fall of Perimadeia because I lived there, and you wanted me out into the big wide world again, where you could take care of me, see me right, make it all up for me for what you'd done. You brought me the Guelan sword, you as good as warned me about what was going to happen, you came looking for me in the fighting; you had a ship waiting to pick me up and bring me on. All that trouble you went to, just to make up with your brother. You know, in a way that's really *sweet*.'

Gorgas looked at him, but there was nothing to see.

'In a way,' Bardas went on, 'that was real brotherly love. I can't think of anybody else who'd do something like that, someone so obsessively – loving. Really, making you the bow is hardly a fitting recompense.'

'It was all I ever wanted from you,' Gorgas replied.

'Think nothing of it, please. But I thought I'd mention it; you see, if it was just what you'd done to Dad and the rest of us all those years ago, I'd never have made you the bow. But when I found out about the City, it set me thinking; I was thinking about it just now, a few minutes before you arrived. Gorgas, you know what? Your actions have always caused mine; in a sense, you made me, just like I made the bow. The only difference is, I made the bow out of dead tissue; you used me while I was still alive.'

Gorgas looked up. 'What do you mean?' he said.

Bardas stood up and walked to the door that separated the main room from the small bedchamber. 'You were asking me about what the bow was made of,' he said.

'That can wait,' Gorgas interrupted. 'Bardas, what do you mean, my actions caused yours?'

Bardas leant against the doorpost. 'I met your son a short while ago,' he said. 'What was his name? Luha? A good boy, I thought. I liked him.'

'He's all right,' Gorgas said.

'I mentioned that I was going to make you a bow,' Bardas went on, 'and he said he'd like to help. In fact, he helped a whole lot. Have you been home lately?'

Gorgas got to his feet. 'Bardas,' he said, 'what's all this about?'

Bardas stood out of the doorway, gesturing Gorgas to come across. 'You asked me what I made the bow out of,' he said. 'Come and see.'

In the bedchamber was a low wooden bed. On the bed were the remains of a body. About half the skin had been flayed off the flesh, which was in an advanced state of decay. The ribcage was exposed; all the front ribs had been neatly sawn out, and the intestines were missing. There were long, neat slits up the sides of the arms and legs, across the chest, up the sides of the neck, where every last fibre of sinew had been carefully removed. Half the scalp was shaved. There was no sign of any blood apart from a brown residue in the bottom of a brass dish on the floor.

'It's wonderful,' Bardas said. 'Everything you need to make the perfect bow's in there somewhere, except for a little strip of wood. I'd heard about making bows from ribs years ago. I even tried it once but it never worked; I used buffalo ribs, and I guess they just can't take it the way human bone can. Human sinew, too; it's marvellous stuff, far better than deer or beef tendon. Then there's the skin, for rawhide and glue; blood, for glue again; guts for the bowstring – some waste, obviously, but not too much. There's even fat for waterproofing and fine hair to make into serving thread; I read somewhere that human hair makes good bowstrings, but I thought I'd stick with tried and tested gut.' He put a hand on Gorgas' shoulder. 'And I bet there were times you thought Luha'd never amount to much. Instead, look, he's helped you win the war.'

Gorgas was still and quiet for a long time, thinking. Bardas sat down at the foot of the bed, waiting for him to speak. 'Good tactics, don't you think?' he went on, as Gorgas stayed quiet. 'Your wife thinks her son's here with me, staying with Uncle Bardas. Which he is, of course, though in a sense he also went with his father to the wars. That's neat, really; he's learnt soldiering with you and bow-making with me. Really, the best of both of us.'

'It's all right,' Gorgas said.

Bardas looked at him. 'What did you say?' he asked.

'It's all right,' Gorgas repeated slowly. 'It doesn't matter.'

Bardas jumped up and grabbed him; he didn't resist. 'What the hell do you mean, it doesn't matter, it's all right? Gorgas, I just killed your *son*! I killed your son and I made him into a bow, and you're telling me it's all right. What is wrong with you?'

Gorgas had his eyes shut. 'What's done is done,' he said firmly. 'Luha is dead, we can't bring him back. I've lost a son, but I can always have another one, I can make sons, I can't make brothers. If I - if anything happened to you, you'd be gone for ever, and there'd be no point in that, it'd be a *waste*.'

Bardas let go of him and slumped against the wall. 'I don't believe it,' he said. 'You're forgiving me. Gorgas, I always knew you were evil, but I never thought you were as bad as this.'

Gorgas shook his head. 'Not evil,' he said. 'Unlucky. There's no such thing as evil, Bardas, it's a myth, a sloppy, wasteful way of thinking. There's just bad luck that makes us do things, even though we're trying to do what's best. You can't fight bad luck, you've just got to accept it, the way I did when I—'

'When you killed our father.'

Gorgas nodded. 'It was bad luck, but I was practical, I knew I'd done a bad thing but I knew I could make amends for it, if I really tried hard. That's why it doesn't matter, Bardas, what either of us has done. I'm still your brother.'

Bardas walked away, back into the main room, and sat down. 'Well,' he said, 'if that doesn't beat cock-fighting. What have I got to do to stop you loving me, Gorgas? There must be something, short of killing you. I can't kill you, Gorgas, that'd mean you'd have won, you'd have escaped, got away free.'

Gorgas came through and sat opposite him. 'What are you going to do now?' he asked.

'Me? The gods know, I haven't given it any thought. I'd assumed I'd be dead about two minutes after you saw that thing in there.'

'You don't know me, then, do you?'

'Apparently not,' Bardas replied. 'I made the mistake of thinking you'd react like a human being rather than a Loredan.'

Gorgas grinned at him; his face was like the face in the other room. 'We're one hell of a family,' he said. 'On balance, it's probably just as well there's not more of us.'

CHAPTER TWENTY-TWO

Anaut Mogre stood in front of his army and gazed across the downs to the southern gate of Scona Town, wishing he'd kept his mouth shut.

The horrible fact was that the three thousand or so men behind him were more or less all that was left; if they went the same way as the armies led by Sten Mogre, Avid Soef and the third man whose name he couldn't for the moment remember, the Foundation would have more senior staff officers than halberdiers. Unlike his three predecessors, he was proposing to lay siege to the enemy in a highly defensible town, as opposed to fighting a pitched battle in the open with an overwhelming advantage in numbers. For a man who hadn't left the Citadel for thirty-two years, it was a daunting prospect.

'The scouts are back,' said a sergeant, appearing at his side. 'No sign of any activity. The gates are shut, but if there's anything more than the usual number of sentries on the wall, we can't see them. It's as if they aren't interested.'

Mogre said nothing. So far, if what he'd been told was correct, twenty-six members of the Mogre family had been killed in this war, or were at the very least missing in action and unaccounted for. Two of them, Juic Mogre and his son Imerecque, had been pulled out of the disused stone quarry in the mountains a few days ago, starved to death; not, as far as he knew, by deliberate malice, but simply because they'd been forgotten about.

Twelve men were all that were left of cousin Sten's army.

So far, he'd met with no resistance at all. He'd sent detachments to the sites of the three battles, found out as much as he could about what had actually happened, taken his time, all without seeing so much as a single archer. He felt like someone who's come a long way to pay a visit, only to find he's come on the wrong day and everybody's gone out.

'Well,' he said, 'there's Scona Town. If anybody's got any suggestions for what we do next, I'm willing to listen.'

There was a long silence; then somebody said, 'Why not try talking to them?'

Anaut Mogre thought about that. 'It has the merit of originality,' he said. 'How do you suggest going about it?'

Half an hour later, he was standing under the gatehouse with a small escort, all visibly unarmed, with a nervous-looking lance-corporal trying to hide behind a long banner with the pennant reversed. When he'd asked, he found that nobody knew what the Scona convention for a flag of truce was, so he'd ordered them to set up a flag using the Shastel protocol and hoped to hell that the enemy were better informed than he was. It had been a long and nervous walk from his camp to the gate, but the storm of deadly arrows he'd been more than half expecting hadn't materialised. There was, in fact, no indication that anybody inside the city had even noticed that they were there.

'This is ridiculous,' he said, looking up at the empty rampart above his head. 'What do we have to do, ring the bell?'

'There isn't a bell,' someone pointed out.

Anaut Mogre stepped back a pace or so and craned his neck upwards. He wanted to pick up a stone and throw it, or shout; something he hadn't done since his student days, when he'd tossed pebbles at the shutters of girls' bedrooms while their fathers slept.

'Look up,' someone observed behind him. 'Signs of life.'

A man's head appeared above the rampart. The face was vaguely familiar, or at least it reminded Mogre of faces he knew. 'Hello?' the man called out.

'Hello,' Mogre called back self-consciously.

'Sorry to keep you waiting,' the man replied. 'Are you the commander of the Shastel army?'

'Yes,' Mogre called back. His neck hurt. 'My name is Anaut Mogre.'

'Bardas Loredan,' the man replied. 'Have you come to demand the surrender of the Town?'

'Yes.'

'You've got it.' Something flew through the air and landed in the dust with a metallic clang. Everyone had jumped back, Mogre included, as if they'd been expecting some diabolical weapon; a jar of burning pitch, or a hail of white-hot caltrops. It was, in fact, a large steel key.

Mogre looked up again. 'Who are you?' he asked.

The man smiled. 'I think I'm the Director of the Bank of Scona,' he replied. 'Do you mind talking like this, or would you rather let yourselves in and we can talk somewhere more comfortable?'

Mogre hesitated. 'Explain what you just said,' he called back. 'Then we'll come in.'

'Fair enough,' the man said. 'Niessa Loredan's gone and so has Gorgas Loredan; between them they've taken all the money and the movable valuables and skipped off. Since I'm their brother, arguably I've inherited the Bank. More to the point, I found that key in Niessa's office. One thing, though. If I've got this right, it's the Bank you're at war with, rather than Scona itself, yes?'

Mogre had to think before he replied. 'That's right.'

'I thought so.' The man made an all-reasonable-men-here gesture with his arms. 'Well,' he said, 'rather than any more fighting and killing and waste of resources, wouldn't the simplest thing be if I were to give you the Bank – what's left of it, anyway; like I said, Niessa and Gorgas took pretty well everything that wasn't pegged down, but there's still the realty and the mortgages, of course. I mean, you can't be at war with something you own, can you?'

A sergeant had picked up the key and handed it to Mogre. He took it without looking at it. 'What about your army?' he said.

'That's a good question,' the man replied. 'And to tell you the truth, I don't know the answer. I haven't spoken to any of them. In fact, the closest I've come to an official act since I acquired the Bank was to go into my sister's office to look for that key. To the best of my knowledge, the army sort of disbanded itself when the news broke about Niessa and Gorgas running out on them. I don't think any of them wanted to be associated with government authority around here when you arrived.'

'You mean they've run away?' Mogre asked.

'Sort of, though not really as energetic as that,' Bardas replied. 'I gather they just dumped their weapons and kit in the street and went home. What do you think of my proposal?'

Mogre rubbed the back of his neck where it hurt most. 'I'll accept it as your unconditional surrender,' he said.

'Whatever,' Bardas replied. 'If you feel nervous about coming in, bring up the rest of your army. All I can do to prove it's not a trap is give you my word.'

'You could open the gate,' Mogre replied.

'I can't. You've got the key.'

Mogre scratched his head. 'How do you know we won't burst in and start killing and looting?' he said.

'Up to you,' Bardas said. 'But from what I know of you people, I don't see you as the types who'd go smashing up your own property, or killing your own citizens. To be honest with you, the way things have been going, I imagine you'll be grateful for all the manpower you can get.'

'I'll be straight with you,' Mogre said. 'I don't know what to make of this. Even if what you're saying is true, I find it hard to believe that your army, which has killed thousands of our people, wouldn't be actively defending the wall.'

'Like I told you, I haven't talked to anyone in authority. I don't think there's any authority left to talk to, except conceivably me. But Gorgas is their commanding officer and he's jumped ship. Who exactly are they supposed to fight for?'

'So, after three massive victories, you're just going to let us walk in and take over the Town?' Mogre shook his head. 'I don't see it.'

'Please yourselves.' Bardas Loredan shrugged his broad shoulders. 'Anyway, you've got the key. If you'll excuse me, I'm getting packed ready to leave.'

'Wait.'

Bardas hesitated and turned back. 'Well?' he asked.

'Here's the deal,' Mogre said. 'Provided there's no resistance, nobody will get hurt and there won't be any looting or damage. The first sign of any trouble, though, we're going to burn this Town to the ground.'

'Entirely up to you,' Bardas said. 'It's all yours, you do what the hell you like with it. I'll leave it up to you to announce the terms.'

'Where do you think you're going?' Mogre shouted.

'Haven't decided yet,' Bardas replied. 'And now, if you'll excuse me, I want to get down to the dock while there's still space on a ship out.'

As it turned out, he needn't have worried; there was a berth reserved for him on the *Squirrel*, Venart Auzeil's ship. What had prompted Venart to come back to Scona at this precise moment, with a war in progress and a severe risk of Shastel privateers in the Straits, he couldn't say. But the privateers all flew the Island pennant and paid him no attention; and as soon as the news spread that Scona was being evacuated, they immediately pulled into the Strangers' Quay and started taking on paying passengers. By midday, the harbour was flecked with heavily laden Island ships setting out for the open sea, and Shastel no longer had anything to ferry its army back home in except a few lame, slow-moving barges.

Most of the people who left Scona, however, went by the land gates rather than the Quay. They went light, generally taking with them only what they could carry in their hands or on their backs. Some of them had families inland to go to; some were talking about heading for the burnt, empty villages in the middle and the west. But the number of people leaving was relatively small; fewer than five hundred out of a population of over ten thousand. There was a substantial minority prepared to welcome the halberdiers as liberators, most of them workers in Gorgas' factories, though the majority of these people either went quietly home or hung about at the workshop gates, waiting for someone to tell them it was all right to carry on working. Once Anaut Mogre had made his proclamation, there was no hint of any attempt to try and stop him entering; Scona Town was holding its breath, as if to say of the Loredans that they'd never seen these people before in their lives.

'That's all very well,' Venart said, not for the first time. 'But you still haven't told me what she wanted you there for.'

Vetriz Auzeil sat down on a wooden crate full of Tornoys pottery lamps and looked across the bay to the harbour. 'I'm not sure myself,' she said. 'It was something to do with magic, but I don't know any more than that because I can't remember what happened when I was - well, doing the magic. Whatever it was it can't have done her much good, or she wouldn't have lost the war.'

Venart sighed and sat down beside her. 'So long as you're all right,' he said. 'That's the main thing.'

'I think I'm all right,' Vetriz said. She moved her eyes a little, so that she was looking at Bardas Loredan, sitting on the stern-rail looking back. 'I have an idea there were lots of dreams, or visions or whatever you're supposed to call them, with him in. It's a great pity I can't remember them, because I have a feeling that some of them were *fun* ... Oh, stop pulling faces, Ven, it was just dreams or hallucinations or whatever. I bet you have dreams like that sometimes.'

Venart frowned a little. 'No,' he said, 'I don't.'

'Really? Oh. Anyway, whether they were Niessa's magic or just stuff I had in my head already, I really don't know. A bit of both, I suspect.'

'Triz,' Venart said, 'sometimes I – well, I don't know. If you can come through being abducted and held hostage during the most bloody war in history, I suppose you can look after yourself. Still, I worry.'

Vetriz smiled. 'I was worried too. About you, I mean. I had this dreadful idea that you'd try and rescue me, and then we'd probably all have ended up dead or in prison.' She looked up at her brother. 'Have you looked in on Alexius? Is he all right?'

'Oh, I should think so. He's just a bit seasick, that's all.'

'Ven! He's an old man, he needs looking after.'

'Tough as old boots, more like,' Venart replied, standing up. 'But before you ask, yes, I suppose he can come and stay with us, at least till he finds something he wants to do. Isn't there a branch of his what-d'you-call-it on the Island, his Foundation or whatever? He can go and be the boss of that.'

Vetriz nodded. 'Actually,' she said, 'it was more like a Perimadeian embassy-come-trade-mission, and it's looking a bit run-down these days. But I'll mention it to him.'

'Good idea.' Venart furrowed his brows and jerked his head towards the stern of the ship. 'What about him?' he asked.

'I don't know,' Vetriz replied. 'I haven't said a word to him since we left.'

'I suppose you'll want me to look after him as well, find him a job or something.'

Vetriz laughed. 'Ven, all he's good at is making bows and killing people. And somehow I don't see him settling down to learn book-keeping. Besides, I expect Athli'll want to do something for him.'

'Athli Zeuxis? Oh, I forgot, she used to work for him.'

Venart thought for a moment. 'Were they ever ... you know?'

'I don't think so; too straight-grained and wholesome for his taste, I think. Mostly, though, I guess he just had other things on his mind.' She lowered her voice a little. 'I think he had some kind of confrontation with his brother before he left; at least, there was a story going around that they had a big falling-out and that was something to do with why Gorgas suddenly upped and left like that.'

Venart shook his head. 'I don't think so,' he said. 'Gorgas saw that he couldn't possibly win in the long run, and for once did the decent thing by clearing out and making the peace possible. Or, more likely, he lost his nerve and ran, especially once Big Sister had slung her hook. Everybody knows she's the one with the real brains.'

'Really?' Vetriz wrinkled her nose. 'Ven, he slaughtered six thousand halberdiers virtually without loss; Anaut Mogre's army's practically all the Foundation's got left. He'd *won* the war. That's what's so odd about it. I shall have to ask Gannadius if he knows anything about what really happened there.'

'What, Doctor Gannadius, the one who used to work for us? Triz, if you think we're going to Shastel just so you can—'

'Doesn't matter,' Vetriz replied. 'Go and steer the ship or something.'

Alexius?

'Go away,' Alexius replied, 'I'm asleep.'

Of course you're asleep, otherwise you couldn't hear me. You seem to be still in one piece, I'm glad to see.

'Never felt better,' Alexius grunted. 'Leaving Scona has a wonderfully therapeutic effect.'

You don't mean that. After all, I did what I promised I'd do. I taught you about magic.

'You did not,' Alexius replied stiffly. 'Oh, you used me as a pair of supernatural lazy-tongs, I'll grant you that. I suppose you'd hammer a wedge into a block of wood and then say you'd taught it carpentry.'

It was there for you to learn. If you chose not to, that's your fault, not mine.

Alexius sighed. 'I can't envisage myself ever wanting to learn the sort of thing you'd have taught me,' he said.

Really? How ungrateful. I've given you, on a plate, the key to understanding the true nature of the Principle – something you'd never have figured out in the abstract if you lived to be two hundred.

'That's true,' Alexius admitted. 'And how I can ever have been interested in something so – so banal, I really can't imagine. Wonderful, isn't it, finding out that your whole life's work's been a complete waste of time.'

Alexius, Alexius. You sound just like my brother.

'Which one?'

Both.

'Is there anything I can do for you?' Alexius asked. 'Or is this just a social nightmare?'

One small favour. You remember my daughter? She was your student, for a very short while. Iseutz Hedin.

'I don't suppose I'll forget her in a hurry.'

Splendid. And you remember that curse you laid for her? On Bardas?

'In the same way as a one-legged man remembers the cart that ran him over. What of it?'

I want you to go back and lift the curse. No, be quiet, you can do it now. I've taught you how.

'I – Yes,' Alexius reflected, 'I suppose you have—'

—And he was standing in the courtroom in Perimadeia, under the high-domed roof with the peculiar acoustic, the one that made the clack of swords meeting echo. The floor under the thin soles of his shoes was sandy, and scrunched when he moved. There was a man directly in front of him, his back turned, Bardas Loredan, in a fencer's white shirt; and over Bardas' shoulder he could just see the girl, Iseutz Hedin, holding a sword in fingers she no longer had.

'Nothing we can do about that, of course,' said the short, dumpy woman by his side. 'A pity. What I really need most is a good clerk, but with no fingers to speak of on her writing hand she's never going to be much use to me.'

The red and blue light from the great window burnt on Iseutz's sword-blade, a long, thin strip of straight steel foreshortened by the perspective into an extension of her hand, a single pointing finger.

'Unless,' Niessa went on, 'she learns to write with her left hand. A surprising number of people can, you know. Look sharp, Alexius, this is the bit where she kills him.'

Alexius saw Bardas move forward; Iseutz reacted, parrying backhand, high, then recovered into a fluent lunge that bypassed Bardas' attempted parry –

– That was stopped and flicked aside by Bardas' masterful defence, leaving her to stumble forward a step and catch hold of his shoulder to steady herself.

'Damn,' she said.

'Never mind,' Bardas replied. 'You're getting there. Let's try it once more, and this time, *anticipate*.'

'Oh, very neatly done,' Niessa said, as Alexius looked up and saw the hammer-beam roof of the fencing schools where the dome of the courtroom had been a moment before. 'Very economical. Stylish, even.'

'Thank you,' Alexius replied. 'What did I do, exactly?'

Niessa patted his arm. 'Let's see,' she said. 'Let's start with what you haven't done. You haven't changed what's actually happened; Iseutz did fight Bardas and have her fingers cut off, and she did want to kill him, and she did get a really rather horrible sort of revenge on him by telling him about Gorgas opening the gates. What you have done is set her mind at rest; now she reckons that what she did was far better than killing him, because – well, I don't suppose he'd have minded all that much being killed, but right now I should think he's feeling quite awful. And she'll be pleased because she'll figure she's paid out Gorgas and me as well as Bardas. In consequence, maybe she'll stop hating me and start making herself useful. As I told you, I really do need a helper – right-hand man, I almost said, but really that's *not* the best way to describe Iseutz.'

Alexius thought for a moment. 'To replace Gorgas, you mean?'

Niessa nodded. 'He was hopeless. My own fault for putting family above business. His ridiculous war ruined a successful business and wasted years of hard work; but he always wanted to be a soldier, bless him, just like Bardas and Uncle Maxen.'

Alexius watched the fencing lesson for a few moments. 'You don't seem too upset,' he said. 'About losing the Bank.'

'One must be practical,' Niessa replied. 'When something's in such a mess that there's nothing to be done about it, you turn around and go away.'

'Like Gorgas did?'

'Exactly. And between you and me, it wasn't as great a loss as you'd think. Given our position and the way Shastel saw us, there wasn't a future in the business. Getting out when I did, at least I was able to salvage the ready money and negotiable assets. And,' she went on, 'being brutal about it, I've got rid of a serious liability, namely Gorgas. Time now to move on to better things.'

'Niessa—' Alexius said—

—And opened his eyes.

'Alexius,' said Bardas Loredan. 'Are you all right?'

Alexius' brow furrowed. 'I'm not sure,' he said. 'What's going on?'

Bardas sat down on the edge of the bed. 'It's all right,' he said. 'You're in the master's cabin aboard the *Squirrel*, Vetriz Auzeil's ship. We're going to the Island. You had a funny turn up on deck. How are you feeling now?'

Alexius smiled. 'A bit of a headache, that's about all.'

'I see. A *headache* headache, or an industrial injury?'

'A genuine headache, I think,' Alexius replied. 'So what happened? With Anaut Mogre and the army?'

Bardas shrugged. 'It all seemed remarkably quiet and

tame when we left,' he said. 'If all goes well, there won't be any trouble.'

Alexius nodded. 'That's good,' he said. 'You saved a lot of lives, handling it the way you did.'

'Did I?' Bardas shook his head. 'Well then, good for me. To tell you the truth, I didn't particularly care what happened. It made better sense not to have another battle.'

Alexius reached out, put his hand on Bardas' wrist. 'Tell me,' he said, 'what happened between you and Gorgas? You did something that made him cut and run.'

'I don't want to talk about it,' Bardas said.

'Please yourself. In any event, it ended the war, so whatever it was it was worth it.'

Bardas laughed. 'I suppose I did, yes,' he said. 'I guess you could call that coming to good through evil. But it was the last thing on my mind at the time, so it doesn't really count.'

Alexius looked at him, but there was nothing to see in his face. 'Have you thought what you're going to do next?' he said.

Bardas shook his head. 'Something that has nothing to do with carpentry,' he said. 'I think I've suddenly become allergic to the smell of glue.'

A man and a child, in flight from the fall of their city—

The big bald man grinned at the thought; city after city, a pattern emerging. He could elaborate; *city gates opened by a brother* – he'd heard the news from Scona when they made landfall at Boul. Bardas had done well.

'Niessa.'

The little girl in his lap opened her eyes and looked up at him.

'What's the matter?' she said. 'I'm sleepy.'

'Niessa, Mummy won't be joining us. She's staying at home.'

'Oh.' Niessa looked thoughtful. 'Why?'

Gorgas sucked at his lower lip. 'Mummy and Daddy don't want to live with each other any more. So you're going to come and live with me on the farm. It'll be great fun; there's cows and sheep and horses and all sorts of animals.'

'Oh.' Niessa considered the matter for a moment. 'If we're going to live on the farm, can I have a rabbit in a cage?'

'I don't see why not,' Gorgas said. 'Your Aunt Niessa had a rabbit when she was a little girl. In fact, the hutch is probably still around the place somewhere.'

The girl nodded. 'And then we'll go home and see Mummy again, won't we?' she said.

'We'll see,' Gorgas replied. 'Go back to sleep now.'

When she was fast asleep, Gorgas tucked her into the bed and went up on deck. 'How much longer?' he asked the helmsman.

'At this rate, a couple of hours and we'll see Tornoys Point,' he replied.

Gorgas nodded. 'That's good,' he said, and looked back over the stern of the ship at the two sails following close behind. 'Where's the master-at-arms?'

The helmsman pointed, and Gorgas hopped down onto the main deck. There were details to be sorted out - always details to be sorted out, whether the army is fifty or four hundred - and one neglected detail can destroy an army as easily as a shower of arrows.

'It ought to be child's play,' he told the master-at-arms. 'After all, they've got no standing army, no government, most of them haven't even got weapons, and there's no towns or even villages, so there's nowhere for them to gang up on us or hide.'

The master grinned. 'A bunch of peasants stand up to the man who wiped out the Shastel army? Don't see it myself.'

Gorgas accepted the compliment with a polite nod. It was touching, the faith these men had shown in him, their loyalty; enough for them to leave their homes and families and follow him. Now, the army was their family, and his too.